Vyper
World-Class Hacker
Novice Covert Operative
Trouble by Any Name
A Laynie Portland Sequel
VIKKI KESTELL
Faith-Filled Fiction™
www.faith-filledfiction.com | www.vikkikestell.com

VYPER
A LAYNIE PORTLAND SEQUEL
Laynie Portland | Book 5
Vikki Kestell
Also Available in eBook Format

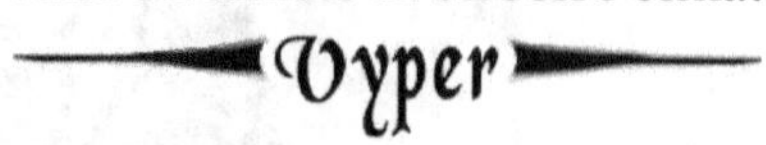

BOOKS BY VIKKI KESTELL

LAYNIE PORTLAND

Book 1: *Laynie Portland, Spy Rising*
Book 2: *Laynie Portland, Retired Spy*
Book 3: *Laynie Portland, Renegade Spy*
Book 4: *Laynie Portland, Spy Resurrected*
Book 5: *Vyper, A Laynie Portland Sequel*

THE TAHOE MYSTERIES

Book 1: *Number 1 with a Bullet*
Book 2: *Be Quick or be Dead, 2025*
Book 3: *Death on the Big Blue, 2026*
Murder by Accident, A Miss Finch Prequel, 2025

A PRAIRIE HERITAGE

Book 1: *A Rose Blooms Twice*
Book 2: *Wild Heart on the Prairie*
Book 3: Joy on This Mountain
Book 4: *The Captive Within*
Book 5: *Stolen*
Book 6: *Lost Are Found*
Book 7: *All God's Promises*
Book 8: *The Heart of Joy—A Short Story*
Book 9: *Rose of RiverBend*

NANOSTEALTH

Book 1: *Stealthy Steps*
Book 2: *Stealth Power*
Book 3: *Stealth Retribution*
Book 4: *Deep State Stealth*
Book 5: *Stealth Insurgence*
Book 6: *Stealth Triumph*
Book 7: *Stealth Genesis,*
A Nanostealth Prequel

GIRLS FROM THE MOUNTAIN

Book 1: *Tabitha*
Book 2: *Tory*
Book 3: *Sarah Redeemed*

VYPER
A LAYNIE PORTLAND SEQUEL

Laynie Portland | Book 5
Vikki Kestell
Also Available in eBook Format

TASK FORCE Resolute holds a mandate to hunt terrorists online. Director Wolfe provides the funding and agency umbrella under which Resolute operates, while Bella Tobin serves as Resolute's team leader. Bella, however, is not this woman's actual name. It is the current identity of Laynie Portland, *spy extraordinaire*, a covert asset who operated under deep cover in Sweden and Russia for more than twenty years before "coming in from the cold."

Enter Resolute's top intelligence analyst, Jasmine Jessup, or *Jaz* as she prefers. In front of her teammates, Jaz cuts a touchy, solitary, and peculiar figure. Few individuals alive, including her team, are aware that she, like Laynie, has a shadowed past, a dark history hidden behind a barricade of counterfeit identities—more aliases than even Laynie Portland could boast.

At the same time, Wolfe, Bella, and Task Force Resolute guard Jaz's most precious secret: Within the upper echelons of international hacking, Jaz's brilliance and reputation are legend—for behind a keyboard, Jaz reigns as *Vyper, the Venom Queen*, a computer guru who instills both dread and reverence across the global hacker community.

Despite her renown in cyberspace, Jaz is not a trained field agent. So why would Director Wolfe recruit Jaz for a dicey undercover assignment—one he insists has *her name* written all over it?

Turns out, it isn't Jaz but *Vyper* Director Wolfe desperately needs for this high-risk assignment.

As Jaz prepares for her assignment, uppermost in her training is operational security. Her handlers stress the peril that would await her should she be recognized as Vyper by someone in the hacker community, thus blowing her cover. Even so, no one could predict that Jaz will soon face a dangerous figure from her past—an individual *who will hold her life in his hands*.

ACKNOWLEDGEMENTS

All my thanks, appreciation, and love
to my esteemed teammates,
Cheryl Adkins and **Greg McCann**
continually demonstrating that they are
—BEST IN CLASS—

SCRIPTURE QUOTATIONS

New International Version (NIV)
The HOLY BIBLE,
NEW INTERNATIONAL VERSION®.
Copyright ©1973, 1978, 1984
International Bible Society.
Used by permission of Zondervan.
All rights reserved.

—

New King James Version® (NKJV)
Copyright ©1982 by Thomas Nelson.
Used by permission. All rights reserved.

COVER DESIGN

Vikki Kestell

PROLOGUE

REGINA, SASKATCHEWAN
OCTOBER 1975

"THAT CHILD is staring at me." The group home's foster mother, Maude Northam, pursed her lips. The lines between her brows deepened and drew closer together. "It is unsettling."

The overtaxed caseworker, a few years past her prime, glanced at the girl standing in the foyer just inside the group home's doorway. She set the child's suitcase on the floor before she answered.

"Don't let it bother you. She is simply sizing you up."

"Really, Miss Timmons! *Her,* sizing *me* up?"

Miss Timmons massaged her tired eyes. "Yes. She does that." The caseworker's equally weary smile seemed to blend wry humor with regret. "Such a clever little thing she is. I have known Jenny since she entered the system, and it grieves me that we must place her in yet another new environment."

The two women studied the child. The girl, her dark hair parted in the middle and plaited into two tidy braids, studied them back. Her pale green eyes did not shift or blink.

Mrs. Northam sniffed. "I hardly think our home an appropriate fit for her. My husband and I care for children ages seven to thirteen. This girl is what? Four or five? Not our age bracket, I'm afraid. No, not a fit at all."

"She will be six come spring, but is small for her age. However, as I said, she is intelligent and, I am sorry to again impress upon you, no other options are open to us on such short notice."

"So you say. How long has she been in care?"

"Her mother left her at the entrance to our offices when she was two years old."

"Why? Was there something wrong with the girl?"

"Nothing wrong with *her*. More likely the mother was unfit. From the bits and pieces the child told us, we deduced that her mother was a sex worker who, because of her line of work, could no longer care for an active toddler."

"From what the child told you, you say? Surely a two-year-old couldn't tell you much. I assume the mother left a note with her?"

Miss Timmons' chuckle was sardonic. "A note? Not so much as a scrap. What we pieced together was that the mother left Jenny on our steps early on a Monday morning thinking we'd find her as we arrived to work. Regrettably, it was autumn—quite chilly, you know—and the day her mother left her was a holiday. Offices closed. I arrived at work early Tuesday morning and came across her sitting on the steps, just as patient and unruffled as can be."

"Merciful heavens! Left alone through the cold of night? Why, how did she survive? And did no one notice her?"

"We think not. Rather, the evidence suggests that Jenny took it upon herself to provide for her needs. Next to the office steps we found a package of cookies, half-eaten; a pile of bubblegum wrappers; an empty juice bottle; and a rumpled stadium blanket—new, with the price tag still attached."

Miss Timmons inclined her head toward the girl. "Evidently, Jenny had spent the night curled up in the flower bed."

"So her mother left her with a blanket and food."

"Doubtful. We believe Jenny was left with nothing but the clothes on her back."

"Then someone *did* notice her and gave her those things."

"No."

"But someone had to have helped her. Why would you think otherwise?"

"Just this: When we asked Jenny where she got the items, she pointed to the little market on the opposite corner. We showed the blanket and trash to the store manager. He verified that the items could have come from his stock—and the tag on the blanket proved that it, at a minimum, had. However, his evening employees swore that they never saw the child, nor did they recall selling those items."

Miss Timmons shrugged. "It seems that Jenny crossed the street by herself and 'appropriated' what she needed."

"At two years of age? Preposterous!"

Miss Timmons turned and smiled at the girl, who puffed out a tiny, aggrieved breath in response.

"I would not have disagreed with you—that is until Jenny volunteered her full name, her age, even her date of birth, and declared that she was hungry and would like pancakes, *if you please*. According to the DOB she provided, she was all of two years and five months. However, when we asked her about her mother, her father, or where she'd lived, she would only lift her little shoulders as if she did not know . . . or was, perhaps, *unwilling* to tell us. That was when I began to realize what a special child we had on our hands."

"Special?"

"Yes, special. I have come to the conclusion that Jenny is abnormally bright and precocious, a child who, because she was neglected, learned early on to be self-reliant."

"And yet a child that special has not been adopted since entering care?"

"That is correct. You can see that she is a healthy, comely little mite, and we had no lack of prospective adoptive parents. Nonetheless, out of three adoption attempts, not one worked out."

"Why is that?"

"My experience tells me that most children in the system long for loving parents, whereas Jenny is content to live in a bubble of her own making. She keeps to herself, does well in school, and requires little help."

Miss Timmons glanced at the child. "I think it highly regrettable that the majority of prospective adoptive parents these days desire a child who will need and love them. Parents such as I've described are less receptive to a child who scarcely notices them, is less than affectionate, prefers her own company, and will not assimilate into the family. For those reasons, Jenny has never stayed long in an adoptive situation—or in a foster home for that matter. Eventually, an uproar ensues, and like today, we're called in to remove her."

"Eh? So you have brought me an unruly child, is that it?"

"No. It is not that she's unruly or difficult; it is more that she is *different* and, therefore, frequently misunderstood. And as I said, she is intelligent. Frankly, Mrs. Northam, Jenny is probably smarter than the two of us put together."

Maude Northam grimaced. "Is she, now? I suppose that remains to be seen. So what did she do to lose her place at her most recent foster home?"

"Truth be told, I cannot fault *her*. I believe the family's ten-year-old biological son bullied her. According to Jenny, he pulled her hair, teased her about her name, and pinched her. Hit her when he could get her alone."

"The parents didn't notice what was happening? Didn't take steps to stop him?"

Miss Timmons sighed. "Theirs was not the best of foster homes, and you know how overburdened the system is. The girl insists she did try to tell the parents, but they turned a deaf ear to her. My observations told me they doted on their son and barely tolerated little Jenny."

"Jenny is a common enough name. Why would the boy tease her about her name?"

"According to the child, her full name is Geneviève Zenibaa Simard. We call her Jenny."

"Simard is a good French Canadian surname, but Zenibaa? That is an indigenous name, isn't it?"

"It is a First Nations name, yes. However, the child does not look to be even a quarter Native—not with those green eyes of hers. Her cheekbones and the slight cant to those eyes might point to Indian blood but, without the identity of her parents, we could only surmise that she was of Native ancestry. Even with Jenny providing a date of birth, we found nothing. Without proper documentation, her lineage was purely conjecture on our part, and she was classed as Non-Status Indigenous."

"Huh. So the boy in the family teased her and called her names? Surely that was no reason for his parents to surrender her."

"Oh, they had reason enough."

Mrs. Northam folded her ample arms across her chest. "Then it's like I said! You've brought me a budding delinquent—and I do not appreciate it, I really do not. I will not have a willful, troublemaking child disrupting the entire household."

"She will not be a problem if you handle her fairly."

"What? If *I* handle her fairly? Fair or not, I expect obedience, I do."

Miss Timmons' mouth tightened as she faced the other woman. "Let me speak frankly, Mrs. Northam. I have received less-than-glowing reports about this house, and I will return frequently to ensure that Jenny is thriving here. I had *better not* find any reason to remove her from your care."

"Well, I never. I will not be intimidated by the likes of you!"

Miss Timmons had been a social worker for twenty-five years, and she had seen it all. Her expression did not shift an iota. "Mrs. Northam, you would do well to remember my warning. If you treat Jenny fairly, she will give you no grief."

"And if the girl feels she isn't treated fairly? What then?"

"As I said, the older boy in her last home bullied her, and his parents did not believe Jenny when she complained to them. The last straw for Jenny was when she told them the boy had cut off the end of one of her braids and still they disbelieved her."

"Easy enough to check such a story. Did she lie to them?"

"Jenny is no liar. They found an inch missing from the end of her left braid. However, when they asked their son if he had cut her braid, he denied it. His parents decided Jenny had done it herself to get attention. Instead of believing her, they punished her for defaming their little darling."

The foster mother's eyes narrowed. "And then?"

The caseworker tendered a uncharacteristically sardonic grin. "Let us just say that the parents came to regret their choices."

Maude Northam backed up a step. Her eyes jinked to the child then back to the caseworker. "Y-you cannot leave that girl with me—not if she is given to violence. I won't stand for it! We have other children in this home, you know, and we must protect them."

"Oh, I assure you, Mrs. Northam, Jenny hasn't a violent bone in her body. She is merely what I call . . . a creative problem solver."

"Nonsense! You must disclose the reason the parents in her last placement surrendered her. I insist that you tell me *exactly* what the girl did!"

Across the vestibule, the child unwrapped a piece of bubble gum, exhaled a longsuffering sigh, slipped the gum into her mouth, and slowly chewed it.

Miss Timmons quirked a fond smile on her. "I know we have kept you waiting, Jenny, but please be patient a little longer. Thank you; you're a good girl."

The girl replied with a small nod.

Mrs. Northam snorted. "My, my, don't you behave as though the child were an honored guest! Well, she won't be a guest *here*."

Miss Timmons leaned toward the foster mother. "What I do is address Jenny with respect, Mrs. Northam, because when I do, she is docile and biddable."

Mrs. Northam bristled. "Well, she'll mind her Ps and Qs for me, she will! And she will show proper respect to her elders—*if*—if I even allow you to leave her with us in the first place. Now, I insist that you tell me what mischief she got up to for her last foster parents to toss her out."

Miss Timmons echoed the little girl's resigned sigh. "All right. I will tell you. And afterward? You would do well to mind my warning and manage Jenny in an equitable manner. If she has a complaint, listen to her. *Believe* her. And act on her complaint."

"Yes, yes. So you've said."

Miss Timmons turned her back on the child and began quietly, "When little Jenny encounters a problem or is the recipient of a perceived insult and cannot get an adult to address her grievance, she sets about solving the situations herself. Several of her foster parents have told me the same, and her most recent foster parents, Mr. and Mrs. Placard, confirm it."

"What can you possibly mean by 'she sets about solving the situations herself'?"

"Mrs. Northam, really! I am getting to it—and I will get to it quicker if you do not continue to interrupt me."

The group home mother scowled; her pinched lips thinned further.

Shaking her head, Miss Timmons continued. "The first event occurred one evening after dinner when Mrs. Placard noticed money missing from her purse."

"What? *Now* you tell me the child's a thief? I'll have you know, I abide no thieves here, Miss Timmons."

"Mrs. Northam, kindly *shut up* until I am finished."

The sneer Mrs. Northam sent Miss Timmons could have frosted window panes in July—but Miss Timmons had seen worse and had stared down the best.

"As I was saying before you interrupted me, *Mrs. Northam*, that evening, Mrs. Placard discovered that a twenty-dollar bill had gone missing from her purse. She suspected Jenny had taken the money. Mrs. Placard searched Jenny's room but found nothing. When Mrs. Placard demanded Jenny return the money, Jenny asked if Mrs. Placard had also searched Howard's room— Howard being the Placards' ten-year-old son and Jenny harboring a need for equal treatment.

"When Mrs. Placard retorted that her 'little gentleman' was no thief, Jenny answered by asking where Howard had gotten the candy. Mrs. Placard wanted to know what candy. Jenny said she'd seen Howard eating a candy bar before dinner.

"Howard was out playing at the time, so Mrs. Placard went into his room. She spied a crumpled candy bar wrapper in Howard's waste basket and turned on Jenny, accusing her of putting the wrapper in the trash herself. Jenny then asked why Howard had no appetite at dinner.

"Mrs. Placard recalled that Howard had not seemed hungry over dinner, and so, with reluctance, she searched the remainder of Howard's room. She discovered cash—several small bills and some change—and two candy bars tucked under Howard's mattress. When she and Mr. Placard confronted Howard, he denied taking the money or buying any candy. What he *did* admit to was seeing Jenny holding a candy bar before dinner and he confessed to taking the candy bar from Jenny so that she would not ruin her appetite—his reason for taking Jenny's candy bar delivered in a most pious manner, I'm certain."

Mrs. Northam's sneer drained away. "Are you suggesting that little Geneviève took the money, bought some candy, then put the change and candy under Howard's mattress? But wouldn't that also mean she intentionally allowed Howard to see the candy bar she had in her hand, knowing he'd steal it from her?"

Miss Timmons did not alter her expression except to raise one eyebrow, so Mrs. Northam finished her line of reasoning. "But what you are *insinuating*, however implausible, is that Geneviève planned these many details in order to discredit Howard—all because he bullied her and his parents didn't believe her?"

Miss Timmons' mouth twitched. "Have I your attention now?"

"But that's diabolical . . . and she's just a child!"

"A brilliant child, Mrs. Northam, as I have said more than once. Do you care to hear the rest?"

Mrs. Northam swallowed. "I-I do. Yes. If you please."

"Very well, since you asked politely. Even though the Placards found money and candy under Howard's mattress, they did not act. They were unconvinced that Howard had taken the money in the first place but they could not prove Jenny's guilt, so they let the matter lie—which was a mistake.

"One night, a few days later, after the children were abed, Mr. Placard poured himself his evening libation, only to discover that his bourbon tasted 'off.' Watered down. He and Mrs. Placard checked on both children. Jenny was sound asleep with no hint of bourbon about her person. Howard was sleeping also, but the faint odor of bourbon lingered near his mouth. When the Placards awakened him, they discovered that his pillow, rather than *he*, held the odor . . . as though alcohol had been dribbled on it."

"*Mon Dieu!* The child is a demon!"

"Are you daft, Mrs. Northam? I have told you repeatedly that she is intelligent and will not tolerate being treated unfairly. More accurately, from what I have observed and documented, she can hold a sizable grudge if her plight is unjust and nothing is done to amend the unfairness. Case in point, this prank was not the end of her 'setting things right' between herself and young Howard and his biased parents."

Miss Timmons forged ahead. "A week later, Howard's school principal phoned Mr. Placard at his work. A book report Howard had turned in was found by his teacher to contain a number of profane lines and disturbing phrases. The language was so concerning that the principal required Howard be evaluated by the school psychiatrist. That was when the Placards called me in, because by now they were convinced Jenny was behind this incident as well as the previous two events.

"They rehearsed the first two episodes to me, and then I looked over Howard's book report. It was written in pencil, you see, and while I was reading it, I detected faint erasure marks. And although the rewritten text bore a striking similitude to Howard's handwriting, Mr. Placard insisted Jenny had to have taken the report from Howard's book bag and revised it. I agreed that she likely had. As Howard was known to be rather a poor student, Jenny probably presumed he would decline to reread the report before he turned it in."

Miss Timmons chuckled. "She was right about that."

Lifting a hand to forestall additional questions from the disquieted Mrs. Northam, Miss Timmons added, "I set about finding Jenny another placement at once, but a week passed without success. The final incident, which occurred yesterday, is what generated Jenny's emergency removal to your group home."

Mrs. Northam grew pale. "What," she implored in a whisper, "what did she do yesterday?"

Miss Timmons checked over her shoulder to assure herself that the child was paying their murmured conversation no mind. Jenny had her back to the women. As far as Miss Timmons could ascertain, the child was engrossed in tracing the woodgrain on the home's entrance door—which, in Miss Timmons' experience, was no assurance at all.

She lowered her voice to a whisper. "A schoolmate of Howard's, one Jonathan Wexler, came upon a note taped to his locker when he arrived at school yesterday. Jonathan, according to his school records, is intellectually challenged and thus is older—and larger—than his elementary classmates. He also possesses a nasty temper and has been suspended twice for fighting."

"The note?" Mrs. Northam's interjection was breathless. "What did it say?"

"The note, Mrs. Northam, contained a stick figure of Jonathan with the word 'RETARD' in all caps pointing to the figure."

Miss Timmons bent a knowing nod on the other woman. "The note was signed with Howard Placard's name."

Mrs. Northam gasped; her hand went to her mouth.

"Yes, just so. Jonathan sought out Howard Placard straightaway and thrashed him. Thoroughly, I might add. Jonathan was expelled, of course."

"Why, this child you've brought here is a budding sociopath!"

"Not at all. With proper oversight, she willingly obeys the rules—as long as they are enforced equally and impartially. All she requires is that you treat her justly and leave her, for the most part, to her own devices."

Multiple misgivings etched themselves across Mrs. Northam's face and began to work their way out of her mouth, but the foster mother's objections did not deter Miss Timmons from her mission.

"I have here an order to place Jenny in your care, Mrs. Northam, and you have no choice in the matter. On the other hand, you have the power to ensure that Jenny feels welcome in this home. You also have the power to demonstrate to her that you are willing to protect her from older, *less friendly* children. If she comes to you with a complaint? Hear her out. Show her you care and are trustworthy. Believe what she asserts, act to help her, and all will be well. If you follow my advice to the letter, I predict that she will give you little to no grief."

Miss Timmons witnessed the other woman's struggle. She watched Mrs. Northam glance several times at the waiting child, who now sat cross-legged on the floor, chin supported by one hand, the other hand twirling a braid, the embodiment of boredom.

"I . . . I see," Mrs. Northam finally breathed.

"Right, then. I am glad we had this conversation."

Slowly and purposefully, Mrs. Northam straightened and unclenched her arms. She somehow managed to muster a smile and affix it to her face. On a long exhale, she walked toward the little girl, bent down, and held out her hand.

"Jenny? I am Mrs. Northam. I bid you welcome to our home. I hope you will be happy here. Please do, um, come to me right away if you have any problems, yes? Any worries? I assure you that I or my husband, Albert, will take steps to ensure that the other children in our home treat you well. But should they, er, pick on you, you must let me know straightaway, yes? I promise we will handle them."

Jenny ignored Mrs. Northam's outstretched hand but nodded in the affirmative.

"Well. Very good. Shall I show you to your room now, Jenny?"

To Miss Timmons' mind, Mrs. Northam appeared shocked when Jenny answered, "Yes, please."

"Jenny? Before you go . . ." Miss Timmons knelt on the floor in front of the child and gently placed her palms on Jenny's shoulders. The girl squirmed some, then settled. "Do you remember me telling you about Jesus?"

Jenny's chin bobbed once.

"I am glad! I pray you never forget that *he loves you.* If you need him, do call on his name. Can you remember to do that?"

The girl shifted her gaze aside. An impatient sigh escaped her mouth.

"I understand. You have been alone a long time and things have not always been pleasant, dear child, but please do not forget how much Jesus loves you?" It was more a plea than a reminder.

Another clipped bob of the chin was the only answer Miss Timmons received.

"Come, Jenny," Mrs. Northam murmured.

The girl waved goodbye to Miss Timmons and followed Mrs. Northam out of the foyer.

TASK FORCE RESOLUTE

Vyper

CHAPTER 1

TASK FORCE RESOLUTE
MID-MARCH 2002

GRIFFIN INDUSTRIES resides in one of hundreds of similar and unremarkable commercial office suites within a Germantown business park approximately thirty miles north of Washington, DC. Griffin Industries occupies one quarter of a building in such a park, a two-story slice of the building.

Tomlinson Technologies occupies the remaining three quarters of the overall structure, but the two tenants do not share a parking lot. Tomlinson and other businesses within the park are welcoming to client and customer visitors. Not Griffin Industries.

Griffin Industries' plot of ground is fully fenced. It offers neither visitor parking nor public entrance. Sole access to the building is via an underground parking garage and the elevator within the garage. Admission to the parking garage is through a guarded and fortified gate; access to the elevator is by key card and PIN only.

Within Griffin Industries resides Task Force Resolute, the team of anti-terrorism analysts that blunted an attempt to poison thousands of New Year's Eve partiers with fentanyl-laced ecstasy. On the heels of the foiled New Year's Eve attack, Resolute also prevented a shipping container packed with several thousand pounds of carfentanil—a drug one hundred times more powerful than fentanyl—from landing in a US port. That single act thwarted a plot to pollute the Washington, DC, water system with massive amounts of water-soluble carfentanil. Even a few drops of carfentanil-spiked water on human skin would have been lethal, would have turned DC's morning coffee and showers into weapons of mass destruction.

Griffin Industries is Task Force Resolute's home base—its secure base. Four months ago, the facility hadn't been secure enough. Griffin Industries had been attacked, the building's defenses breached, and Task Force Resolute nearly cut down. Resolute's Director, Jack Wolfe, evacuated the team to Broadsword, a specialized training facility in the mountains of Virginia, and a secure fallback location. Then Wolfe took steps to ensure that such a penetration of the facility would never happen again.

He ordered that the gate and the fence surrounding Griffin Industries be upgraded, a fortified guard shack at the gate be added and staffed by an armed, two-person security team, and that two additional guards and a dog would patrol the perimeter 24/7. A state-of-the-art camera system now studded the exterior of the building. Finally, in place of a lone security officer checking IDs in the open lobby where the elevator arrived, two armed security specialists stood post behind a reinforced wall, prepared to defend the facility's single access point.

Oddly enough, Griffin Industries' two-story suite possesses no windows. The center of the suite is open from the ground floor to the upper floor's ceiling, allowing external lighting to filter down from a skylight. The upper floor's offices, built around the suite's perimeter, are mostly unoccupied, but the rest of the floor surrounds and overlooks the open center where a staircase of eight steps descends to a landing halfway to the ground floor. At the landing, the flight of steps turns back on itself and continues down to what had originally been an atrium encircled by individual modular cubicles.

The ground floor of Griffin Industries, stripped of those modular walls and reconfigured, presently provides two large areas, the guarded lobby and the task force's joint work space. Their work space, now an open area, is walled off from the lobby. Someone has slapped a crude hand-scrawled CLASSIFIED sign on the door leading from the lobby to the task force's domain.

The task force members (six crack computer analysts and the team's administrative assistant) refer to this area as "the bullpen." Their seven work-stations are laid out in a rough, somewhat haphazard semicircle with a view to a large LCD monitor and four whiteboards. The semicircle is back-stopped by a rack of servers. Cables supply power and network access to the workstations via conduits under the floor of the bullpen.

Throughout the day, task force members huddle over their respective key-boards. With the exception of tapping keys, the occasional squeak of a chair, or muffled cough, the team labors with intense concentration. The bullpen may appear messy and disorganized to the unpracticed eye, yet it is not unusual for any member of the team to interrupt the quiet concentration to announce a finding or request input.

Long sessions of group discussion and deep analysis—including question-ing their own assumptions—keep the task force members razor sharp. Like a well-oiled machine, they complement and feed off each other's specialties and expertise.

The task force leader, Anabelle Tobin (*nee* Anabelle Garineau; *Bella* to her team), is responsible for the task force's unconventional seating arrangements. It was Bella who ordered the team to tear apart the first floor to accommodate the bullpen and their frequently lively (and loud) discussions—loud as a result of the task force's three rules of operation, also established by Bella.

All members participate; no one slacks.

Everyone's input is equally valued.

All assumptions are suspect and subject to scrutiny.

But who, exactly, *is* Bella Tobin? Few people in the world are privy to her true identity—not even the team she now leads. However, since not one member of that team could be labeled a slouch when it comes to data mining and analysis, they have stitched together less than half a dozen salient details surrounding Bella's past. They know she spent two decades as an undercover intelligence operative, and had operated in Russia as one (supposed) Swedish citizen, Linnéa Olander. They know, too, that she had been the long-term mistress of a powerful and wealthy Russian politician/oligarch.

Despite the information her team has uncovered, only Bella's family and Director Wolfe know her as Laynie Portland, now permanently "in from the cold," and newly married to Deputy US Marshal Quincy Tobin.

Although Bella oversees the task force, it is Canadian national Jasmine Jessup (Jaz to her teammates) who has drilled her strict expectations and world-class hacking skills into every member of the team. As it turns out, Jaz is not *her* real name either. Neither is the handle she is best known for in the global hacker community: *Vyper*.

In the scant time the task force has been operational, through difficult adjustments, interpersonal conflicts, and grievous attacks from outside enemies, Bella, Jaz, and their teammates have bonded. Indeed, the dangers and ordeals they endured together have forged from the individual members a single unrelenting and highly effective terrorist-stalking weapon.

Welcome to Task Force Resolute.

JAZ, HER eyes never straying from the lines of code scrolling down her computer screen, unwrapped a stick of Black Jack gum, folded it in half, folded it again, brought it to her mouth, then tossed the wrapper into the trash.

One handed.

Without looking.

She chomped down on the gum, jaws firing like pistons, until the new stick of gum joined the three-piece gob already in her mouth. Ten minutes later, a wicked smile curved her mouth.

"Bingo."

Jaz called aloud, "Yo, Vincent!" Eyes still riveted to her screen, she motioned the group's admin to join her.

"Yes, Jaz?"

"Add Amsterdam to the board."

"And the bank?"

"Rabobank." One of the Netherland's top financial institutions.

"Got it." Vincent strode to one of the whiteboards in front of the team's work stations and carefully printed "Amsterdam" and "Rabobank" under previous lines that listed three other cities—London, Paris, and Madrid—and three other banks—Standard Chartered, La Banque Postale, and Bank of Spain.

The task force was on the hunt, and they were motivated. The six analysts bent to their tasks with the ferocity of a ravenous wolf pack stalking a wounded bull moose. They could scent their prey. They knew they were closing in. And that knowledge made them salivate. Drove them harder.

Their quarry was a jihadi extremist whose followers had planned and executed three bombings to date, each bomb intended to kill innocent civilians, primarily *children*. Jaz growled low in her throat as she replayed the terrible details burned into her memory.

The first attack, a Saturday seventeen days ago, had targeted unsuspecting moviegoers in a UK cinema. The terrorists had selected a family-friendly film for their assault, a deliberate choice to ensure that the resulting thirty-seven lives lost would include youngsters. Sixteen kids and twelve adults had perished at the scene. Nine more young lives, their small bodies broken and maimed, still hung in the balance.

A week later *to the day*, the terrorists detonated a second bomb, this one in the food court of a Paris video gaming center, a popular venue for children's birthday parties. The explosion ended three such parties and twenty-three lives—nineteen of which were under the age of twelve.

The third bomb, *six* days later rather than seven, had taken out a school bus in Madrid when it arrived at its elementary school destination. The bus was filled to capacity with students. Not one child survived the blast.

After the third bombing, an anonymous account posted a video message on multiple online bulletin boards. In the video, a lean young man gloated, "You have bombed our mothers and our children. Now we bomb yours. This is Attaf, protector of the weak and oppressed. You shall hear from me again."

Profilers in the FBI's Behavioral Analysis Unit set Attaf's age to be between twenty-five and thirty. Based on their analysis of his accent they concluded he was Pakistani. His verbiage and body language seemed to suggest a Messiah complex. And the FBI analysts were unequivocal concerning his intentions: Attaf's final sentence had promised further carnage.

It was obvious to the world that this terrorist's perverse objective was to strike fear and horror at the very heart of the nations they chose to attack. How? By killing or maiming the most precious and innocent treasures these countries possessed.

Jaz had absorbed the man's every feature, the shape of his head, the color and tilt of his eyes, the width of his nose and mouth, the folds of his skin. It was clear to her that the man leading this terrorist movement was evil incarnate. A heartless, soulless being. The lowest of the low.

What no one to date had uncovered was the man's real name. Rusty had slapped an unflattering moniker on the man, *Gandagi*. Gandagi in Urdu meant dirt or filth. It was not a name Bella would have allowed them to use, had she overheard them calling him that, so the task force analysts kept the name to themselves.

Regardless of the man's identity, Jaz now believed she knew how to find Gandagi. She and the task force had tracked the terrorists' money trail, had painstakingly followed every financial lead they unearthed, however small or inconsequential, until a faint but cogent pattern emerged and with it, a precedent that predicted where the terrorists would strike next.

Amsterdam.

"Come to me, my pretty," she crooned under her breath. "Come to Vyper, Gandagi. You do not see me, but I see you and am slithering through the grass, silent as the grave, drawing ever closer to you and the little hole where you are hiding, where you feel safe. You do not sense danger approaching, do you? No, not yet—but you will. On the day I strike, you will know the fear you have inflicted on so many others."

A voice behind her interrupted. "Talking to our suspect, are you? I hope you are giving him a piece of my mind too."

Jaz sat up and stretched her tight back. "Happy to give him any message you like, Bella. Yah, we're getting close."

Jaz's Canadian roots were most perceptible when she used "yah," instead of that American staple, "yeah."

Bella rolled a chair to Jaz's work station and sat. "How close is close?"

"They're in Amsterdam. They opened a Rabobank account yesterday and funded it from a familiar source—just as they did in London, Paris, and Madrid. Oh, they laundered the money well enough, so they thought, and they routed the transfer through sixteen IP proxies across ten countries, but their attempts to hide the source of the transfer weren't as clever as they believed. Not nearly clever enough."

Jaz glanced at the large calendar taped to one of the whiteboards. "The Madrid attack was four days ago, but the terrorists changed their schedule on us when they hit those kids on the bus. *Six days* following the Paris bombing to Madrid, not seven days as with the previous attacks."

"But only because school buses don't run on Saturdays."

"Right."

"It's very possible that Attaf's band of terrorists will return to their original schedule and attack again this Saturday."

"Wow, I hadn't figured that out, boss."

Bella snorted. "Don't get sassy with me, missy."

"Missy? *Really?* Now you're channeling your husband's southern schtick?"

At Bella's grimace, Jaz laughed aloud.

Half a dozen sets of eyes swiveled toward them.

Jaz scowled and barked an order. "Back to work, you scurvy crew!"

Grumbles of "Yeah, yeah," and "Slave driver!" percolated through the bullpen.

One voice rose over the grumbles. "Aye aye, Captain Black Jack!"

"Belay that drivel, Brain Pan," Jaz retorted.

"Aye aye, Captain Black Jack!"

A ripple of titters circled the room; even Bella chuckled. Jaz sighed and slid a woeful glance toward her.

"That dude is gonna be the death of me. Or the death of *him*. Haven't decided which yet."

Bella grinned. "Classic Brian, right? But to be fair, you did start the pirate talk. That's on *you*."

Jaz cracked her gum and grinned back. "Yah. Guess I did."

"So, the next attack is Amsterdam?"

"That's our working assumption. We'll monitor that account and what it's paying for, but Wolfe should deploy his tactical team to the Netherlands, ASAP."

A small frown flickered across Bella's face. She eased into another position in her chair, and shifted the sling in which her right arm rested.

Jaz recognized Bella's actions as unconscious adjustments intended to relieve discomfort. She ran an assessing eye over her friend. Her *best* friend. The only best friend Jaz had ever had.

Not that I had friends before. Before I was forced to flee my life in Canada. Before Director Wolfe offered me safe harbor here as part of the task force. Before Bella showed the task force members how to work together. Before she hammered her expectations into us and we became a team. Something greater than a team.

Jaz's assessment didn't catch more than the twinge that had crossed Bella's face or the minute adjustments she'd made in her chair. Visible or not, though, the weeks Bella had spent as Sayed's prisoner in his Dagestan fortress had left indelible marks on both her body and soul.

Profound and profuse cuts and contusions, particularly about her face and scalp. Still visible.

A dislocated right shoulder requiring ongoing physical therapy as it healed.

A wicked burn to her left forearm that had developed into bacterial cellulitis and near-fatal sepsis.

Jaz's friend had not fully healed, and she was often in pain. Jaz had to also admit that those experiences had changed Bella in other ways too. Intangible ways. She seemed calmer. Settled. At peace.

If Jaz was honest with herself, she could not attribute those changes solely to Bella's marriage to Quincy Tobin nor to Ksenia, the daughter Bella had brought back from Dagestan, whom she and Quincy were adopting. As happy as those tandem events appeared to be, the alterations Jaz saw in Bella were deeper. More fundamental and significant.

Jaz turned inward.

She addressed someone in whom she didn't *quite* believe but to whom she often found herself speaking, nonetheless.

You saved Bella.

Marshal Tobin dared me to pray to you. I didn't know how, so he prayed in my stead. I just added that 'amen' part, and you . . . well, you answered our prayer.

You saved Bella.

I don't know what to do about that. Yet. But I thank you again for saving her, for bringing her home. I will never forget that you did.

At least Bella's hair was growing back. She might never again own the long blond locks she'd once had. Her newly grown hair, now about an inch in length, was tawny instead of blond and had a twisty bit of a wave to it. The tawny color was also shot with soft silver. *Silver!* For some reason that encroachment hurt Jaz inside more than the rest of the abuses Bella endured.

It signified that her beautiful friend was showing her age.

Jaz's eyes welled with tears. She turned away from Bella to hide the moisture. Not that the emotions that had ambushed her *yet again* had gone unnoticed.

"You okay, Jaz?"

"Yah. Whatever."

Jaz heard Bella sigh.

"I have my moments too, Jaz. Ruth says it's a kind of grieving and a normal response to trauma. She tells me it's okay to mourn."

Ruth was Bella's therapist and a dear friend to Bella's family.

Jaz tried to swallow, but her throat was too tight. Eventually, she was able to mutter, "Okay to mourn? Nobody died. At least nobody who didn't need to."

"No, God was very gracious to us. To me. I'm alive, and I'm healing. Getting stronger each day. Tobin and I have each other, and we have a precious daughter now—Lord help us, a teenage daughter! Even our task force is intact and functioning well. That doesn't mean that some *things* didn't die in the process."

Jaz lifted her head. Peered over her shoulder at Bella. "Things died?"

"In a way. Take my hair, for example. Every time I look in the mirror, it hits me. Steals my breath away. Ruth and I talked about how someone forcibly and violently chopping off my hair was a grave trespass. A trauma akin to . . . rape. Yes, I'm mourning the loss of my hair, and Ruth says it's okay to grieve over it."

"Oh." Jaz again turned her face away. Always suspicious of newcomers, she had not taken to Ruth initially.

Like I ever "take" to anyone new, she admitted to herself. *But Ruth, well, she has proven to be good for Bella, and anyone good for Bella is all right in my book.*

Jaz shuddered when Bella's warm hand touched her shoulder and rested there.

"I know you're struggling, Jaz, but you're not alone."

Every fiber of Jaz's being itched to throw off Bella's hand. Every habit of a lifetime demanded that she reject Bella's friendship and love.

Jaz forced herself to sit still. To endure the discomfort.

The truth was, Bella's touch was like precious oil to Jaz's cracked and dry heart.

She never wanted it to end.

CHAPTER 2

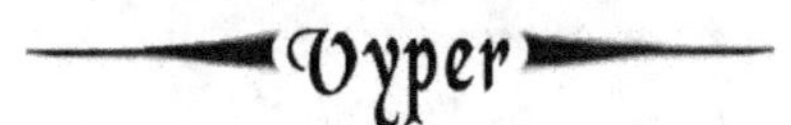

LAYNIE STOOD as her unexpected visitor entered her office.

"Good morning, Director Wolfe."

He took the seat in front of her desk and motioned her to sit as well. "Good morning, Bella. I hope you don't mind my stopping by unannounced."

"Not at all."

Wolfe put his head to one side and said, "I must say you look healthier each time I see you."

Laynie shrugged. "It would be hard for me to look worse than when I returned to the US. Still, I'm grateful for little improvements each day."

"Your forearm?"

"Another round of antibiotics finished clearing up the infection. The skin, however, remains tender and discolored. The discoloration is likely permanent."

He gestured toward the sling holding her right arm. "And your shoulder?"

"Improving, although I have weeks of physical therapy ahead of me to regain its full strength."

"I'm glad to see that your hair has grown out some."

A small shudder rippled across his features, and Laynie's fingers automatically crept to nape of her neck. Rather than finding the heavy cascade of hair she expected, she was surprised, once more, to encounter inch-long strands. At least those feathery strands were beginning to conceal the many scabs and scars crisscrossing her scalp.

Laynie didn't blame Wolfe for shuddering. She had not been a pretty sight.

"Mmm? Yes, my hair has grown some. Like I said, I'm grateful for small improvements."

Wolfe snorted. "Small improvements? I wake up every morning grateful that you're *alive* and safely back home, which is no 'small improvement' in my book. By the by, are you getting enough sleep? You appear tired."

Laynie didn't respond right away. Not long after she, Quincy, and Ksenia had returned to the States and settled into a new apartment, nights had become problematic, her family's slumber often disrupted. If Ksenia's nightmares didn't wake them, Laynie's disturbing dreams, although less frequent than Ksenia's, did.

Thank you, Lord God, for my husband! For his comfort in the dark when the demons try to creep in.

Her heart resounded with the Bible passage that had sustained her during the awful weeks as Sayed's prisoner.

Whatever happens . . .
conduct yourselves in a manner
worthy of the gospel of Christ . . .
For it has been granted to you
on behalf of Christ
not only to believe in him,
but also to suffer for him . . .

Yes, Lord. Whatever happens, I have determined to conduct myself in a manner worthy of the gospel of Christ—worthy of you.

Laynie twitched and came back to her surroundings when Wolfe murmured, "I'm not surprised that you have bad dreams, Bella."

"Sorry?"

"Before I came here, I dropped in on your husband. I may or may not have grilled him."

"I don't suppose he told you to mind your own business?"

"Nope. Folded like a deck of cards—and if you don't point that glare in another direction, Bella, I may just spontaneously combust."

"Kind of the idea, *Director*."

Wolfe smiled to diffuse Laynie's ire. "Frankly, I'm glad I spoke with Marshal Tobin. Glad that he told me about Ksenia's night terrors . . . and yours."

Laynie was only partly mollified. "*Quisling*. Wait till I get my hands on him."

"I need to know these things, Bella. You should have told me yourself."

Laynie slowly deflated. "Honestly? It's not as bad as it was when we first returned to the States. Our therapist, Ruth, has been a godsend. She flies into town once a week so Ksenia and I can meet with her individually, then our family as a whole. She is a wise, godly woman who is teaching us how to pray through these issues as a family. She assures us that as we lean upon the Lord, the nightmares will subside. Eventually."

Laynie paused to take a sip of water. "As for Quincy and me? We're good —happy to be together and content in our newly married state. Our common concern is that we provide a stable, loving home for Ksenia to heal and grow in. Quincy has shouldered the lion's share of that job, ferrying her to and from school daily, helping her navigate its demands, coaching her as she learns English, and overseeing her homework."

She didn't need to tell Wolfe that Tobin had taken a leave of absence from the US Marshals Service and his assignment with the task force to devote himself to Ksenia's needs. His absence from the task force had left a pothole the size of Kansas in Laynie's team. Although not an analyst, Quincy's background in law enforcement and his calm and steadying presence were sorely missed.

Wolfe nodded. "Marshal Tobin has a way about him."

Laynie blinked back the moisture that sprang so easily to her eyes these days. "Yes, he does. He's given himself wholly to our girl. I love . . . I love seeing them together, love seeing how Ksenia adores him."

"Seems to me that Ksenia dotes on the both of you."

A flush of joy crept up Laynie's neck and brightened her face. "I am astonished daily, I truly am. I have a daughter whom I love and who loves me back. A daughter! Who would have ever imagined I would, at this time of life, become a mother?"

"And a darned good one, if Marshal Tobin is to be believed."

Laynie grinned. "Take Quincy's opinion with a grain of salt, Director Wolfe. That man is in love with his wife. Totally smitten—and I with him."

It was Wolfe's turn to try to master his emotions. "I'm not . . . not a religious person, Bella, but when I think of the night you and I met, the woman you were when we brought you in from the cold? Nothing but thankfulness fills my heart."

Laynie's eyes lost focus as she stared into the wreckage of her past. "Yes, that woman was broken. Shipwrecked, if I'm being honest. But Jesus? Jesus makes all things new. He is making *me* new."

Laynie, preoccupied with her own musings, missed the spiritual longing that flickered over Wolfe's expression. He managed to mask it before he cleared his throat.

"Yes. Well, I wanted to check in with you and with the task force. Jaz tells me we're closing in on Attaf?"

Laynie snapped out of her reverie. "Indeed. I expect Resolute to have actionable intel later today or tomorrow—intel detailed enough for a tactical team to identify Attaf and his band of terrorists, follow them to their base, and take them down before they can strike their next target."

"I'll host a celebration for Resolute when this threat is off the table."

"Thank you. This team deserves a celebration. They have given their all to their work."

They sat in silence for a few moments before Wolfe's lips thinned, and Laynie felt the little hairs on the back of her neck rise.

"Was there something else, sir?"

"There is something, actually."

Laynie girded up her heart and waited. *Whatever it is, Lord, I will trust you.*

"I want to borrow your lead analyst for a few weeks."

Nothing could have been further from Laynie's mind, and she didn't hide her surprise. "You want to borrow Jaz?"

"Yes. Jaz."

A protective objection surged inside of Laynie. Still, she chose her words carefully. "Jaz is integral to Resolute's work, Director. May I ask what you want her for?"

She watched Wolfe as he framed a reply. His expression stilled and his eyes shuttered—but only a little. A less observant, less experienced individual wouldn't have seen the minuscule alteration.

Laynie was not that person.

Oh, I get it. You've decided that whatever task or plot you've cooked up for Jaz is 'need to know,' and I don't need to know. As if! And that song and dance you're about to lay on me? Pure fabrication.

Wolfe hadn't gotten to where he was without skills, though. He was smooth, and the words dropped effortlessly from his mouth. "Jaz is an important asset, both to this task force and to my other organizations. I'm sending her out for additional training. Two or three weeks, I estimate."

Laynie sat back. "Huh."

The fiery trial Laynie had endured at the hands of Sayed and Gupta had refined her. She no longer felt chained to the defensive and rebellious attitudes that she'd once struggled with. It meant that she was more settled inside, more at peace. It did *not* mean that she'd stopped reasoning or that she'd gotten the expected deportment of a government bureaucrat "down pat."

Nope.

But she could be "sweet." Right?

Brows lifted, genial smile fixed, she murmured, "Additional training, is it? See, I find that interesting, Director, because I cannot construe a single skill in Jaz's field of expertise where she wouldn't already far outstrip her instructors and end up schooling *them*—can you? It makes me think that the 'training' to which you refer to has nothing to do with Jaz's position on my team or her ability to perform the duties for which you hired her."

She chuckled inside as Wolfe sat straighter to assume his "I'm your boss" posture and readied himself to reply. She spoke again before he did.

"Puh-*leeze*, Director. Please don't ply me with the tired vagaries of 'security' and 'compartmentalization.' You've decided to cut me out of whatever this is, and you know that I know it, so you may as well tell me what the endgame is, what exactly you intend to train Jaz to do and, more importantly, *why.*"

Wolfe's eyes hardened. "You seem to have, *again,* forgotten your place and for whom you work, Bella."

"No, sir. Hasn't slipped my mind at all. Rather, in the spirit of cooperation, I'm electing to be transparent, utterly and intentionally so. See, Jaz is both my employee and my friend. Perhaps that's not the objective, professional admission you would prefer to hear, but it is what it is.

"Instead, I suggest that we take stock—shall we? You, sir, are a spymaster, whereas Jaz is but a 'lowly' analyst. She's brilliant at what she does, but she's *not a spook*, not a trained agent. You didn't see her when the assassins sent by the Ukrainian mob attacked our apartments and tried to abduct her. I did. After Tobin and I had neutralized the threat, Jaz was curled up on her apartment floor weeping, traumatized, and helpless.

"I, on the other hand, am perhaps one of your most experienced operatives. Given the breadth of my skills and regardless of you cutting me out, do you think I won't suss out what's going on? That I won't rest until I do? And *I will* find out, you know.

"Being entirely forthright with you, Director, I will not allow you to put Jaz in harm's way. She's not cut out for it."

Their eyes locked. Laynie refused to look away.

"Are you done?" Wolfe growled.

Laynie shrugged. "For the moment."

After a long, tense staredown, Wolfe broke the silence. "Yes, I have a task for your lead analyst. A special assignment to address what we believe is an emerging threat of importance. I expect her part to be a short-term mission, but something only a world-class hacker and a woman with her, shall we call it *personal style*, could pull off."

"I would like in on the op."

"That's not your prerogative."

"Nevertheless, I want full access."

Wolfe pretended he hadn't heard her. "I need to know how effectively your team will operate without her while she's out."

Laynie shook her head. "We can assess that after we've nailed Attaf and after I have access to the op."

"You know I could replace you. Today, if necessary."

Laynie laughed aloud. "Could you? The thing about highly effective teams, particularly *this* team? You can't treat its members like replaceable cogs and wheels. People who fight together through great peril forge deep bonds that are difficult to sever. And why would you want to do that? *These people will walk through fire for one of their own.* If you don't believe me, why don't you ask Resolute's members who oversees them? Then tell them you're removing me. See what happens next and just how 'effective' the team becomes overnight."

She leaned forward on her elbows. "I'd pay money to watch Jaz's response to your 'special assignment' if you ditched me."

Wolfe's mouth flattened. He stared across the desk with barely restrained anger.

Laynie shrugged and softened her voice. "Why do you feel the need to cut me out of the loop, Director? I've proven my loyalty to this agency and to you, personally, again and again. And with my years of covert experience, wouldn't my input be of some value both to you and to Jaz?"

Finally, Wolfe released an exaggerated sigh. "Fine. I was hoping to spare you unnecessary stress, given that you and your family are still adjusting and recuperating. But since you're an incorrigible glutton for punishment, I'll read you in. *Later.* After I hear how Jaz handles her training and whether we think she can hack the assignment—pun intended. But before I send her out? I need your assessment of how her absence will affect Resolute."

Laynie gnawed her bottom lip. "Her absence will alter the team's dynamics and its efficiency, certainly."

"Give me a percentage of loss if you can."

Laynie tilted her head and considered his question. "Jaz's technical expertise cannot be replaced nor her value to this task force understated. If I were to step into the bullpen and replace Jaz—as titular chief analyst only—I estimate at least a fifteen- to twenty-percent degradation to Resolute's effectiveness in the near term. But as time goes on? Jaz's loss would be devastating. You say her training will be short. How short?"

"Two weeks, if all goes well."

"And the op? How long for it?"

He shrugged. "Depends entirely on Miss Jessup's success. If and when she gains access to the target's communication system from the inside, our hope is that the info she provides will blow things wide open for us."

"Okay, but if she's gone longer than a month at a stretch, I think the task force begins to seriously degrade. I don't have a replacement who possesses Jaz's real-world acumen and shrewdness, both theoretical and experiential, or who has her connection to the other analysts. She is continually honing the team's computer and analytical skills. I can lead the team, but I can't provide technical guidance."

"Perhaps we can work within those parameters." Wolfe shifted in his chair. "I'd like to speak to Jaz now. Sound her out."

Laynie dug in her heels . . . gently. "One second, please. You said 'we.' 'If *we* think she can hack the assignment.' You also said, 'Perhaps *we* can work within those parameters.' By we, you weren't referring to me. Who, then? What training, exactly, and where? Surely not Marstead's agent training campus."

"No. We intend to customize her instruction and provide it off book, much of it behind closed doors and without witnesses. This is too important a mission to risk a security breach."

"Again with the 'we.' Who and where?"

Wolfe smiled. "Who wants to know? A mother bear protecting her cub?"

"Who and where, please."

He sighed. "At least you said please.

Laynie effected a proud smile. "I did, didn't I? See? My respect for the chain of command is growing—while you, *sir*, are avoiding my question."

With a soft snort, Wolfe capitulated. "I'm sending Jaz to Broadsword, Bella. Richard and Harris are, as we speak, devising an instructional package customized to Jaz's part of the mission. Richard and Harris will school Jaz, measure the outcomes, and determine whether she can handle the job I have in mind. Harris will fill the role of training officer and handle most of the actual instruction; Richard will advise."

"Good. I know and trust them both."

"Glad to have your approval, Bella."

"Happy I could provide it, sir. Now, about the op—who's the target and what's the threat level?"

Wolfe leaned back and steepled his hands. "Have you heard of American Equality for All? AEA?"

"I can't say that I have. Resolute's focus has been jihadi terrorist threats; our theater of operation has been Russia and the former Soviet states—with the Brighton Beach Ukrainian mobsters thrown in by association. Recently, Attaf's bombing campaign has shifted our attention to Europe. This AEA must be homegrown, yes? I don't think it likely that Jaz would fit in with white supremacists or some kind of neo-Nazi group."

"Oddly enough, we don't believe they *are* 'homegrown,' or at least not exclusively so, nor are they white supremacists. The evidence leads us to think they are something altogether different, an emerging threat with a unique profile. On the surface, AEA is an ultra-liberal, socially progressive but non-militant, non-violent alliance only about a year old. Publicly, they advocate for drastic social and governmental change and employ the usual liberal change tactics such as protests, lawsuits, and electioneering."

"Publicly, you say? They have a hidden agenda?"

"We believe so or we wouldn't be as concerned as we are. It's been three months since AEA first popped up on our radar, yet their organization doesn't fit the mold or category of any known subversive American group, nor do their outward behaviors. They are the proverbial horse of a different color."

"Different how, sir?"

Laynie didn't blink, shift in her seat, or massage her arm—despite the urge to alleviate her discomfort. She kept herself still because, contrary to Wolfe's "*later*," he was giving up the op's intel *now*, and she did not wish to disturb the flow.

"Different demographically for starters," Wolfe said. "Most questionable or openly radical American groups tend to separate along racial and ethnic lines: Caucasian, Black, Latino, Native American, and so on, with agendas to alleviate injustices along the same racial and ethnic lines, the exception being when liberal Caucasians join their efforts to an ethnic group they themselves are not part of."

"AEA doesn't follow either pattern?"

"Not on the surface. Their regular membership is racially varied, almost purposely so. AEA cells are also urban-based. Their members tend to be young, educated, gainfully employed, well-placed, and yet—and this is the anomalous part—holding terrorist leanings. We don't generally see 'well-placed and gainfully employed' coupled with your run-of-the-mill terrorist group. These contradictions are what made us pause and look closer."

"And their organizational doctrine?" Laynie asked.

"Ah, that. The supposed and binding commonality is a deep dissatisfaction with the prevailing social order—or at least their perceptions of said social order. We find it ironic, since most of the members seem to have good-paying jobs with clear, upward mobility."

"The better to infiltrate you with, my dear," Laynie muttered, "but to what purpose?" Her brow furrowed. "Wait. You said the 'regular' membership was racially varied, Director, and intentionally so?"

"That's right. First of all, you don't 'join' AEA. Membership seems to be by recruitment only. Second, they have taken pains to attract the best and brightest, but they've also made a point of recruiting a diversity of races and ethnicities—perhaps 'the better to blend in, my dear,' to follow your line of thinking. In fact, if I showed you a photo lineup of the AEA's New York cell, you'd appreciate how easily Jaz could blend in."

"What? Really? They're all *Goth*?"

"No, not that extreme, but unquestionably 'edgy.' However, New York isn't where we hope to insert Jaz. Our surveillance believes that the primary leadership mechanism of AEA resides in Houston, Texas, of all places. We're constructing an appropriate cover for Jaz, the right sort of job included, so she might troll AEA's primary cell and snag their interest. For her to match AEA's member profile, even in this forward-looking year of 2002, we'll need to dial back her look a notch or two. Have her grow out the shaved side of her hair. Lose the purple-tipped hair and some of her piercings."

Laynie's reply was wry with humor. "Oh, she'll love that."

Wolfe finally cracked a smile. "It gets better. Remember when I said members were recruited? What makes an individual recruitable? Our surveillance operatives have done extensive background checks on these cells and their members. Each cell has between twenty and thirty members—Black, White, Latino, East Indian, Asian, Native American, and so on, along with a balanced ratio of male to female. When we finish building Jaz's cover and adjusting her appearance, Jaz will make an excellent candidate. Then we'll arrange for her to "happen upon" some of the cell members and, hopefully, engage with them."

"But you haven't said who's actually behind these cells or what about them is nefarious enough to put them front and center on your radar."

"Getting to it, Bella. What first piqued our interest was when our surveillance picked up on a commonality from cell to cell, a trait easily overlooked but telling when noticed. Here it is: Each cell has three or four leaders, and these leaders, whether American, Canadian, or British born, are invariably of Asian extraction."

He paused on a note of "gotcha." "Those of Asian extraction, you see, are *always* the leaders of these cells and the key to whom or what is planning these attacks."

Laynie huffed. "I don't get it. What in the world does that mean when the rest of the membership is so diverse? Is AEA affiliated with the Triads or the Yakuza? Are they a front for other Chinese, Japanese, or South Korean organized crime syndicates? And where does their funding come from?"

"All good questions, but you may be surprised to hear that we've found no connection between AEA and organized crime—no drug or weapons running, human trafficking, or other criminal endeavors. No illegal activities at all. And while we have cataloged more coincidences than we can ignore, we have no real proof of who's behind the AEA front. Nothing actionable. Certainly, we've attempted to trace their funding back to its source, but on that count, too, as much as it pains me to admit it, we've also been unsuccessful."

"Sort of Jaz's specialty, sir. She could bore into their servers without ever leaving Resolute's bullpen."

Wolfe shook his head. "The members of any given cell are tech-savvy, and each cell has an embedded cybersecurity specialist. They are rabidly security conscious, which adds to our concerns. Why so secretive if they aren't dangerous? At present, they don't suspect we are surveilling them, and we don't wish to risk tipping them off."

"Then what's your working hypothesis?"

Wolfe leaned forward and placed his hands, palm down, on Laynie's desk. "If I read you in on this op, Bella, nothing I say leaves this room. Absolute, ironclad OPSEC. I trust you to confide in Marshal Tobin but not another soul."

Laynie nodded. "All right. Agreed."

Wolfe said softly, "We think the CCP is preparing to make a big move on the US. An actual attack."

Laynie's mouth slowly fell open. *The CCP? Not organized crime but the Chinese Communist Party? The* government *of Communist China?*

She shivered. "That's unexpected . . . and concerning."

"Not so unexpected, actually. America is under relentless cyberattack from the Chinese. Oh, they aren't the only ones probing the cyber defenses surrounding our critical sites. The Russians, Ukrainians, Pakistanis, Indians, and more? All of them have their fingers in our pies, but the Chinese are behind the majority of attacks, primarily through remotely dispatched bots.

"They run relentless bot attacks against US Government entities, particularly DOD and DOE. Bots probe and test our military defense systems and our power and transportation grids seeking and exploiting vulnerabilities.

"And they don't assault just government sites. Their best coders hack and steal American corporations' intellectual property. Then China manufactures knockoff products and undercuts American merchandise on the open market. They hide behind proxies and buy into our companies in an effort to leverage them against us.

"But this organization, AEA? We think AEA, although in its infancy, is something we've not yet seen. We have only an inkling of what they're planning, but we cannot afford for them to bring their plans to maturity and catch us unprepared."

Laynie slowly exhaled. "Not my area of expertise. I don't quite see their endpoint."

"We don't either, which is why we want to dangle Jaz in front of the AEA and make her as tantalizing as possible. If we successfully insert her into that primary AEA cell, she may provide the missing context we need—particularly if she can sell how we're going to bill her."

"Bill her how?"

Wolfe drew a photo from his suit pocket. Laid a full-color headshot on Laynie's desk.

"That's Jaz's badge photo, but we had one of our techs alter it. We toned down her *style*, shall we say, because, as I indicated, AEA isn't as transparently nonconformist as our Jaz is. But look closely at her eyes."

Laynie studied Jaz's eyes, focusing first on their striking color before attending to their slight palpebral slant. "You're suggesting that she may have some Asian in her ancestry?"

"That's it exactly. That's how we'll build her background—raised in America with Chinese grandparents on her mother's side—grandparents who were avowed Communists of the heavy-handed Marxist variety."

"But with *green* eyes?"

"We'll fold that physical trait into her background by adding an absentee Anglo father. Actually, we think her green eyes will work in our favor. 'The better to hide in plain sight, my dear,' not unlike the rest of AEA's leadership."

Laynie nodded. "I get you. But still . . . Jaz cracked under pressure when the Ukrainian mob assassins attacked our apartments. I'm not altogether convinced that she has the temperament for high-pressure covert ops."

"We disagree. Perhaps she was simply caught outside of her element—she was jerked out of a dead sleep when the assassins attacked, right?"

"Well, yes. I give you that."

"Bella, Jaz has never struck me as a shrinking violet. She's street savvy, aggressive, and highly independent. Before she came to us, she was the Royal Canadian Mounted Police's top cybersecurity expert with unfettered access to the RCMP's system and networks. I hear she was also running cybersecurity gigs around the world, not to mention any odd job that called for her type of expertise—enriching herself 'on the side' so to speak, with the Canadian Security Intelligence Service's tacit consent.

"As one of those side jobs, when the FAA detoured your plane to Canada on 9/11, Jaz ran the Ukrainian mob's op to hunt you down. When she decided instead to save you from that charming fellow, Zakhar, and hack the mob's financials into the bargain, she made an enemy of them. That was when she needed a safe haven and we took her in."

"That's all true," Laynie admitted, "But . . ."

"You say Jaz hasn't the temperament for high-pressure covert ops? Why, then, do her international hacker friends, to this day, call her *Vyper, the Venom Queen?* That doesn't paint Jaz as weak, helpless, or blubbering like a baby on the floor. Sorry, I can't picture it because that's not the woman I know."

Wolfe cracked a smile. "I mean, have you ever sat back and watched Jaz lie?"

Laynie couldn't help it; she grinned. "Like a rug."

"Precisely. She has a will of steel and can prevaricate in real time. As for basic spycraft? She learns quickly, and Richard and Harris will train her hard. The proof is in the pudding, as the saying goes. If she passes Richard and Harris' exacting standards and earns a thumbs up from them, *well and good.* If not? She returns to Resolute, richer for the experience."

Laynie slowly acquiesced. "All right."

"Good. I had wanted to speak to her today, but I understand that we can't take our eyes off Attaf and his fellow terrorists at this critical juncture.

"However, once the strike team takes Attaf down, do I then have your *permission* to speak to Jaz—our most wonderful 'The-Task-Force-Can't-Get-Along-Without-Me' senior analyst?"

The tips of Laynie's mouth curved upward. "Yes, Director, and I'd like to be in the room when you do, sir. Just to watch."

She smirked. "Mainly, I want to see Jaz's expression when you tell her you're sending her to Broadsword—especially the part about Harris being her training officer."

Wolfe bent a sharp look on her. "Something I should know? An interpersonal conflict?"

Laynie's expression smoothed. "No, sir. Not a conflict."

Wolfe even believed her—until she allowed a snicker to escape.

"Harris? Oh, yeah. She'll *love* that part."

CHAPTER 3

WOLFE DISPATCHED an agency strike team on an overnight flight to Amsterdam. The strike team spent two days surveilling the Rabobank branch where Attaf had opened an account; in addition, they inserted a female agent into the bank as an employee. During the bank's operating hours, while strike team members watched every entrance and egress, the female agent monitored the bank's computer system, keeping her eyes on the account Jaz had identified as belonging to Attaf.

Late on the second day of surveillance, the strike team's careful work paid off when the inside agent radioed her team leader. "A customer just made a sizable cash withdrawal, then closed Attaf's account and wired its remaining funds to a bank in Yemen. The individual who completed the transaction is exiting the bank as I speak—male, five ten, dark hair, blue-and-black patterned shirt."

At her alert, the strike team moved into a predetermined order for following the young man. The team members leapfrogged over each other, one in a van, another on a motorcycle, yet a third in a commandeered taxi, a fourth on a moped, each of them radioing the suspect's position and direction before handing him off to the next agent in the rotation, so that no individual followed the suspect more than a few blocks at a time.

Their suspect led them to a dozen narrow, two-story buildings on a damp and decaying street. The conjoined structures' tall, peaked roofs towered over a crumbling part-commercial, part-residential ghost town of a neighborhood. While a pair of concealed strike team members observed and photographed, the suspect unlocked the fifth ground-floor door in the row and disappeared inside. Signage on the building he entered announced that it was a tailor's shop, but the shop was permanently shuttered—as were the bakery to the left, the shoe repair shop on the right, and the remaining street-level storefronts up and down the street.

As darkness fell, the strike team's careful reconnaissance of the area revealed only front and rear exits from the tailor's shop. Consultation with certain Amsterdam housing authorities (yanked without apology from their suppers) told them that the second floor over the defunct tailor's establishment had once been living quarters for the shop owners below. Indeed the entire row, as far back as eighty years, had once housed twelve shop owners, their families, and their modest enterprises—but that was before the buildings with their outdated plumbing, primitive sewage systems, and frayed electrical wiring had been condemned.

According to the disgruntled Amsterdam housing authorities, no apartments in the rat-infested buildings should have been occupied.

The strike team's leader contacted Wolfe directly. "Sir, we have ascertained Attaf's location. We will execute the op thirty minutes prior to dawn, Amsterdam time."

LAYNIE GLANCED—for the umpteenth time—at her watch. The time difference between Amsterdam and Germantown was six hours. For Task Force Resolute, thirty minutes before daybreak in Amsterdam would be 11:00 p.m. Thursday evening.

That night, while across the ocean the strike team made their preparations to take down Attaf, Griffin Industries was the only building alight in their section of the industrial park. By 10:25, Laynie, Director Wolfe, and Task Force Resolute—all members present and accounted for—were gathered around a powerful radio unit set up in the center of the bullpen.

Although they would be nonparticipant listeners, no member of Resolute wanted to miss the strike team's op. By unspoken consensus, task force members were willing to spend the night at Griffin Industries, if necessary, to see the operation through. To that end, they had stepped out for a quiet dinner as a group in anticipation of the prolonged workday. Laynie had arranged for fresh coffee, tea, and fruit to fortify them as the evening progressed.

At 10:40, the strike team's leader called with an update. He had staged a six-man breaching team across the street facing the shop's front door and positioned two three-man teams at either end of the alley behind the row of buildings. As the strike team completed its preparations, the task force— collectively holding its breath—leaned toward the radio. However, Resolute heard only the occasional clipped strike team exchange.

By 10:50, the tension in the bullpen was palpable. Laynie needed to stretch, so she got up and walked behind the workstations in the bullpen.

"One of these days," she heard Brian grouse softly, "we'll have the technology to watch live, right there with a strike team as they take down the bad guys. This listening to a bunch of disembodied voices and trying to piece together what's going on is for the birds."

Wolfe shifted his attention to Brian. "What would technology like that look like, Mr. Tayhill? And how would watching a live op work from such a distance?"

Brian sat up, eager to prognosticate on future tech. "Through the team members' individual helmet or body cameras, most likely. The strike team guys are already wearing helmet cams that send live video signals to the strike team leader. It's the tech necessary to 'live stream' that signal to distant end users in real or near-real time that's currently undeveloped."

"We desperately need improved video quality too," Rusty chimed in. "Let's say that somehow we were simultaneously viewing the dozen individual feeds from our strike team members' helmet cams and watching it on our big monitor here in the bullpen. With present-day streaming video quality, the feeds would be low res, jumpy, grainy, and grayscale."

Wolfe frowned. "The reason for such poor resolution, Mr. Buchen?"

"Video bitrate, mainly," Rusty said. "The higher the video quality, the greater the bitrate. Standard computers don't yet have the memory, computing power, or graphic display hardware and drivers to process and display high-bandwidth video streams, nor can our 'state-of-the-art' T1 or T2 Internet pipelines feed them to us fast enough. Someday they will, someday soon, hopefully—but those are just a few of our technological obstacles."

"I see. And how would video be—what did you call it? 'live streamed'?—from across vast distances, Mr. Tayhill? Will it ever be possible?"

Brian nodded thoughtfully. "Sure it will. I figure the helmet cam video feed would upload to a satellite in orbit above the action, across to another satellite in orbit above us, then download to us in *near*-real time—gotta allow for a slight time lag. But in addition to what Rusty said, we also don't have enough satellites in orbit to cover the populated parts of the earth at all times.

"See, right now, US military or intelligence can task a satellite to fly over a specified target and continuously photograph the target until the satellite moves out of range of the target. The satellite sends its still images to the tasking element, *us*, for example. Watched in rapid succession, the still images provide the illusion of video, but only from above, not from the ground, not at all like being embedded with one of the strike team members, seeing the action from his or her perspective. And again, the satellite's window over the target is temporary. And until we get higher resolution cameras, the images taken by the satellite will be a grainy grayscale."

Rusty shrugged. "For all those reasons, we're still years from true live stream capability—"

Brian jumped in, "Yeah we are, but when all that pie-in-the-sky surveillance tech does emerge? It'll explode. Why, we'll be able to—"

Jaz made a slicing gesture across her throat. "Can it, boys. It's time, and some of us want to listen."

Director Wolfe dipped his chin toward Jaz. "I apologize for distracting your people."

Jaz had the grace to blush. "Not a problem—"

The strident order of the strike team's leader cut in. "Breaching team, you are go, go, go!"

What Laynie and the task force heard next were the crashing sounds of doors breaking, the panting of strike team members as they hustled through the shop's front entrance, followed by thundering feet on the stairs leading to the second floor, overlapping shouts, more garbled noise, and a brief exchange of gunfire.

Then they heard, "Alpha, this is Bravo. We've found bombmaking materials and an explosive device. We have one suspect in custody. Be advised that the remaining suspects, count four, climbed a ladder into a crawlspace inside the peaked roof above us. We can hear them moving away from us. I say again: Four suspects are no longer directly above us. They are moving north in the crawlspace above us."

Confounded mutters filled the bullpen.

"Stow it!" Jaz barked.

The task force lapsed into silence while waiting for more information.

Bravo spoke again. "Alpha, we've determined that the attics of these apartments can be accessed across the entire row of buildings. I've sent two of my men in pursuit. Sending the rest down to cover all street-level exits. Again, we need to cover *all exits* from the row, street level."

Although no one on the task force spoke during the pounding and heavy breathing of the strike team's rush to reposition themselves, Laynie shared a look of frustration with Jaz. The strike team may have deprived the terrorists of the bomb they'd intended to detonate in *this* city, but had they lost Attaf in the process? Would he and his people escape and reemerge later to bomb another unsuspecting city?

Brian couldn't handle the suspense. "What's going on? I can't make out what's happening!"

No one on the task force spoke, because no one had an answer for him.

Then, through the jumble of a dozen mingled feeds, sudden shouted commands rang out.

"Freeze! Stop where you are!"

"Get on the ground! Get on the ground! Get on the ground!"

A brief exchange of gunfire punctuated the commands.

"I said *down!* Get on the ground!"

More muffled words followed. For several minutes, the task force waited, the tension so thick that no one dared move or utter a word.

Finally, a now-familiar voice spoke. "Alpha, this is Bravo. We have them. Repeat. We have them! Five targets in custody; one casualty. No friendlies wounded."

It was a decidedly good thing that the radio in the bullpen was receiving only, not transmitting—a good thing that the strike team could not hear Task Force Resolute's reaction—because raucous pandemonium broke out. Gwyneth, Jubaila, and Soraya, bouncing up and down in a group hug, shrieked their delight. Rusty, Brian, and Vincent shouted, hooted, whistled, and high-fived.

Laynie glanced at Jaz. She was draped over the back of her chair like a wet dishrag, the poster child of exhausted relief.

She managed to exhale and nod to her boss. "Guess we did it."

Laynie smiled. "We sure did."

As the noise started to die down, Wolfe clapped his hands to get the task force's attention.

"Thank you. Thank you all—each and every one of you. Your work to end this threat has been exceptional, your devotion and perseverance worthy of great commendation."

Applause and shouts disrupted him, but he just grinned at the task force's joyful antics.

"As I was saying, Task Force Resolute is worthy of great commendation. And, as a small acknowledgement of my appreciation for your labor, please take tomorrow off—or should I say take the rest of today off? In any event, it's now past midnight, so technically Friday morning. Sleep in a few hours and enjoy some down time."

Interrupted by more cheers, he waited until the din died down.

"Although you'll have the rest of today and all of Saturday off, please report back here Sunday evening at 5:00 p.m.—but not for work. Instead, I want you to dress up. Put on your best party duds and your dancing shoes. Get ready to let down your hair and prepare to be formally and thoroughly feted. I intend to have an unforgettable dinner catered in, along with a dance floor and a DJ, all to celebrate your accomplishments. Afterward, you are free to finish out the evening as you wish."

Over cheers and more enthusiastic applause, Brian exclaimed, "Rockin'! Totally rockin'!"

"Yes!" his teammates shouted in agreement.

Wolfe spoke again when he was able to regain their attention. "I apologize ahead of time, but you'll need to come in Monday, regular time. Resolute has a lot of reports to write and file."

A low "boo" went around the room.

"I know, I know. I hope Sunday evening's party will make it up to you."

The team cheered and applauded. Wolfe extended his hand to Laynie and said for all to hear, "Outstanding, Ms. Tobin. Outstanding."

"Thank you, sir."

Laynie watched as Wolfe then worked his way around the bullpen, shaking hands with individual task force members, adding a personal word of thanks to each one.

He ended at Jaz's workstation, and Laynie joined him there. At the last possible moment, Jaz caught Laynie's repeated gesture from behind Wolfe's back and jumped to her feet as he reached out his hand.

"Excellent work, Miss Jessup. Well done. Well done, indeed."

Jaz tucked the wad of gum in her mouth to one side. "Thank you, sir."

She was openly nonplussed when he added, "By the way, I have a proposition for you, Miss Jessup, something that may appeal to your adventurous side. To that end, would you be amenable to meeting with me Monday morning at, shall we say, 9:00 a.m.?"

Jaz jinked her startled gaze toward Laynie and received an almost imperceptible nod in return. Jaz tossed the wad of gum in her mouth to the other side before answering.

"Yah. Okay. Uh, I mean, *yes*, sir. That would be . . . amenable for me. To me. Er, *with* me."

"Glad to hear it. I'll see you at the party Sunday evening and then nine o'clock Monday morning."

He looked to Laynie. "Shall we meet in your office?"

"Of course, Director."

"Excellent."

To Laynie, Wolfe added, "And if it's convenient, Ms. Tobin, feel free to bring your family to the Task Force's celebration."

She knew that what he really meant was, "Everyone wants to see Ksenia; don't come without her."

Laynie laughed. "I'm pretty sure I can manage that."

"Good." He turned and waved goodbye to the task force. "I will see you all at our celebration party."

CHAPTER 4

Vyper

JAZ SLEPT hard and long the remainder of that night and took her slow, sweet time waking up. She stretched while the kettle heated on her stove, then took her morning tea out onto her apartment's veranda. She smiled at the ornamental trees in bloom, closed her eyes while a light breeze riffled her hair. She was truly relaxed and enjoying herself for the first time in weeks . . . until an unwelcome notion wormed its way into her head.

Her tea cup clenched in one hand, Jaz retraced her steps to her bedroom and stared into her closet. The walk-in was filled with clothing she liked and enjoyed wearing. Soft, loose sweaters, blousy tops, calf-length broom skirts, two "funky" dresses, and a wide variety of jeans. Clunky sandals, knee-high boots, and thick-soled and thicker-heeled Doc Martens lined the closet floor.

Jaz loved her wardrobe. She believed it spelled out the five "Cs" necessary for clothing: Cool. Campy. Chic. Classy. Comfortable. But . . .

She abandoned her cooling cup of tea to the little table next to her bed. Starting on the closet's left and working her way through her clothing, she ended her search with a muffled curse. Practically everything in the closet was dark—from midnight black to shades of gray, with the occasional sparkle of silver, a swatch of madras, or a colorful scarf thrown in.

She added two other Cs to her attire: Completely Casual. She had not one blessed thing that would achieve Wolfe's expectations of "dressy" or "best duds." And absolutely no "dancing shoes."

Get ready to let down my hair? Too much time has elapsed since I last ventured into local nightlife, and apparently I've lost my touch.

She growled low in her throat, "Celebration dinner? *Fine.*"

Disgusted but determined, she turned on her heel, grabbed her shoulder bag, and slouched out her apartment door.

SUNDAY AFTERNOON at the Tobin residence, Laynie fastened a clasp behind her neck and watched in her dresser mirror as a riot of silver strands trickled like rain drops across her fair skin. The strands came to rest at the perfect length for the neckline of a shimmering blue gown.

In the mirror's reflection, Laynie spotted Ksenia standing shyly in Laynie and Quincy's bedroom doorway. The girl had changed her apparel three times already and asked Laynie her opinion with each wardrobe change.

"*Mader*, am I now looking right?"

Knowing how uncertain Ksenia was of American expectations and the insecurities with which she struggled, Laynie stopped what she was doing to give her daughter a thorough examination.

"Oh my. How lovely this dress is on you, Ksenia," Laynie murmured, "The russet color makes your hair gleam like gold. Yes, it suits you well, and I do believe you've made the right choice for the party." She raised her voice to include Tobin in her next comment. "By the way, Ksenia, who thought of adding a few highlights to your hair?"

Ksenia giggled. "The girls at school are doing it. Papa took me after classes tomorrow when you were late to be waking up."

"My goodness—your English is improving by leaps and bounds, my darling girl. But I believe you meant Papa took you *yesterday* when I slept in late." She added, "And evidently Papa loves to spoil you to pieces."

She tipped her head to one side, "I must say, I like the highlights. They add the perfect touch of brightness to your hair." She looked deeply into Ksenia's brown eyes. "But then you were already perfect, my daughter."

Ksenia beamed. "Thank you, *Mader*. I-I wish to be looking like you someday." She stroked the soft fabric of Laynie's gown. "This is being same color of your eyes. You are being so very beautiful!"

"She sure is," Tobin called from deep within his closet. "My wife is *hot!*"

Laynie blushed, and Ksenia giggled again. Laynie's arm went around the girl's waist to pull her close. "Are you about ready, Papa Tobin? We don't want to be late."

Tobin dropped into his countrified jargon. "Hey there, missy! Don' be rushin' me—takes a fair mess o' time to turn out m' *full* manly and studly style. 'Sides, y'all, we have plenty of time."

As he emerged from the closet with a suit swathed in dry cleaners' plastic, he took one look at Ksenia and Laynie, faked a groan and a stagger and, clutching his heart, fell onto the bed. "Behold! I'm knocked over, fair flattened by beauty! Seriously, m' ladies—one at a time you are drop-dead gorgeous, but the two of you together? I can't take it! Can't take it, I tell you! Arghhhh!" His head lolled to its side in faux death.

"Oh, *brother*," Laynie drawled.

"Oh, *brother!*" Ksenia repeated. She tipped her chin toward Laynie in puzzlement. "Who is brother, *Mader?*"

It was Laynie's turn to giggle. She crooked one brow at Ksenia. "Let's get him, shall we?"

"Yes, *brother!*"

She and Ksenia pounced on Tobin.

"Wait! Stop!" Tobin tried to get away but failed miserably. Within seconds he was laughing and squirming.

"You should never have told me you were ticklish, Quincy Tobin," Laynie said.

"Yeah, Papa," Ksenia laughed, digging her fingers into Tobin's ribs. "You should never have told *Mader* you were being ticklish!"

———————◆———————

FIFTY MINUTES later, after Laynie and Ksenia had pressed the wrinkles out of their dresses and repaired their hair, and after Quincy had achieved his "full manly and studly style" he pulled their car into Griffin Industries' garage and parked. Even with the car doors and windows closed, the pounding rhythm of house music reached into the garage.

Quincy, eyes wide, muttered, "Uh, *wow.*"

"Yes, wow," Laynie replied.

"I suppose Wolfe did say 'dancing shoes.'"

"That he did."

They got out, and Quincy called for the elevator. When the doors opened, the throbbing beat thundered down the elevator shaft. Ksenia, her eyes bigger than Quincy's had been, pressed into Laynie's side.

"Don't worry; it's just music, Sweetheart," Laynie murmured. "Or what passes as music in some circles."

"I kinda like it," Quincy said with a grin. "'Tis makin' m' feet twitch."

With a snort, Laynie replied, "Yeah? Well, it's making my eyes jump right out of my head." She muttered to herself, "Girl, you are a world away from the Moscow Symphony."

They rode the elevator up to Griffin Industries' lobby . . . and stepped out into a pulsing, strobing fairyland. Twinkling lights festooned the walls and ceiling. A long, candlelit table set with fine china and crystal stemware for eleven, awaited the team on the right side of the foyer. A modular dance floor, presided over by a grinning, jiving DJ, properly screened and vetted, of course, took up the other side. Above the dance floor, a disco ball twisted and sparkled.

Ksenia, her expression slack, pointed. "*Mader*, look!"

"Oh, believe me. I'm looking."

Members of Task Force Resolute had gotten there ahead of them and were already on the dance floor, fully invested in cutting up and having a good time. Someone had issued them noise makers, bubble pipes, and party blowouts.

"But *Mader!* See my uncles and my aunties?"

Laynie laughed. "I see them, all right."

Truthfully? She scarcely recognized her team. Gwyneth, Jubaila, and Soraya shone in party dresses of saffron, emerald, and scarlet, with strappy heels to match. It was obvious, too, that they had spent part of the day having their nails done and with stylists who had curled, primped, and pinned up their hair while weaving sparkling "bling" into the curls.

As for Vincent and Rusty? They were resplendent in suitcoats and slacks—but Brian? Brian had the disco look down cold, and the moves as well. His shiny gold suit, crimson shirt, and gold tone-on-tone tie moved in perfect sync with every throb and thump of the music.

Laynie gawked when, at the end of a particularly "hip" move, right on the beat, Brian actually "shot his cuffs" so that an edge of crimson popped out of the end of his suitcoat's sleeves. But if that wasn't enough, she also caught a glimpse of matching crimson socks above Brian's black shoes.

Laynie had to hide her mirth against Tobin's chest.

"Oh, Brian," she muttered, "you are in a class of your own."

Tobin agreed. "You're not wrong, Sweet Pea."

Ksenia, with a sage nod, added "Oh, *brother!*" and that tore it for her parents. Laynie and Tobin fell together in choking laughter. They were still snickering when Director Wolfe, dressed in a fine evening tux, joined them.

He fixed his gaze on the dance floor, his expression carefully neutral. "Never know what you're going to get at an office party."

"Good one, Director," Tobin snarked. He added, "Well, this evening confirms my suspicion that tech geniuses hide the inner depths of their lives by day—and that Brian has cornered the market on nerdiness."

Laynie feigned incredulity. "You needed this evening as confirmation?"

Ksenia, unable to take her eyes off the dancing, asked, "What is *nerdy-ness, Mader?*"

"Tell you in the morning, Sweetheart."

The music broke off, and a voice boomed through the lobby. "Good evening everyone! I'm Dave, your DJ for this rockin', hoppin' party!"

Whoops and shouts greeted him.

"Thank you, thank you, thank you! Tell you what, I'm going to take a short break now. I'll be back in five."

Groans of disappointment followed, until those on the dance floor noticed Quincy, Laynie, and Ksenia and rushed toward them. Rather, they rushed as one toward Ksenia.

"Ksenia!"

Director Wolfe retreated, wisely moving out of the herd's path. Laynie and Tobin stood their ground yet were neatly sidled aside as six of Ksenia's honorary aunts and uncles jockeyed for position to hug their honorary niece.

As they surrounded her, they complimented her dress and hair, and generally loved her to pieces. Ksenia, smiling shyly, basked in their attention.

Even with the music off, Laynie's ears itched and tingled, but at least she could hear again. In fact, she heard when the elevator dinged, announcing someone's arrival. Smiling at the general melee around Ksenia, she idly wondered, *Huh. Who isn't here yet?*

She turned as the doors parted.

So did the others.

For a long moment the person within the elevator car did not move—no doubt taking in the extent of the lobby's alteration. Backlit as the individual was, all Laynie saw was the outline of curvy hips, tiny waist, and an ample bosom . . . wrapped in glistening, floor-length, figure-hugging neon purple, one purple-gloved hand resting on said hip. The figure, on three-inch spike heels of matching neon purple hue, slid a single foot forward, and a side slit in the dress revealed a long leg sheathed in glittering thigh-high black fishnet stocking.

"Holy *cow!*" Brian gulped. "Someone fetch the defibrillator—my heart just stalled out!"

Rusty threw an arm over Brian's shoulder. "Steady there, bro. We'll get through this together . . . or should I say, may the best man win?"

Vincent muscled his way in front of them both. "Get thee behind me, gents. *Yowza!*"

The figure paused to leisurely draw a second purple satin glove up her sleek arm where it ended inches above her elbow but below her bare shoulder.

The ticking of the foyer's clock was the only audible sound . . . until Ksenia piped up, "It's Auntie Jaz!"

Brian stumbled. "What?"

Jaz, a gloved hand still resting on her hip, stalked—one loooong leg at a time—into the lobby.

"Heard there's supposed to be a party. What's the holdup?"

CHAPTER 5

MONDAY MORNING, following Resolute's Sunday evening celebration, Wolfe plopped into the chair in front of Laynie's desk. "Not with it yet. Having trouble recovering from last night. Short on sleep."

Laynie lifted a brow. "You and everyone else. And I can't *unsee* what we saw last night."

"Exactly. Certain, er, *scenes* hijacked any hope for peaceful slumber. Ran on a loop like a gerbil on a wheel, they did. Thus, I did not get much in the way of sleep."

"Uh-huh. At least you didn't have Ksenia humming *YMCA* all the way home—thank you for that, by the way. When she started back up this morning at breakfast, Quincy actually growled at her. He was *that* close to bending his fork in half."

Wolfe cracked one eye toward Laynie. "I confess that I must now mistrust my own judgment when it comes to arranging appropriate celebratory rewards. I offer my sincere apologies, Ms. Tobin."

"As you should, sir—what with the pinnacle of the evening being Jaz and Brian doing their rendition of a *very* spicy tango. *Really, sir?* I need to bleach my eyes."

He shuddered. "Jaz and Brian. Who'd have thought? That exhibition is forever emblazoned on my brain. Again, I apologize."

Laynie inclined her head. "It's true that Task Force Resolute has been strung too tight for most of its short life. I mean, it hasn't been a year since you ordered us to stand up this task force. To be blunt, sir, our people have experienced nothing but go, go, go and danger, danger, danger since Resolute's inception. And six months ago, when this facility was attacked? They gave up their homes and gave up their Thanksgiving and Christmas holidays to push through dire circumstances and to snatch victory from those who sought to kill innocent civilians. Sure, all of us in Resolute got a vacation after the threat passed, but shortly after their return to work, they were dumped right back into the same level of stress due to Attaf and his merry band of child killers.

"For weeks now, the task force has lived and breathed Attaf and his bombs, knowing that if they failed to stop him, more innocent children would lose their lives. Sadly, stress of that kind takes a mental, physical, and emotional toll."

"Yes, well . . ."

"Right. Our people needed and deserved an immediate celebration, and you went all out to give them one. Just . . ." Laynie took a moment to choose the right words. "I think that because of the work they do, they needed more than a nice dinner, and perhaps you sensed that. They needed an outlet for the unrelenting pressure they live under—hence the rather uncharacteristic behavior we witnessed last night."

Laynie snickered. "I mean, group karaoke? The seven of them belting out *Sweet Caroline* followed by *Love Shack*, and reaching an epic finale with *Bohemian Rhapsody*? And then when we witnessed Brian and Jaz—"

Wolfe's hand shot out. "Please. Don't go there again."

"Right. Thank you for saving us both. Would you care to discuss our upcoming meeting with Jaz, Director?"

He sighed. "Frankly, I can't function without more coffee . . . but I'm afraid to walk through the bullpen alone."

Laynie assumed a solemn expression and did not allow it to crack or slip. "I'd be happy to hold your hand all the way to the breakroom and back. *Sir*."

—■◆■—

AT THE appointed hour, Jaz tapped on Bella's office door. When Bella called, "Come in," in response to her soft knock, Jaz opened the door and stepped inside Bella's office.

Her furtive scan noted nothing of concern. Nothing ominous. Wolfe and Bella seemed to be chatting amiably over coffee. They glanced up as she entered.

"You wanted to see me, Director Wolfe?"

"Yes, Miss Jessup. Please take a seat with us." He indicated the chair next to his in front of Bella's desk.

As soon as Jaz settled, Wolfe got down to it. "Back in January when Marshal Tobin and I returned to Broadsword with Bella and Ksenia, Seraphim and I conducted a classified debriefing to tie up loose ends and to ensure that everyone on the task force had some closure to the op."

Jaz, slowly chewing her gum, nodded. "Sure. I remember the debriefing."

"Good. Do you also recall after we concluded the debriefing, while people were still mingling, that you and I shared a moment? We spoke of the Ukrainian mob's encrypted files in the FBI's custody. How the New York FBI

Field Office believed they had experienced a cyberattack and that something had happened to the files, but no one knew what, given that the contents of those files were and remain encrypted."

Jaz forced her eyes to remain fixed on Wolfe while she kept her features carefully neutral.

So that's what this is about?

On the one hand, she was relieved. On the other? She fought the smirk that threatened to tweak her mouth.

Glad to hear the FBI still hasn't got a clue. They'll never be able to prove that I replaced those files with encrypted junk—or how I managed to do so.

"Yes, I remember our conversation."

The sardonic glint in Wolfe's eye overrode his mild reply. "I'd be surprised if you didn't, Miss Jessup."

Jaz nodded and blinked once, slowly. A second time, in complete innocence. "Well, sure."

Wolfe's shrewd gaze drilled deep into hers, and the corners of his mouth turned up—just a fraction. In Jaz's overly fanciful imagination, it was enough. She saw his expression morph into a sinister facsimile of his namesake.

She clenched her teeth to keep a shiver at bay.

After a long, charged moment, Wolfe added, "I believe that day I also expressed my hope that we might have opportunity later to talk about your future with us, Miss Jessup. Specifically, I said that, with proper training, we might expand the scope of your duties. Well, today is 'later.'"

Now Jaz looked from Wolfe to Bella and back to Wolfe.

Might what?

"Might expand the scope of my duties, sir? What does that mean? You don't think I'm doing enough? Working hard enough?"

"No, that's not what this meeting is about. We have an emerging situation for which I feel you may be suited and of assistance to us." He paused before adding, "In the field."

"Who, me? A field agent?"

"Yes, you. I'm proposing that we send you out for a spot of training to see how you take to it."

"But . . . why me?"

"As I said that day, you have an aptitude for prevaricating. I believe my exact words were, 'You lie with the best of us professional liars. We should make better use of you.'"

Jaz's upper lip itched. She wanted to either gnaw at the itch or spew a nervous laugh, but she knew better than to give in to her inclinations. They were watching her reactions, judging her responses.

Well, let them look; *she* was all business.

Jaz nonchalantly chewed her gum. "What's the play?"

Wolfe, his eyes still fastened on her, got down to it. "The play, as you call it, is to insert you into an organization of growing concern to us. It's a US-based organization, although we believe the group is a front for the Chinese."

"What? The Chinese as in the Chinese government?"

"Yes. We may refer to them going forward as the CCP—the Chinese Communist Party. We also fear this group is planning a terrorist attack."

"That's what Resolute does, hunt down terrorists, but the Chinese fronting a terrorist org? Wouldn't that be an improbable move on their part?"

"It would be, yes. Furthermore, if this group *is* a terrorist organization, they've chosen a strange way to form and run it. Their demographics are atypical, for one thing. The problem is, we don't know enough about them, but we think you would fit right in."

Wolfe swiveled his chair around so he could more easily speak directly to Jaz and watch her responses. "This organization promotes itself as American Equality for All, AEA for short. They style themselves as social justice crusaders and have attracted American adherents who view the US as a less-than-just society built on European colonial conquest and the subjugation of minority races.

"Publicly, AEA is an ultra-liberal and socially progressive alliance of urban-based cells in thirteen states, with a significant presence in large cities across those states. While professing to be nonmilitant and nonviolent, they advocate for drastic social and governmental transformation, employing the usual activist change tactics such as protests, lawsuits, and electioneering."

Jaz shrugged. "Hundreds of groups like that in the US. Maybe thousands."

"Yes, and those numbers make it easy for AEA to blend in—just one of many such groups one might encounter in a big city, do you see? But what if I were to tell you that membership in AEA is by recruitment only, that AEA recruits only the best and brightest from a wide spectrum of ethnicities, yet we believe all top AEA leaders are CCP sleeper agents?"

Jaz's jaws slowed to a stop. "I think I'd be reasonably concerned, sir."

"Concerned how? For typical terrorist activities? Bombings? Mass transit violence? Radiological attacks?"

"Uh-uh. Nope. I'm no expert on the CCP, sir, but I don't think bloody mayhem abroad reflects China's preferred public image, do you? I mean, at home where they control the media, maybe, but that's not the self-portrait they present to the world."

"Well, you're right so far. We have seen no evidence of typical terrorist activities in AEA's behavior. AEA's members may be racially and ethnically diverse—in other words, intentionally wide-ranging at a glance—but beyond their surface appearance? What we've noted is that these same AEA members share multiple commonalities. They are well-educated, gainfully employed, highly skilled in one technical capacity or another, and of course, they share similar extremist geopolitical leanings."

Jaz's mouth tightened. "Gainfully employed how and for whom, sir?"

"Architects, civil and electrical engineers, attorneys, communications specialists, journalists, city planners employed across a spectrum of companies. Their resumés and work profiles are so varied, we've not been able to pinpoint a common target. That's why we need someone on the inside."

Wolfe reached for his briefcase and removed a rolled-up document.

"May I?" he asked Bella.

"Of course, sir."

The two of them unrolled a map of the continental US, stretched it across her desk, and secured its corners with books. Red dots identified two cities along the Pacific coast states with a solitary dot in eastern Washington State. The majority of the dots appeared in the American South and up the inland East Coast, stretching from the Gulf to the lower Great Lakes.

"Not a *single* terrorist target then," Jaz muttered, talking to herself and no longer to Wolfe. "Also not a political figure or entity. Not a bloodstained 'statement.' Something bigger or broader . . . or designed to occur in stages?"

She shook her head. "Sorry, Director. Nothing's coming to me. And if I'm honest with you, I'm not interested in going out into the field. Thanks, but no thanks."

Wolfe didn't appreciate Jaz's flip but firm response. He managed to remain civil though. "I see. Well, in any event, I thank you for what you do here with Resolute; it's important work. Vital work. *So is this.*" He rolled the map, stuck it back into his briefcase, nodded to Bella, and walked out.

Jaz offered Bella a sheepish shrug.

Bella smiled. "Don't worry about Director Wolfe, Jaz. He's disappointed, but he'll get over it. As for me? I'm relieved."

"You and me both. I don't do undercover, role-playing stuff."

Nope. Not for me.

Not anymore.

She shivered. "Frankly, gives me the creeps just thinking about it."

CHAPTER 6

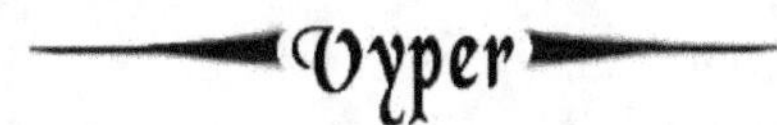

EARLY MORNING the next day, Jaz knocked on the jamb of Bella's open office door. "Hey, Bella. Do you have a minute?"

"Sure. What's up?"

Jaz sat. Played with her pack of gum. Grimaced and shook her head. "Last evening, I went over what we talked about with Director Wolfe. I thought about it. A *lot*. Couldn't get it out of my head, to tell you the truth."

"But as I already said, Jaz, Director Wolfe will get over it. You don't need to beat yourself up because you declined an assignment you're not suited for."

"No, it's not that," Jaz sighed. "It's about the map he showed us. I kept seeing it in my head all night long, so I got up and did some research online, checked out some bulletin boards, chatted with a few people and . . . I think I've figured it out. Figured out *something*, at any rate. I have a theory about AEA's activities, and I'd like to run it by the Director. See if it holds water?"

Bella stared at her. Took her time responding.

"You believe this 'something' you've figured out is important enough to ask Director Wolfe to come back? You know he's not in the habit of sitting around waiting for things to happen. He's a busy man."

"We could go to him if he prefers."

Laynie probed deeper. "You're certain he should hear your, what? Notion? Idea? Working theory?"

Jaz vacillated momentarily, then bobbed her head. "I really hope it's not true, but *crud*. Yes, I think it's important."

"And you'd like me in on this meeting?"

"Yah, please."

"All right. I'll set it up."

WOLFE APPEARED in Resolute's offices two hours later. Jaz and Bella were waiting for him.

"Thank you for coming back, sir," Jaz said. "I apologize in advance if this ends up being a waste of your time, but . . . I don't think it will be. Thanks, too, for bringing the map with you."

"You said you had something?"

Jaz shifted with discomfort. "I believe so. Uh, could we look at the map together?"

Wolfe and Bella again spread the map across her desk and weighted its corners.

"You said yesterday that AEA members share multiple commonalities, that they are tech savvy and employed across a broad spectrum of companies. What if AEA is positioning their people in companies and organizations that are the linchpins of . . ."

Her words petered out.

"Yes? Finish your thought?"

Instead, Jaz said, "Tell me again about AEA's leadership. You said AEA leaders were sleeper agents for the CCP. How have you identified them as such?"

Jaz was asking him to divulge sensitive information, but Wolfe didn't object. Jaz had one of the sharpest minds he'd encountered in his lengthy career, a career that spanned decades as an intelligence operative and foreign asset manager culminating in his role as "spymaster," overseeing several specialized "off book" intelligence branches, one of which was hidden within the tech giant, Marstead International. Yes, Wolfe knew brilliance when he saw it—idiosyncrasies and all.

"To date, all AEA leaders we've identified, and their immediate deputies, are the American-born children or grandchildren of Chinese immigrants. As we dug deeper into these immigrants, we often hit a wall, finding that their history in China had been erased. Expunged. *But*, in every instance where we were able to find traces of their past lives in China, we determined that those immigrants to the US had been hardline Chinese communists back in the old country."

"If they were hardline communists, does it make sense for them to immigrate? *No*. It makes me wonder why they would want to leave China," Bella observed.

Jaz snorted. "If they *were* hardline communists? May I guess at your conclusions, Director? You and the team that's been surveilling AEA suspect that these parents or grandparents were selected *expressly* for their communist loyalties and that they were tasked to immigrate to the US to facilitate a long-term operation. You believe that their assignment was to radicalize and train their children or their grandchildren to carry out that op."

She laughed without mirth. "Why, that's old-school Soviet spy doctrine."

"Yes, we infer that the CCP has taken a page or two from their communist cousins. Some of those parents or grandparents even intermarried with white Americans, purposely diluting their offspring's Chinese ethnicity."

Jaz nodded, still more in her own thoughts than in conversation with Wolfe. "What's the name of that classic film, an old Charles Bronson movie? Oh, yah. It's called *Telefon*. The movie's premise is that fifty or so Soviet sleeper agents were embedded in America years ago while they were young. They don't know they are sleeper agents, though, because they were all hypnotized before they were placed—hypnotized and programmed to marry Americans and live typical American lives, until they received a phone call and the caller quoted a certain poem to them."

Wolfe spoke lines from a Robert Frost poem. "*The woods are lovely, dark and deep, but I have promises to keep, and miles to go before I sleep.*"

"Yah, that's the one. In the movie, those lines awakened the sleeper agents from their hypnotic state and activated them. Sent them out to complete detailed, preprogrammed acts of sabotage."

"Yes, but in this case nothing so dramatic as that, I hope," Wolfe said softly. "While AEA's members are frankly anti-capitalism and they publicly protest a variety of US policies, including capitalism, as so many naïve young Americans do, they also profess to be nonviolent."

"Nonviolent? I doubt it," Jaz said, her words cold.

"You could be right, I suppose. As a rule, the leap from ardent 'nonviolent' socialist ideology to brutal Marxist totalitarianism is but a short step down—and yet it is a destination to which the proponents of 'compassionate' and 'democratic' neo-socialism are commonly blind."

"They don't believe socialism's historical record," Bella whispered, "but I lived a long time in the Soviet Union. I didn't just see the oppression; I was immersed in it."

"You were rich and pampered," Wolfe reminded her, "the mistress of a wealthy oligarch. I doubt you were oppressed."

"It is true that I was one of the privileged elite, but I was also under unrelenting scrutiny, as are all people within a totalitarian regime. I was also a spy sent to steal Russia's emerging tech—particularly weapons technology—which compounded my jeopardy. If I had been caught . . ." She shuddered. "I never drew a free breath all the years I was there."

Jaz brought them back to the topic at hand. "I think you've missed my point entirely, Director."

Wolfe returned his attention to her. "Have I?"

"Yes, sir. As we discussed yesterday, bloody attacks on the public at large—bombings and such—are not AEA's usual public persona. You've also determined that AEA's recruits are educated, tech-savvy, and upwardly mobile.

Well, since their members are chosen for those characteristics, I'd bet they are also carefully placed in the companies where they are employed."

"We thought so too, but placed to do what? As I mentioned earlier, their placements, as you call them, are literally, all over the map. We haven't been able to identify AEA's objective."

"I may have."

Jaz spoke so quietly that Wolfe said, "Say again?"

Jaz sighed. "I think AEA may be planning a coordinated, multi-state attack on the single most necessary and also most *fragile* of American infrastructures—the US power grid."

Wolfe looked incredulous. "You got all that just from scanning this map, did you? I don't buy it. For years, various government branches, including the military, have warned that a high-altitude nuclear explosion would create a giant electromagnetic pulse, an EMP. They consider an EMP to be the greatest threat to our grid because a large one could fry electrical systems and their vulnerable components, such as integrated circuits, over a sizable geographic area. However, while an EMP might be the goal of a non-state terrorist group, we're talking the Chinese government here, not a terrorist organization."

He shook his head. "I see three problems with your idea. One, why would the CCP position sleeper agents inside the US if an EMP was their plan? The nuke would need to be dropped by plane and detonated while still at a high altitude or launched from ground or sea into the atmosphere. If that was their plan, they have no need for an intricate sleeper-agent plot.

"Two, one EMP wouldn't be enough. They'd need to launch and detonate several nukes over the US. Still no need for sleeper agents.

"And three, the Chinese know we have subs armed with nuclear ballistic weapons roaming the oceans and that we'd retaliate in kind. Do you really think the Chinese would be so foolish as to launch such a public attack on the US?"

"No, the Chinese government would not, sir. Use of nuclear weapons, even in the atmosphere, would be an undeniable act of war. Again, not the CCP's style . . . at this juncture."

Wolfe huffed. "Then I'm not following your logic, Miss Jessup. I've just debunked your EMP theory."

Jaz lifted one shoulder. "I never mentioned an EMP. You jumped to that theory. I didn't."

Wolfe frowned then laughed softly. "I suppose I did. My mistake. So your theory is what?"

Jaz glanced at the map. "Well, sir, electricity can't be effectively stored, can it? Not realistically. It has to be used directly, that is, generated and transmitted immediately to its users. That means the grid needs to supply an uninterrupted flow of electricity, twenty-four hours a day, three-hundred-sixty-five days a year.

"Simply put, generation stations and power plants produce the electricity, transmission lines conduct it across large areas, and transformers step the current's voltage up or down as needed to deliver electricity to end users in the required form."

"An overly simplistic description, but we get it."

"Then you already know that the continental US has three major interconnected electrical networks—the Eastern Interconnect, Western Interconnect, and Texas Interconnect."

"Yes; I'm following you."

Jaz scooted closer to the map. "Let's ignore the sprinkling of red dots on the western side of the US for a moment and focus on these."

She placed her palm, diagonally, on the map. It covered a rough majority of the remaining dots. "Notice anything?"

Bella leaned over the map. "No, I don't see it, Jaz."

"But you do, don't you, Director?" Jaz asked.

Wolfe stared at Jaz. "Your palm is covering most of the Eastern Interconnect?"

"And a chunk of the Texas Interconnect—all the way to the Gulf."

Wolfe rubbed his chin as though something there itched. "Go on, Miss Jessup."

"The main thing to consider at the moment, sir, is that the US grid is stretched pretty thin. You know how, during a really hot summer or a particularly cold winter, when power consumption goes way up, we get those rolling brownouts?"

"Yes."

"Sir, if AEA members managed to impair even three or four power plants? The grid would struggle, then start to collapse. The cascade effect across those areas served by the grid would produce catastrophic results."

Wolfe shook his head. "You're saying AEA is going for our power plants? That's your big theory? Well, they won't succeed. Those things are hardened targets. Highly protected."

"I don't dispute that, sir, but just for a moment, imagine this scenario with me. How many cells have you marked on this map? I counted fifteen cells covered by my hand.

"But what would be the point of such an attack? That's what I struggled with. Some of my online contacts had ideas . . . and one of them started making sense."

"Go on," Wolfe said quietly.

"See, if an attack were to take down a major portion of the grid and do so in such a fashion that power could not be restored inside of a week? It's the big cities that would suffer the most, say, New York City, Newark, DC, Baltimore, Philadelphia."

Jaz placed her hand on the map again. The cities she'd listed were covered. The heel of her hand touched Houston and New Orleans. She spread her fingers; Pittsburgh and other moderately urban cities were included.

"What the biggest of these cities have in common are *dense* urban environments with complex infrastructures, meaning the services necessary to maintain that many people within a relatively small metropolitan area. Ask yourself, what would happen if not one but several high-population, urban-concentrated cities lost power for an extended period?

"Conjures a nasty scenario."

"Only a nasty scenario, sir? Aren't we talking the complete breakdown of urban social structure and a significant number of deaths?"

"Inside of a week?" Wolfe asked, not believing her. "A significant number of deaths in only a week?"

Jaz's shoulders and neck were tight and hard. She could only lift one shoulder.

"Think about it a sec. What would a densely populated city deprived of electricity look like? The first to die would be the most vulnerable—those hospitalized in critical condition, those dependent on medical devices such as respirators, and others unable to fend for themselves, meaning the very elderly and bedridden. Why? Because the city would be engulfed in total darkness after sundown. Who would come to work in utter darkness even if they had a means to get to their job? And they would have *no* means of commuting. We're talking no subway or busses, likely no cabs. Gas pumps wouldn't function, either, so people would be reluctant to drive their cars—if they owned one, and most urban dwellers don't. The cost of parking alone makes owning a car untenable.

"Let's move on to the basic services we take for granted. Phone and cable services would go down, leaving people with no communication at all—no tv, no radio, not even the Web. You've seen how people about lose their minds when their computer bandwidth drops out and they can't sign in to their email to download the latest photos of their precious grandkids. How do you think they would react if they couldn't reach their loved ones at all?

"And what about heating and cooling? Nope to both. No elevators, no microwaves, no refrigeration. Perishable food would spoil inside of forty-eight hours; other foodstuffs would be used up before the week was out. Stores would close, but desperate people would loot them. Pick them clean. Then there's water. Without pumping stations, taps would run dry. And don't get me started on backed-up toilets.

"The police would try to convince people to shelter in place, but for the urban apartment dwellers counting on their building's security? When power fails, the electric locks securing the entrances of most residential buildings *unlock* and stay unlocked. It would be open season on apartment residents.

"Every desperate reprobate in the city would be hunting for food and water and would take what they needed from anyone who had it."

Jaz swallowed. She was starting to breathe hard. "So, yes, sir. We'd see massive death tolls within the big cities, and that's just the first week. If *how* AEA takes down the grid supplying those cities means we couldn't restore power after a week? These vital parts of the US would start to go under. No communication anywhere civilians live, no food or water, no transportation— no ambulances or fire fighters, no law and no order. Fires would burn, looters would loot."

"The government?" Bella asked quietly.

"The government would deploy the national guard and the military into some cities to render aid and bring order, of course, or at the very least, try to bring order. It depends upon how many cities simultaneously go down and which ones. More than five cities at once? We're talking twenty million or more people, and the only means of saving them would be to evacuate them."

"Evacuate twenty million people? Evacuate them to where?" Wolfe asked. "Where could they go? And how would they get out in the first place?"

Jaz exhaled. "People would either find a way to walk out of the cities or they would die off in droves. Sadly, in that scenario, only the vilest of city dwellers would survive and only by the most heinous of means. Gangs would rule the cities."

Wolfe snarled at Jaz. "Did you call me here to waste my time listening to this improbable nonsense, Miss Jessup? You haven't provided a single shred of evidence even hinting that AEA might be targeting the power grid. The people we're surveilling are not commandos trained to attack our hardened power plants and overcome armed security forces!"

Bella, sadness on her face, added, "I must agree with Director Wolfe, Jaz. I get the horrifying 'what ifs' of your scenario, but realistically, how could a bunch of career-minded twenty-somethings blow up even one power plant, let alone the several it would take to crash the grid?"

Jaz, afraid to meet the disappointment and censure in Bella and Wolfe's gazes, stared instead at her hands.

"I haven't made my point, Director, and I've said nothing about blowing up power plants."

"But . . ." Wolfe stopped himself. "Wait. That was us. Jumping to conclusions. Again."

"Yes, sir." Jaz was having a hard time catching her breath. "Director Wolfe, aren't most power plants run by computer these days?"

"Yes, but their networks are isolated. Air-gapped. Not connected to the outside. To the Internet."

"Right, but didn't you also say these AEA members were technically trained and competent? All I would need to render these plants inoperable for days, perhaps weeks—or even permanently—is an 'in' to their mainframes."

She swallowed. Hard. "A single individual on the inside, someone like me, could do precisely what I think AEA is planning to do."

Wolfe got up with such force that his chair toppled over behind him. He stalked Bella's office like a predator at bay, swearing under his breath.

Jaz chanced a quick look at Bella. Bella's hands covered her mouth. Jaz was surprised to realize Bella was praying.

She was more surprised to find herself wondering, *If ever there were a time to pray, wouldn't it be now?*

Wolfe stopped pacing. He stood still, hands deep in his trouser pockets, his mind even deeper in concentrated thought.

Minutes later, he picked up his overturned chair. Set it to rights. Sat in it.

"I will present your theory to my other team. I can't promise they will agree with your rationale, but I also can't ignore it."

Wolfe was the most intense Jaz had ever seen him when he said to her, "If this doomsday scenario you've described is possible, if it is what AEA has planned, you make it sound like a CCP-backed first-strike scenario. An act of war."

Jaz tucked in her chin as she framed her words. "That is precisely what I'm saying, sir. If it is what AEA is planning, then we need to account for all of AEA's cells and members—every last one of them—because their plans won't stop there. What's next? What is the second-most fragile component of the US infrastructure? Isn't it the financial system? If the CCP takes down the power grid, the markets go down too. Stocks would tank as a result. Our currency on the world money market would fall."

Wolfe nodded. "With significant reservations, I see your point."

"A second strike could be worse than the first, sir. If AEA were to 'prearrange' certain moves on the markets before the grid collapsed, those moves would likely be detrimental to the US and beneficial to China and other enemies."

Bella spoke up. "If taking down the power grid was the first strike and the financial system second, what would follow after?"

Wolfe licked his lips. "I hate to say this, Miss Jessup, but yesterday when you muttered, 'Something bigger or broader or designed to occur *in stages*,' I immediately visualized Chinese ships docking in those marked West Coast ports, conveniently loaded with emergency supplies in the aftermath of the grid collapse, of course—followed by Chinese boots on the ground to perform 'humanitarian work.'"

"I don't like the sound of that," Bella replied, shaking her head.

"Right, but then think longer term. A couple of staged events that resulted in Chinese casualties, and the Chinese would drop troops into our cities and shift from humanitarian aid to 'restoration of order.'"

He leveled his gaze on Jaz. "The vilest city dwellers you mentioned, Jaz? The Chinese would shoot them in the streets. They don't tolerate civil disobedience."

"Not the worst outcome I can think of," Jaz admitted, "but only in that moment."

Bella asked, "Do you think the Chinese would stay, Director? Would they occupy the US cities they brought under order? Refuse to leave them?"

It sounded to Jaz as if Bella was hoping Wolfe would correct her.

Wolfe took his time answering. "I think . . . that if the Chinese could make the argument that their move to 'rescue America' was for the good of the world? Yes, Chinese troops certainly would stay."

"The map. Those few AEA cells on the Pacific coast," Jaz reminded them. "Wouldn't the CCP want to get a toehold in Los Angeles, San Diego, Portland, or Seattle? Wherever they could dig in and cement their standing?"

She moved one of her fingers to the dot in eastern Washington. "This dot struck me as a curious outlier, and I had to ask myself why AEA, an urban-based organization, has a cell in Spokane. It's just a middling-sized city, after all, not a dense urban environment."

She shifted her finger minutely. "But, see? That's Grand Coulee Dam, right there, about ninety miles east of Spokane, yet it's the closest city from which AEA could operate one of their inconspicuous cells. Obviously, in this example, AEA's objective wouldn't be to 'kill' another metropolis. They would have another goal in mind."

She added softly, "Grand Coulee is the US's largest hydroelectric dam. It generates enough electricity to power around two million Pacific Northwest homes. Taking out the dam's generation capability, even temporarily, would further disrupt the nation. It would weaken the US's ability to respond to those Chinese incursions into our Pacific coast cities you just described."

Wolfe, silently taking in Jaz's words, said nothing.

Bella, however, nodded and said, "I'm sorry to say this, Director, but I can visualize the end result: Two nations effectively occupying the continental US."

Finally, Wolfe said, "Thank you, Miss Jessup. A lot of what you've said today could fit our little puzzle and make sense. Terrible sense. Do you now understand why we need you to infiltrate this group?"

Jaz wagged her head from side to side, unwilling to commit herself to Wolfe's plan. "What about hacking AEA from here? Why would I need to physically get inside their organization?"

"Good people from my other teams have probed AEA's organization, but not only could they not find a way in, they couldn't even find a network to hack."

"Interesting. Well, you did say AEA members were hired for their technical competencies, and that might account for the absence of AEA hackable tech. Regardless, the cells need methods of passing important communications. I suppose they could have gone low tech or perhaps they have new technology we're unaware of."

"And that's why I need you on the inside, Miss Jessup. You're the best we have for this kind of job. And now that you have provided us with a working hypothesis and if it proves true, if AEA's target is any part of our infrastructure, we need to know more. Whatever technological gadgets you need, we'll provide them to your specifications . . . but we need you and need you *now*."

Jaz sighed. "Yah, I suppose I get it. All right; count me in."

"Thank you, but before we insert you into an AEA cell, I want you to undergo that round of intensive field training I spoke of yesterday. We'll see how you do. Evaluate and go from there."

Jaz shrugged off her reluctance. "Okay, but if AEA membership is by recruitment only, how would inserting me into AEA even work?"

"We'd give you a tantalizing cover and dangle you in front of the right people—something we're already working on."

Jaz tugged a stick of Black Jack from her pocket. Unwrapped it. Folded it in quarters. "Have you identified those 'right people'? If we knew who calls the shots, we'd have a better idea how and where to insert me."

She looked at the neatly folded gum she held in her fingers. "Sir, I'd like to start investigating AEA now. You know, from a distance. Do I have your permission?"

"As I said, other people with skills like yours have tried; they haven't even found an AEA network they could hack or how they communicate from cell to cell. If you were to figure this out and they were to detect your intrusion, it would put them on high alert. They *cannot* find out we're on to them."

"They won't detect me, sir."

"Do you mean they won't detect Vyper?"

Jaz dipped her chin. "I've heard she is both silent and deadly, Director."

"Very well. I authorize you to make a careful start on AEA. However, you will shortly be immersed in field training, and trust me when I say that training will take everything you have."

Jaz shivered. "Where, exactly, would I go for this so-called field training? And when?"

"We'll be sending you to Broadsword as soon as possible. Within days."

"Why Broadsword, sir?" Jaz asked, the unexpected prospect setting her teeth on edge.

"Broadsword has the secure facilities for your training, and Richard is an authority on spycraft. Rick Harris, however, will be your principal instructor."

Jaz slipped the folded stick of gum in her mouth, a temporizing act as she tried to slow the thundering of her heart. She took the opportunity to cut her eyes toward Bella, but Bella was studiously jotting something in her Day-Timer.

Jaz knew her friend better even than Wolfe did: Bella was using her peripheral vision to keep one eye on Jaz's reaction.

Jaz lowered her brows and telegraphed a single word across the desk. *Traitor.*

Bella's mouth twitched.

This isn't over, Jaz glared.

Wolfe glanced between Bella and Jaz. "Er, Miss Jessup?"

"Yes, sir?"

"I'll email my orders to Bella. She will brief you. Any questions?"

Yah, I've got a question. The Ukrainian mob is no longer a threat to me, and I could, at this very moment, be ensconced in a beach chair in Cabo, sipping piña coladas while watching the waves roll in from the Pacific.

So how did I let myself get wrangled into this mess?

"No, sir. No questions."

"Good." He stood and addressed Bella. "I'll see myself out now. You may expect my orders no later than tomorrow."

Wolfe closed the door behind him. Jaz made no move to leave.

Bella batted her eyes. "So . . . Broadsword."

When Jaz didn't answer, Bella tried again. "Are you all right, Jaz?"

Jaz growled at her. "What do you think?"

"I think I'd pay big bucks to be a fly on the wall while Harris trains you. He did love showing you how to shoot. And helping you disassemble and clean your gun. And—"

Jaz slammed the door on her way out, the muffled sound of Bella's soft laughter following her down the stairs and into the bullpen.

"Hey, Jaz! So, you had a meeting with the director, huh?"

It was Rusty who greeted her, but every ear on Task Force Resolute was canted like so many satellite dishes toward Jaz, all of them hungry for news.

Jaz dropped into her chair. She spit her wad of gum into the trash and grabbed a fresh pack of Black Jack.

"Mind your own beeswax, Rust Bucket."

<hr>

LATE THAT night, Laynie and Quincy sat at their apartment's breakfast bar, and Laynie related the conversation between Wolfe and Jaz. She explained Wolfe's plan to send Jaz to Broadsword for training—training customized for Jaz toward an operation into which Wolfe hoped to insert her.

"Seems like a big move, and I can tell that you're concerned," Quincy said. "You don't think Jaz will be able to handle the op, even after Richard and Harris work with her? I mean, it *is* Jaz we're talking about—*Vyper, the Venom Queen,* and all that hacker-centric blather?"

"It's not the training or lack of it that bothers me. I told Director Wolfe how we found Jaz the night the assassins sent by the Ukrainian mob tried to abduct her."

"Yeah, guess she was a mess," Tobin said, recalling the situation, "but so was I after tussling with the assassin sent to my apartment."

"You had recently escaped getting blown to bits, Quincy. Why, you nearly lost a kidney to that car bomb! And if I recall, you tore your surgical stitches fending off the assassin that night."

"Okay, fair enough, but Jaz is sturdy inside and out. What's really bothering you about Wolfe putting Jaz in the field?"

There it was.

Laynie's anxiety forced her from her chair. Without realizing it, she paced the length of their kitchen and back again.

"Marta?"

Laynie smiled and paused to drop a kiss on the top of Quincy's head and wrap her arms around his shoulders. "Did I ever tell you my name isn't Marta?"

"You may have mentioned it. 'Course, Bella isn't your name, either—and Marta is the woman I fell in love with. Linnéa? Oksana? Elaine? Laynie? All the other names you've had to use are *okay* and all, but *Marta?* That girl's m' main squeeze."

"If Ksenia hears you call me Marta, you'll confuse her. She already heard Cossack call me Magda."

"If our girl hain't already been confused by th' trauma she's been through, my callin' you Marta on th' rare occasion ain't goin' push her over th' edge. 'Sides, she saw things back in Sayed's mountain fortress. She saw you stand up to th' guards and wale on 'em. She knows her mama ain't no helpless, suburban housewife."

"You slip that fake hick accent of yours on and off like you slide into and out of that nasty pair of loafers stinking up our closet."

"Hey! Them shoes and I, we hev *history*. Impo'tant history."

"Those shoes are going to *be* history if you don't install some Odor-Eaters in them ASAP."

Quincy shucked off the accent, "And you, my lovely wife, often avoid difficult conversations."

"Huh. Do I?"

"Yep. But no worries, Sweet Pea. We'll gitcha over thet."

"That so? This is your last notice, darling husband of mine: It's either Odor-Eaters or those loafers can stink up the balcony from here on out."

CHAPTER 7

Vyper

EARLY WEDNESDAY, Jaz stood outside Bella's open office door. She wrestled with her tangled feelings inside before she finally knocked.

Bella glanced up. "Hey, Jaz."

Jaz nodded. Sighed. "Could we talk?"

"Sure; come in. I've kind of been expecting you." She gestured toward the small table in the corner. Jaz took a seat there while Bella made them both a cup of tea before she joined Jaz.

Jaz stirred a spoonful of honey into her steaming cup. "You said you were expecting me?"

Bella nodded. "Yesterday's meeting was a nail biter. Tense doesn't begin to describe it. Great job briefing Director Wolfe on your theory, but frankly? It shook us both. Then after you accepted his assignment, I recognized the weight of responsibility Director Wolfe had laid on you. I imagine that responsibility has been pretty much the only thing on your mind since then."

"Oh? I wonder why."

"I teased you yesterday, too. I'm sorry and apologize. None of that today, okay? Today I hope to help you prepare for what awaits you during your time at Broadsword."

"Broadsword—*gah!* Why couldn't Wolfe send me someplace else?"

"Because this training has to be fast and effective, and you already know Richard and Harris. You know for a fact that you can trust them—isn't that true?"

"Well, yah, but—"

"No buts, Jaz. From here on out you must choose to maintain a positive mental focus. Mental strength determines a great deal of success while undercover. Literally, you must 'focus on your focus.'"

Bella opened a folder on her desk. "I have already received your orders. Let's go over them, shall we?"

Bella looked down at the folder's contents. "A car will pick you up from a specified neutral location, Friday morning, 8:00 a.m. Let the driver approach you. He will ask if you know Adrian Romero. You'll reply with, 'He's my mother's brother.' The driver will say, 'I thought you looked familiar.' Then you will get into his car, and he will drive you to Broadsword."

She slid a sheet of paper toward Jaz. "This is a list of clothing you're to pack and bring with you. Your pickup location is at the bottom. Have a taxi drop you there. You'll have time during the drive to consider my advice before you reach Broadsword."

"Your advice?"

"That's why you're here, isn't it? To pick my brain? Get a head start on your upcoming training? Additionally, I hope you're here to talk about what happened when I was Sayed's prisoner and Quincy dared you to pray with him for my release . . . you know, when he threatened to toss you into a snowbank after he, I believe the term was, 'double-dog dared you' to pray?"

Jaz squirmed. "Oh. *That.*"

"Must have been a sight to behold, him holding you head-down over the drift?"

"Who ratted me out?"

"Oh, basically every member of the task force." Bella tapped her forehead "Believe me, between their individual descriptions and Quincy's, I have my own vivid image."

Jaz's attitude soured further. "Super."

"But then Tobin prayed, you said amen, and God answered—that's the important part, yes? And I am so very glad he *did* answer. I will be forever grateful that the Lord rescued me from Sayed. So grateful that he gave Ksenia to us, to Quincy and me, and brought us home safely."

"I'm . . . grateful too."

"Good! So, isn't it time for you to acknowledge that the Lord of heaven does exist? That the God Tobin and I worship and pray to is real? You know he is real. You witnessed the many miracles he performed and the details only he could have coordinated in order to rescue me—and Ksenia—from Sayed. Can you deny him any longer?"

Jaz didn't say anything. What could she say? She stared at her hands instead.

"All right; moving on. Let's consider what's ahead. If you work hard and take your training to heart, you should leave Broadsword with enough basic spycraft to get you through this assignment. I will also try to pass a few things to you before Friday.

"After you finish your training to Richard and Harris' satisfaction, Wolfe's people will set you up in the alias they are constructing for you—identification papers, apartment, job, background, life in general—and steer you toward the AEA members they've selected as your targets. You, then, must find a natural way to introduce yourself to those targets without raising their suspicions. You must dangle yourself before them like a worm on a hook but allow them to make the first move.

"The introduction itself may take weeks, but let's say they take the bait, discover what a technological asset you are, and they slowly welcome you into their cell. Every hour you are with them? You will be in ongoing danger, living exclusively by your wits. Nearly always alone and without immediate support."

As Bella paused, Jaz shuddered. She couldn't help it. *I already know what living exclusively by my wits entails—and I don't care to go back to that.*

Bella asked softly. "Instead of being alone, wouldn't you like to have Jesus go with you, Jaz? To counsel and comfort you? Lead and guide you?"

Counsel and comfort? Lead and guide? Could he? Would he?

Jaz spread her hands. "How? I know he answered Quincy's prayer and my amen, but don't get how . . ."

"I can make the introduction, so to speak, and pray with you to commit yourself to Jesus as your Lord and as your Savior. Are you willing to pray with me?"

Some last bit of resistance crumbled inside her. "I . . . yes."

Bella slid from her chair to her knees on the floor. Jaz, her heart racing, slowly followed. Bella took one of Jaz's hands; Jaz's fingers quivered inside Bella's, so Bella clasped Jaz's shaking hand between both of hers.

Then Bella prayed, and Jaz trembled at the power in her words.

"Lord God, maker of heaven and earth! Thank you for seeing us, for seeing Jaz and me as we come before you. Lord, you know Jaz's heart, the very depths of her being. You've known Jaz her entire life. She is ready now to acknowledge you as her God, ready to repent of her sins and receive the gift of salvation you offer her through your Son, Jesus."

The thundering of Jaz's heart intensified. Her grip on Bella's fingers tightened.

Jaz was staring at Bella when she opened her eyes and stared back. "Jaz, I'm going to help you pray to repent of your sins and commit yourself, your entire being, to Christ. If you are serious, if you mean the words you hear me say, then repeat them—but only if you mean them. All right?"

Jaz swallowed. Nodded. Bella again bent her head, so Jaz followed suit. She focused on every word Bella uttered.

"Lord God, I confess that I am far from you, that I have wandered down my own paths."

Jaz managed to mumble, "Lord God, I confess that I am far from you, that I have wandered down my own paths."

My entire life, I have lived only for myself. I have ignored you, disregarded those you placed before me, those who knew you and spoke of you. Iris. Miss Timmons . . .

Bella said, "I confess that I have sinned."

Jaz choked out, "I confess that I have sinned."

So many sins! So many lies, deceptions, thefts . . . even deaths. How can you forgive me for any of them?

"Lord, I turn from my willful ways."

Jaz's voice began to shake. "Lord, I turn from my willful ways."

Willful. Yes. My way! Always what I wanted.

"I repent of all my sins, Lord."

Jaz looked up. "Wait. Repent? What does that mean?"

Bella offered half a smile. "Repentance is a decision to turn away from sin and turn to God. It is a solemn, holy thing, and we do not do it lightly. At the same time, we acknowledge that without God's help, we're unable to turn away from our old lives. We're incapable of making ourselves 'good.' Only Jesus can do that; only Jesus can forgive our many sins and change us from the inside out."

Joyous relief flooded Jaz's heart. *Forgive my many sins?*

"Yes. That. I want to repent."

Bella prayed, "Jesus, I repent of my sins and willful ways. Please wash me clean through the power of your death and resurrection. I surrender my life to you, Lord Jesus. Please come and make your home in my heart and make me clean and new, inside and out."

As Jaz repeated Bella's words, the Holy Spirit of God came down. Like a cloud, he filled Bella's office and enveloped them. Jaz and Bella remained on their knees, weeping and worshipping . . . for some time.

———————●———————

THURSDAY, JUST before the task force members shut down their computers for the night, Bella entered the bullpen and asked for a moment.

"Everyone? Before you leave for the evening, I have an announcement."

Her team stilled.

"Tomorrow morning, Director Wolfe is sending Jaz out on assignment. We don't know yet how long she'll be gone. It's likely to be several months."

The team's attention shifted to Jaz.

She acknowledged them with a sharp nod.

Bella continued. "While she's away, I'll be sitting with you in the bullpen." She laughed at the humor of it. "I suppose the goal is not to wear out the carpet between here and my office door, okay? Look, I know I'm not Jaz;

I don't have her skill set. I can, of course, facilitate any needs you have as we go forward, but tech wise? That's not me."

"So, do we have a new assignment?" Soraya asked.

"Yeah," Gwyneth tacked on, "and what, exactly, will Jaz be doing?"

Bella answered Gwyneth's question first. "You should not be surprised to hear that we're not at liberty to discuss Jaz's assignment."

Six sets of eyes swiveled toward Jaz. Of course, it was Brian who spoke the obvious. "Wait—Wolfe is sending Jaz into the field?"

Bella glared at him. "Again, *Brian*, we're not at liberty to discuss her assignment."

As if Bella hadn't said a thing, Brian added, "But if Jaz will be out in the field, why aren't *we* backing her up?"

Rusty piped up. "Right? That's what I want to know. We're best equipped to support her."

Team chatter kicked in until Bella lifted a hand to silence it.

"No more questions."

It was Jaz who signaled Bella. "May I say something?"

Brian gawked. "May I? Who are you—and what have you done with our Jaz?"

"Stow it, Brain Pan."

"Aaaand she's back, folks. Just returned from a stint on the Vegas strip."

Jaz glowered; Brian shut up.

"What I want to say is that, in my absence, I'd like Rusty to serve as the task force's interim technical lead and liaison with Bella. If you need technical guidance or anything else? See Rusty. Got it?"

Bella opened her mouth, then shut it. "You heard her. Guess I don't need to sit in the bullpen after all. Rusty, you have point while Jaz is out of pocket. Now everyone say your goodbyes to Jaz and wish her well."

———◆———

FRIDAY MORNING, Jaz rolled her suitcase out to her apartment's parking lot. The waiting cab driver popped his trunk and swung her suitcase inside while Jaz got in the back seat.

The driver climbed behind the wheel. "Destination?"

"Holy Cross Hospital, please."

He glanced at her in the rearview mirror. "You checking in?"

The lie rolled off her tongue with ease. "Just a minor procedure, but I'll be admitted for a night or two."

He nodded and the cab pulled away from the curb. "I'll keep you in my prayers. I believe my Jesus will help you."

Jaz nearly choked. "Th-thank you."

Did you do that . . . Jesus?

Jaz looked down. Her folded hands gripped each other, reminding her of the prayer she'd prayed with Bella. *Jesus, I repent of my sins and willful ways. Please wash me clean through the power of your death and resurrection. I surrender my life to you, Lord Jesus. Please come and make your home in my heart and make me clean and new, inside and out.*

Clean and new. Inside and out.

Even the skin Jaz was in felt different. Foreign.

Instead of being alone, wouldn't you like to have Jesus go with you, Jaz? To counsel and comfort you? Lead and guide you?

Under her breath, Jaz whispered, "Yes, Jesus, please don't leave me. I really need you."

"Here you go, lady. I hope and pray your procedure and recovery go well."

"Thank you. I . . . I really appreciate your prayers for what's ahead."

Yah, for what's ahead.

She got out at the hospital admissions entrance, took her suitcase from the cabbie, tipped him generously, and walked through the door, rolling her suitcase behind her. Through a window, Jaz watched until the cab had left the parking lot and driven away. She waited five more minutes before she emerged from the hospital entrance and made for a nearby bus stop. She stood at the curb, several car lengths ahead of where the bus would take on passengers, and glanced at her watch.

Ten minutes to eight. She was early.

Mentally, she reviewed the list of clothes she was told to bring with her to Broadsword, a list that signaled the level and nature of physical activity ahead for her: six t-shirts, two pairs of jogging pants, four pairs of shorts, two pairs of sturdy running shoes, six pairs of athletic socks, a light jacket.

Inside, she snarked. *I hope Harris includes dancing in my training. It's the only physical activity I've ever been any good at—and until Resolute's party last weekend, I hadn't been dancing in years. My hips are still hurting!*

She laughed under her breath. *Dancing, yes. Because I don't do jogging. Or calisthenics. Or weight training, or fighting, or shooting. But give me a computer, and I'll take home the gold every time.*

At 7:59, a sporty Land Rover pulled up alongside the curb. The passenger-side window rolled down. "Hey, do you happen to know Adrian Romero?"

Jaz walked to the window to get a better view of the driver. "He's my mother's brother."

The driver nodded. "I thought you looked familiar. I'll pop the back hatch. Put your case in there."

Jaz did as she was told, then climbed into the backseat. The driver put the Land Rover in gear and his foot on the gas. They soon merged onto northbound Highway 270. Several hours of travel time stretched ahead for Jaz, and she recalled what Bella had said to her. *You'll have time during the drive to consider my advice before you reach Broadsword.*

Bella's advice? Yes. Jaz's head was filled with it.

Wednesday after they had prayed together and again Thursday morning, Bella had drilled Jaz on standard spy protocol. The things that would keep her alive, Bella said.

"Know your cover backward and forward. Be prepared for anyone to ask unforeseen questions. Build little stories into your cover, bits of detail that will make your alias come to life."

Bella doesn't seem to appreciate my eidetic memory. I have an accurate and vivid recall of anything I've seen and much of what I've heard. Maybe she doesn't realize that a single read of my cover, and I'll have it down cold.

Bella had shared other pearls of wisdom with Jaz. She'd touched on spiritual lessons as well, drawing on the verses the Lord had used to keep herself trusting in him during the time she was Sayed's captive and while that monster Gupta was torturing her.

Jaz rehearsed those conversations again and again. Her favorite was the moment Bella had pulled a book from her desk and given it to her.

"I bought this for you, Jaz. Your first Bible. It wasn't that long ago that I began reading the Bible. I started with the Gospels while I was on the run from Zakhar. Since you don't know much about Jesus, that might be the best place for you to start too."

Bella had looked her in the face then and said, "Jaz, if you read this book faithfully, it will change you on the inside. Of course, you won't be able to take it with you on your assignment, but you should have time to read while you're at Broadsword. I recommend that you memorize a few verses like I did."

Bella's gift had touched Jaz deeply. As she took it from Bella, she said, "Thank you. I will . . . treasure it."

And memorize everything I read in it. Without hardly trying.

But Bella hadn't stopped there. "This morning, in my Bible time, I was reading in 1 Peter—that's a letter Peter, one of Jesus' disciples, wrote to some of the churches. Why don't we read part of it together and talk about it?"

It took me a while to even find 1 Peter so we could read it together, Jaz thought, *but those words! They pierced my very being.*

> *Praise be to the God and Father*
> *of our Lord Jesus Christ!*
> *In his great mercy*
> *he has given us new birth into a living hope*
> *through the resurrection*
> *of Jesus Christ from the dead.*

"He has given us new birth into a living hope," Jaz breathed. "Yes, in his great mercy, God has given *me* new birth into a living hope."

My entire life, I have lived for myself. I believed many wrong things, many lies and deceptions. And I used my talents to get whatever I wanted.

What I wanted.

Lord, I turn from my willful ways.

"Yes, Lord, I turn from my willful ways. Please . . . show me *your* way, the way you want me to go?"

As she watched the scenery pass by, she began to wonder again, *How in the world did I get here? After everything I've seen and done, how did I end up being recruited to spy on terrorists?*

As unacquainted with prayer as she was, she found herself asking, *God, you could have chosen anyone for this. Why did you choose me?*

Without being conscious of it, her mind drifted elsewhere, back to a place and period she'd scrabbled and fought to escape . . . and leave forever in the dust of time gone by.

JENNY

Vyper

CHAPTER 8

Vyper

REGINA, SASKATCHEWAN
1982

EASTER AT the Northams' group home was acknowledged in a marginal manner. The Northams did not attend church, but on Easter Sunday morning, Maude and Albert served a special breakfast of scrambled eggs, sausages, and toast, and each of the five children in their home found a chocolate bunny next to their regular place setting. Maude even set a dish of jam on the table and allowed the kids to spread small amounts on their toast.

The best part of the day in the children's eyes came after they were excused from the table and had finished clearing up the kitchen and dining room. Then they were allowed to eat their chocolate bunny—the entire thing. Some disappointment inevitably followed, as soon as the children bit into the bunnies and discovered that the chocolate confection was hollow. For such a big bunny, it meant the candy disappeared in a few bites.

AN ADDITIONAL event occurred during Easter morning that year. The social worker who occasionally visited the home knocked at the Northams' front door. The woman's unexpected appearance vexed the Northams.

Chiefly Maude.

Albert and Maude opened the door together, and Maude set her jaw. "Miss Timmons. We weren't expecting you today. It is Sunday, after all."

"Pardon the intrusion, Mr. and Mrs. Northam. My visit is not entirely in an official capacity. Since I was in the neighborhood following Easter service, I wanted a moment with Jenny. Her twelfth birthday is next week, you see, and I have a small gift for her. That is the unofficial part of my visit."

"Oh? And which is the official part?" Maude demanded.

"Right. Being that Jenny is the only child of her age in your home at present, I wish to remind you that when a Permanent Ward reaches age twelve, he or she is to receive a weekly allowance of five dollars—not out of your pocket, of course. Your monthly stipend for her will increase to reflect Jenny's allowance."

"We know that," was Maude's tart reply.

"Very good." Miss Timmons cut her gaze to Mrs. Northam exclusively, an unmistakable warning glittering in her eyes. "Then when I speak to Jenny, you won't mind if I tell her that she can expect to receive her first allowance on her birthday?"

Maude's lips flattened. "Not at all. Is that everything?"

"Not quite. A year from now, Jenny will turn thirteen. Since your home has an age cutoff of thirteen, I'll begin now to seek a new placement for her, one suited to her growing needs."

The skin around Maude's mouth tightened. "Actually, Miss Timmons, because Jenny has been with us most of her life, Albert and I have come to regard her as our own, and Jenny is beloved by the younger children in our home. We feel Jenny's departure would be deeply injurious all around. For those reasons, we are willing to make an exception to our age rule."

Miss Timmons observed the other woman closely. "You're saying that you're willing to keep her on?"

"Why, yes. We would miss her terribly if she left us."

"I see. Well, I will discuss it with her and allow her to decide. I would like to see her now, please."

<hr>

MISS TIMMONS waited for Jenny in the living room. When Jenny walked in, Miss Timmons noted with pleasure that Jenny had grown several inches, although she still did her hair in two neat braids.

"It's lovely to see you, Jenny."

Jenny nodded without much change of expression.

Miss Timmons soldiered on. "Er, did you remember that your birthday is next week? You will be twelve years old."

That got Jenny's attention. "Oh. I suppose I had forgotten."

"Well, it *is* next week, and I have brought you a little gift."

She seemed amazed. "You have?"

"Why, yes. Here it is."

Miss Timmons placed the small but artfully wrapped box in Jenny's hand. The girl studied the bright paper and the curling ribbon that trailed across the paper and down the sides of the box, running her fingers over them as if to absorb their textures and colors.

"It's very pretty. I like the ribbons and paper. Thank you."

Miss Timmons beamed. "You're welcome, dear girl. I wrapped it myself."

Jenny, still examining the package, added, "You've never given me a present before."

"You are correct, but this birthday will be a special one."

Jenny's eyes slid from the package to her visitor. "I didn't know some birthdays were special."

"Yours is special this year because when you turn twelve, you will begin to receive an allowance. Five dollars a week."

Jenny's lips formed a small "o." Finally, she said with some wonder, "I've never had five dollars."

"Well, then I hope my gift will come in handy when you do."

Jenny nodded again but made no move to open the present.

"Wouldn't you like to open your gift, Jenny?"

Miss Timmons watched Jenny consider her question. The girl seemed reluctant to undo the paper and ribbons, so Miss Timmons added, "Let me share a little trick with you, Jenny. You can slide the curly ribbons off the box without ruining them. And if you find the bit of tape on the folded ends of the package and gently slide your fingernail under the fold, you should be able to pull the tape away without tearing the paper. That way you can keep the ribbons and paper, perhaps use them to liven up your room."

Jenny brightened and began to carefully work the ribbons and tape off her gift. When she finally got to the box inside, she took the same care as she lifted off the lid.

"It's a cat," she announced. "A pink cat."

Miss Timmons, holding an invitation to Easter brunch with friends and desiring to be on time, glanced at her watch. "Why don't you take it out of the box, Jenny?"

At last Jenny held the miniature "cat" in her hands and saw that it was more. The cleverly shaped face of the cat, enhanced with cute glued-on googly eyes and embossed whiskers and ears, was actually a flap that snapped shut.

Jenny unsnapped the flap. "Why, it's a purse!"

Miss Timmons breathed a sigh, relieved and delighted that Jenny liked her gift. "Yes. A safe place to carry your allowance, but small enough to fit in the pocket of your jeans."

Jenny tucked the purse into her pocket and smiled. "Just right," she exulted. "It fits just right."

"I'm so glad you like it."

"I do. Thank you, Miss Timmons."

With Jenny still smiling, that moment was everything Miss Timmons had hoped for.

"You're welcome, dear girl. Now, I have a question for you. Are you happy here with the Northams, Jenny?"

She considered the question. "I am not *un*happy."

"I see. Well, I ask, because on next year's birthday you turn thirteen, and in the fall after that, you'll be attending high school. I can arrange for you to move to another group home then, one with children your age. Would you like me to do that?"

"I have to move out at thirteen. It's a rule."

Miss Timmons cleared her throat. "Mrs. Northam tells me she and Mr. Northam would like you to stay on. They are willing to bend the rule so that you can stay until you're sixteen."

Jenny frowned. "Bend the rule?"

Miss Timmons understood. Bending rules was difficult for Jenny—unless the rules were unjust or got in the way of something she felt she needed.

"You do not need to decide today, Jenny. Here is my card. My office number is on it. Why don't you keep the card in your purse? If you decide you'd like to move next year, give me a call, and I'll find you another placement."

Jenny glanced at the card. "I have your number memorized, but I will keep the card anyway." With no other response than that, Jenny pulled her new purse out of her pocket, unsnapped the face, slipped the card inside, and snapped it closed.

Miss Timmons blinked. "You have my number memorized? When did you do that?"

Jenny looked at her with some amazement. "Why, just now. When you gave me your card."

Now Miss Timmons was flummoxed. "I . . . I see." She again stole a glance at her watch. "I am sorry, but I must be going now. A happy Easter and a happy birthday to you, Jenny."

With an enigmatic little smile for the little cat purse in her hand—and as though Miss Timmons hadn't taken her leave—Jenny launched into a different subject.

"I got a chocolate bunny for Easter. We all did."

"That sounds lovely, dear."

Nodding, her fingers zipping and unzipping the small coin pouch under the flap, Jenny added, "I don't know what it means, getting a bunny for Easter. What is Easter?"

"Ah! Easter is the day we celebrate Jesus coming back from the dead."

Jenny's head swiveled toward her. "When people die, they don't come back. It's sort of a rule."

"Well, Jesus is different, Jenny. He is God's Son. I guess you could say that Jesus lives outside of our rules, because God can do anything."

Jenny frowned as she considered Miss Timmons' explanation.

<hr>

THE THURSDAY following Easter, Jenny did her chores as usual, including making the oatmeal for breakfast. After the household sat down, Albert handed Jenny a card and everyone said together, "Happy birthday, Jenny!"

All birthdays at the Northams' were the same. This one was no different.

Jenny opened her card and read it. Then she passed it to the other children who wanted to see it.

"Today is my birthday?" she asked Maude.

"Well, we don't give birthday cards if it isn't."

"Then today I get my first allowance?"

Maude reddened. It was Albert who grinned and answered. "Sure enough, kiddo."

Jenny looked back to Maude.

Maude huffed. "I'll give it to you after breakfast and cleanup, Jenny. It's in my handbag."

But after cleanup, when Maude opened her handbag and wallet, she doled out three one-dollar bills into Jenny's hand. "I'll be keeping two dollars each week for you in a savings account. It will be safe there. That way, you won't be tempted to spend it all and will have something to show for yourself later on."

—————— ● ——————

OCTOBER 1982

"WHAT DO you mean, she's gone? *Again?* Why, I'd like to twist her scrawny little neck, I would!" Mrs. Northam wrung the wet dishrag in her hands with a fervor that underscored her vexation.

As he usually did, her husband tried to placate her. "Now, Maudy, you know well as I do Jenny'll be back by morning—and she won't come to no harm, neither. Never gave us trouble before now. Not like she goes out stealin' or carousin' y'know."

"Won't come to any harm? Never gave us trouble before now? And just how do *you* know whether she goes out stealing or carousing?"

"Well, she ain't hungover next day, is she? And she don't come home with clothes we never seed before or with cash money in her pockets. Always looks a bit tired like she stayed up too late, but her grades don't suffer none."

Maude Northam wasn't discontent in her marriage, all things considered. But on the rare occasion, such as this one, she had to remind herself that she'd married "down," had fallen in love with a man of lesser culture and education, a man whose coarse and "common" language skills were somewhat beneath her own loftier ones.

"Those points are neither here nor there, Albert Northam. We simply cannot allow this behavior to go on, we truly *cannot*. A twelve-year-old-girl sneaking out at night? And gone for hours? The next time Child Protective

Services springs a surprise inspection on us, it could be late of an evening. And if Jenny isn't in her room, tucked into bed, you know full well they will shut us down. I'm too old to go back to working in a shop, Albert, and I refuse to mop office floors!"

"Now, Maudy, you know, same's I do, that CPS ain't never done an inspection past nine o'clock. Bless me if Jenny don't know that, too. Never once has she gone out her winder before that." He beamed with pride as he shook his head. "Tricky little thing, that one is."

"Albert Northam, if you don't favor her, I'm a one-eyed rooster. You always have favored her, you have."

"I wouldn't 'zactly say I favors her, Maudy. More like I admire her spunkiness. Going places, too, I 'spect."

"Her 'spunkiness' as you call it will be the death of me—how much will you admire and prefer your little trickster then, eh? Think you can run this group home without me? As for 'going places,' just where *does* she go every Tuesday and Thursday night like clockwork, hey? You tell me! I'd lay odds that she has a boy waiting for her, I would. She'll end up preggers and we'll be tossed out onto the street straight off."

Mr. Northam rubbed the stubble on his chin. "Don't think she has some boy a-waitin' on her, Maudy. No, our Jenny ain't boy crazy. That one has loftier ambitions than just a man and a passel o' kids."

He squinted a bit. "I'd pay a spot o' money to know what she's up to, I would."

"You'd pay money to know what mischief that girl is up to? But you won't part with a dollar to take me to the cinema?"

Muttering an uncomplimentary descriptor of her husband, Mrs. Northam threw the strangled dish rag into the sink and stomped out of the kitchen.

━━━◆━━━

JANUARY 1983

IN THE dead of a winter night, an insistent knocking on the group home's front door aroused Albert and Maude Northam from sleep. By the time they threw on their robes and slippers and staggered down the stairs, the knocking had progressed to a window-rattling pounding accompanied by shouts of, "Regina Police! Open up! Police, I say. Open up!"

"All right! All right!" Albert shouted through the thick wood. "Hold your horses; Got t' unlock th' door, I do!"

Albert flipped on the porch light, fumbled with the locks until they turned, gave the knob a quick twist, and pulled the door toward himself. He squinted at the sight on the house's porch. Maude gripped Albert's shoulder and stared out from behind him as if he were a protective brick wall.

A frowning female police constable faced him. Behind her stood Jenny, the collar of her lined jean jacket bunched up tight in the unyielding grasp of a burly male constable. The faces of both officers were set in severe lines, but Jenny seemed unfazed, her attention focused elsewhere, her jaws gently working.

The female constable nodded. "Sir, ma'am. Sorry to awaken you. I'm Constable Pikkus; this is Constable Ramsey, RCMP." She gestured toward Jenny. "Do you know this girl?"

Albert cleared his throat. "Aye, we know her. We be a Child Services group home, and Jenny lives here."

"Permanent Ward is she?"

"Yes, Constable."

"She is how old?"

"Twelve last spring."

"That young? And you didn't know she was out in the middle of the night?"

Albert huffed. "Course not. We do a bed check at 9:30 of an evening 'fore we turn in. She was abed when we checked her room as was our other children. Had to have left after we was asleep. Tell us, please, what she's done?"

The constable's mouth puckered as she thought how to phrase her response. "Constable Ramsey and I saw a light through a window and investigated. Found young Jenny inside."

Maude's grip on Albert's shoulder tightened.

Albert lifted his chin. "Inside o' where, Constable?"

The woman frowned. "Thom Collegiate Secondary School. Kid says she goes to school there."

"Yah, that she does. Started lower secondary this past fall term—"

"Little vandal!" Maude hissed, interrupting him.

The female constable exhaled. "Actually . . ."

Maude stepped from behind her husband. "Actually what? What damage has she done? Broken windows? Sprayed paint on the walls? I can assure you Jenny will be fitly punished and will pay for the repairs out of her own pocket."

The constable managed an awkward shrug.

"That's the thing, ma'am. We found nothing amiss. Frankly, we couldn't discern where she'd broken in, although we did find an unlocked door. That's how *we* got in and discovered her."

Albert's eyes crinkled in puzzlement. "So . . ."

The burly male constable released the collar of Jenny's jacket and nudged her toward Albert. "Looks to be simple trespassing, so we're not pressing charges at present. We will notify the school of her actions and ask them to do a thorough inventory. If anything is missing or damaged, the school admin-istration will decide then whether to press charges against the girl or discipline her themselves."

Constable Pikkus added, "The school will be in touch with you." She touched the bill of her cap. "Good night."

As the two constables trod down the porch steps, Maude leaned upon Albert and exhaled in relief. Albert, his brow still crinkled, automatically patted her hand.

"Dodged a bullet there, we did, Maudy."

Maude's sense of relief gave way to outrage. "Dodged a bullet? I'll teach that child a lesson, I will!"

She whirled around, but Jenny had slipped past them through the doorway and crept upstairs.

"Leave her be for now, Maudy."

"Leave her be? She could have cost us our livelihood!"

"I said leave her be."

"Well, I never, Albert Northam. What's gotten into you?"

"What's got int' me? I'll tell you, Maudy. If *school* is where Jenny's run off to twice a week since fall term started, I want to know why. I want to know what she's a-doing there, what's so all-fired fascernatin' to that child—that's what's got int' me."

"But I—"

"I said leave off, Maudy. I mean it." To appease her, he added, "Come on, now. Let's get you tucked back int' bed again, eh?"

———◆———

"MR. AND Mrs. Northam? I am Principal Charpentier. This is our guidance counsellor, Ms. Bobet. Please come into my office and have a seat."

A week after the police officers brought Jenny home in the middle of the night, Albert and Maude Northam followed the principal of Jenny's school into his office and sat on the short sofa where he indicated. Principal Charpentier and Ms. Bobet took chairs opposite them across a small coffee table.

"Thank you for coming, Mr. and Mrs. Northam," Principal Charpentier began. "Of course, we are here to talk about little Geneviève Simard—I believe you call her Jenny?"

The Northams both nodded.

"The main thing, of course, is the trespass last Thursday night. Have you any insights into why Jenny might have been trespassing, what she was after?"

Maude licked her lips but remained silent. Albert had insisted that she let him do all the talking.

"Well, we had no idea she had left that night or even how, since we lock our doors, real religious-like. Asked her in th' next morning and found out she had gone out her bedroom winder. Coulda knocked us over with a feather, certain."

He noticed how the guidance counsellor, Ms. Bobet, watched and listened closely although she had yet to speak.

"And did you ask Jenny why she entered the school that night?"

"Well, yah, we did," Albert answered, "but she wouldn't say. Jenny is usually such a good girl, but she ain't much fer talkin', that one. Like pullin' teeth sometimes."

"Is she a discipline problem in your home?" Principal Charpentier asked.

"Our Jenny? Not a bit of it. Does her chores without fussin' none, finishes her homework on her own. Don't argue nor talk back."

What Albert did *not* say but was at the forefront of both his and Maude's minds, articulated often by Maude in her own words, *If Jenny sets her cap on something, Jenny gets what she wants—one inventive, unconventional, and even imprudent way or another. And our other children, all considerably younger than Jenny at this point, know better than to cheat or taunt her. But years ago, children older than her who tried to bully her, found out the hard way just how rash and injudicious their actions were—and gave her a wide berth thereafter.*

"Would you say Jenny going out at night was unusual behavior on her part?"

"Aye," Albert answered smoothly, "and we don't understand what she was about, breaking int' the school. Did she do much damage?"

"No, no damage."

Maude reached the end of her forced patience. "But how did she get inside? The police said they found no signs of a broken window. Did someone leave a door unlocked? Were other children involved?"

Principal Charpentier and Ms. Bobet exchanged a glance. Charpentier tapped his index fingers together. "No, we don't think a door was left unlocked and no other children were with her."

"Then how—"

The toe of Albert's shoe connected with Maude's foot. She subsided and swallowed her question.

No one spoke for a minute or two.

Finally, Principal Charpentier asked, "Do you know in which part of the school the police constables found Jenny?"

Albert and Maude looked at each other. Shook their heads.

"No, sir. The coppers—er, *constables*—they din't tell us," Albert said.

Principal Charpentier nodded to the guidance counsellor. "Ms. Bobet?"

She smiled and clasped her hands in her lap. "Mr. and Mrs. Northam, the police found Jenny in the school's computer lab."

The Northams stilled. Maude turned pale—and found her mouth again. "Oh, dear, oh dear, oh dear, oh goodness me! What . . . what *has* the girl done? Computers, now, they are awfully expensive machines, are they not? How many of them has she broken? We don't have that kind of money, truly. Not us!"

Ms. Bobet was momentarily confused. "What? Oh. No, not at all. As we already said, Jenny did no damage."

"Then what . . . oh, dear!"

Maude was lost. Albert wasn't far behind her.

Ms. Bobet smiled again. "Our computer lab might not be strictly up to date, but we do have some nice machines—six Commodore 64s. I believe we also have a brand-new Apple III."

The Northams weren't tracking with Ms. Bobet.

The woman tried another approach. "You see, when Jenny enrolled at Thom Collegiate, she wanted to take a computer class. But being as she was only twelve and in the lower secondary form, she wasn't eligible for those classes. I can attest to her disappointment."

Albert Northam's haze thinned. Started to lift.

If Jenny sets her cap on something, Jenny gets what she wants—one inventive, unconventional, and even imprudent way or another.

"You say that's where th' police found her? In th' computer classroom?"

"Yes, it is. I asked our lab instructor, Mr. Truesome, to do some investigating, and he ascertained some fascinating particulars. It seems that last Thursday wasn't Jenny's first nocturnal visit to our computer lab."

Albert labored through the big words and muttered, "Oh? Wasn't, eh?"

"Mr. Truesome found records—in the machines themselves, I mean—of Jenny's presence in the lab every Tuesday and Thursday night of the entire term—and *every* night of the term break over the Christmas holiday."

"We're ruined," Maude moaned under her breath, more to herself than to anyone else. "They'll put us out on the street. We'll be left in the cold and the snow."

With a concerned glance toward Maude, Ms. Bobet redirected her comments to Albert alone. "Really, it's remarkable, Mr. Northam. Think of it! Jenny not only taught herself how to create a new user ID and a login for the lab's machines, she also taught herself BASIC."

He seemed intrigued. "Er, basic what, if'n I might ask?"

"Not basic what, Mr. Northam, but BASIC, a computer programming language—Beginners' All-purpose Symbolic Instruction Code—a language spoken by some computer machines, such as the Commodore family of computers we have in our lab."

Albert's jaw dropped. "The machines can talk?"

"No, no, not talk as in how we're talking now, but rather in the manner the machines operate. The language is all typed out, you see, not spoken aloud, and Jenny has already taught herself how to type commands into the machines."

Maude's head wobbled back and forth, and Albert's fingers started rubbing holes in his trousers. The Northams were sinking fast.

Principal Charpentier tossed them a lifeline.

"Please, Mr. and Mrs. Northam—what we're trying to tell you is that little Jenny is quite brilliant—didn't you know? We wish to rescind our earlier decision not allowing her to take computer courses. She has an aptitude for computers, you see, *a gift,* and we wish to help her grow that gift. Therefore, we have enrolled her in the beginner's class and the lab that goes with it. She won't have to sneak out at night any longer to use the computers."

"You're saying she's not in trouble?" Albert asked, a bit of hope in his voice.

Principal Charpentier and Ms. Bobet nodded their heads in concert.

"That is correct. She is not in trouble. We've decided to grant her a pardon for the time being," Charpentier said. "If she keeps her grades strong and doesn't sneak into the school at night, we'll forget this little, er, bump in the road."

Albert's entire being relaxed. "Maude and I, we thank you, we do, but . . . I'm supposin' I still have a question."

"Yes?"

"What I mean is, well, how did Jenny get int' the school at night in the first place?"

"Ah, yes." Principal Charpentier delayed a little before answering. "We asked Jenny the same thing, of course, and we're not saying that we approve—"

"No, we're not saying we approve," Ms. Bobet hurried to agree, "and we'll work to discourage that sort of behavior in the future, certainly."

"Discourage what sorta behavior?" Albert demanded. "Speak plain, God save th' Queen!"

Principal Charpentier folded his hands together. "Yes, yes, we're coming to it. It is just that when we asked Jenny how she got into the school at night, well, she told us she opened the lock herself."

"Opened the lock? She had a key, then?"

Ms. Bobet answered. "No, Mr. Northam. Jenny did not have a key."

The counsellor sighed, reluctant but forced to use a coarse term Albert would understand.

"Jenny . . . picked the lock."

Albert gasped. "She what! You're jokin' are ya?"

"I'm afraid not, Mr. Northam."

Unlike Albert, Maude had a very different response. As clear as a bell, she recalled Miss Timmons' voice from the fateful morning Jenny came to live with them.

Oh, I assure you, Mrs. Northam, Jenny hasn't a violent bone in her body. She is merely . . . what I call a creative problem solver.

Under her breath, Maude ground out, "Should have put my foot down that day. I really should have."

CHAPTER 9

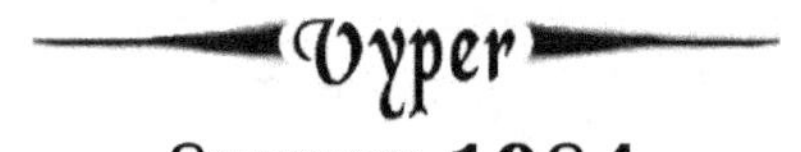

SUMMER 1984

THE COMPUTER lab at Jenny's school became a lifesaver in more ways than one. Foremost, it kept her occupied and contented during the school year, which made her life in the Northams' group home more tolerable. Secondly, Jenny's more settled attitude was a godsend for the Northams too, and for a time, Maude's sentiments toward Jenny moderated and calmed.

Jenny found that the logic of programming came to her as easily as breathing. By the time she turned fourteen, she'd worked her way through the entirety of the school's computer instructional materials and despaired of finding fresh information. As a result, she'd been bored and despondent during the spring term. Mr. Truesome, the school's computer instructor, had tried his best to keep her engaged, but Jenny had plumbed the man's supposed wealth of computer know-how, and drained his shallow cistern to its very dregs.

When spring gave way to summer break, closing the school's computer lab to her, Jenny feared endless months of tedium. She turned to reading and visited Regina's public library system weekly. Unexpectedly, she found a reprieve when she stumbled upon the shelves housing the library's modest selection of computer books. Jenny checked out and read the majority of the books in the system—six at one time being the library's limit—in order to feed her roaring thirst for anything computer-related.

She devoured the brief history of computers beginning with Boolean logic, binary arithmetic, the first relay-based calculators, the ideas of Polish code-breaker, Marian Rejewski, and the resulting British Bombe conceived by Alan Turing and Harold Keen and used to decrypt the Nazi's Enigma cypher machines. She moved on to read about the work of Atanasoff and Berry, Bell

Labs, Bletchley Park, Curt Herzstark, the summer lectures at University of Pennsylvania's Moore School, and Project Whirlwind.

She studied the first computers themselves—the Manchester "Baby," IBM's Selective Sequence Electronic Calculator (SSEC), Mauchly and Eckert's ENIAC, CSIRAC, ERA 1101, MADDIDA, Manchester Mark I, and 3C DDP-116. She mentally followed the steps of competing scientists, universities, businesses, and governments and scrutinized the new approaches they took to build more advanced machines, machines that pushed their visions forward.

The envisioned computer applications (principally automation) heralded by their inventors drove a mad rush to develop machines specifically for communications, manufacturing, business, military, and even entertainment. Eventually, ongoing design efforts led to smaller computers built on transistors instead of cathode-ray vacuum tubes. Smaller models birthed the idea of "personal computers" rather than the institutional mainframes that took up large rooms and generated so much heat that they required continuous cooling strategies.

When Jenny's reading arrived at present-day personal computers, she explored their hardware, inner workings, and useful peripherals. She knew BASIC but tried to teach herself programming languages such as FORTRAN, C, and Turbo Pascal. Unfortunately, she had no computer on which to practice —a source of unending exasperation.

She moved on to network structures and read that computer users could use a "modem" and a regular phone line to "dial up" to connected computers and visit with other computer users in "chat rooms," post comments on informational "bulletin boards," or exchange email via FidoNet or CompuServe.

Jenny had never been "online," had no practical sense of what a modem was, nor had she seen what was being dubbed email. She certainly did not consider email a necessity or even a "nice to have."

Who would I ever send email to? And why?

Jenny's reading blazed onward. Entirely by accident, she stumbled onto *2600: The Hacker Quarterly,* a brand-new magazine on computer "hacking," yet another novel term. She devoured the magazine. One article referenced a whistle found in a box of Captain Crunch that, when blown into a phone during a long-distance call, was the exact frequency (2600 hertz) to access "operator mode" and use aspects of the phone system not available to the public.

Jenny also snagged a fictional book from the New Releases display. She devoured the story, titled *Neuromancer*, told in a strange future setting and featuring Henry Case, a washed-up hacker-for-hire.

Jenny frowned. *There's that word again. Hacker. And what is this evil "artificial intelligence" he's fighting?*

Intrigued with the idea of hacking computers, Jenny looked for and found a book on the topic, primarily a lofty overview of the subject. Still, Jenny devoured it and thought she understood its basic principles.

Although she had no access to computers that could dial up to the modest offerings available online, and although what she read in those weeks lived mostly in her head, what she visualized was real *to her*. The clear and unchanging logic of computers hummed and resonated within her.

Nevertheless, what she needed, *what she craved*, existed in a world she was not part of. It was an environment a fourteen-year-old Permanent Ward could not hope to access.

She gathered the books she intended to check out that day. Angered and thwarted, she shoved *2600: The Hacker Quarterly* back into its place on the magazine racks.

❖

ONE SULTRY August day, Jenny sauntered into the library branch she frequented. She browsed the stacks and selected six new books to investigate. If she liked what she read in their opening chapters, she would check them out and take them home. She carried the books to the study area of the library to peruse them.

There she came upon three young adults quietly discussing a group project due in two weeks. From what she gleaned of their conversation, the project was for a sociology class—a subject of disinterest to Jenny. However, she also overheard them decide when and where to meet in order to type up the project's findings. When they used the sacred words "computer lab," a jolt ran through her.

She scanned the study area from behind one of her books. After a moment, she meandered to a table closer to the students. She sat with her back only feet from them and listened in earnest. Soon she understood they were summer-session students at Regina University.

Jenny had heard enough; it was time to act.

She padded to the front desk, checked out her book selections, and used the opportunity to inquire about the university. She was directed to some brochure racks. On the racks, she found what she sought, a recent course catalog that included a map of the campus. Jenny ran her finger over the map, learning it, until she located the computer lab. As soon as she saw how to get to the lab from the bus stop, she returned the catalog to the rack.

Jenny then looked for information on Regina's city bus system and found a stack of the bus system's routes and schedule. From a quiet chair in a corner, she plotted her next steps, until a disheartening revelation nearly swallowed her whole.

I'm not a university student. I'm just a kid! Without a student ID, I won't be able to get inside the computer lab. Even if I had a student ID, there's the problem of a student login.

She pondered this dilemma and sorted through a very short list of options. *What if . . .*

Still in deep concentration, she returned to the computer book shelves and ran her finger down the rows of books until she found and retrieved the book she hoped would help her. On her way to substitute that book in lieu of one of the six she'd already checked out, a small warning flashed through her mind. *I shouldn't put this book on my reading record.*

She slipped the book into her bag with the six already there and rationalized her actions. *Well, I'm not stealing it, am I? Only borrowing it. I'll bring it back with the others.*

Then she crept along the narrow aisle between the shelves' end caps and the windowed wall until she reached the study section. Screened by the last row of shelves, she peered at the students who'd been hashing out their project. Apparently, they had finished their meeting. Jenny watched as they gathered their books into backpacks. One of the students, a tall blond guy, slid his wallet into his hip pocket.

It wasn't as though Jenny decided then and there to become a thief. It was more that she had a pressing problem to solve, and solving that problem was of the highest importance to her, higher even (temporarily, of course) than the rules she largely abided by.

She sprinted back along the wall until she reached the row of shelves nearest the front entrance of the library. As the students meandered by, she barged out from the row and collided with them.

Or at least the blond guy.

"Hey! Watch where you're going, kid!" he growled.

"Sorry," she muttered. She retreated between the rows to search the student's wallet. Once his university ID card was safe in her hip pocket, she returned to the check-out desk and handed the wallet to the helpful library employee.

"I guess someone dropped this," she told the woman.

"Why, thank you, deary. What a good girl you are."

IT TOOK Jenny two hours to catch the right bus to the university, walk across campus, and find the computer lab. Her next steps were scary, but necessary.

At the door to the lab, while keeping her thumb over the photo, Jenny flashed the pilfered student ID card at the bored lab monitor and scribbled something illegible on the sign-in sheet. That being the extent of the ID's help, she navigated the lab's perimeter in unhurried fashion, reading the notices on the bulletin boards, or sitting in front of an idle computer, watching for a careless student to leave the machine he or she was using . . . without first logging off.

There.

Jenny counted to five, then slid into the girl's seat and hit the space bar to continue the girl's session. She pulled up the computer's directories and studied the machine's operating system and installed programs, then viewed the user profile of the girl whose account she was using. As she browsed . . . a door opened before her, the entrance to a wondrous world she'd only dreamed about: The computer lab had dial-up service.

I'll be able to go online at last! But to use the lab regularly, I will need my own ID and login. I can't keep using someone else's ID to get in here, nor can I count on a random student forgetting to log off.

Jenny brought up the command prompt and began to query the university's network. Within moments, she was stuck. Surreptitiously, she unzipped her backpack and removed the book on hacking she'd "borrowed" from the library without checking it out. The book wouldn't tell her exactly how to do what she had in mind, but it would lay out the elements. Jenny opened a new file and tried to follow the book's logic.

An hour went by. Jenny felt like she was getting closer, but something she'd typed wasn't working right, and she couldn't figure out what. On top of that, she knew she had to leave soon or risk being late for dinner—and being on time for dinner was an inviolate house rule. She started to sweat. Was anyone watching? Had she been in the lab too long?

She shifted in her seat and shot her eyes around the lab—only to encounter the gaze of a scruffy-looking guy two seats to her left. Jenny froze. The guy sported several piercings and dark, unkempt hair half covering his eyes. He smirked at her scrutiny and jerked his chin toward her screen.

From behind his upraised hand, he whispered, "Trying to build a fake student profile, huh?"

Jenny frowned. "No. Absolutely not."

He snickered under his breath. "Sure you are—but you made a rookie blunder two lines back." He wheeled his chair closer and pointed. "Look. What you need to do here is this."

Pulling up his chair and practically pushing Jenny aside, he appropriated her keyboard and erased and retyped the lines, adding a third. "There. See that? Now enter the rest of the info it asks for and you're in. That's not the tricky part, though. The tricky part is picking up your student ID card from the bursar's office. You gotta show them a valid form of ID with name and info that matches the name and info on the student ID card—and for heaven's sake, don't use a *real* ID for your profile, one that can be traced back to you. The profile needs to be one hundred percent bogus."

Taking in the helpful information, Jenny felt a burst of gratitude toward the guy, slovenly as he was. "How can I get a fake ID?"

He stopped smirking. "How much money you got?"

Jenny turned inward and mentally counted the money she kept stuffed inside a shoe in her closet. "Maybe thirty dollars?"

The guy shook his head. "Fifty bucks, minimum—and that's for a *cheap* fake."

Looking her over, he added, "You had to show a student ID to get into this lab, didn't you? Where'd you get it?"

"I-I found it. Some guy dropped it at the library."

He snorted. "Sure he did. Well, good luck to you."

He rolled his chair back to the computer he'd been using, gathered his things, and started to get up. Jenny snagged the tail of his t-shirt. She opened her other hand and showed him the ID.

"Huh. Nice. New, too. You offering a trade?"

"Um, yah."

"I might be able to help you. Meet me behind this building tomorrow. Bring this ID and the thirty dollars. I'll bring you a driver's license you can take to the bursar's office so you can pick up the student ID card for your fake student profile. Oh. And don't finish setting up the fake profile until after we meet."

Jenny narrowed her eyes. "Why not?"

"Because the profile and ID have to match, dingus."

Jenny had been called many names in her short life. She'd learned to school her expressions, keep her emotions in check, and plan an appropriate payback—a teachable moment for the individuals who bullied her. This was different, though. She needed this guy's help and would, for the present, let the name-calling slide.

"Oh. I see."

"Man, you're green as grass, ain'tcha? Surprised the lab monitor didn't give you a second look. I mean, what are you, twelve?"

Jenny drew herself up, the lie prepped and ready to go. "I'm seventeen."

"Wow. I'm impressed. This your first hack?"

Jenny set her mouth in a firm line. "I can learn. I *am* learning. And I-I learn fast."

He eyed her with speculation. "I could show you a few things. For a price."

"I won't have any money after I give you the thirty dollars tomorrow."

He looked away. Brushed the hair out of his eyes. "You seem like a nice kid. I might let you work off a few lessons. We'll see. Tomorrow, 11 a.m."

Jenny blinked. "Wait. What's your name?"

His mouth twisted on one side. "We don't use our real names, you dope. Only hacker handles. *Ever*. You call me Syntax. Got it?"

"Yah. Got it." Jenny swallowed. "Wait. You said, 'we.' 'We don't use our real names.' Are there many more people like you?"

His laugh was softly scornful. "You're as witless as a newborn chick, but if you prove that you can learn—like you said you could—you'll get around to meeting more of us. Eventually."

He started to turn away, glanced over his shoulder. "What do we call you? And I don't mean your real name, *sweetheart*."

Jenny moved her head side to side. "I don't know yet."

"I get you. No rush. Give it time." He looked her over again. "Don't get ahead of yourself, either."

"What do you mean?"

"I mean don't go painting yourself with some grandiose title. You don't warrant an impressive name, nor do you look the type to grow into anything epic—so don't hype yourself with an ambitious handle."

Jenny didn't move. The guy's dismissive comment angered her, but she wasn't going to jeopardize this vital connection by allowing that anger to show. She knew better than to tell him off . . . just like she knew how to bide her time. She'd spent her young life perfecting the art of payback.

Pressing her lips together, she nodded.

"Good. Just make sure you show up tomorrow at 11 o'clock. This is a one-time offer."

"Yah. I'll be there."

JENNY GOT up early, before anyone else in the house was up. The fact was, she had hardly slept at all through the long hours of darkness. Instead, she had relived yesterday's encounter with Syntax again and again during the night—almost to the point of madness. It was a relief to climb out of bed and get moving, to fix her thoughts on *today's* meeting with him and what it meant.

The fake ID Syntax had promised to sell her was key to Jenny's objective: unfettered, unlimited access to the computers in the university's lab and their dial-up connection.

Jenny shivered with anticipation.

She made her bed in the tidy manner she was accustomed to. Being as quiet as she could, she dressed, washed her face, and carefully combed out her hair, parted it in the middle, and re-braided it. Afterward, she studied the four pairs of shoes lined up on the floor of her closet. She pulled out an old pair and chose the left shoe. She tugged a wadded up sock from its toe and emptied the sock's contents onto her bed.

She already knew the amount she'd find—$67.25. For months, Jenny had saved two of the three dollars she received from her five-dollar weekly allowance. Mrs. Northam kept the first two dollars and Jenny spent one dollar on gum, leaving her two dollars which she added to her "cash on hand."

She had lied to Syntax about how much money she had.

I'm not stupid. I'm not telling anyone how much money I have—or where I keep it.

Syntax's dismissive words echoed in her head. It may have been the hundredth time she'd remembered them, yet it didn't matter. They stung her afresh with each repeat.

You don't warrant an impressive handle, nor do you look the type to grow into anything epic—so don't hype yourself.

"Yah? Guess we'll see about that."

From the crumpled bills on her bedspread, she counted out thirty dollars. She neatly folded the bills and pushed them into her jean's right hand pocket along with the blond guy's student ID. Then she took a single dollar bill and put it into her left pocket. That dollar would purchase her weekly allotment of bubble gum. (Jenny rationed her gum with care so she never ran out. That would not do. *At all.*)

She stared at the remaining money. The change dumped on her bed totaled maybe two dollars. The rest, the folding cash, amounted to thirty-four dollars. Slowly, she picked up the bills, smoothed and folded them together. Stared at them. Unzipped a pouch in her book bag and tucked the wad inside.

Even though she couldn't conceive of any need at the moment, she muttered to herself, "Just in case."

The house was quiet. No one got up before eight o'clock during these summer months. If she hurried, she could complete her chores, snag something to eat from the kitchen, and be out the door before Maude dragged herself downstairs.

Jenny grabbed her book bag, crept down to the ground floor, and headed to the laundry room behind the kitchen. Three baskets of clean laundry waited for her, one basket of linens and two baskets of clothes that belonged to the other kids of the house—Donny, Trey, Kit, and Mary. One of her jobs was to fold and put away the previous day's clean laundry.

She didn't mind. Folding laundry was a soothing, somewhat satisfying task. When she finished, she'd have a pristine tower of towels for the linen closet and smartly folded stacks of pants, shirts, undies, and socks, all sorted by child. Later, when she put the stacks into each kid's dresser, she'd tidy up the drawers' contents, leaving them orderly. *Again.* Also, *again,* she would remind each kid to keep their drawers organized.

Her admonitions didn't make much of a difference, but she couldn't help repeating herself. She derived a fair amount of gratification from keeping her own things organized, and it bothered her to see unchecked disarray in the younger kids' rooms—kids younger than her by a handful of years but who often acted (in her estimation) like they were five instead of seven through nine.

Jenny didn't—couldn't—tolerate chaos. She required order, order in her room, her things, and her life. It never occurred to her that most kids were messy by nature, whereas she was not. She didn't give her desire for structure a second thought. She hadn't yet realized that her behavior, compared to other kids her age, was anything *but* normal.

When she finished folding the laundry, Jenny moved on to her next chore, breakfast preparation. She lifted down the kettle, measured and added water, a dash of salt, and turned the burner under the kettle on high. While she waited for the water to boil, she measured out four cups of rolled oats and set them aside. When the water began to roll, she added the oats, placed the lid on the pot, and turned down the heat.

Next came the Northams' coffee. She filled the percolator, measured out the right amount of ground Hills Bros Coffee, and plugged the cord into the wall. She knew *exactly* how the Northams preferred their morning brew and strove to deliver it as expected. Maude invariably woke up grumpy. Coffee made to Maude's specifications was the easiest means of keeping the woman off Jenny's back and out of her business.

Jenny's last morning chore was to dust the living room and dining room and open the drapes for the day. Donny was supposed to close the drapes after dinner and sweep the floor under the table, but at seven years of age and being the youngest child in the house, he wasn't much good at sweeping up. Jenny finished the dusting, then swept the floor herself, catching the dried bits of food Donny had missed.

Jenny's evening chores were to do the dishes and clean the kitchen with Trey, Kit, and Mary's help. Trey was eight years old and shared a bedroom with Donny, while Kit and Mary, who shared the other bedroom, were both nine. Jenny, at fourteen, was the odd duck in the house age wise. It was easier for Jenny to do the work without help from the other kids, but she assigned them tasks anyway and kept after them until they were done. Who else was going to do it? Certainly not Maude. On the upside, supervising the younger kids' chores was one way to avoid Maude's loud harangues—and all the kids in the house were in favor of that.

Jenny had wondered why Albert and Maude kept her on after she aged out of the home's designated upper age limit of thirteen. After Jenny had puzzled over the question a while, she felt it had to be because she rarely complained about the work they expected of her. She did it without being told and did it well.

For herself, Jenny looked on the arrangement as an equitable one. She completed the tasks they asked of her, and they gave her the little freedoms she lived for. Each morning, after she finished her morning chores, she could either isolate herself in her room to read or go to the library—and that "deal" suited Jenny just fine.

Today, though, she had more momentous experiences on her agenda.

Grabbing two bananas, a juice box, and her book bag, she tiptoed to the front door, unlocked it, and stepped outside. The sun was up and starting to warm the air as she walked two miles to the park adjacent to the library. She had hours before her meeting with Syntax, and the library wouldn't open until 9:00 a.m., but that was fine. More time to read, and the park was her preferred place to wait for the library to open.

Jenny dropped her book bag under her favorite tree. She sat down next to the bag with her back to the tree trunk, opened the book she was currently reading, and cracked the lid on her juice box.

———————◆———————

JENNY EXAMINED the driver's license Syntax held out to her. The name on it read Carol Hanover. The face staring back at her was that of a bored college-age woman with short, bobbed hair.

"But that's not me," Jenny protested. "The picture doesn't look anything like me! I won't be able to pick up a student ID using this."

"She's got your hair *color*; that's close enough."

No, it isn't! Jenny fumed internally. *My hair is brown. Hers is practically black!*

He leaned in and poked her shoulder with his finger, "It's up to *you* to make yourself look more like *her*."

Jenny started to panic. "But how?"

He flicked one of her braids and sneered. "For one thing, lose the kiddie tails. You're seventeen, right? Well, these braids make you look like a ten-year-old. And put on some makeup while you're at it. Eye liner. Mascara. Lipstick."

Syntax's words shook her. *I look like a ten-year-old?*

Down deep in her gut, in a place she hardly knew existed, let alone had considered, Syntax's advice made her shiver. Then his mocking disdain began to resonate.

Until this exact moment, Jenny's self-awareness had lain dormant, immature and stunted. She'd had no feminine figure to look to for feminine behavior. No mother to emulate. But within the span of mere seconds . . . momentous self-realization took root, budded, and bloomed within her.

I look like a child?

*A **child**? I'm fourteen!*

Wait. I don't have to keep looking this way—do I?

Do I?

No. I can change how I look.

I can? Dare I?

Yes . . . but how?

Only a real university student ID would grant her unfettered access to the university's computer lab, and her chest already ached over this crushing loss of opportunity.

*If I can't pick up the student ID until I look more like the woman in this driver's license, then I **must** change how I appear.*

All these observations and strange feelings passed through her mind in mere moments.

Syntax gestured toward the fake driver's license in her hand. "Hey! You owe me thirty bucks and that other student ID you pilfered."

Jenny tore her attention away from the novel notions jinking around in her head. "If I give you the ID, I won't be able to get into the lab to finish Carol's profile."

He squinted. "Good point. Let's get that done. I'll let you use one of my student logins, but I'll keep the driver's license until we're done and you've paid up."

Jenny swallowed and handed back the license. "Okay. Shouldn't take long to finish the profile."

He snarked. "Yeah, right. Don't worry; if you run into problems, I'll step you through them."

Jenny gritted her teeth. "Fine."

⎯⎯◆⎯⎯

THIRTY MINUTES later, they exited the lab separately and met up behind the building, under the building's eaves.

Syntax gave her a grudging nod of acknowledgement. "You did better than I thought you would. Maybe you do have some potential."

Jenny bit back a retort and held out her hand. "Can I have the license now? And you said you'd show me a few things—things I don't already know."

"I also said, in return, you would do some work for us." He withdrew a five-and-a-quarter-inch floppy disk from the notebook he carried. "Got some good code on here. Basic stuff, but essential. Study this code, figure it out. Practice and learn it. Then meet me in that parking lot over there Friday at noon. You and I will take a ride to a friend's house. He's got a sweet setup in his basement, and we have an op running that day. We'll put you to work. See how you do."

Get in a car with a guy she barely knew? Go to a stranger's house? They'd put her to work? Alarm bells jangled in Jenny's head.

"Um, what kind of work?"

He grinned. "The kind that makes money, kid. You'll learn a lot that day, and if you're any good, if you catch on quick enough, we'll cut you in. But first off? Pay up."

Jenny pulled the folded bills and the blond student's school ID from her pocket. Syntax took them from her, gave them a cursory examination, and stuffed them into his hip pocket. He placed the license and floppy disk in her hand.

Nodding, Jenny zipped them into the pocket of her book bag.

When she looked up, Syntax had folded his arms.

"Okay, kiddo. Just for your information? You've passed your first test— and avoided a nasty bit of comeuppance at the same time."

Jenny gaped. "W-what?"

"Yah, see, you welsh on a deal with us? That earns you a beatdown and a swift kick to the curb. Can't say I was looking forward to roughing you up, but it's standard practice. We don't do business with cheats, but we *do* teach them a lesson. It's a rule."

It's a rule?

Her head started to spin. "You were going to beat me up?"

Syntax shrugged. "Welshers always get a beatdown. They gotta learn not to mess with us. After that, they're marked for life. Nobody in the community will give a welsher the time of day, cuz nobody, but *nobody* messes with one of us."

She swallowed. "Us? The hacker community?"

"You think we're alone out there in cyberspace? The hacker community in Canada is growing. At a rate."

Cyberspace?

At a rate?

Mystified, Jenny asked, "What's cyberspace?"

"The global computer network, kiddo. It's not quite here yet, but it's coming soon! One day all computers will be connected, and us hackers will understand computers better than anyone. We'll breach any and every kind of security they can come up with. They won't be able to keep up with us, let alone stop us. And then? Then we're gonna rule the world."

Then we're gonna rule the world.

While he was talking, he pulled a pack of gum with a red wrapper from his front pocket and began to twirl it between his fingers. When he slid a stick from the pack and unwrapped it, a spicy scent tickled Jenny's nose and throat.

Curious, Jenny asked, "What is that?" She pointed to the red pack.

He sniffed his disdain. "Do you live in a cave? It's Clove gum. The only gum I chew."

CHAPTER 10

Vyper

JENNY STOOD across the street from the neighborhood drug store. In her hand was Carol Hanover's driver's license. As she studied the image on the license, Syntax's voice resounded in her head. "It's up to you to make yourself look more like her. . . Lose the kiddie tails. They make you look like a ten-year-old. And put on some makeup while you're at it. Eye liner. Mascara. Lipstick."

I don't have to look like a ten-year-old.

I can change how I look.

Can I really change how I look?

Maybe I can.

Jenny had thirty-four dollars burning a hole in her book bag and an excitement bouncing around inside her that refused to be calm or rational—and yet didn't she plan everything? The unreasoning, impulsive excitement twisting her stomach scared her more than a little.

The store beckoned to her, but she couldn't get her feet to move. First, she had to have a plan, a strategy, right? But she'd never done anything like this. She didn't know how to start.

She licked her lips. *I don't have to buy anything. I can just browse. See what is there. Maybe then I'll know what to do.*

Syntax's declaration also boomed in her head. "We're gonna rule the world."

"We're going to rule the world," she murmured. "The hacker community is going to rule the world." Those words pulled on Jenny in a way she'd never experienced. She felt a desire welling inside, a longing to belong to that community, to know what they knew, to do things they could do.

If she'd looked deeper inside, if she'd been brutally honest with herself, she would have acknowledged another desire lurking there.

I want to be as good as Syntax. As good as his friends. Maybe better.

Instead, her thoughts returned to the problem at hand. *How do I make myself look like Carol Hanover?*

She found herself pushing through the door and wandering the personal care aisles—rows and rows of makeup, hair products, and skin care. She stopped in front of hair color. Glanced at the photo on the license.

Carol Hanover's hair is nearly black.

She fingered one of her braids. Studied its color, mousy brown. Picked up a box of brown-black hair color. Put it back and chose a solid black. With it in her hand, she felt empowered.

I need makeup. Specifically, eye liner, mascara, and lipstick.

After vacillating for twenty minutes between brands and prices, she made her selections and moved toward the checkout counter, passing through the candy aisle where she normally picked up her bubble gum for the week.

Bubble gum? Really? What am I—a kid?

Nope. Not anymore.

It took her a few minutes to hunt down Syntax's preferred Clove gum. She found the red packs at the bottom of the gum shelf. Lifting one pack to her nose she inhaled—and jerked the gum away.

"*Gag.* Too strong. I want . . . something else."

Not far from the red packs were blue ones with the words Black Jack on them. She lifted a pack and, tentatively, sniffed it. The tang of black licorice was faint but unmistakable.

"Maybe I'll give this one a try."

She added five packs to her shopping basket and got in line to pay for her purchases.

Before she left the store, she stuffed the plastic shopping sack into her book bag—with the exception of one pack of gum.

When Jenny left the drug store parking lot and headed home, she had fifty-nine cents in her pocket, a stick of Black Jack in her mouth, and a strange exhilaration blooming in her chest.

———◆———

THE UNIVERSITY'S catalog said it would take three business days for the student ID from the profile she'd created to be ready to pick up. She needed to be certain, so she called the bursar's office when the three days were up, identifying herself as Carol Hanover.

"Yes, Miss Hanover, your student ID card is ready to be picked up. Please bring another form of identification with you when you come in."

The woman on the other end chuckled. "Can't be too careful these days, what with people forging student accounts and all."

"No. Uh, I mean, yes, I'll bring ID with me," Jenny answered.

She hung up and wiped her sweaty palms on the legs of her jeans. If she was going through with her plan, it was time to act.

"I'm going to take a shower," she announced later that evening. "If you need the toilet, use it now."

Four sets of legs thundered toward the bathroom. Five minutes passed before it was available again. Jenny took everything she needed down the hall to the bathroom, locked the door behind her, and set the contents of the hair color box on the sink. She had already read the instructions six times and went straight to work.

The big constraint was the twenty minutes she had to wait before washing out the hair color. Hopefully, no one would come knocking at the door before she finished.

Forty minutes later she stared at the results.

"Huh." Her towel-dried hair was now a deep, glossy black . . . and she didn't hate it. The next step, however, was more radical.

She parted her hair in the middle from forehead to crown, and pulled the two sides into pigtails. Using the scissors she'd "borrowed" from Maude's sewing kit, she carefully cut through each tail about two inches below her jawline. When the two sides looked reasonably the same length, she pulled out the ponytail holders and watched her hair fall into its new shape.

The ends were noticeably uneven, and Jenny began to sweat.

"I-I'll blow dry my hair, then even things up."

She used the handheld dryer, brushing her hair as it dried, pulling most of the curl out of her hair. As best as she could, Jenny trimmed the uneven places.

"Curlers," she muttered, "to turn the ends under like the picture on the license."

With the curlers in place, she cleaned up her mess, stuffing all the evidence of hair color into the same plastic sack she'd brought things home in from the drug store.

"I'll get rid of it first thing tomorrow."

———◆———

JENNY WOKE with a start. She'd gone to bed anxious, but had slept soundly until morning. In fact, the clock read 7:30. She nearly panicked.

I overslept! There's no way I can do my chores and put on makeup before the Northams or the kids start to get up. She weighed her options. *I'll rush through my chores and take the makeup and whatever else I need with me.*

She ripped the curlers from her hair and dressed like the house was on fire. She gathered her new makeup, a small mirror, and a hairbrush and stuffed them into her book bag. Thought for a moment before she grabbed an old washcloth, dampened it, tossed it into the bag's pocket, and fled down the stairs as quickly and quietly as she could.

Her feet skidded to a stop when she reached the kitchen. There sat little Donny. He'd pulled a block of cheese from the fridge, hacked off a chunk, and was slowly gnawing away at it. The end of the block had been butchered under Donny's unskilled hands; crumbled cheese had spilled on the floor and over the counter.

"What are you doing?" Jenny demanded.

His eyes widened and his thin shoulders lifted a little. "Woke up with a big growl in my tummy." His expression shifted to puzzled. "Whadya do to your hair, Jenny?"

Jenny set to work. "That's none of your business."

"It looks funny."

"Does it?" she sneered. She didn't say anything further though. At the moment, her thoughts were racing, sorting through several ploys she could use to keep him quiet after the rest of the family got up. *I'll face the Northams at dinner, but I don't want Maude stewing all day on what I've done to my hair. I'd rather surprise her—hit her while she's in shock.*

As she finished her tasks, an idea came to her. Slinging her bag onto her back, she faced the boy. "You know you'll be in trouble when Mrs. Northam finds out you snitched food, Donny."

He looked at the bit of cheese clenched in his hand. When his eyes met hers, they glistened with unshed tears. "But I was hungry!"

Jenny played it cool—the way she always did. "Hmm. Well, what if . . . I clean up your mess? I won't tell on you . . . if you don't say anything about my hair today. To anyone."

He snuffled. "Okay."

Jenny pried the last bit of cheese from his hand and was about to toss it in the trash when she noticed his woebegone expression. "Here. Eat it quick."

While he chewed and swallowed, she evened up the end of the cheese block, wrapped it up "right" and set it back in the fridge, then wiped the counters clean and swept up the cheese crumbles.

"Done? Good. Now, go back upstairs. Stay in your room until the other kids get up and come downstairs. Then you can come down too."

Without a word, he scampered away, and Jenny left the house.

———◆———

JENNY HAD never handled makeup before. Consequently, she made a mess of her first two attempts to draw the eyeliner right and had to wash her face twice, rinsing and rewetting the rag from a sprinkler head. Under her tree in the park, with the mirror propped up against the tree trunk, she made a third attempt.

This time, she finally got the liner to a decent state. She began to add mascara—and poked herself in the eye several times, making herself cry and the liner run in dirty rivulets down her cheeks.

"*Gah!*"

Tired and disheartened, Jenny sat still for a long time. She couldn't, however, halt her mind. Her thoughts, on their own, attacked the problem with the same ferocity they attacked every problem she ran up against. Eventually, she nodded to herself.

I need that ID. I need access to better computers than the ones at my school—and somehow I need to get online. It's the only way I'll learn anything new—and I must keep learning if I ever hope to join the hacker community.

She scowled. *Makeup is just another kind of skill, one I haven't figured out yet. If other girls,* stupid *girls, can do it, I can do it too. Just gotta get the hang of it.* **I can and I will.**

After washing her face clean for the third time, Jenny picked up the eye liner and declared, "You will not beat me. Putting you on right is no different than working a keyboard right. It requires a sure, steady hand and muscle memory."

Jenny applied the liner and deemed it a fair job. She picked up the mascara and alternately daubed and brushed it over her lashes, poking her eye only once, blinking hard to keep her eye from watering. By now, the curled hair she'd released from curlers first thing that morning had relaxed some. She used the brush to turn the ends under and to smooth the rest of her hair. Last of all, she dabbed on a thin coat of lip gloss.

The morning was half spent when she figured she was finished applying the makeup. She muttered darkly, "What a bother."

But that was before she held the mirror out at arm's length and viewed the full effect.

She would have gasped—if her mouth hadn't dried up and her tongue hadn't gotten stuck. As it was, the individual she beheld was a stranger—a child no longer, a girl who was very nearly a woman. Her green eyes shone like cats' eyes, their exotic, tilted shape pronounced and mysterious.

Blinking breathlessly, she put the mirror away. Packed up and headed for the nearest bus stop on the route to Regina University. Self-conscious at first, she stood straighter. On the bus, she kept aloof as usual, yet she couldn't help notice that other occupants of the bus were less likely to overlook her. Several young guys actually eyeballed her, speculation etched on their juvenile faces.

Jenny ignored them—she wasn't interested in boys at this point—but inside she was smiling and wondering how she might use this new look to further her goals.

Who knows? I just might start to like this.

———————•———————

COLLECTING CAROL Hanover's student ID had been a cakewalk. No one in the bursar's office so much as batted an eye when she showed Carol's driver's license. Entering the computer lab and logging in as Carol for the first time had been just as easy. Jenny blended in with other university students so effortlessly, that she relaxed into her role.

Not a child, she reminded herself. *Not anymore.*

She inserted Syntax's floppy disk into the machine she was on and viewed the disk directory and its five files. She opened the first file and slowly scrolled down the lines of code. Right away, she began to decipher the logic behind the commands and follow the flow and direction of the code. That wasn't, however, all she needed to do.

Syntax had been explicit about his instructions. *Got some good code on here. Basic stuff, but essential. Study this code, figure it out. Practice and learn it.*

Today was Tuesday. She had until Friday to learn the code. Syntax and his friend expected her to know both how and when to use the code, too. Jenny's mouth compressed in determination as she scrolled down the file a second time. The thing was? The code made perfect sense to her.

I can do this.

Jenny read through the code two more times before she closed the file. She opened a new file. Sinking into herself, she recalled Syntax's code and began to type. Line after line flowed from her fingers, each line sublimely ordered, the precision language humming a sweet melody in her soul, a gift that sang down deep in her being.

On and on she typed, each line necessary to the code's unfolding artistry, each command specific, the logic perfect—

"*No.*"

Jenny had said it aloud, and a couple of heads turned her way. Ignoring them, she muttered to herself, "That's not right."

She hadn't typed it wrong, had she? No, she had not. The *code* was wrong.

Exasperation thrumming in her chest, she sent what she'd typed to the lab's printer, saved the file, then pulled up the original file and compared the two. Line by line, they were the same, but . . .

"It's wrong."

She stared up at the ceiling. *What do I do now? Syntax expects me to know this file's code . . . but it's faulty. Broken.*

"Clunky, too," she muttered.

Closing her eyes, she mentally read through the remainder of the code file and released her subconscious to do the problem solving like it always did.

Eye pressed shut, she whispered to herself, "As the code is presently written, the use of that variable will make the code hang up here. Requires a tweak to restart and finish its task. But if I rewrite the variable options, it won't hang up, and the outcome will be faster. And if I add in this query—

Up jumped a series of warning thoughts.

Just who do you think you are?

Will Syntax and his friend applaud when you tell them they made a mistake, and you've "fixed" it?

When you announce that you've altered their code? Is it possible that they will give you a "beatdown" instead?

Jenny ground her teeth. "But it's *wrong!* And what if . . . what if they're testing me to see if I catch the error?"

Guys with big egos don't like little girls telling them off.

Jenny closed the first file. She opened the other four one at a time and worked her way through them, grasping structure, elements, and style as she went, not realizing she was absorbing them, learning them, acquiring a new language in much the same way a child acquires their native tongue.

From memory she typed out each set of code into a fresh file. As she did, she again analyzed what was there and looked for ways to streamline and add function while checking for errors. She found two typos in the third file and fixed them.

Guys with big egos don't like little girls telling them off.

"Well, I refuse to stay a child," Jenny whispered. As her agitation intensified, a seed of upheaval planted itself in her heart. As it swelled, it told her that she didn't have to remain the same, assured her that she was changing.

Growing.

"Everyone tries to put me in a box. The Northams. Mr. Truesome. Syntax. Well, I'm not going to cower to Syntax or his friend. I know I'm smart. I can learn—I *am* learning. I shouldn't have to hide what I can do or who I am becoming. I can and will work hard and contribute to the hacker community . . . but no one gets to treat me like a child anymore."

She reopened the first file on the disk that she'd typed from memory, scrolled to the error at its bottom, and began to edit the code. She fixed the hang-up and added further utility to the coded function. Then, starting at the top, she went through it again, streamlining several lines. Finally, she resaved the file and logged off.

By the time she finished, the afternoon was far advanced. She slung her bag over her shoulder and headed for the bus stop.

On the way home, Jenny turned inward to examine this day's novel revelations. How easy it had been to pass herself off as a university student! And like the icing on a cake, an entire world had opened to her as she reviewed, learned, then revised the files Syntax had given her.

But below those positives, a thread of disquiet tickled her. How might Syntax and his friend respond to her edits on Friday? And what about the Northams? What would they say when they saw her shorter and very black hair? Jenny had lived with them for nine years. She had a realistic idea how Maude would react.

I won't let her put me down, Jenny vowed. *I may be only fourteen, but I am no longer a child. I can make my own choices.*

When Jenny left the bus and walked toward the house, she lifted her chin. She had determined her course of action.

———◆———

JENNY CREPT up the front porch and slipped through the door minutes before dinner. She was quiet and no one heard her, so she kept out of sight until Albert called the household to the table.

When she sat down at her usual place, her face was free of makeup, as it normally was.

Her hair was anything but normal.

Maude took one look and screeched, "What in heaven's name did you do to your hair?"

Jenny toyed with her food. She forked a bite of potato and answered quietly, civilly, "As you can see, Maude, I cut and colored it."

Affronted, Maude slammed her palms onto the tabletop. The littles stilled in anticipation of a major blow-up. Albert, though, watched Jenny cautiously. He couldn't have known what was brewing within her, but perhaps he sensed it.

Jenny, for her part, was calm—at least on the outside. But inside? The seed of rebellion in her heart had sprouted and put down roots. Her new mantra was a battle cry: *I am not a child.*

Again, Maude slapped the table with her hand. "You will wash that trashy color out of your hair right now, Jenny. Now. Leave the table immediately," she commanded.

When Jenny did *not* leave the table but continued to eat, Maude roared, "I said, *now*."

"No."

The response was so quiet and unexpected, that Maude gaped.

Jenny put down her fork and glanced from Maude to Albert and back to Maude. "I've been thinking I should give Miss Timmons a call."

Maude blinked. "You . . . whatever for?"

"You have always said that this group home's age limit is thirteen, yet I'm fourteen now. I should ask Miss Timmons to find me a placement for teenagers, one that gives me the freedom to express myself. Miss Timmons will understand. She gave me her card. I will call her tomorrow."

Jenny paused before adding, "That is, unless . . . " Jenny watched the Northams' expressions swing from puzzled to shocked. Jenny knew the gambit she'd set in motion, and from the dumbfounded realization settling on the Northams, she saw that they had reached the same conclusion.

Jenny had engineered a shakedown.

She didn't break eye contact with Maude, and although she said nothing, the meaning her unwavering gaze conveyed was clear. *Go ahead. Push me and see what happens. Miss Timmons likes me. She will bend over backwards to find me another placement. Then who will do my chores around here, the chores the littles are too young to do? And who will see that the littles take their baths and clean their rooms?*

It wasn't that Jenny actually wanted to leave the Northams. No, what she desired and what she was determined to do was *bend them.*

Maude licked her lips. "Perhaps we should talk about this, Jenny, dear . . . but after dinner. Go ahead and eat your food. We'll talk after.

With a choking cry, Donny shouted, "Well, I-I-I *like* Jenny's hair!" He planted the butt of the fork in his hand on the tabletop and scowled. "And I don't want Jenny to leave!"

Mary, Trey, and Kit's eyes widened like saucers. Such an outburst from a child was unheard of.

Jenny swiveled toward Donny's seat and, with the one eye out of the Northams' view, dropped him a slow wink.

She turned back. Took another bite. "I'd prefer to talk now."

"You do not make the rules in this house, Jenny," Maude shouted.

Albert put a placating hand on her arm. "Now, Maudy—"

"Don't you 'Now, Maudy' me!"

The pressure of Albert's hand on Maude's arm intensified.

"Maude, perhaps Jenny has a point. She *is* fourteen. Be emancipated a year from her next birthday. Think, love. Do we *want* her to leave just now? Eh?"

Maude reddened. For a long, tense moment her jaw worked. She refused to look at Jenny.

It was Albert who finally spoke. "What d'you want, Jenny?"

Jenny swirled her bite of potato in a little dab of gravy. "Jenny is a child's name, and I am no longer a child. I want you to call me Niève. Not Jenny, not Geneviève, but Niève."

"*Neeve?* What sort of a name is that?" Maude demanded. "In all my born days, I never heard of the name *Neeve!*"

Albert squeezed Maude's arm. "We can do that, can't we, Maudy? Call her Niève?" He squeezed harder. "Right, Pet?"

Maude jerked her chin once in the affirmative. She did not move otherwise.

Albert tried to smile. "Anything else, er, Niève?"

"Yes. I want you to raise my allowance to ten dollars a week. Five dollars more for all the chores I do." She let the demand hang in the air for a minute.

"And from now on, I'll choose how I do my hair, what clothes I wear . . . and makeup too."

Albert grimaced, then said, "That sounds all right, doesn't it, Maudy? The girl will be fifteen in nine months, after all."

When Maude did not respond, Albert tried to smile. "That's all right too, er, Nième."

"And I want the rest of my allowance."

Albert looked confused. "What do you mean?"

When Maude's arm tensed under his hand, Albert rounded on her. He was no longer smiling. "Do you know what she means, Maude?"

Not "Maudy," not "Pet," but *Maude*.

When Maude didn't answer, Nième did. "Maude has taken two dollars out of my allowance every week since I turned twelve. She *said* she put it in a savings account for me."

Albert wagged his head. "I don't know about that."

Turning to his wife, he demanded, "Did you do that, Maude? Did you take money from Jenny's—I mean *Nième's*—'lowance? Did you cheat that girl? Did you? *Did you?*"

The kids had experienced the rough side of Maude's tongue on a daily basis and lived with the fear of her formidable temper, but they had never seen Albert livid, let alone heard him raise his voice, and certainly not at Maude.

Maude withered under Albert's fury. "It's in our savings account. All of it."

For a long, tension-charged moment, Albert stared at Maude. Finally, he ground out, "T'morrow, I will take Nième t' the bank first thing. I'll pull Nième's money outa our account and give it to her."

He looked at Nième. "Can ya say how much we owe you?"

"Yes. Two hundred and eighty-four dollars as of last week."

Albert sighed. Shook his head. "I'm that sorry, Jenny—I mean *Nième*. I'll round it up t' three hunnerd dollars, if you promise not t' tell on us t' Miss Timmons."

Nième considered the offer. "All right, but I would like to have my own savings account. I'll put the money she took from me into it," Nième answered.

"Need an adult t' sign for you to open that account."

Nième thought a moment. "I trust you, Albert—but it will be my account and my money."

"Won't touch a cent of it, promise. When th' statements come, you'll get 'em, unopened. You have m' word, Jenny."

"Nième."

"Right. You have m' word, *Nième*."

Knowing she'd won her battle, the girl newly born as Nième looked around the table. "You can go ahead and eat, kids. Everything's all right. Now."

With her chair's legs scraping the floor, Maude pushed her chair back from the table. She stomped out of the dining room, shouting, "Creative problem solver, my left foot!"

BROADSWORD

Vyper

CHAPTER 11

◀ Vyper ▶

APRIL 2002

IT WAS coming up on eleven o'clock when the driver of the Land Rover turned off the state road and rolled onto a dirt track winding up the mountain. The thick forest surrounding the vehicle was familiar (and oddly comforting) to Jaz, as was the manned guard shack when they rolled toward the top of the road.

Resolute had been safe here. When the task force had been driven out of their offices in Germantown by the threat of additional attacks, they had holed up for weeks within Broadsword's hidden mountain compound—a secure facility operating under Director Wolfe's oversight. The task force had remained at Broadsword until Director Wolfe and the new head of the Ukrainian organized crime mob out of Brighton Beach, New York, had worked out a compromise that removed the threat.

Richard and Harris were waiting for Jaz on the front porch of Broadsword's lodge, no doubt given notice of her arrival by the guard at the compound's checkpoint. They stepped down as the Land Rover came to a stop.

Richard, looking the part of genial butler but with a long and distinguished military and intelligence career behind him, opened her car door. "Welcome back, Miss Jessup."

"Thank you, Richard." Jaz glanced at Harris.

He was grinning like a Cheshire cat. "Welcome back, Jaz. Good to see you."

Jaz rolled her eyes. "Hey."

After the greetings, Richard was all business. "Your driver will see to your luggage, Miss Jessup. You'll be upstairs in the room at the end of the hall. As soon as you've freshened up, please join us in the conference room. We'll go over your training schedule and then adjourn for a spot of lunch."

Recalling Richard's gourmet skills in the kitchen, Jaz perked up. "Lunch? I'm looking forward to that! Resolute still talks about your muffins."

Her anticipation crashed to the ground when Harris shifted on his feet and said, "Yeah, well, we should probably let you know up front that we're modifying your meals as part of your training regimen. Strict calorie count. No breads, rice, pasta, and so on."

He grimaced apologetically. "Need to knock a few pounds off you. Make you lighter on your feet. More agile."

"Make me lighter on my—" The look Jaz leveled on Harris could have drilled through rock and smelted steel. She envisioned her hands reaching for his neck. *I'll show **you** what needs to be knocked off, buster. I—*

Her own voice, lifted in sorrow-filled prayer, interrupted her internal rant. *Lord, I turn from my willful ways.*

Jaz's jaw dropped. "What the—" All on its own, with no forethought on her part, a curse word popped out of her mouth.

"Whoa! Where did that come from?" Then she heard herself again, this time declaring, *Yes, in his great mercy, God has given me a living hope!*

"Well—" She bit off another "colorful" word. "No, I shouldn't say *that,* either."

"Uh, say what, exactly?"

She blinked several times before she came to herself and realized Harris was studying her, waiting for her to respond. Richard, too, watched her, a small frown creasing his forehead.

"It's, uh, nothing. Just . . . trying to break a bad habit. Swearing, actually. Uh, yah, that's it."

Her eyes flicked back to Harris, and she could have sworn—*Good grief! Stop with the swearing already!*

She shook herself and hazarded another glance at Harris.

Yup. There it was.

But what is it?

A glint of something. Was it, perhaps, speculation?

Harris tipped his head. "I get it. Been where you are. It's a tough habit to break."

You get it? You've been where I am?

Professional again, Harris added, "And speaking of tough habits, I'm afraid we need your stash."

"My stash?"

Richard stepped in. "Yes, your supply of that aromatic chewing delight. I believe you call it Black Jack? We'll be relieving you of your supply."

"What? Uh-uh. Nope."

But Richard was adamant. "Miss Jessup, your habit is, shall we say, *legend,* a distinguishing idiosyncrasy of your celebrated online notoriety and a predilection so well versed across the cyber community that it cannot, *must not* be indulged while you are in the field. You can envision, can you not, that you may encounter members of the hacker community while on this assignment? We simply cannot permit this characteristic of your vaunted cyber-persona to jeopardize your undercover persona."

Jaz's lips parted to reply, but nothing came out.

Richard continued, "As we have it on good authority that you come well-provisioned, Travis will search your luggage and handbag and confiscate the offending items. Please relinquish what you carry on your person to Harris."

Harris waited, hand outstretched.

Jaz balked. "I didn't agree to this."

"Give it up, Jaz."

"But I need it!"

"Our point exactly," Harris said.

"Hand it over, please, Miss Jessup," Richard ordered.

Richard and Harris were obdurate.

Swearing under her breath and not caring a whit who heard her, she emptied her pockets.

Mostly.

— ● —

JAZ UNPACKED her clothes into the empty dresser and put her toiletries in the bathroom, then started down the stairs on her way to the conference room. She was giving herself a good "talking to," the kind of scolding she was not accustomed to giving *or* receiving.

"Okay, so Bella says I need to focus. Focus on my focus. Can't do that if I'm ready to throttle Harris, then Richard, then back to Harris. *Grr!* Add to that, because I prayed with Bella yesterday, now I'm supposed to be all religious and perfect? Ha! Right? What a pile of . . . er, doo-doo."

She reached the landing and stopped short. "Oh, man! What if I—oh, wow. I need to call Bella. Ask her if I undid our prayer yesterday. I mean, I did curse a couple of times since then—*okay a bunch of times*—and I wanted to choke that smarmy grin right out of Harris. I still do, frankly. So, did I undo that prayer? Sheesh. I need to figure out how this Christian thing works. And fast."

She sighed. "This is a lot harder than it looks, God—if you're still listening to me. And no gum? Are you kidding me? Do they really expect me to function without my Black Jack?"

Her fingers twitched in response.

"There you are, Miss Jessup. Ready to join us?" Richard stood at the bottom of the staircase, prim, proper, and placid as always.

That's all it took for Jaz to become angry all over again. *Oh, I'm ready, all right*, she seethed silently. *Ready to wring someone's neck!*

She stalked down the remainder of the stairs. "I need to make a call."

"Pardon?"

"I need to ask Bella something. Important."

"I see. Very well. I will accommodate your request this one time."

"You will *accommodate* my request? This one time? What is this, kindergarten? Do I also need a hall pass to use the bathroom?"

"While you are in training here, Miss Jessup, we will keep you totally immersed in your cover identity. No distractions and no calls. So yes; we will accommodate your request, but only this one time."

Jaz stared hard at Richard, her teeth clenched. Inside, her rebellious self-will was cussing a blue streak while attempting to claw its way up her throat and fight its way out of her mouth.

Oh, the things I'd like to say to you right now, Richard.

Unexpectedly, another desire piped up.

I really don't want to curse Richard. He's a sweet old guy, and he's been very kind to me, remember? Besides, I'm sick at heart from living a self-centered life, putting what I want ahead of everything and everyone else. Ahead of you . . . Lord.

Jaz blinked. The memory of what Bella had prayed and what she had repeated—*but only if you mean it, Jaz*—stood clear and strong in her heart.

Lord, I turn from my willful ways. I repent of my sins. Please wash me clean through the power of your death and resurrection. I surrender my life to you, Lord Jesus. Please come and make your home in my heart and make me new, inside and out.

"Miss Jessup, are you all right?" That worried pucker had made another appearance in the middle of Richard's forehead.

"Mmm? Oh. Yah. Sorry—I get it. One call, then radio silence. Thanks, um, for accommodating my request."

He didn't reply right away and kept watching her. Finally, he said softly, "We've temporarily locked out the lodge's landline. Requires a code to unlock it. I'll just dial out for you, shall I?"

"Thank you."

She followed Richard into the conference room where Harris was sitting, a stack of paperwork in front of him. Richard explained, then pushed the required numbers on the phone's face to access an outside line, and handed Jaz the receiver.

"We'll give you some privacy."

"Thank you . . . again."

When Richard and Harris had closed the door behind them, Jaz dialed Bella's office number. She knew it by heart, of course, like she knew every phone number at Griffin Industries and the cell number of every task force member. Their addresses. Their birthdays. Their car's license plates. Bank accounts.

The social security numbers of their firstborn.

"Just kidding, Lord. Being facetious."

"Bella Tobin speaking."

"Bella, this is Jaz."

"Jaz! Aren't you at Broadsword yet?"

"Yah, I'm here. We're about to get started, but I-I . . . I said some things."

"You said some things?"

"Curse words. And I feel . . . all wrong inside. Strange." Now that she'd said it aloud, the enormity of how she felt started to choke her up. "Really strange, Bella!"

"Strange how, Jaz?"

"Like I'm somebody else and I don't fit in my own skin anymore. And I'm . . . I'm hearing things. I-I think I'm cracking up, Bella!"

Jaz's last words ended on a high note, a desperate plea for help.

"You aren't cracking up, Jaz."

"I'm not? But, there's like this voice in my head!"

Jaz heard Bella's soft chuckle on the other end of the call, and it irritated her.

"You don't believe me?"

"Oh, yes, I believe you, Jaz."

"Then you know I can't do this, the training and the assignment. Not if I'm a-a-a paranoid schizophrenic!"

"Jaz, you're not cracking up, and you're not a paranoid schizophrenic."

"But—"

"Did you ask Jesus to make his home in your heart? Did you surrender your life to him and did you ask him to change you? Did you? Did you mean it?"

Jaz collapsed into the nearest chair. She couldn't speak, but her brain started shifting gears.

What if . . . what if Jesus actually is *inside me? Is that him, reminding me of what I prayed? Does that mean I'm* not *a fruitcake—or does it mean I* am *a fruitcake?*

"Jaz? Are you still there?"

Jaz slowly exhaled. "Yah. I'm here."

"You're going to sense the presence of Jesus in your life, Jaz, inside your heart and thoughts and in your circumstances. He's going to 'speak up' or whisper little warnings to you when you're tempted to sin. He's going to prompt you to trust and obey him. Believe me when I say your old life is over.

You gave it to Jesus, and he's not giving it back. Going forward, he's going to remake you entirely . . . one curse word at a time."

"So, I didn't blow it?"

"Well, sure you did, and I'm not saying you should take it lightly when you do. Instead, the Bible gives us instructions for when we sin. We are to go to Jesus and ask for forgiveness, sincerely, thank him for forgiving us, ask him to help us do better, then move on. And Jaz? You can't get rid of Jesus just by losing your temper or spouting some swear words. Jesus said, 'Never will I leave you; never will I forsake you.' He wasn't kidding."

"Never will I leave you; never will I forsake you," Jaz repeated.

"Right. So when you blow it, remember to ask for forgiveness. Do it right away. Be earnest, thank him for his mercy and forgiveness, and ask him to help you do better."

"Okay," Jaz answered meekly. "Thank you, Bella. I have to get off now. Richard and Harris are waiting for me and . . . this is the only phone call I'm allowed to make while I'm in training."

"I understand. We had strict rules like that when I was in training. The Lord bless you, Jaz; Quincy and I are praying for you and for your success."

Jaz hung up. Inhaling deeply, she whispered, "I'm sorry. Please forgive me? Thank you. I'll . . . I'll try to do better, but I think I'm going to need *a lot* of help."

She opened the conference room door. "Hey. I'm done."

Richard said, "Very good. Harris? Over to you."

They took seats around the table, and Harris handed Jaz a folder. "This is your alias, your cover identity. It is *you* until the op is concluded. You'll need to study it and memorize all the details—and I do mean *all* the details. It's vital to your safety that you know every scintilla of information forward and backward; it's my responsibility as your TO—training officer—to ensure that you do."

Jaz was already reading, nodding as her eyes scanned the first page.

"Because we can't cram every aspect of fieldcraft into the two or three weeks you'll be spending with us, much of your training will be op-specific. We've designed scenarios to get you used to introducing your alias to new people and answering their questions—and, again, while we're on the topic of your cover ID? From this moment forward, we will interact with you only as that persona. Furthermore, you will need to lose or switch out words, phrases, or pronunciations that would tag you as a Canuck, not an American. For example, instead of 'yah,' say 'yeah' and instead of 'aboot,' say 'about.'"

Jaz finished the second page and moved on to the third. "Yeah, not yah. About, not aboot. Right."

Richard said, "We'll give you ample time to learn your cover, but when we start the scenarios, you should bear in mind that your personal safety and the success of the operation will depend upon how well you sell that cover. More than 'get used to' the situations we've designed, you'll need to be adept. Proficient. Utterly foolproof."

Jaz finished the fourth and last page. "Got it."

She tried to hand the folder back to Harris.

"You need to keep that and study the info, not just read it."

"I have it down."

Harris and Richard exchanged a look Jaz found humorous.

"You don't believe me, do you? Go ahead. Test me."

They again exchanged a look. This time, Jaz snickered aloud.

"Not funny," Harris warned. "We need your complete and unassailable attention."

Jaz leaned forward across the table. She smiled and offered her hand to Harris. "Hey. I'm Darcy Walken, from Lindale, Texas, but I live and work in Thompsons outside of Houston."

Harris played along. "Hi, Darcy. I'm Rick Harris. My friends call me Harris—*haha*. Tell me about yourself. What do you do?"

"Me? I'm just a drone, an underappreciated computer security drone, pretty much bored out of my mind nine hours a day."

Harris laughed. "Computer security? Maybe it's your vocation rather than your employer, that's boring, huh?"

"No kidding. I need some action, you know? Actual 'find the intruders' security-type work? I didn't earn a master's from MIT just to eyeball lines of code scrolling by all day long."

"MIT? Wow. You should have your pick of jobs with that degree on your resumé."

"Yeah, well, I slipped up big time by accepting an offer that promised to pay off my student loans. See, the company I work for will make the monthly student loan payments for me, but as it turns out, I have to *stay* with this company five years or repay them the amount they've paid out on those loans. But if I can stick it out another, uh, four years and nine months? I'll have hit that five-year mark, and my company will pay off the balance of my loans in a lump sum. Once they've done that, I'll be free of them. Free to go elsewhere."

"Whoa," Harris said. "Interesting employee retention plan they've got going on. More or less coercive, if you ask me."

"I agree. I'm still new there, but from what I've seen and heard, they have trouble keeping cybersecurity people with them because the job is so freaking monotonous. Well, most of the time. I hear that once in a blue moon we detect an intrusion, and I'm told that's exciting—while it lasts—except it always turns out to be an employee trying to hack us from the inside."

"Why always an employee? Doesn't anyone ever try to hack in from the outside?"

"No can do. We run a closed network. No outside connections at all. Only way 'in' is from the inside. You know. What DOE calls the 'insider threat.'"

"DOE? Insider threat? Just what is this place where you work, Darcy?"

"Oops. Sorry; not supposed to blab too many details—well, not until you've bought me a couple drinks, anyway."

When she batted her eyes at Harris, he leaned in and whispered, "I may not drink, but you have no idea how much I wish you were flirting with me for real."

"Uh . . ."

Richard dropped the hammer. Hard. "That's enough of that, Mr. Harris. This is neither the time nor the place—nor will it be until this op is completed."

He turned to Jaz. "Tell me everything you know about your cover. Start at the top and run it down."

She did. From the top of the first page of her cover, she repeated all four pages—but not verbatim. Rather, she talked them through every line of information by couching it within a running narrative.

"Darcy Walken. My middle name is Anne, after my mom and Grandma Annie on Mom's side. I'm twenty-nine and was born on March 3, 1973, in Wichita, Kansas. My folks are Robert Zhang Walken—my dad's parents emigrated from China—and Damaris Anne Walken. Dad would have turned fifty-six last month, but he suffered a stroke and passed away five years ago. Mom will be fifty-four in July.

"I'm the oldest kid of three; I have a younger brother and a little sister— she's only nine, a change of life baby. It's been hard on Mom, raising us kids without Dad around."

She slouched in her chair and blathered on without pause or hesitation.

"Right now I work at the W.A. Parish Generating Station in Thompsons, Texas, but I hope to get out of this hick state and find a more exciting, cutting-edge gig. In the meantime, while I work off my five-year sentence at Parish, driving into Houston and spending the weekends immersed in some notable nightlife is about the only thing keeping me sane. I love to dance, see. I can dance for hours! Pretty sure they wrote that song, *Dancing Queen,* about *me.* Anywhere I can find decent dance partners or a great, nonstop DJ, does it for me. Keeps the boredom from eating me alive. I—"

Richard held up his hand. "That's sufficient, Miss Walken. Thank you."

Harris folded his arms. "I wouldn't have believed it if I hadn't seen and heard it with my own eyes and ears." He looked at Richard. "We'll be revising our schedule?"

"More than likely."

Jaz interrupted. "I have questions. Why the Chinese grandparents on my dad's side?"

Richard answered. "We were told you have a spot of Indigenous blood in you. It shows enough in the shape of your eyes that we can pass you off as being part Chinese. We hope that small detail plays well with the leaders of the cell you'll be infiltrating."

"You'll spend an hour a day with a tutor," Harris said. "A woman who will, with the limited time we have, ground you in a bit of Chinese culture and a small vocabulary."

"I spent a year in Taiwan. I already speak some Standard Mandarin."

Harris whistled softly. "Did not know that."

"Indeed," Richard agreed.

"There's a lot you don't know about me."

Nor does anyone, for that matter.

"Well, your time with the tutor won't be wasted. She can refresh and perhaps add to what you've already learned."

"Okay, but on another point, why am I new to this job with W.A. Parish? Wouldn't AEA consider me a more valuable recruit if I had some tenure at my job, some seniority?"

"We've vacillated on that detail," Richard answered. "Yes, you would be a bigger catch if you had more on-the-job cachet. On the other hand, we need to safeguard your legend, your cover. You mentioned the concept of the insider threat?"

"Yah—I mean yeah. What of it?" Then Jaz snorted. "Oh. I get it. You don't know if AEA already has someone inside Parish."

Harris replied, "That's our concern. We can't backstop a long tenure with that company if an unknown AEA cell member is already employed inside and would know differently."

"Got it."

Richard nodded. "Shall we adjourn for a spot of lunch?"

Jaz sat up straight. "Lunch? Yum! I've thought a *lot* about your apple pie since I was here last, Richard."

Harris moved his head minutely.

Jaz deflated. "Oh, yeah. Calorie count and all."

Richard replied, "Afraid so, Miss Walken, but I promise you will enjoy what fare we set before you."

"Well isn't that just *dandy.*"

CHAPTER 12

FOLLOWING LUNCH—which for Jaz was a few slices of grilled chicken and a plate of greens not unlike a condemned rabbit's last meal—Harris took charge of her. He provided her with khakis, a long-sleeved t-shirt, and good, sturdy shoes for the firing range. Then they crossed the grounds from the lodge to the gymnasium.

Harris unlocked the fortified room at the back of the building that served as Broadsword's armory. He drew a number of different handguns and a long gun from secure lockers, signed them out, and laid them in a row on a table.

"Your training objective, Miss Walken, is to learn these weapons inside and out, not intellectually, but experientially, so that you become proficient in handling them. A shooter becomes proficient through repetition and only repetition, so that's what you will do. You will load and shoot these sidearms; disassemble, clean, and reassemble them each time you shoot; and you'll do it over and over until you can do it in your sleep—until you can reassemble and load every gun before you while blindfolded."

Jaz was suitably cowed. "You won't mix the pieces of different guns together, will you?"

"Now that you mention it, we just might."

"*Shoot!*"

"Yup. That's the idea. When you and the rest of your team arrived here before Thanksgiving last year, you were newly certified on the Glock 43, a sweet subcompact 9mm semiauto sidearm. We worked with you and your team to improve your facility with your sidearms, but I'll bet you haven't touched a gun since we drilled you here, have you?"

"Uh, no. Nope."

"Well, let's remedy that. We'll start by identifying and distinguishing ammo types."

He drew a baker's dozen boxes of ammo from another locker and set the boxes on the table and put all but five boxes to the side. He opened the ends of those five boxes and slid out the cardboard bullet carriers.

First he pointed to the box with the largest rounds and then to the long gun on the table.

"This box contains 12 gauge shotgun shells or cartridges for the Mossberg 500 pump-action shotgun. The 500 is easy and fun to shoot and will stop just about anything or anyone. Take the safety off, point, and pull the trigger. To advance the next shell, grab hold of the grip under the gun's barrel—the forend—pull the forend toward you, and shoot again. That's it. "

Jaz shivered. "Do I have to shoot that?"

"No, you *get* to shoot that. Don't be such a wuss."

He pointed in turn to the remaining four boxes. "Here we have 9mm rounds. The rounds in this box are .38 Spl+P, for the .38 revolver. The last two boxes contain .40cal and .45cal, respectively. Fifty rounds to a box. You'll learn to identify ammo on sight and know what ammo each sidearm takes. You with me?"

"Okaaay." Jaz dragged out the word to mask her anxiety. Learn the ammo and which gun shoots which? *No hay problema.* Shoot, disassemble, clean, and reassemble? Over and over and over? More than a little outside her comfort zone. But shooting these guns with Harris hanging over her shoulder? Breathing down her neck? Reaching around her to adjust her "stance" or her "grip"?

Making me all shivery? Gah!

Anxiety sparked a craving. She wanted a stick of Black Jack, and she wanted it *bad*. What Harris did not know is that she just so happened to have a lone stick of gum riding in her hip pocket. Travis had missed half a pack of gum when he searched her purse, and Jaz was saving back the three sticks for emergency use.

Like right now. In fact, she thought she heard the stick in her pocket calling to her. Crooning her name.

Oh, Jaz! Come get me, Jazzy! I'm juicy and luscious and I'm all yours!

"Uh, bathroom break?"

"Three minutes."

Jaz no sooner had the bathroom door locked than she clawed the stick of gum out of her pocket, tore it in half, pulled the paper off one part, and shoved it into her mouth. She sighed and leaned her back against the door, chewing and trying to suck every morsel of flavor from that bit of gum.

I cannot believe I let these troglodytes browbeat me into giving up my gum, she fumed. Immediately, that other voice, the new one, spoke up, but Jaz shoved it to the back of her mind where she could ignore it.

Harris pounded on the bathroom door. "You about done in there? Let's go, Miss Walken. Time's a-wasting."

Jaz tucked the gum in her mouth between her lower teeth and cheek and returned the remainder of the stick to her pocket. She flushed the toilet, ran water in the sink, unlocked the door, and sauntered past Harris.

Cool and calm. Back in control.

Just don't breathe in his direction.

Harris's head swiveled. "What . . . what's that smell?"

Uh-oh.

He got in front of her. "Where is it?"

"Where's what?" Oops. Opened mouth.

"You've got gum in your mouth. Give it to me, Jasmine Jessup."

"My name is Darcy Anne Walken."

"Fine. Give it up, *Darcy*. Now."

"I don't know what you're talking about." Inside, she cringed over the lie.

"You know what? You're worse than a junky. No, actually, you *are* a junky." He began to pat her down. "And like a junky, you probably have more drugs hidden on you."

"Hey! Get your hands off me!"

"Think this is invasive? Just wait until we toss your room—junky."

He slid his hand into her hip pocket, and pulled out the half stick. "Got it."

Jaz exploded. "Give me that, you-you-you *Cretin!* You beast!"

"Give it to you? *Make me*. And since we're getting you clean, spit out what's in your mouth!"

Jaz grabbed for her gum, and they engaged in a game of keep-away in which Harris' longer arms stymied and infuriated Jaz. When he held the gum beyond her reach *and laughed*, she lost it.

She screamed and cursed him out. When that got her nowhere, she stomped on Harris' left foot and kicked his knee.

"Ow! You *brat!*"

Their scuffle-turned-brawl went downhill from there, or rather down onto the gym's floor which, fortunately, was covered in thick mats.

Jaz, screaming every epitaph she knew, fought Harris tooth and nail, but she found herself on her back atop Harris, and he, using wrestling holds, had his legs wrapped around her legs and had both of Jaz's arms pinioned inside one of his piston-like arms. His free hand pinched her nostrils in an effort to force her to spit out her gum, but Jaz clamped her teeth together and threw her head back and forth to break his hold on her face.

"Spit it out! Spit it out, you miserable little . . . *stinker!*"

About the same time, the two of them spotted Richard standing there, arms folded across his chest.

"My, my. How very disappointing."

━━━●━━━

IT WAS Wednesday, noon, Jaz's fifth full day at Broadsword. Richard was preparing lunch when the phone rang.

"Good afternoon, Richard."

"Ah, good afternoon to you, Director. I presume you're calling for a sitrep?"

"Yes. How is our Miss Jessup doing?"

Richard chuckled softly. "Progressing nicely, sir, all things considered. By the by, on the spycraft and intelligence gathering side, she's unlike anyone I've ever trained. Phenomenal memory, brilliant and intuitive thinker, and excellent instincts—the instincts of a criminal, I'd wager."

"What did you say?"

"Surely you must have deduced, Director, that Miss Jessup owns a storied past? She's a natural to every devious part of spycraft—actually too good in those ways not to have lived by her wits for years. She also possesses a most colorful vocabulary and has put it to good use this week—although she seems oddly contrite after employing said profanity. Why, I've learned a hatful of new swear words myself, and I was forty years in Her Majesty's Royal Navy."

Wolfe exhaled. "The Canadians weren't entirely forthcoming on Jaz's background when they offered her to us. They needed to hide her from the Ukrainian mob ASAP, and we badly needed her skills to hunt terrorists. The Canadians attested to her loyalty and reliability but offered nothing more on her background other than avowing that she had been the Security Intelligence Service's star cybersecurity specialist for a number of years, working out of the RCMP's Rideau Glen compound in Ottawa."

"Well, she's astonishingly fast on her feet, sir—figuratively speaking only. We've rarely seen her miss a beat in any of our mock scenarios or interrogations—and did you know she is conversant in Mandarin?"

"Really? I had no idea. And how fast on her feet is she on the not-so-figuratively side?"

"Underwhelming, Director. Miserable marksman, for starters. Also? She runs like a wounded wildebeest and fights like a feral cat—hissing, scratching, screaming, and cursing. If one can set all that aside for the moment, we feel she's well-suited for this operation and eminently qualified to best any of our adversaries' similarly qualified technical agents."

"Yes, on the cyber side, I suppose that goes without saying. What of her emotional and mental state?"

"Ah, that is the rub, is it not, sir? When speaking on her emotional state, an abundance of adjectives do come to mind, *tornadic* being first, *adamantine* a close second. She is tempestuous yet singularly unyielding. Candidly, sir, the young woman does not quit—particularly when her principles or loyalties are challenged—and we've thrown the lot at her over the five days we've had her."

"If you were to make your recommendation today, what would it be?"

"By the customary rubrics, I would be obliged to pronounce her unfit. However, and I believe Harris would agree with my assessment, she could walk into our adversary's headquarters tomorrow, present her saucy self to them, and have them wrapped around her anise-stained fingers by teatime."

"You mean to tell me you haven't broken her of that revolting habit?" Wolfe's disdain ran straight through the wires to Richard.

"Correct—and on that topic, sir, I can state with confidence that our Miss Jessup can maintain a grudge with the best of them."

"A grudge?"

"Of epic proportions, Director. Case in point, she has not forgiven our appropriation of her 'stash.' To report that she was miffed when we confiscated her drug of choice would be the equivalent of saying Nero was mildly put out when they took away his prize fiddle."

"What! Has she burned Rome into the bargain?"

"Only *us*, sir. Toasted our ears, she did. Medium-well, crispy on the outside. Such is Miss Jessup's strength of will, that we've resorted to a démarche that employs Black Jack as both carrot and stick, interchangeably. Not an ineffective stratagem, if I do say."

"Miss Jessup cannot go into the field with a disgusting black gob in her mouth, Richard."

"We are aware, Director, and are adjusting our training stratagem to the need. Our scenarios today and tomorrow must take on a brutish quality, I'm afraid. It is imperative that we impress upon Miss Jessup's pain receptors the excruciating nature of being found out and tortured whilst undercover. I believe that, after several unpleasant experiences—such as being hosed down and left alone all night, or being subjected to nonstop audio abuse—she will not, at least during the short run of this one-off assignment, indulge her vile habit and thus risk the reality of an actual interrogation."

"I see."

Wolfe was quiet for a time. Richard waited while Wolfe's remarkable mind chewed through the information Richard had provided.

When Wolfe spoke again, he said, "If it's all the same to you, Richard, I would like to recommend an alternative tactic."

"Of course, sir."

"Let's give our Miss Jessup an enemy other than yourselves. Team her up with Harris and perhaps another member of your security force. Pit the three of them against that shared enemy. I believe then you'll see the best Miss Jessup has to offer."

Richard considered Wolfe's suggestion. "I appreciate your advice, Director, and shall endeavor to put it into play."

"Good. Call me next Friday, Richard. I want to know how your adjusted strategy is working out."

"Yes, sir. Next Friday it is."

❖

WEDNESDAY, THURSDAY, and Friday passed without much change to Jaz's training regimen. Daily, Harris had her shoot, dismantle, and clean the handguns and the shotgun he'd laid out on her first day. And actually, to her surprise, she was beginning to prefer shooting the Mossberg.

Harris and another Broadsword guard, Bo, put together a small outdoor range in order to emulate an active shooter scenario. They stacked bales of hay as "cover" throughout the course and set up lifelike targets for Jaz to shoot at.

Of course, Jaz whined and complained.

"I'm not going to be carrying a weapon during my op, so why do I need to learn all this-this *killing* stuff? Why so much target practice and pretending to shoot people?"

"Because, *Darcy Walken*," Harris hissed at her, "it's better to be prepared for the unlikely rather than be killed while exclaiming, 'Oh, my goodness gracious! I didn't know the bad guys would have *guns!* Why didn't anyone tell me?' Bad guys, by definition, *Darcy*, have it out for you. Do you want to be prepared or would you prefer *dead?* Huh?"

"Well, when you put it like that," she grumbled.

"Then straighten up and take the Mossberg. I want you to run this course, stopping behind cover, then popping out to shoot the targets."

"Just like that? Just shoot them without provocation?"

"The targets are pointing guns at you. Again, by definition, that is provocation, so *yes*. Shoot them."

"*Fine*."

Jaz picked up the shotgun. She liked the fact that it wasn't all that long of a gun. And with the collapsible stock folded to the side, the gun fit her nicely.

"Safety on?"

Jaz's eyes flew to the safety. It was all the way back, but she thumbed it anyway. To be certain.

"Safety is on."

"Ready to load?"

She depressed the action release and pulled the gun's forend toward her.

"Ready to load."

"Receiver clear?"

"Receiver is clear."

"Load!"

Jaz palmed the first shell, slapped it into the receiver, then pushed the forend away from her to load the shell into the firing chamber. The movement made a nice, solid, reassuring sound that she kind of liked.

She flipped the gun over so that the loading port faced up and placed the next shell into the magazine, using her thumb to push it forward, into the magazine tube, until she both heard and felt the cartridge *snap* into the magazine. She repeated the same step with the remaining three shells.

"Loaded!"

"Place five cartridges in a left-side pocket."

"What? Why?"

"Because you don't know how many bad guys are out there. You may need to reload."

Jaz growled under her breath, "Stupid macho games."

"What?"

"Nothing. Five spare cartridges in my pocket."

"Stand on the firing line and await my start command."

"Ready."

"Don't forget to take the safety off."

Darcy scowled at herself for forgetting. "Safety off. Check."

"Ready? Go!"

The object wasn't to go fast. It was to shoot with accuracy. With the Mossberg angled forward and down, her finger off the trigger, Jaz jogged to the first stack of hay bales, put her back to the stack, and sidled toward its edge. Then she whirled around, cleared the bales, acquired the target, and fired.

She immediately ran to the next set of bales. As soon as her back was against them, she pulled the forend toward her and heard that satisfying *thunk* as the next shell loaded into the firing chamber. She whirled to the side, facing forward, "acquired" the next target, and shot it.

What she really liked was how easy it was to *hit* said target.

Kinda hard to miss with the spread of a 12-gauge cartridge.

She repeated the same maneuver, moving in a zig zag farther down the course until she'd shot five targets—but at least two more remained.

I'm out! Time to reload.

As she went through the reloading process, she noticed that her movements were smoother, surer, and marginally faster. She patted the Mossberg's stock affectionately.

Would you look at that? I'm starting to get the hang of this thing.

OVER THE weekend, however, Jaz didn't see much of Harris. Instead, she couldn't help but notice that Richard *and Travis*—not Richard *and Harris*—were holed up in the conference room, hours at a time, whereas Harris had vanished altogether. Dematerialized into Broadsword's mountainous thin air. She sought out Bo, but he, too, was absent.

"I've given them the weekend off," was all Richard would say when Jaz asked after them.

Jaz wouldn't admit to herself that she missed Harris, would certainly not entertain such a notion. So why did she catch herself looking for him, expecting him to appear at any time?

Stupid Harris. Go ahead—you can just stay gone for all I care—and I don't care a whit.

But where are you, anyway?

Saturday and Sunday, twice daily, one or another of Broadsword's guards led Jaz through a rigorous physical fitness routine in the gym, had her shoot stationary targets, then coached her through endless and taxing laps around Broadsword's perimeter.

Slave drivers. Sadists—all of them.

As for the remainder of the weekend? Jaz was left practicing her Mandarin or twiddling her thumbs and wondering what fresh new torture Richard was concocting with Travis' input.

Time hung heavy on Jaz's hands. With nothing better to do, she picked up the Bible Bella had given her. She held it for a long time before she cracked it open and located the table of contents.

Huh. Old Testament. New Testament.

What the devil are those?

She scanned the list of Old Testament books, then moved on to the New Testament. The first book listed there was the Gospel of Matthew.

Bella said she started with the Gospels. Guess I should start with them too.

Matthew began with Jesus' genealogy. Jaz slogged through it and was gratified when she arrived at verse 18: *This is how the birth of Jesus came about.*

"Finally! Sheesh."

After that, she couldn't stop. She gobbled up chapter after chapter while she ate her meals, thought on what she'd devoured before and after her workouts, and "reread" whole chapters while jogging the worn path around Broadsword's perimeter, goaded by her taskmaster of the hour.

But not everything she read made sense, which irritated her to no end.

If I were allowed to call Bella she'd know what this means. Or if I had access to a computer, I could look things up, but noooo. No phone calls and no Internet, she grumbled to herself.

Surely others have had the same questions I have.

Her unanswered queries didn't keep her from reading on. Even without perfect understanding, line after line spoke to her.

Touched her.

Humbled her.

She was horrified as she read through Jesus' crucifixion. She wept as he hung on the cross and died. She cried with relief and joy at his resurrection. And something deep within her budded. Began to open . . . and flowered.

Bella's words echoed in her heart. *Jaz, if you read this book faithfully, it will change you on the inside.*

The Bible on her lap, her finger on the open page, Jaz wondered, *Is this what you meant, Bella? Am I changing on the inside?*

She charged into the Gospel of Mark only to stop short in Chapter 3, verses 16 and 17.

These are the twelve he appointed:
Simon (to whom he gave the name Peter),
James son of Zebedee and his brother John
(to them he gave the name Boanerges,
which means "sons of thunder")

"Why did Jesus change Simon's name to Peter? For that matter, why did he call James and John 'sons of thunder'?"

As Jaz deliberated over those bothersome questions, she repeated aloud, "*These are the twelve that he appointed.* Was it because being his disciple was a big deal, an honor, that he changed their names? If so, why didn't he change all of the disciples' names? Why only a few?"

She read verses 18 and 19. "*Andrew, Philip, Bartholomew, Matthew, Thomas, James son of Alphaeus, Thaddaeus, Simon the Zealot and Judas Iscariot, who betrayed him.* Wait. Wasn't Matthew called Levi in Chapter 2 while he was a tax collector? But here he's all of a sudden called Matthew. Did Jesus change Levi's name like he changed Simon's name?"

She didn't know where the idea came from, but when it came out of her mouth, it was fully formed. "Maybe Jesus changed Simon's name to Peter to signify that something *in* him had changed—and the same with Levi?"

Jaz stilled. She turned her hypothesis around in her mind, examining it from all sides and wondering why it resonated, why it struck such a profoundly familiar chord.

When the answer hit her, she gasped. "But isn't that what I did? When I realized that there was a world outside of the Northams' group home and outside of my own thoughts and needs, when I became self-aware, didn't I change my name? Insist that I be called by that new name?"

Jenny is a child's name—and I am no longer a child. From now on, I want you to call me Nième. Not Jenny, not Geneviève, but Nième.

"Except that situation was different. Sure, adopting a new name implied a change in me, but it was not a name Jesus had given me. Not a name that proclaimed what *he* had done in me.

"No, it was a name *I* took on . . . and only the first of many names, each alias a tool, a means to an end. To get what *I* wanted.

"I, I, I. *Always me.* Always what I wanted."

For a long time, Jaz sat there, her Bible cradled on her thighs.

Lost in her past.

NIÈVE

Vyper

CHAPTER 13

Vyper

BREAKFAST, THE morning after Nième announced her demands, was again tense. Maude said little. Neither did anyone else until the meal ended and Albert spoke up.

"Nième, th' bank opens at nine o'clock. You go on an' get yourself ready. I'll take you t' open your account. An' at the bank, I'll withdraw your 'lowance money from our savings t' put in your account."

Cursing under her breath, Maude threw her napkin on the table and stomped upstairs. Everyone knew when Maude reached her room. The resounding slam of the Northams' bedroom door punctuated her arrival.

Albert tipped his head toward the littles. "You kiddos manage th' cleanup, right?"

"Sure, Albert," Mary answered for the four of them. She beamed at Nième with something very like hero worship. "We can do it."

Albert and Nième returned home an hour later, Nième with a savings passbook in her pocket. She kept running her fingers over the little booklet's outline.

I have my own savings account, my own money.

FRIDAY, NIÈVE walked to the library, took the bus to the university, and started toward the parking lot adjacent to the university's computer lab where she would wait for Syntax to show up. Syntax hadn't seen her since she cut and dyed her hair. Nième had chosen to wear makeup that day, too.

*I'm a lot younger than Syntax and his friend, but they don't know **how** much younger. If they did, they would try to take advantage of me, the way Maude did.*

If I'm going to work with these older guys, I had better not look like a kid or behave like one either. I need to look older—no, I need to be older. I must fool them into thinking I'm college-aged like I fooled the people in the bursar's office.

How she *should* act around the older, more mature hackers had eluded her until she had witnessed two students, a guy and a girl, arguing in the breezeway outside the computer lab. The guy was furious; the girl was . . . altogether something else.

The young man wagged his finger inches from her face. "I *saw* you with Zack, Brie! I saw what you were doing!"

The girl's response was cold and disinterested. "You must be mistaken, Gary."

Gary, shaking with rage, stepped back and pointed to his eyes. "You think I'm blind? I saw you with my own eyes."

Brie slid a pack of cigarettes from her pocket, removed one, and lit it, her movements casual, indifferent, her smile mocking. Deliberately so. The smoke of her cigarette curled around her head before she answered him.

"I didn't mean you are mistaken about Zack, Gary. I meant you are mistaken in thinking I belong to you."

"What the—? We've been together three months!"

"News flash? You don't own me nor does any man. You're yesterday's headline, Gary. I'm with Zack today. Run along now, like a good boy."

An aghast Gary stared, his mouth working but unable to speak. Niève, goggle-eyed, stared too.

"I said, *beat it*, Gary. Move on." Brie leaned her shoulder on the building's brick wall and watched him, her mouth spread in an insolent smirk. What struck Niève most profoundly was how Brie seemed to enjoy Gary's anger and his *pain.*

Niève was fascinated, but she also shivered, unable to grasp how Brie could be so completely audacious and callous. Niève watched Gary slink away, defeated and demoralized.

That girl put Gary down hard. *She demolished him.*

Niève's thoughts returned to her upcoming meeting with Syntax and his friend. *I must be bold and confident like Brie. Daring, but maybe not as cruel as her. She outright trashed Gary, and that's not my goal with Syntax and his friend. I need them, need to work with them and learn what they know. But I want to be equal with them too.*

Pondering her situation, Niève concluded, *I won't get an introduction to the hacker community by burning bridges between me and Syntax and his friend. So maybe my behavior should land somewhere between Brie and how I handled Maude and Albert. Older and tougher but not mean. Well, not exactly* mean. *Firm and no-nonsense.*

Nième kept walking until she reached the parking lot. She sat on the adjacent grass to wait. While she waited, she added a second stick of Black Jack to the one already in her mouth.

I think I like this gum. It's better than bubble gum and a lot *better than that nasty stuff Syntax chews.* She winced. *Clove gum? Gross. Me? Guess I'm a Black Jack girl.*

Syntax arrived shortly after noon driving a dinged-up red Ford Pinto. Nième walked to the edge of the lot, but Syntax rolled right by without seeing her. He drove the circuit of the lot then pulled into a parking spot and got out. He swept the lot with a glare, again sweeping over Nième . . . until she lifted her hand to signal him.

He stared in disbelief. "Holy guacamole! I didn't recognize you."

Keeping a mental image of Brie before her, Nième shrugged. "Whatever."

The look on Syntax's face was priceless. "But you—"

"Are we going or what?"

"Uh, yeah. Sure. It's just—"

Nième got in the car, slamming the door on his words.

Syntax went around the car and got in behind the wheel. He cut his eyes toward her. Nième stared straight ahead. He didn't speak until they were on the road.

"You seem . . . different."

"Was that a question?"

"No. Maybe. It's just that when I met you last week, I got the impression that—"

"Whatever impression you 'got' last week, Syntax? Was the impression I intended you to get. Today you 'get' the real me, so move on."

"Um, sure. Okay."

BY THE time they arrived at his friend's house, Syntax had recovered enough to make introductions. "This is my friend and business associate, Azteca. Azteca, this is . . ." He turned to Nième. "What did you say your handle was?"

"Who says I did?"

Somehow, by casting herself in Brie's mold, Nième had stepped into playing a part, a role.

This isn't the real me but . . . as she kept Brie's image front and center and continued to emulate her hard-edged behaviors, Nième settled into the act and her confidence grew.

The act had to be working, because Syntax's shoulders twitched like they were tense. Tight and uncomfortable. "Okay, so what do we call—"

Nième cut Syntax off and spoke directly to Azteca. "I'm Jinn."

Azteca—the hollow-cheeked *artiste* type—slender, dark-eyed, dark-haired, and sporting a thick soul patch beneath his bottom lip, swept his eyes over Nième. Nième, having never heard the word "alpha," nevertheless recognized Azteca as the dominant of the two hackers. She forced herself to reach out her hand while cringing on the inside.

I loathe anything touchy, but I have to make nice with these guys. Because I want to learn. I need to learn.

Azteca chuckled as they shook. "Your handle is Gin? What, as in gin rummy or gin and tonic?"

Nième smiled indulgently around her gum. "Neither. Jinn as in the genies of Arabic mythology. According to legend, the Jinn are shape-shifting spirits. Some say they are made of fire and air."

Azteca grinned, charisma dripping from every cell in his body. "Jinn it is."

Syntax's eyes jinked from Azteca to Nième and back. "I told you you'd like her, Az."

"So you did. But can she follow instructions and, what is more important, can she code?"

"Well, I gave her—"

Nième had already withdrawn the floppy disk from her backpack. She held it out to Azteca. "I streamlined and enhanced a few things. Fixed an error in the first file. Corrected a couple of typos."

Syntax scowled, but Azteca's black eyes gleamed. "Did you now? Forgive me if I check your work . . . Jinn."

Nième unwrapped another stick of Black Jack. Folded it and put it in her mouth with the other pieces. Managed to keep her hands from shaking.

She gave Azteca a nonchalant nod. "Sure. I get it. But if we're gonna do business together, we need to have each other's backs, right?"

Azteca approved of her reply. "Most definitely." He gestured down the hallway. "We work from downstairs. Let's get started, shall we?"

Azteca's setup was in a basement room finished out to about thirty feet square. On one side, a long, cluttered workbench took up the length of the wall. Nième went directly to the workbench, her eyes perusing the disarray like a greedy child drools over the selection in a candy store. Half the bench was covered in bits and pieces of computers. Hard drives, motherboards, ventilation fans, and various expansion cards littered the bench's surface. Three monitors had been shoved to the back of the workbench. A box on the floor was piled with used keyboards. On the more organized half of the workbench, Nième spied a computer in the making.

I could spend days here, she thought.

"I build my own machines," Azteca murmured.

"I'm salivating." Nième wasn't kidding.

He chuckled. "I can see that." He pointed across the room. "That's the business side."

Reluctantly, Nième turned her attention to Azteca's setup. She saw a chair-height countertop that extended from the corner out along both adjacent walls. Six machines sat on the countertop, three on each wall. She also spied a length of coax cable snaking down from the ceiling to the countertop.

"Nice. You built all these?"

"That I did. Let's pick one for you. Syntax, find Jinn a chair, would you?"

Nième sat in the rolling office chair Syntax provided and clicked to the login screen.

"Create a login ID for yourself using Cyberdyne$ystem$ as your preliminary password. Let me know when you're ready."

"I like the Terminator reference," Nième breathed. She hadn't seen the movie, but she'd overheard kids at school talking about it. She created her login identity and chose a new password.

"Ready."

"Good. Gather around now."

Nième and Syntax wheeled their chairs to Azteca's machine and watched over his shoulders. Syntax knew the drill, apparently. Nième did not. Within moments, though, she began to figure out what Azteca was doing.

It was Friday, and for a great many people, Friday was payday, the afternoon or early evening when they conveyed their paychecks to their local bank to cash or deposit them. Azteca had somehow acquired the network dial-up number for a Winnipeg bank—and a fairly large bank at that. Dialing up to the bank's network was his first step. He then had to overcome the bank's login processes.

Nième's skin tingled. Azteca had hacked the bank's login!

How did he do that?

Once he was logged on to the bank's system, she followed his keystrokes, his logic, the bold yet simple audacity of his processes, soaking up knowledge and methods as she watched.

"Listen up, Jinn," he murmured, "I have just three rules here. We don't get greedy. We don't hit the same place twice. We leave no trace of ourselves behind."

Nième had questions, but she swallowed them. "Good rules."

"I'm glad you can appreciate them."

She watched as Azteca queried the bank's recent deposits. He chose a deposit of $876.49 and jotted the timestamp on a sheet of paper in front of him. Next, he entered the bank's restricted edit mode and modified the deposit amount by transposing the eight and the seven. The net difference was ninety dollars. He jotted the amount on the paper opposite the time stamp. He moved on to another deposit farther down on the query list.

"Won't people notice that their account balance doesn't match what they deposited?"

"Probably not as soon as you would think. When was the last time you checked your bank balance?"

Niève frowned. Made a mental note to revisit the question later. *I had better pay attention to my account balance. No telling what Maude might try.*

"What becomes of the difference between the actual check and the revised deposit figure?"

"That, Jinn, is precisely why we're here. The bank closes its doors to customers at 5:00, but before 6:00, the end of the tellers' work day, I will total up the money we've skimmed and move the exact amount into another Winnipeg account, one I set up weeks ago. In fact, I drove to Winnipeg last month and opened fifteen accounts in fifteen different Winnipeg banks as prep for this op—that's a $750 investment right there plus travel expenses—not to mention what I paid to acquire the banks' dial-up numbers."

"Providing I shift the adjusted deposit amounts into my own account before the bank's system closes out the day at 5:55 p.m., the bank's closing balance will be correct. The bank's computer system will not notice a balance error or send an alert signifying an unauthorized withdrawal."

"Whose ID did you use to open those accounts?"

"I know a guy. He's good. *Very* good. What I pay him is another investment *I* make into our ops."

"I'm impressed, but how do you retrieve the skimmed money?"

Winnipeg was about six hours from Regina by car.

"On Monday, I will wire all but fifty dollars in that Winnipeg account to an account in Montreal. From there, I send it here, to an account in Regina. I have fifteen such 'landing' accounts here in town under various aliases—another $750 investment plus the cost of the fake IDs. As soon as the wired money arrives, I will use a drive-through lane to withdraw all but fifty dollars from the account. Once I've make the wire transfers and the cash withdrawals, I never touch those accounts again. They are dead to me."

"Huh. I'm following so far. But don't banks have cameras? How do you deal with them?"

"I 'borrow' a car and make sure the license plate is obscured. Also? Not even my mother would recognize *the woman* in the drive-through lane—a scarf across her mouth—who made that withdrawal."

Niève snickered. "I'd like to see that."

"Any other questions, Jinn?"

"Yah, just one. Why alter some deposits and skip others? Why not change them all?"

"Because *we don't get greedy*. And you see this number alongside the deposit? It's a teller ID number. Today we tap only the deposits made by *this* teller. Each teller usually processes forty to fifty deposits on a Friday afternoon."

A light went on in Nième's mind. "When the bank finally realizes something isn't right, they will think it's this teller's fault."

"Yes. They will call the first one a teller error. A one-off mistake, transposing two digits. When more deposits are reported as wrong, the bank will think it's a deliberate act on the teller's part. Eventually, they will realize they've been hacked, but if we follow our three rules, they will never catch us."

"We don't get greedy. We don't hit the same place twice. We leave no trace of ourselves behind." Nième smiled. "It's a brilliant plan,"

Azteca nodded. "Thanks."

"Have you . . . have you ever hit any banks in Regina?"

"We did that last month as a test run, but we only hit three of them and for small amounts. We don't want to soil our own nest, y'know? Going forward, we won't use any Regina banks. When we're done in Winnipeg, I'll pick a new city, pay them a visit, and we'll rerun our op on that city's banks."

Nième's head was spinning, but she was utterly enthralled.

Azteca went on. "The plan today is to hit three of our fifteen Winnipeg banks simultaneously. The three of us will each handle one bank. Now I have a question for you, Jinn. Can you, on your machine and on your own, follow the steps I've just shown you?"

"Easy peasy. What about the actual hack on the bank?"

"I handle that part from your machine. I estimate our take will run between $1,500 and $3,000 apiece. Not *too* much, because—"

"We don't get greedy," Nième finished for him.

"You're catching on. Just remember, *greed will get you caught*. And don't forget to log every single deposit switch you make. When we're finished for the day, I'll tally your deposit switches and move that exact amount into my account, so make sure you log the switches accurately. I will double check by querying the bank's daily deposits total to ensure that the amounts you've logged are correct.

"And after we're done for the day, I'll check the changes you made to the disk Syntax gave you. If I think you can learn tasks other than these simple deposit switches, I'll train you."

Nième nodded. She had no qualms over Azteca checking her work on the disk. She was more excited about learning the new skills he could teach her than she was about the money she would be earning today.

Stealing. The money she would be stealing today.

She shrugged off the thought without examining it too closely. What were a few dollars to most people? That's all she, Azteca, and Syntax were taking. *Rob from the rich; give to the poor. As in poor me.*

Three hours later, Niève trudged up Azteca's basement stairs, both elated and sated by the steep learning curve and the intense workout she'd received. At the front door, Syntax looked to Azteca.

"Same time next week?"

"Yes. I'll have the next three banks set up for us."

Azteca turned to Niève. "You did well today, Jinn, and I believe you have talent." He stepped back and again studied her. "Of course, you're young, only a year or so out of school by the looks of you."

Niève let her features harden. It seemed that Brie was more and more comfortable inside Niève's skin. "Young, am I? So what?"

You have no idea how young I am, do you? Good.

He smiled. "Everyone has to start somewhere. Can you make it next Friday? Friday is our payday too. I'll give you your cut from today's job then."

"And what is my cut?"

"Twenty percent of your take—the total of the deposits you altered."

"Just twenty percent? Because I'm 'young'?"

Azteca grinned. "No, twenty percent because *I* get sixty percent off the top of everything—my setup, my plan, my cash investments, my hack, and the personal risks I take, operating from my home. This week, Syntax gets ten percent of your first take because he recruited you, and I get the balance. But if you continue to work for me and do well next week, you'll keep forty percent of your take. Got it?"

Forty percent of $1,500? Or $3,000? Niève was elated.

"Got it."

"Can you make it next Friday?"

"If Syntax gives me a ride I can."

Azteca tipped his head and studied her from her feet to the top of her head while Niève channeled Brie's indifference.

"I like your style, Jinn, but if I may? I'd like to suggest an enhancement to your 'look.'"

Niève studied him back. During her part of this afternoon's job, she'd added three more pieces of Black Jack to her mouth. She tossed the wad of gum to one side. "I suppose."

"Great. A good friend of mine, Tozi, owns a hair salon. Tell her *Andy* sent you. Have her cut and style your hair."

Nieve's first thought was, *Huh. Like that's not a strange suggestion or anything.*

Azteca went on. "Tozi is a bit of a radical, so I give you fair warning. Actually, that's why I think you'll like her. Oh, and I'll let her know that the cut and style are on me. Consider it a sign-on bonus."

Is that what I should call the weird vibe you give off? A sign-on bonus?

He drew a pristine business card from his wallet and extended it to Niève. "Show her this."

Intrigued by Azteca's description of his friend, Niève took the card. Then she looked for the agenda in Azteca's eyes. Because everyone had an agenda.

What she encountered was mild amusement, and she didn't know what to think of that.

She had Brie answer, "Cool. Thanks."

Niève walked in the front door of the Northams' house only minutes before 6:30 p.m. Albert called the house to the dinner table shortly after.

I've pushed Maude and Albert as far as I can for the time being, so I'll need to watch my timing next week, she thought. *Make certain Syntax drops me at the library earlier than he did today.*

———————— ● ————————

IN THE morning after her chores were done and breakfast was over, Niève reread the card Azteca had given her. His suggestion bothered her. *Why? Why would he offer to pay his 'good' friend to cut and style my hair? Sign-on bonus? I don't believe it.*

Niève's neck and face heated as, in a rush, the answer came to her. She didn't want to voice it, though. Saying it aloud would make it real. She said it anyway.

"Azteca saw the raggedy ends of my hair and the uneven sides. He knows I chopped it off myself. It must look awful. Way worse than I thought it did."

At her core, Niève was a pragmatist. As embarrassed as she was in this moment, she was not one to deny or hide from the truth. At the same time, she still figured Azteca was hiding an ulterior motive behind his offer.

"*Fine.* I'll deal with Azteca and whatever he's hiding when the time comes."

She went downstairs to the house phone and called the number on the card.

"I'd like to make an appointment with Tozi."

"For what service?"

"Um, to fix a bad haircut?"

"I have a 9:30 three weeks from Monday."

"I meant today."

"I'm sorry, but Tozi is booked up today and for the next three weeks."

Niève exhaled. "I'm . . . I'm supposed to tell her that Andy sent me."

"Oh! That's different. We've already cleared a slot for you this afternoon and have you booked for 3:00 p.m. The name is Genie, correct?"

Niève almost snort-laughed into the phone. "Uh, yes. Genie."

As in *genie* . . . in place of Jinn.

Well done, Azteca. Or should I call you Andy?

"We'll see you at three o'clock, Genie."

———————— ● ————————

NIÈVE STEPPED through the doors of Tozi's salon and into a wild and alien world. Exotic sights and pungent smells assaulted her senses, but the chatter, laughter, and busyness of three stylists, two manicurists, and half a dozen customers were harder for Nième to stomach. She was never comfortable in crowded spaces or with this much noise.

At the same time, the salon wasn't at all what Nième expected, what she'd seen portrayed in magazines or television programs. It was different because *the people* were like nothing she'd ever encountered. They were . . . "out there," to put it mildly. What was the word she'd heard tossed about at the university to describe people like them?

Goth. Yes. That was it.

And what had Azteca said of his friend? *Tozi is a bit of a radical, so I give you fair warning. Actually, that's why I think you'll like her.*

Nième struggled to settle her nerves. Was this foreign atmosphere what Azteca thought she would like? She peered more closely around the salon, taking in details. A guy at a station in a far corner caught her eye. She hadn't noticed him during her once-over. Nième was startled to realize he was applying a tattoo to the shoulder of a young woman.

"Are you Genie?"

Nième yanked her attention from the tattoo artist and gave it to the woman who'd spoken. Nième gaped, then muttered, "Yah. I'm . . . Genie."

"And I'm Tozi."

Tozi was gorgeous, tall with milky-white skin and brilliantly blue eyes. The upper two-thirds of her hair was elaborately braided and skillfully woven together atop her head while a few lone braids artfully dangled. Most of the braids were as black as night, but a few of them were silvery white. The lower third of Tozi's head was shaved to the scalp, and she had multiple piercings: nose, lips, and left cheek.

Tozi took Nième by the arm. "Andy said you'd like to refine your look, and I think I see what you were going for."

"Er, yes. *Andy.*"

Nième found herself seated in a chair with a cape fastened around her neck. The cape covered most of her body. In her lap lay a thick book opened to a colorful photo spread.

Tozi pointed her scissors at one of the pictures. "This one, yes? It's called an asymmetrical cut. You have just the right shaped head and face to carry it off."

Nième's heart skipped a beat. "I . . . *yes.* I *love* that. But maybe don't shave my scalp?" Despite her arrangement with the Northams, even Albert had his limits.

Tozi laughed. "Would that be too much, Genie? No problem; I'll just do the asymmetrical cut.

"What about color? The black is great, but perhaps a touch of color in the front would accent your stunning green eyes." She reached for a color swatch. "I suggest this intense turquoise—but not a lot. Like I said, just a flash of color, nothing extreme. What do you think?"

Dunno about Albert, but I think Maude will suffer a seizure.

"Yes. Please."

STUPEFIED, GAWKING silence met Niève as she joined the table for dinner that evening. Before the tension grew any thicker, she made a point of addressing Maude and Albert head-on . "I went to a salon to have my hair done today. I hope you haven't forgotten our agreement."

Albert was quick to jump in. "No. Nope. Haven't forgotten. You . . . can choose your own hairstyle. Er, right, Maudy?"

Maude couldn't seem to find her tongue, but the kids had no difficulties expressing themselves.

"Cool!" Mary whispered.

"I love it," Trey agreed.

Kit and Donny nodded enthusiastically.

Maude left the table.

CHAPTER 14

Vyper

NIÈVE RETURNED to the university computer lab Monday morning, determined to spend every possible hour she could logged on to a machine in the lab. Once online, she haunted bulletin boards populated by computer enthusiasts, devotees, and gurus and perused the articles on coding she found posted there.

She soaked up the nuggets of information they dropped and sought out chat rooms led by the best of them. She bought two boxes of disks and downloaded reams of code, learning, then honing, new coding skills.

With the tricks she'd gleaned from Azteca on Friday and the online computer world opening to her, Nième felt like a kid with a sweet tooth, sucking up new information to feed her sweet addiction—the university's lab being the proverbial candy store. She lay back on her bed that evening, reveling in the glorious ideas cascading through her head.

Exploring the online world through Regina University's connection had opened the door to a fantastic new realm. Nième's imagination ran wild, over-whelming her with . . . possibilities. She hadn't been this excited or this engaged *ever*, not even when Thom Collegiate opened the doors of the school's computer lab to her.

School.

As thrilled as she was, she was also vexed. The end of summer loomed ahead. *What will I do when fall term starts and I'm stuck all day in class? My school's computers are a joke compared to these machines. The school's computer lab doesn't even have a dial-up modem. Why should I be forced to waste my time learning nothing new?*

Without realizing it, her mind began to gnaw away at the problem, even while she looked farther into her future.

When I turn sixteen, I will age out of the foster program. I won't be required to live in a group home or be obligated to attend school . . . then what? I won't stay in Regina—that's for sure! Saskatchewan is altogether too tame for me. What I need is to be around others like myself so I can grow my skills.

She stared at her bedroom wall visualizing the less than two-year gap between the Northams' group home and a life of freedom. It was the chasm between now and then that loomed before her, disheartening and unbearable. She had to shake herself mentally.

Start planning today, Nième. You need to make money, a pile of it, and build up your savings account. Find or make a safe place here in my room, too, and squirrel some cash away for immediate needs.

Nième found it interesting that so many of the comments she read online mentioned the free spirit of the growing cyber community. Apparently, a large hacker faction believed evolving computer knowledge was to be shared, not hoarded, not sold for profit.

She frowned. *I want to improve my skills, and I'm grateful to be learning, but what Azteca, Syntax, and I do is all about the money. Well, everyone needs money, right? Can't exactly get by without it.*

I won't ever be free without money. Free of CPS and the Northams. Free to live my own life. Yes. Make money. Money is my ticket out of here.

———— • ————

ON FRIDAY, Syntax picked Nième up in the parking lot adjacent the university's computer lab. "Wow. You look great! *Really* great."

"Thanks." Nième felt that Tozi's work on her hair was nothing short of a masterpiece. Nième was getting better with the makeup part, too, but she was annoyed to sense an unwelcome vibe emanating from Syntax.

Her inner Brie whispered, *Best to shut that down the instant it pops up. Shut it all the way down.*

"Say, Jinn, would you like to come with me—"

"Nope. I don't 'do' dating, Syntax."

He coughed and cleared his throat. "Right."

Sheesh. Will I also have to fend off Azteca because I've suddenly got a great hairstyle?

"Nothing personal, but I don't mix business with my private life."

"Sure. I get it."

"Appreciate the ride, though."

"Uh-huh."

———— • ————

BEFORE THE three of them got started on the afternoon's work, Azteca paid them both. Nieve's envelope contained $410—almost doubling her savings account.

"Are you good with your take from last week's job?" Azteca asked. "By the way, I'll have to compliment Tozi on her work. You're stunning."

Not "your hair is stunning," but "*you're* stunning."

Nieve nodded, then skipped straight to his question. "Yes, I'm good with my cut—as long as I get forty percent from now on. And I'm ready to get started on today's job."

The afternoon went about the same as last Friday's, only Nieve was faster this time and "her" teller assisted by logging more deposits than last week's teller had. When closing time loomed, Azteca totaled up the amounts they'd "adjusted" in each bank and moved the money to his own accounts.

"Great. We're done for the day. Three Fridays from now, we'll have exhausted our Winnipeg marks. We'll break for a couple of weeks while I select a new city and set up the accounts."

Nieve lifted her chin. "I'd like to understand how you hacked the banks' login processes. Do you have time to show me?"

He stroked his "soul patch" and thought about it. "Are you willing to pay for the lesson?"

Nieve withdrew the envelope from her pocket. "How much?"

"No money. Instead, how about I drive you home afterward so Syntax doesn't have to wait around. It will take a couple hours to get through the lesson anyway."

Inside, Nieve sighed and called upon her memories of Brie. "Nope. It has to be a business deal. Nothing more."

Syntax snorted. "Rejected! Nice to see you get the same treatment I got, Az."

Azteca shrugged. "Never hurts to try—but now the lesson will cost you a hundred."

She shrugged. "Fine."

After Syntax left, Nieve and Azteca returned to the basement, and Azteca showed Nieve how he hacked the banks' administrative login and gained access to the account editing functions. Nieve soaked up the lesson, and she intuited more than Azteca was prepared to show her.

"You're smart, Nieve," he admitted. "I'm copying some of my code onto a disk for you. I think you can figure things out from there."

Nieve forked over five twenty-dollar bills and had Azteca drop her two blocks from the Northams' house. All was good in Nieve's mind until she reached the front door.

It was locked.

Well, the time was 9:15. She'd missed both dinner and lights out.

No worries. It's part of my deal with the Northams.

Nième shimmied up the tree outside the house and crawled inside through her bedroom window.

<hr>

AFTER DINNER the following evening, Albert said, "Nième, we need to talk." Maude stood behind him, tight-lipped but with a triumphant gleam in her eye.

"Yah. Okay. Talk about what?"

"About where you go all day long, every day—plus you didn't come home last night until after lights out. We're concerned."

"Concerned about what?"

"We don't want you to get into trouble, Nième. You know, hanging out with the wrong crowd, smoking or doing drugs?"

She laughed. "Drugs are a waste of time and money and smoking *stinks*. I don't do either of them."

"But where do you go, Jenny?" Maude interjected.

"It's *Nième*, Maude. And it doesn't matter where I go as long as I'm not getting into trouble."

Albert shook his head. "Maude's got a point. If'n CPS comes callin' and does a bed check, what do we tell 'em? I mean, you're gone from breakfast 'til dinner most days—and now after bedtime?"

Nième shrugged. "I don't intend to make a habit of staying out late. Last night was an exception. But, should it happen again, and should CPS do a bed check? Tell them I'm spending the night with a friend, that it was all prearranged."

Albert shook his head. "Don' think that's gonna cut it. They'd ask the name of your friend, and so far's we know, you don't got any friends. Looky, Nième, Maude and me? We could find oursels' in a patch o' trouble."

"A *lot* of trouble," Maude echoed him.

Nième thought for a moment. "How much?"

Albert looked confused. "How much trouble?"

Maude, though, understood perfectly. "Fifty."

Nième softly snorted. "All right. Fifty each month—but only if you cooperate with me."

Albert's eyes jinked from Maude to Nième and back to Maude. "Maudy?"

"I think we can live with that," Maude replied.

Nième pulled two twenties and a ten from her hip pocket and handed them to Maude.

"Wh-where'd ya get that kind of money, Nième?" Albert sputtered.

Brie answered for her. "I worked for it, Albert. Want to know what I do all day? I work. Now lay off the third degree."

Nìève wasn't sure what she saw reflected on Maude and Albert's faces. Concern? A measure of respect? And was that speculation in Maude's eyes? Yes. Definitely speculation.

Oh, Maude, you don't fool me. I can see the wheels in your head go 'round and 'round. Nothing of mine is safe from your greedy hands.

Nìève went straight to her room. She nudged her bed away from the wall and yanked on the envelope taped to the headboard's back side—the entirety of her cash on hand.

From now on, I'll deposit all but twenty dollars into my savings account as soon as I get it—and carry that twenty with me at all times. Why? Because dearest Maude cannot be trusted.

THREE MORE weeks rolled by before Syntax, Azteca, and Nìève completed their fifteen-bank op. On the next Friday, Syntax and Nìève drove over to Azteca's, and he paid out their shares for their work the previous week.

"I'll call you both when we're ready to roll with the next town?"

"Sure," Syntax replied.

"I don't have a phone," Nìève said.

Azteca scratched his chin. "I see. Wow."

"How about I call you in two weeks to check in?"

"That works."

"Uh, one more thing?"

"What's that?"

"The school term starts in two weeks. I'll have classes."

"Will you, now? Got us a college student, eh?"

Nìève let him believe his own words. "Yah, but I think I can work my class schedule so I get out early on Fridays."

She hoped she could.

"See that you do—if you want to keep working for me."

CHAPTER 15

Vyper

JUNE 1985

THE JUST-completed school year had been torture for Nième. Excruciating, mind-numbing torture. Added to that was the unexpected ridicule she'd encountered. The previous year, no one had paid her any attention at all, but when she'd returned to classes in the fall with her new "style," she'd been jeered and mocked for her Goth look.

She didn't care. The year finally passed, and a summer of freedom stretched before her—not that school had halted her forward progress. It may have slowed her down, but Nième had continued learning, kept honing her programming skills.

She'd managed to keep working with Azteca and Syntax throughout the year, too, although she'd missed several Fridays due to unavoidable exams. Despite her absences, the three of them had skimmed thousands from banks, hitting seven cities to date, and Nième saved every dollar she earned.

I could buy a little house if I wanted to, she thought with growing wonder as she studied the balance in her savings account's passbook, *but the banks are going to catch on eventually. When they do? The police will start looking for us.*

She frowned. *And Azteca isn't careful enough.*

Anxiety sharpened its claws and took hold of her.

I don't want to go to jail. I need to find a better way to make money. A legal way. I should stop working these scams and get away from Azteca and Syntax.

ON A FRIDAY afternoon, two weeks into the summer break, Azteca, Syntax, and Nième assembled in Azteca's basement to launch their attacks on his next set of banks. The city this time was Edmonton, Alberta, roughly three quarters of a million people and seven and a half hours from Regina by car.

As before, Azteca wanted to hack the individual banks himself before the three of them began altering deposits.

"Hold up a sec," Nième asked around the three pieces of gum in her mouth. "Take a look at the modifications I've made to your code." She loaded a disk, brought the code up on her monitor, and slid her chair aside. Azteca scooted closer and slowly scrolled through it.

"You . . . you've made *a lot* of changes."

Wanting to blunt Azteca's rising ire, she pointed to the screen. "See this line? If any of the banks are using Sawtooth Security code, this line deactivates their incursion algorithms."

Azteca frowned. "Sawtooth is new, just hit the shelves. None of the banks are using it yet."

"It's new to consumers, but the commercial branch of their company started offering free 90-day trials two months ago. That info isn't public knowledge."

He frowned again. "Then how do you know about the free trial?"

Nième lifted one shoulder. "I've been studying various network security software packages. First I figure out how they work, then I identify their weaknesses. After I write code to get around their defenses and test it out, I add it to my library of hacking code."

"*Your* hacking code? Don't you mean my hacking code?"

Nième's jaws slowed. "I started with your code, but I've tripled its size since then. When I hacked into the Sawtooth company network, I found their campaign to attract commercial customers. That's when I downloaded their commercial product and located its vulnerability."

"And this line addresses that vulnerability?"

"Yah."

Azteca continued to peruse Nième's code. He found multiple additions that addressed issues he hadn't thought of. "Fine. Today *you* hack the banks. Let's see what you can do."

Nième didn't want to do the hack, but now she had no choice. Besides, she knew the banks were increasing their security efforts, and Azteca was not as careful as she was.

Caution may as well be my middle name.

"Okay. I'll do it."

Azteca and Syntax waited while she wormed her way into the three banks that were today's targets. Partway into the third bank, she pushed back from her keyboard. Unwrapped another stick of gum and folded it in half, then quarters while, with her other hand, she pointed to her screen.

Azteca scooted in and perused the code. Suddenly he cursed. "Sawtooth? Son of a—" He rubbed his face. "I would have tripped their algorithm."

He nodded to Nière. "They would have had us but for your code. From now on, you do the hacks."

"Yah? What about a raise?" Niève didn't know where such moxie had come from—this demand was way beyond Brie!—but she managed to keep her features calm and immobile.

Still nodding and now gnawing the inside of his cheek over their close call, Azteca replied, "Fifty percent of your take."

"Sixty percent of my take." *What in the world . . .*

A protest erupted from Syntax. "Hey! I've been here longer than she—"

Azteca shut him down. "Look, bud. I have a couple thousand dollars invested in our Edmonton op. If I'd tripped Sawtooth's incursion code while hacking in? We would have kept going, oblivious to the fact that we'd been made. By tomorrow, the bank's security people would have identified our incursion, seen the deposits we'd altered, and passed our MO off to the police.

"Just how long after that do you think it would it be before they came *here*, beating down the door to *my house?* Every op we've conducted could come back to haunt us."

No one spoke as Azteca's chilling words sank in.

When Azteca did speak, it was to Niève. "From now on, you do the hacks and take home sixty percent of your take."

"Agreed."

Because of Niève's diligence, they'd dodged a bullet. She was both glad and relieved; nevertheless, she knew in her bones that it was only a matter of time before bank computer security evolved and made Azteca's scheme obsolete.

Would she be able to stay ahead of that evolution?

Doubtful. I need to pull out of this arrangement soon. Before we get caught. And then? Then I need a better and safer way to grow my bankroll.

The thought of the police banging on the Northams' front door utterly terrified her.

———◆———

ANOTHER FALL school term was almost upon her, and she hadn't found a way to get out of it. Awaking early the next morning, Niève began to panic.

Two weeks! Classes start in two weeks, but I don't think I can tolerate another year of tedium, particularly in the company of the mindless juveniles at Thom Collegiate.

Try as she might, she could think of no way around the legal requirement that she attend school until she was sixteen, and that birthday was more than half a year away. *Even if I could somehow transfer to another school, it would be the same old thing, me stuck in class day in and day out,* she fumed.

"I can't stand it! I can't—" She stopped, struck still. "Even if I transferred to another school?"

An audacious—no, *outrageous*—idea took shape in mere moments.

Nième tossed her stacks of floppy disks on her unmade bed and shuffled through them until she held the disk she needed—her advanced code to hack the banks. She threw it and a couple of blank disks into her bag and readied herself for the day.

Downstairs, she raced through her chores, then ran toward the bus stop. When she reached the university's computer lab, she logged in at her preferred machine and inserted the disk, calling up the code she used to hack the banks. She copied the code and pasted the code into a new file and began to amend it, to customize it for today's purposes. Finally, she saved it to her blank disk. Then she fed a folded stick of Black Jack into her mouth and went to work.

Regina Public Schools boasted a new and "cutting edge" computer system, a network that housed the administrative functions of the entire district: grades, attendance, parent-teacher conference notes . . . and student transfers. As Nième found out, cracking their "state of the art" system was easier than cracking a bank. A *lot* easier.

Nième laughed softly to herself. "You guys need better security. Maybe I could help. Ha!"

She wormed her way into the node assigned to Thom Collegiate and accessed her own student record and began the transfer process. "Transferring where? Let's see. How about Campbell Collegiate? Yes, that will do just fine."

She moved her enrollment out of Thom Collegiate, designating Campbell Collegiate as her destination school. Of course, the transfer would trigger Campbell Collegiate's enrollment process and a request for her academic record—if Nième allowed it.

"Nope. Don't think so," she whispered with glee. She switched to Campbell Collegiate's node, located her enrollment process and student record request and deleted them both. Switched back to Thom Collegiate, accessed her academic record, and marked it "Closed" and "Records Forwarded."

As far as Thom Collegiate's administration would ever know, Nième had transferred out of that school and her records had been duly passed to Campbell Collegiate.

And Campbell Collegiate itself? They'd never heard of her and never would, thus they wouldn't log her absence when the term began. But on the same note, they wouldn't be sending report cards to the Northams or CPS.

"Not a problem," Nième said under her breath. "I will generate bogus report cards and send them myself."

She smiled to herself. "Congratulations, Geneviève Simard. You've completed your high school education. Great job, by the way!"

CHAPTER 16

Vyper

FALL, 1985

ALTHOUGH NIÈVE had successfully disenrolled herself from school, it was essential to her plan that she keep her liberation a secret from both the Northams and Child Protective Services. In a big way, that necessity worked on her behalf. Each morning she got up, did her chores, then alternately cajoled and threatened the littles to dress, eat, and get out the door in time to catch their bus, so she could do the same—or so the Northams thought.

Instead, she walked to the nearest city bus stop. For the rest of the day, she was free, *entirely* free, to spend what should have been her school day elsewhere—in other words, at the university's computer lab.

Using her upgraded version of Azteca's code as a jumping-off point, Niève began to break into and explore commercial networks far and wide, adding to her knowledge with each new hack. As she learned, she revised her code, making improvements and streamlining her approach until Azteca himself would not have recognized the result as having originated with him.

Behind every move Niève made, money was her objective. As confident as she was becoming, she wasn't ready to pull off a "job" on her own just yet, because another factor held an even higher value for her, *security*. Deep down, the possibility of spending part of her life caged terrified her.

Syntax and Azteca are always on the hunt for "easy money" opportunities, quick cash ops rather than quiet, passive, and safe income streams. Azteca is careful, but not careful enough in my book. One of these days, he's going to get caught, and I don't want to get caught with him. As soon as I can, I need to pull out and distance myself from him and from Syntax.

Nième also suspected that, given time, she would far outstrip Azteca's abilities. *I'm already more creative, more inventive than he is. If Azteca is a blunt but powerful object, then I am a thin, penetrating blade. A stiletto.*

Hmm. Stiletto. Not too ostentatious. Not too grandiose. Maybe I will use Stiletto for my next handle. After I discard Jinn. A time will come when, for safety's sake, I must cut ties with that handle and everything I did as Jinn.

Nième drove herself hard. She rewrote, tested, and refined her code. With each new network incursion, she was careful to cover her tracks, but that wasn't good enough for her. She began to devise little "traps" that, if triggered, would alert her to the fact that her network incursion had been detected.

The traps themselves weren't too difficult to code. It was the alert that stumped her.

Sure, when I revisit a network, then I'll see that a trap has been tripped, but what I really need is to receive some kind of external notification, but how in the world do I make that work?

The only possible means she could come up with was email.

Yah, but most email programs are network-centric. That meant messages could only be sent between and among members within a given organization's network, and not that many organizations had yet established such communications.

She fussed over the issue. *Here we are in 1985. Who has email that can reach beyond its own domain?*

She found several registered dot com email providers—think.com, bbn.com, mcc.com, and symbolics.com.

One by one, Nième perused their systems. When she reached Symbolics Computer Corporation, she found a place to host her alerts—and hide them as well. Symbolics was first in the world to have registered a domain name, symbolics.com.

She hacked into the Symbolics network, then into their email system, and created an account for herself. She added code to the program that would not display her account on a generated list of accounts. Then she returned to her "trap code." She added a command to the code's alert function, telling it to send email to her new symbolics.com email address should the trap be tripped.

The end result was clunky and dependent upon her logging into her email account regularly, but at least whenever she did, she'd know if any of her traps had been tripped. With her trap function finalized, she saved the entire code back to disk.

Guess I've found a need for email after all, she admitted. In any given network, if her traps remained undisturbed for a week or more, she'd come back and penetrate the system a little further, setting additional traps the deeper she went and on her way "out." She was determined not to leave even a whiff of her presence when she exited a network.

When I breach a system's security, I want to be like a serpent, gliding in and out of the smallest of holes.

No one the wiser.

Hmm. A serpent . . .

MID-OCTOBER

A SCHEME had been percolating around in her head for weeks. It had come to her as a wisp of an idea the evening Azteca had nearly tripped the Sawtooth software, a way for Nième to make money and make it legally.

Well, mostly legal, she reminded herself.

In her corner of the university's computer lab, she began drafting a business plan to check her idea's profitability. The exercise was "bare bones" as far as business plans go. She made a list of her services and a price for each and estimated her startup and regular, ongoing costs.

Hmm. My specialty will be network security . . . and after I stage a network intrusion or two, I think prospective customers will flock to me.

What to call my little enterprise? How about Protect My Network?

She planned to deliver flyers to Regina businesses located along the bus route. Her flyer would tout "Complete computer network security assessment, amendment, and ongoing protection." Featured in bold font, Nième's flyer laid out why they needed network protection. She snickered as she typed.

Unscrupulous computer "hackers"
seek access to your computer network.
These hackers are persistent and unrelenting.
They **WILL** succeed.
Ask for a **FREE** network security assessment.
DON'T HESITATE!
The data you save may be your own.
Contact us today!
PROTECT MY NETWORK

Immediately, Nième's proposed plan stumbled to a stop. *How would potential clients contact Protect My Network?* She had no phone or office. Worse yet, she realized that no prospective client would hire *her*—especially to grant her access to their computer network—without glowing, unshakable references and proof of valid experience.

I don't even have a valid ID let alone references. And even if I did, I would still need a business license, business cards, and brochures to go along with references.

She sat back. "I have some problems to sort out—not the least being how I can obtain a new and 'valid' ID."

Niève's brilliant "whim" was going to cost her more in hassle than it would in startup costs. She toyed with expanding her Carol Hanover persona, using it to start her business, but she soon discarded the option.

I've used my Carol Hanover ID exclusively to access the university's computer lab. If something at Protect My Network were to go wrong, would I want the authorities to trace Carol's ID back to the lab? Back to me, Niève Simard?

No. Because . . .

A hard-and-fast set of rules landed in her head. *I should never mix ops. Not ever. I should never allow an op to bleed over into my real life. I must keep the lines between all ops clean and separate, and start every op fresh.*

The rules felt right. Safe, even. And hadn't she lived by rules most of her life?

Okay, if I follow my own rules, then I must start Protect My Network fresh. Separate from all else. Huh. Guess I need a different ID.

Hey! What did Azteca say about the fake IDs he uses to open bank accounts?

Niève breathed out Azteca's words. "I know a guy. He's good. *Very* good." She wouldn't ask Azteca for the guy's name, though. She'd get the name a different way.

Never mix ops. Not ever. What I'm doing for myself is none of Azteca's beeswax. Also, what he doesn't know won't hurt him, right?

Right.

A mischievous smile tugging at her mouth, Niève started a new computer session. "Okay, Azteca. Let's see how hard it is for me to hack *you*."

———◆———

NIÈVE HACKED Azteca's preferred machine and found the online location of the private chat room where Azteca and his document guy conducted their business. The man's name was Bodie, and he should have made himself an anonymous online profile and made his location unknowable, but the guy (obviously) was not a hacker. He didn't know the first thing about how to protect his identity in the nascent virtual world. Bodie was a fake documents guy, an artist type who did his best work by hand.

"And that's a vastly different set of skills, Mr. Bodie."

———◆———

NIÈVE SHOWED up at his door the next morning. She was armed with cash, her appearance as mature as she could achieve.

One jaundiced eye peered at her over the door's chain guard. "Who are you?"

"An acquaintance of Azteca. I have some business for you."

"Not interested. Go away and don't come back."

Nième, slowly chewing her gum, gazed down the empty street. "I have a couple of hundred-dollar banknotes in my pocket. You interested in them?"

She waited. Finally, the door swung inward. "Get in here. For future reference? I don't receive clients except by appointment—and always at my back door. Got it?"

Once she was inside, he vented on her. "I have one hard-and-fast directive, girlie: None of my clients ever speak of me to anyone else. *Ever.* If they do? I'm done with them—and Azteca's blabbing indiscretion means I'm done with him."

Nième understood rules. She had a healthy respect for them. Most of the time. Nodding, she glanced around his living room, feigning indifference, a fresh stick of gum in her hand.

"You shouldn't blame Azteca for me showing up without an appointment. He never mentioned your name to me."

"But you said—"

She put on Brie's persona, hardened her tone, and interjected with a *very* Brie-like impression, "I said I was his acquaintance. Never said he gave me your name."

Bodie's expression soured. "Then who did?"

Nième unwrapped the gum and folded it in quarters. "I hacked you, Mr. Bodie. I dialed into your computer."

"Sure you did. What are you, all of eighteen?"

She smirked. *Close but no cigar, dude.* "First, I hacked Azteca's computer to get the location of the chat room you and Azteca use to conduct business. Then I hacked the chat room and your login ID to find your name and where you live. By the way, nice client list you have on your computer. The Saskatchewan Warriors, for instance, have an exceptionally active account with you."

The Saskatchewan Warriors were an indigenous organized crime group, one of several in Canada. Nième dropped their name for the shock factor.

It worked. Bodie progressed from disbelief to fear to polite compliance within seconds. "But you're just a—" He stopped himself mid-sentence. "Obviously not. Never mind. I, er, apologize for doubting you. Tell me what you need. Please. I don't want any trouble."

"And I'm not interested in making any trouble for you, Mr. Bodie. I would like a driver's license. Could you make one for me?"

"Yes, yes. Of course."

"Super. If I need anything in the future, I will call first and make an appointment, as you prefer. Also? I expect the same circumspection from you that you expect from me. You won't speak of me to anyone—including Azteca. If you live up to your end of the bargain, I won't hack your computer a second time and, perhaps, wipe it and all your records. Are we agreed?"

Bodie, worry cementing the deep lines across his forehead, nodded. "Absolutely crystal. No problem. And it's just Bodie, not Mr. Bodie."

He had a camera and a chair ready. "Let's get your picture taken, shall we?"

Niève sat for the photo, then left Bodie's home by his back door, lighter by two hundred dollars in exchange for the promise of a Saskatchewan driver's license in seven days. Bodie had also agreed to slightly age the photo he'd taken of Niève for the license.

"I do the alteration work by hand," he explained, obviously proud of his skill. "It's sort of my forte."

Niève spent the rest of her day chewing on her other problems, ironclad references being the toughest nut in the bunch to crack.

I could fake references easily enough. Just as easily, a simple phone call would prove them false and blow up my game. What I need is a flattering testimonial from a known and unassailable organization, vouching for my work. She perked up. *Or maybe a single authoritative individual within that organization?*

If Niève had been an outsider, able to listen in on her own musings, she would have been dumbfounded. For whenever she "put on" Brie, she stopped thinking of herself as a CPS Permanent Ward and a high school dropout. Unconsciously, her vocabulary and language skills jumped ahead by years.

Hmm. The one "right" individual's reference letter? I could arrange that, couldn't I?

The method that came to her for obtaining such a letter would be considered blackmail or extortion in most circles, but those terms never entered Niève's mind. Only the means to achieve her objective did. In her eyes, this newly hatched plan was purely an expeditious solution to a tiresome problem.

⁕

A WEEK after visiting Bodie, Niève waited in the park by the library for him to show up. He sauntered into the park at 9:15 a.m. and sat down on a park bench for five minutes. After he got up and walked away, Niève moved to the same bench and spied a tiny envelope on the grass beneath the bench. She bent to tie her sneaker, snagged the envelope, slid it into her sock, then headed toward the library.

She sat down at a study carrel where she would have some privacy. Inside the envelope she found a Saskatchewan driver's license for one Adele Logan, born February 16, 1965, age 20. Niève grinned at her older likeness staring out from the license. It was good.

No, it's really good, she thought. *Bodie did his best work for me.* She fixed her eyes on the row of book shelves opposite her carrel. *Probably because I made him afraid.*

For some reason, the idea that she'd made Bodie afraid tickled her, and she snickered to herself—not because she got off on instilling fear in others, but because she felt a little stronger than she was accustomed to feeling.

I learned a lot about Bodie when I hacked his computer, a lot about his work, even his customers. I suppose that knowledge could be used as a kind of leverage. Yes, leverage, because I could really mess things up for him if I wanted to . . . or if I needed something from him.

And I might need something from him down the road.

Other words replaced the concept of leverage in her thoughts.

Maybe information is a kind of power.

Personal power was new to Niève. Until recently, she hadn't experienced much sway over her life, had certainly never felt that she might someday wield real control over her choices. Over her future.

But in this moment, she experienced something of an epiphany.

Perhaps the more information like this I accumulate, the more power I will have to make other people do what I decide. Like how I made Maude and Albert agree to the freedoms I want. That I need.

She tucked Adele Logan's driver's license into her little pink cat purse. Stopped and stared. Her precious gift from Miss Timmons was now worn around its edges, the cat's expression a bit dull and forlorn.

I'm supposed to be too old for such juvenile trinkets.

She shoved the purse into her pocket.

Where it was safe.

Yah? Well, I don't care.

———◆———

NIÈVE HADN'T been idle while Bodie was making her new ID. She labored two weeks further hacking into and lurking unseen in a number of high-stakes gambling chat rooms, seeking the right mark to advance her plan. These rooms allowed players to bet on horse and dog races, unregulated lotteries, boxing matches, and the outcome of just about any professional team sport.

She wrote code to trace the dial-up connections used by the gambling participants and then worm her way into their computers. Only a few of the participants were savvy enough to unplug their modems when away from their computers. The rest? Not even close to "Jinn-proof."

"I am fire and air," she breathed to herself. "I am a shape-shifting spirit, undetectable and unstoppable."

By hacking the gamblers' computers, Nième was able to strip them of the personas they'd assumed in the gambling chat room, uncover their true identities, and learn their secrets. She then sorted the individuals by employment, position, and gambling *indebtedness*—for without a sizable debt, Nième couldn't leverage the mark as she needed to.

At the end of her search, she'd identified two candidates who fit her ideal profile, two men highly placed in their business or organization, each with the authority to make unilateral decisions. Both of her candidates were also majority shareholders in their companies.

Nième had no intention of pressing either of them for money, however. All she was after was a glowing reference for her emerging company.

"These guys are so steeped in debt, they will find the threat of public exposure to be *highly motivational*."

Just as Nième was poised to make her selection, another interesting individual logged into the chat room. Nieve hacked the account information and sucked in a breath. The woman owed a lot. She then hacked the woman's computer and personal info, one Iris St. Lawrence Dunwoody. Born into an old and respected Regina family, Ms. Dunwoody outright owned her thriving business, St. Lawrence Office Supply. Her growing company had three stores in Saskatchewan and two in Alberta. Moreover, although Ms. Dunwoody was in the process of taking her company public, St. Lawrence Office Supply was, at this time, still completely hers to do with as she wished. In other words, she was accountable to no one but herself.

An impeccable mark.

"Oh my goodness, Iris! Wouldn't even a hint of impropriety on your part derail the killing you hope to net on your company's initial public stock offering?" a smirking Nième asked as she worked, "and I'm sure you don't want that. No, you're counting on the ready cash from your IPO to get out from under your crushing gambling losses."

Nième grinned to herself. "I don't want to spoil your hopes or ruin you, Ms. Dunwoody. At the same time, I'm not averse to using this predicament of your own making to solve my problem."

She created a profile for herself in the gambling chat room frequented by Ms. Dunwoody. Nième then waited for Ms. Dunwoody to log on. As soon as she did, Nième sent a message to her.

> **GreaseMonkey03:** Ms. Dunwoody, I invite you
> to join me in this private chat room to discuss your
> gambling losses.

Ms. Dunwoody did not respond, so Nième tried again.

> **GreaseMonkey03:** Ms. Dunwoody, in looking into
> your history on this site, I found that two weeks ago

your gambling losses amounted to $77,000. Ten days ago, as you tried to recoup a portion of your losses, you added another $11,000 to your debt, bringing the total to $88,000, not including the monstrous interest you're being charged.

The woman read the messages, but she did not reply.

I'm not going away, Iris Dunwoody, Nième thought while she framed her next message. *I've been nice so far, but now I'm going to squeeze you just a bit. You **will** answer me.*

> **GreaseMonkey03:** Ms. Dunwoody, what would happen if your gambling debt were to become public knowledge? Would it not adversely affect your IPO? Neither of us want that. Let's come to an agreement that ensures your IPO has a successful launch. My offer will not cost you any money.

Again, the woman did not respond.

She's panicking, searching for a way out, Nième thought. *If I were her, I would be too.* She messaged Iris a fourth time.

> **GreaseMonkey03:** Ms. Dunwoody, I propose a simple swap. I agree not to release details of your gambling debt to the newspapers. In exchange, you will write a letter of reference for me. That is all I ask for.

Nième waited five minutes before Ms. Dunwoody replied.

> **OceanLover365:** What kind of reference?

> **GreaseMonkey03:** I own a network security startup. In return for my company performing a security assessment on your company's network, you will provide a reference letter that attests to the value of my company's services. I will write the letter for you. You will sign it, return it to me, and keep a copy in your files. If you receive phone calls from my company's prospective clients, you will, in every instance, report that the services I pro-vided were satisfactory. That is the extent of the exchange.

OceanLover365: Sure it is. And next month, you'll threaten me again and demand that I pay you some exorbitant amount.

Niève was losing her patience.

GreaseMonkey03: I could demand money now, lady. That's not what I want.

OceanLover365: I don't know you. I certainly do not trust you.

Niève thought a few minutes before she replied.

GreaseMonkey03: Fair enough. When we conclude our arrangement, you'll have my business' name. If I were to break my agreement with you, you could report me to the authorities, and I do not want that any more than you wish to have your gambling debts made public.

Please note, you will be more than able to wipe out your gambling debt when you launch your IPO, yet I am not asking for money now nor will I later on.

Although it's tempting . . .
Ms. Dunwoody's response was immediate.

OceanLover365: Send your letter.

GreaseMonkey03: I'll deliver it to your downtown offices, marked Personal and Confidential.

Niève had already roughed out the letter. As she reviewed the draft, something struck her.

I should actually perform a network security assessment for Ms. Dunwoody. If I find and fix a deficiency, it might take the sting out of our . . . exchange. I'll also make recommendations on how to improve her network's security. She should appreciate that.

CHAPTER 17

WEDNESDAY MORNING, Nième got to it. Inside of three hours she'd completed the assessment of Iris Dunwoody's simple company network used primarily to track inventory, sales, and other accounting functions across her several stores.

She glanced down at the checklist she'd used and what she'd found. In a surprising turn of events, the assessment had led Nième far afield, requiring her to hack other networks to verify her findings.

Oh, Iris, Iris, Iris. Someone in your accounting department is a naughty boy. He is siphoning off company funds—has done so for three years—and you never noticed. This information, if it were to come to light during a pre-IPO audit, would also damage your opening stock prices.

But that wasn't the worst of what Nième had found. She spent two more hours writing up her findings in a way that someone not computer savvy would be able to follow and comprehend.

When she was certain she had fully explained her findings, she printed the documentation, pages and pages of it, earning the displeasure of the computer lab's attendant.

"Big term project," she muttered to him.

When she left the computer lab, she took a bus to Iris's Regina branch of St. Lawrence Office Supply. There, she bought a yellow highlighter and some file folders before perusing their selection of briefcases. Most on hand were designed with men in mind.

Nième turned up her nose at their masculine lines and colors. She finally settled upon a lightweight burgundy attaché case with a lengthy shoulder strap. It didn't have enough flair for her tastes, but it would do.

She carefully organized her printouts, highlighted several points, separated the documents into two folders, and slid them into the attaché case. It was afternoon when she caught a bus to Regina's downtown area and disembarked at a stop conveniently near Ms. Dunwoody's offices.

<hr>

NIÈVE, ATTACHÉ case slung crosswise across her body, was waiting for Iris Dunwoody when she exited her office building early that afternoon. The woman looked to be in her early thirties, trim and fit. She was dressed in a smart skirt suit and no-nonsense shoes and wore her brown hair in a utilitarian upsweep, her look the epitome of "convention" and everything Nième shunned.

Iris's steps were brisk as she headed for a nearby car park. Nième had to quicken her pace to catch up.

"Excuse me, Ms. Dunwoody?"

Startled, the woman veered toward the curb. She kept moving, even as she shot worried looks over her shoulder.

"Iris Dunwoody. Please stop a moment."

"I don't know you. Stay back!"

"Iris, I'm Adele Logan, your network security analyst."

She halted. "You—you're who? *You* are GreaseMonkey03? You're the horrid person extorting me?"

Nième shifted the wad of gum in her mouth. "Yah, I am. Listen, I finished my assessment of your network, and you have a big problem. Two big problems, in fact."

Iris's countenance hardened. "You must take me for a fool."

"You'd be a fool if you didn't listen to what I've found."

A blotchy red ran up Iris Dunwoody's face and neck. "I told you to stay away from me! You'll get your *precious* reference letter, but you had better leave me alone after that."

When the woman pivoted on her heel, Nième grabbed her arm and jerked her back around.

"You take your filthy hands off me!"

Nième ignored her. "Shem Lewiston."

"I said, *let go of me!*"

Nième hung on. "He's the head of your accounting department."

"That's it! I'm going to scream!"

"Shem Lewiston has embezzled $12,000 a year from your company, three years in a row."

As Nième's words penetrated Iris's rage, she quit struggling. Her face drained of color. "How could you know this?"

"*Duh.* I told you! I finished your network security assessment. I found Shem's little scam during the assessment. I can show you."

"Wait—you actually performed that network security thing? A real one?"

Nième released Iris's arm. Struggled to compose herself.

If I'm going to build a business, I guess I need to learn how to act like an adult and a professional. More like Iris here—gag.

Or maybe I could manage my business entirely online and by phone? Never meet clients face to face? Oh, yah, I like that idea.

But in the here and now, she didn't have such a choice. She cleared her throat and forced herself to speak slower and with more aplomb.

"It didn't seem ethical to ask you for a reference, Ms. Dunwoody, if I hadn't done the work."

"You're worried about ethics *now?*" Nième's reluctant client looked her over. "Why . . . you're just a kid."

Nième laughed under her breath. "I get that a lot. The sceptics usually find out I'm smarter than any hacker they've ever met."

"So, you're a *hacker.*"

The disdain dripping from Iris's words grated on Nième. She growled back, "Let me tell you something, *lady.* It takes a hacker to stop a hacker. Furthermore, I know a scam when I see one. Look, I'm trying to start a legit business here, Ms. Dunwoody, and because I *am* a hacker, I know how to stop your competitors from hacking your network—which, as it turns out *they already have*—conveniently just prior to the launch of your IPO, I might add."

Iris fired back, "*No one* has hacked my company! I have a very capable IT department, and if someone had tried to hack my network, my IT people would have detected them and told me!"

Nième was so affronted, she spat her gum into the gutter. "You call those two clowns capable? Why don't you ask yourself how *I* was able to hack your network? I spent the morning browsing your accounting, email, and inventory programs, even your business correspondence. I found evidence of duplicity within and without your company—and your 'capable' IT blockheads never caught so much as a whiff of me."

Nième moved closer to the woman. "Tell me, Ms. Dunwoody, *who* is your biggest competitor, huh? Is it by chance Braxton Business Machines? Because, when they hacked you last month, they located and copied your plans to take St. Lawrence Office Supply public. Braxton knows the date and time of your IPO and is, at this moment, busily appointing the proxies who will snap up *every share you offer* next month—which will certainly drive your share prices way up. But then Braxton will turn around and immediately *dump* those shares, making a killing on the sale, but sinking your company's net worth in the process."

Iris's anger faltered. "H-how do you know these things?"

"Well, I didn't just hack *your* company, did I? When I noted the intrusion into your network, I traced the intruder's connection back to Braxton.

"And here's something else you need to know. Once your stock tanks? Braxton's board intends to devour your company. To aid in the process of destroying your company's net worth, Braxton's board has bribed journalists at several newspapers to write negative stories about your precious business, stories that will include personal info about *you*. Yes, Braxton's board is aware of your little gambling problem, Ms. Dunwoody. The stories their paid journalists write will run soon after Braxton dumps your stock, and I wonder to what degree that negative press will impact your stock prices, don't you?

"Let's also talk about the loan St. Lawrence Office Supply took out two years ago to construct your office building. You need to know, *Iris*, that Braxton has already bought St. Lawrence's debt from Whitmore Savings and Loan. After your stock drops, Braxton intends to call in the loan. Unfortunately, you don't have the cash on hand to pay off that amount, and by then your stock will be in the toilet, meaning you won't be able to leverage a new loan—and that makes you *very* vulnerable to a hostile takeover."

Nière had just delivered more words to Iris Dunwoody in a single go than she had spoken to anyone in her entire life. Living in her head as much as she did, Nière hadn't even realized she possessed the vocabulary that poured out of her with so little effort . . . yet had concurrently exhausted her.

Having run out of steam, Nière blinked stupidly at the sidewalk. When she looked up, the expression on Iris face had changed from consternation and fear to . . . concern?

"Are you all right, Miss, er, Logan?"

Nière shivered and her fingers twitched. They reached for her pack of gum. "Need . . . a minute."

Iris looked around. Took Nière's arm and steered her toward the nearby bus stop. Sat her down on the bench, then sat beside Nière.

"Miss Logan, you say you can prove the things you assert? That you can show me?"

Nière pulled the stick of gum from her pack. Unwrapped it. Folded it. Stuffed the piece into her mouth. Chewed. All while Iris Dunwoody watched closely, not ready to believe Nière, but more willing to listen than she had been five minutes ago.

A few moments later, Nière sighed. "Yah. I have the proof here in my, er, attaché case."

"Show me."

"Need some table space. Spread things out."

"Feeling better?"

"I guess."

"Right then. Follow me."

Iris Dunwoody retraced her steps back to her offices, Nière in tow. It wasn't a huge building, but it did have three floors. As Ms. Dunwoody and

Niève walked through the front doors into the lobby, Niève's scrutiny took in everything—nice carpet, wood trim, tasteful wallpaper, a prominent board listing the building's tenants and their office numbers, all located on the third floor with the exception of St. Lawrence Office Supply. They took the entire second floor.

They own the building and rent out the third floor as office space for other concerns, Niève thought. *Solid fiscal strategy.*

As they reached the elevator, the doors opened and a suave, middle-aged man stepped out. He paused.

"Er, Ms. Dunwoody? I thought you'd left early for the day."

"I forgot something, Shem."

Niève, jaws slowing, eyed Ms. Dunwoody's head accountant.

He eyed her back. Looked her up and down. "And this is?"

"My college roommate's daughter, visiting from out of town. Have a good evening, Shem."

Niève smiled her approval behind the woman's back. Apparently Iris Dunwoody could think on her feet.

Too bad she's terrible at picking winning horses and football teams.

The two of them took the elevator up to Iris's office on the second floor. Inside Iris's office, Niève spied a meeting table surrounded by chairs.

"Here?" she gestured.

"Yes."

Moments later, they were seated side by side, and Niève had removed the two file folders from her attaché case, separating the two issues she'd uncovered, embezzlement and an imminent takeover plot. Niève withdrew the printouts and set the two piles of documents before them. She walked Ms. Dunwoody through the embezzlement first.

"The first entry I've highlighted is $12,000 for a one-year lease on a delivery truck, three years back, intended for your Saskatoon store. Here's another lease the following year, and a third lease this past January, each $12,000."

Ms. Dunwoody stared at Niève, mistrust springing anew. "I saw the receipts for those leases. You've proved nothing."

"Yes, you did see those receipts. What you didn't see were the lease cancellations for full refunds."

Ms. Dunwoody gaped.

"Your delivery guys in Saskatoon are still driving the same delivery truck they had four years ago."

Iris said slowly, "I directed Shem to donate that truck to a local charity. They needed the truck to pick up used furniture for their secondhand shop."

"Obviously he didn't. See?" Nième tapped a page. "Shem Lewiston paid the license and registration fees on that old truck for the same three years he supposedly leased a new one. Vehicle insurance too."

Nième slapped several other sheets of paper in front of Ms. Dunwoody. "And here are Shem Lewiston's bank records showing three deposits of $12,000, said deposits corresponding exactly with the refunds on the leases."

"But h-how did you get his bank records?"

Nième again pulled her pack of Black Jack from her pocket. "*Pffft.* How do you *think* I got them?"

While Ms. Dunwoody sputtered, Nième unwrapped and fed another stick into her mouth. "Listen. You can prove Lewiston canceled the leases and received the refunds, and you can verify that your guys in Saskatoon are still driving the old truck. What Lewiston cannot prove is that he returned the three $12,000 refunds to your business's bank account. I've looked. No deposits match those amounts."

Nième witnessed Iris Dunwoody's temper rising.

"That miserable cheat! I'll fire him so fast—"

"No."

"What?"

"Not just yet, because I'm not done."

Nième slid another page of Lewiston's bank statements under the woman's nose. "What jumps out at you, Iris?"

Intent as she was on showing her evidence, Nième didn't notice she'd begun using Ms. Dunwoody's first name—and not merely in sarcasm.

The woman ran a manicured nail down Lewiston's bank statement. A few inches from the bottom, her finger stopped. Her nail tapped the page. "This deposit of $75,000?"

"Uh-huh. Don't you wonder how your competitor, Braxton Business Machines, knows so much about your company's affairs?"

Dunwoody's attention jumped back to Lewiston's bank statement. "Braxton paid Shem $75,000; in return, he gave them access to my company's financials—including my IPO plans?"

"Uh-yup."

An hour later, Nième had walked Ms. Dunwoody through her documentation of both issues three times. Three times, not because the woman was slow, but because she was thorough and exacting. Actually, Nième was impressed.

So was Ms. Dunwoody.

"Miss Logan—is that right?"

"Uh, yah. Adele Logan."

Iris gestured at the paperwork on her table, again sorted into two neat stacks. "You did all of this work, this excellent work, in order to obtain a flattering reference from me—and yet I had already agreed to give you the reference to keep you from exposing my . . . unseemly debt. What I mean is you didn't have to go to these lengths."

Niève drew her chin toward her chest. "I suppose."

"Don't worry, Miss Logan. You'll get your reference, but I will also pay you for your work. Heaven knows, I owe you. I would have lost my company but for you."

"What will you do to keep it?"

"That's a good question." She got up and stretched, then paced across her office. "To begin, I should delay the IPO until I have my house in order. Perhaps I will cancel it altogether and instead sell shares only to my employees—giving them some time to consider the option and gather funds for their buy-in. The sale won't net me, personally, as much as I'd anticipated, but why shouldn't my loyal employees share in the profits for the work they do? Offering stock privately would stymie Braxton's attempt to buy up a near-majority portion, although I'm keeping fifty-five percent of the stock in any event."

Niève thought a moment. "I like the employee-owned idea. But if you delay the sale of your stock, how will you pay your gambling debt?"

That essential point had slipped Iris's mind while she tussled over the problem of how to save her company from a hostile takeover. She sat abruptly.

"I suppose I could ask for a repayment extension . . ."

Niève was already shaking her head. "If you did and *if* they chose to give you the extension, it would cost you a fortune in compounded interest, besides which Braxton would smear you in the press for yanking the IPO and halting their plans. Your stock's worth would still drop like a rock, killing your profit from selling stock to your employees. Again, you'd have no way to repay the loan plus interest."

Iris swallowed. "I have to think . . . must consider all options. Perhaps I could sell my company outright to a different buyer. I'd have to walk away from the business my grandfather built from the ground up, but I'd walk away clean. Free of debt. My reputation intact."

Iris laughed a bitter laugh. "Here I am about to lose my grandfather's company, and the one thing your 'audit' didn't detect? The one problem you haven't helped me solve? I've never gambled a nickel in my entire life, Miss Logan. *I'm not a gambler.*"

Niève stared stupidly at the woman. "But . . ."

"Yes, *but*. But my philandering ex-husband is."

"Ohhh." The word tumbled from Niève's mouth on a puff of air.

"We'd no sooner finalized our divorce—me paying him a fortune just to go away and leave me alone forever—than he opened an account in that gambling chat room using *my bank account information* to buy in, so that he might intentionally rack up a debilitating debt *in my name* as his last fond farewell to our marriage. You see, when he was unable to get his hands on my company during the divorce proceedings, he decided that if he couldn't have a piece of it, neither would I."

Iris rubbed her eyes. "He opened an account in the gambling chat room by posing as me, then racked up that huge debt in my name. I was unaware of his actions, of course. I knew nothing of them until just days ago when the site's enforcers showed up *here*, in my office, and threatened me!

"It didn't matter to the site's owners that it was my ex who had run up such an unconscionable tab—I was the one with resources, not him. Of course, I didn't believe their nightmare scenario at first, so my "guests" gave me access to the login my ex had created so I could see the debt he'd racked up.

"And when they began to squeeze me for payment, I realized that if the media found out about 'my' gambling debt? It would kill my IPO. That's why you found me in that chat room in the first place. I had logged on again, hoping to negotiate some kind of lesser settlement or a reasonable payment plan."

Nième wagged her head back and forth, alternately dumbfounded and outraged. The two women were silent while Iris thought and Nième fumed inside.

A moment later, Nième laughed.

Iris was not amused. "You think this is funny?"

"Hardly. But I just figured out how you could pay off your debt. Like tomorrow." Nième shuffled through the first stack of documents, found what she was looking for, and slid the sheet of paper toward Iris.

"This is Shem Lewiston's most recent bank statement. Notice the ending balance in his savings account?"

Iris was a woman who caught on fast. Her head snapped up. "Are you saying . . . wait. You can do that?"

Nième liked Iris's office chairs. The one she sat in rolled and swiveled nicely. It also had a great seatback, all springy and flexible. She bounced a little, enjoying the chair's cushiony feel.

"Sure. I can do that. *Then* you can cancel your IPO because you won't be desperate for the money anymore."

"But if I were to cancel the IPO, won't Braxton suffer a loss? According to you, Braxton has expended money on proxies whom they have ordered to snap up my stock. If I cancel the IPO, won't Braxton's board be suspicious of Shem? Demand to know why I changed my mind? Won't they suspect that he deliberately fed them false information to lead them astray?" Her voice dropped to a whisper. "Might they come after him?"

It had been a long day. Nième let herself lean far back in her chair. She closed her eyes and stretched her aching shoulder and neck muscles. "They might."

Without looking up, she asked Iris, "But is that your problem?"

Iris opened her mouth and just as quickly closed it. While Nième stretched, Iris considered Nième, speculation creasing her forehead.

Finished with her stretch, Nième sat up. The curious look on Iris's face smoothed away, but not before Nième saw it.

What's that about?

She didn't like it.

"Say, Iris, do you have lawyers?" *That should yank her attention off of me.*

"Of course."

"Well, as soon as we wipe out your debt, you should have your lawyers deliver a letter to Braxton's board. The letter should tell them you have proof that they engaged in corporate espionage and that you are willing to publish such proof. The letter should also tell them that you know Braxton paid certain journalists to publish spurious stories asserting that you have gambling debt, but that you do *not*, and should any frivolous story saying otherwise go to press, you will sue Braxton for libel and any newspaper that prints such a lie."

Iris stared hard at Nième. "Miss Logan, I confess that you astonish me. You may be something of a savant. Did you know that?"

Without waiting for Nième to reply, Iris asked, "But for all that, I suppose nothing can be done about Terrell?"

"Terrell? Your ex-husband?"

"Yes."

"I can ensure that he never again uses your name or credit to open a gambling account."

To herself, Nième thought, *Yah, leave him to me.*

Iris shook her head. "You continue to astonish me, Miss Logan. Do you have that reference letter with you?"

"Right here." Nième dug it out of her attaché case.

Iris Dunwoody took it to her desk to read it over.

"Protect My Network, that's your business name? I like it."

She finished reading the letter. "Would you mind if I had my secretary retype this? I'd like to add a few comments. Trust me, they will be positive. I'll send the letter back to you tomorrow."

"I don't exactly have a mailing address yet, Ms. Dunwoody. I'd be happy to come by and pick it up."

Again, a subtle look of perception crossed Iris's face. When it faded, she was all business.

"I'll tell the lobby attendant to expect you." Iris pulled her desk's center drawer toward her and withdrew a pad of checks. "How much do I owe you?"

For more than one reason, Iris's unexpected question flustered Nième.

Never mix ops. Never. Never allow an op to bleed over to my real life.

Then I must not deposit a check from Iris to my savings account. I'll need a new and separate account. For this business only. Preferably a bank in another country, a bank that values its clients' anonymity and uses only numbered accounts. Well, that might be a stretch at the moment.

"Uh . . ."

"Five thousand?"

Niève suddenly couldn't find her tongue.

"You did say you can save my company, Miss Logan, did you not? If you cannot, at the very least, I know who my enemies are, and you've given me a fighting chance. That is worth a great deal to me." She tipped her head to one side. "But you *are* going to save my company, yes?"

"Yah, but . . . I'm not able to cash your check at the moment, Ms. Dunwoody. I really just want the reference letter."

"No one turns down good money. If you can't cash the check today, hold on to it until you can deposit it to your business account. The check won't expire for ninety days."

When Niève didn't respond, Iris again fixed her with that speculative but knowing stare. "Your business has startup costs, no? You need office space, furniture, a phone, business cards, and so on? A startup takes money. So, ten thousand? Will that be enough to get you going?"

The money was too much for Niève to process. At this point, all she wanted was to flee Iris Dunwoody's office and be alone with her thoughts again.

"No."

"You want more? How much more?"

"No! Not more. It's . . . see, the amount you've suggested? It's too much. It might . . . draw attention."

Iris smiled, and the fact that Niève didn't understand *why* Iris was smiling made her squirm.

"Miss Logan? May I ask you something personal?"

There it was. Niève knew it was a loaded question.

She sighed. "You can ask. Doesn't mean I'll answer."

Iris nodded. "How old are you? I mean really."

Niève delayed. Made a production of getting up and spitting her gum into a trash can. She pulled two fresh sticks from her pack, unwrapped and folded them. Fed them into her mouth.

"Nope."

"That's your answer?"

"Yup."

"I see."

And maybe Iris did see. The woman's perceptive eyes drilled Niève until she started to sweat.

"When can I expect to see the results of your, er, debt elimination plan, Miss Logan?"

Nième thought. *Tomorrow is Thursday. I can get it done in the morning and pick up my reference letter midday.*

"Tomorrow. I'll take care of it tomorrow before I come by for the letter."

"Ah, yes—the letter. Now that I've given it some consideration, please grant me a little leeway to finish it. You may pick it up Monday. I assure you it will be ready then."

Nième's eyes narrowed. "You know I can move money both directions, *Iris.*"

Iris licked her lips. "I pray you never find reason to do so, Miss Logan. I am sincere when I say I would not wish to be on the receiving end of your justice."

Iris slid a business card in Nième's direction. "Call my secretary tomorrow as soon as you've finished your job for me. Just leave a message saying that you're done."

Partially mollified and too weary to object further, Nième got up. "Okay. See you later."

She caught a bus to the library, exhausted in body and soul, and arrived home on foot just as Maude was serving dinner.

"Too tired to eat," she mumbled. "Going to bed."

With no other explanation, Nième climbed the stairs, fell onto her mattress, and slept until morning.

* * *

NIÈVE ROSE early, refreshed after a long sleep and feeling like herself again. Her job this day wouldn't be terribly difficult, but it would require coordination on her part, and she was anxious to get to it.

So I can pick up my "precious" reference letter Monday.

With a growl, she added, "For Iris's sake, it had better be ready."

Three hours later, ensconced in her preferred corner of the university's computer lab, Nième mentally listed the steps required to complete her mission. She sorted through her stack of disks, selected one to load into the computer, opened the disk's content, and copied it. She then dialed into the gambling chat room. Using the code she'd copied, pasting it and customizing it on the fly, she hacked into Iris's user profile, and logged into the chat room as Iris.

Almost as soon as Iris's user name appeared on the screen, a user named 'DorsalFin" invited her to join him in a private room.

DorsalFin? Gotta be one of the site's enforcers.

Nième snickered. *Not very obvious, are we?*

DorsalFin: Good to see you back, OceanLover. We need you to cover your losses. Today. If you require an installment plan, we can make an arrangement, but we still require you to make a sizable payment. Today.

Niève snorted. *My dear, my darling little Finny-poo. When do you want your money? Oh, today? 'We can make an arrangement' if needed, but we still require you to make a sizable payment?' Do you mean, like today? Riiight. Of course, the interest you'd charge on the balance of what Iris owes would be so astronomical that it would keep her in debt to you indefinitely—not to mention that if she ever came up a day late or a dollar short, you'd make a move on her other assets or threaten to break her legs. Well, none of that is gonna happen.*

OceanLover365: A payment plan will not be necessary. Please provide my total balance and your bank routing and account numbers. I will transfer the full amount. Today.

DorsalFin went silent, although the user had not logged off or left the private chat. Niève figured he was on the phone to his boss.

Five minutes went by. Ten minutes. Fifteen. Niève began to fidget. She added two sticks of Black Jack to the two already in her mouth. Just as she had decided to log off and come back later, DorsalFin responded.

DorsalFin: We are not entirely confident that you are able to pay off your losses in full. However, we give you one opportunity to do so. Your balance is $93,000, inclusive of interest accrued through midnight.

DorsalFin sent the routing and account numbers then a last message.

DorsalFin: This is a one-time offer. Wire the full amount. Today.

OceanLover365: Understood.

Traffic in the computer lab was low, so Niève didn't log out of the gambling chat room or the private chat. She did press the button to turn the monitor off lest anyone see her conversation with DorsalFin. Taking her stack of disks with her but leaving her bag on the chair in front of her computer, she moved to the computer in the next carrel, selected another disk from her library, inserted the disk, opened it, and copied its content.

"Now to rob Peter to pay Paul."

Niève didn't know where the saying had come from or who Peter and Paul were. She only knew that Maude had used it over the years and that, in this instance, she was an avid fan of the concept.

You know what they say about karma, Shem.

It took her seven minutes to hack Shem Lewiston's bank and another two minutes to access his checking and savings accounts. His savings account balance still read $102,000; his checking account held less than $2,000.

As Niève sped through the process of wiring $93,000 from Shem's savings to the account number DorsalFin had sent her during their private chat, she whispered. "Hey, Shem, don't worry, buddy. We won't clean you out. We'll leave you $9,000. It should be just enough to flee the province and hide out elsewhere before Braxton's board fingers you for the rat you are. Before they hire an exterminator."

Niève jotted the wire transfer number on a scrap of paper, logged out of that machine, and moved back to the other computer where Iris's user name had remained active in the private chat with DorsalFin. She turned the monitor back on and sent her message.

> **OceanLover365:** The wire transfer reference number is 776592210.

A minute later, she saw a reply.

> **DorsalFin:** If the transfer goes through, you may consider your debt expunged. If it does not go through? We know where you live, and we'll be seeing you face to face real soon.

> **OceanLover365:** On another note, please close my account with your company. If, at a later date, should someone attempt to reopen this account, be aware that the individual is likely my ex-husband, Terrell Dunwoody. I DO NOT AUTHORIZE HIM TO REOPEN THIS ACCOUNT. As he has no assets of his own, his activities on this site would likely result in a loss to your company. I WILL NOT PAY HIS DEBT A SECOND TIME.

She waited several minutes to receive a reply.

> **DorsalFin:** We have noted the permanent closing of your account. But perhaps you would care to purchase a different sort of product from us? For a reasonable fee, we can ensure that Mr. Dunwoody does not attempt to reopen your account with us or with any of our business associates for that matter.

"Yikes!" Hands shaking, Nième typed her response.

OceanLover365: Thank you for your kind offer,
but I must decline. Have a good day.

Nième shuddered. *Good grief! Nice doing business with you, DorsalFin.*

She did a screen capture of only the last three chat entries and sent it to the printer before she logged out of the chat room. She grabbed the printout as soon as it was ready. Then she sat back. Breathed slowly in and out until her heart stopped hammering in her chest.

Eventually, she gathered her things into her book bag. Outside the lab, she stopped at a pay phone. She dialed the number on the card Iris had given her, simultaneously pulling an ordinary letter envelope from her bag.

"Iris Dunwoody's office."

"Hey. I mean hi. This is Adele Logan. Please tell Ms. Dunwoody that I have finished the job for her."

"Thank you, Miss Logan. I'll pass that along."

"Oh. And would you happen to have a forwarding address for Mr. Terrell Dunwoody?"

The receptionist hesitated. "I suppose there's no harm in providing it."

The woman read the address aloud, and Nième copied it onto the envelope. On her way home, she folded the screen grab she'd printed out, put it into the envelope, stuck a stamp on the envelope, and dropped it in the mail.

"Don't say you haven't been warned, Mr. Dunwoody."

CHAPTER 18

AT NINE Monday morning, Niève pushed through the double doors of Iris's office building and strode up to the lobby desk. "Excuse me."

The female attendant smiled brightly. "Ah. Miss Logan, is it?"

"Yah."

"Go right up. Ms. Dunwoody is expecting you."

Niève huffed, put out that she couldn't simply pick up her reference letter and be on her way. Hissing under her breath, she got in the elevator and pushed the button for the second floor.

Iris was waiting for her when the elevator doors opened. The woman smiled. She seemed happy. Maybe excited? But in her own understated way.

"The attendant called to say you'd arrived."

Niève shook her head. Iris might be happy, but Niève was not.

"*Duh*. Is that my reference? I was supposed to pick it up downstairs." Niève was still riled up.

Irene passed her a flat manila envelope. "Yes. Here it is."

"Thanks."

Niève pushed the button to recall the elevator. Iris, smiling enigmatically, waited with her until the elevator arrived. Then she got on with Niève, effectively blocking Niève's access to the elevator buttons.

"I'll just ride down with you, shall I?"

Only she didn't push the down button. She pushed the third-floor button.

Niève was not in the mood. "Hey! What gives?"

Iris tipped her head. "Do you know what a patron is, Miss Logan?"

"What, like an art patron?"

"Yes, like that. A patron is someone who recognizes talent, artistic or otherwise, and chooses to invest in that individual so that they might grow and achieve mastery of their talent."

The elevator finished its short climb to the third floor and opened. Iris led the way. Nière, with reluctance, slouched down the hallway behind her. They passed the offices of an insurance company and a financial planning group.

At the end of the hallway a door stood open. Iris paused at the open doorway. She gestured to the glass window beside the doorway.

There, in black and gold lettering, Nième read

PROTECT MY NETWORK
Expert Computer Security

Nième was in such shock that she didn't object when Iris took her by the hand and led her inside. Nième saw that the small office held a desk, a desk chair, and two upholstered chairs for clients facing the desk. She noticed a tasteful credenza behind the desk and against the back wall. A glossy red and black pot holding a trailing philodendron sat on one end of the credenza; a fax machine sat on the other end.

Iris tugged Nième to the chair behind the desk. "Sit."

Nième sat. The chair bounced a little. It was exactly like the chairs around the table in Iris's office.

"Huh."

A phone sat on the desk to her right; two baskets for paperwork were on her left.

Nième couldn't breathe.

Iris opened the desk drawer on Nième's right. She removed a small box and withdrew a single business card. Placed it before Nième.

Nième read it.

PROTECT MY NETWORK
Expert Computer Security

The card listed a phone number, a fax number, and the address of Iris's office building, Suite 312. It did not, however, display Adele Logan's name.

When Nième started breathing again, she realized Iris had taken one of the chairs in front of Nième's desk and was waiting for a response.

When one did not come, Iris whispered, "Adele? Miss Logan?"

"Yah." Nième's eyes stung. She blinked, but they continued to sting. And water.

"I believe I understand where you're coming from, Adele—if Adele is your real name. May I tell you what I think? You don't have to reply or answer any questions. Just listen, please. Can you do that?"

"Suppose."

"You've convinced me that you are a brilliant young woman, but I don't think you've had a warm, loving family life growing up. Certainly, wherever you live at present, they do not 'get' you, do they? Don't realize the gift you have. Haven't a clue, I imagine."

Nièvev's brow creased a little. She swiped at a droplet that plopped onto the desk's gleaming surface.

Iris took a deep breath. "And, I imagine, too, that you are probably not yet sixteen, which makes many of the adult steps you are reaching for somewhat *tricky*. A bit beyond you but not impossible. Steps like applying for a business license and opening a business bank account, particularly with a check whose amount might draw too much attention to you.

"That hasn't stopped you, though, and I have confidence that you'll reach your goals, but I thought—I hoped—that, perhaps, you might allow me to give you a leg up."

Nièvev fidgeted. Put her eyes anywhere but on Iris. "What . . . do you mean?"

"What I mean is that the rent on this office and its furnishings, the phone, fax, network connection—everything you see here? This is all payment in lieu of a check for the invaluable services you have rendered me. I didn't provide a computer though. I assumed you had your own, one that met your, er, rigorous specifications."

She slid another envelope toward Nièvev. "You'll need money to fund your business until you've established yourself and have enough clients to pay your way. In particular, you'll want to upgrade your wardrobe. That said, you don't need to dress like me—I can see that you are developing your own style, a 'look' that suits the type of work you do.

"Even so, I recommend that, whatever your style, you choose high-quality clothing. Clean lines and in excellent condition. Clothing that reflects the quality of service you intend to deliver. The right wardrobe will instill confidence in your prospective clients."

Iris tapped the envelope. "Since you desire to keep a low profile, I'm giving you $5,000 in twenty-dollar banknotes as down payment for services I will commission from you going forward. All my stores and our offices within this building need the network security you can provide."

Nièvev's fists were clenched so tight that when another drop landed on the desk, she used her elbow to sponge it up.

"I probably don't need to tell you not to carry all of this cash around on your person; you need somewhere secure to keep the majority of it. Should you not have such a place, you'll find that I had a small floor safe installed in one of the cupboards in the credenza behind you."

The infernal dribbling from Nièvev's eyes just *would not quit!* No matter how hard she clenched her hands, the drops kept right on coming.

"I should also let you know . . . Adele, that I've spoken to my friends, other business women here in Regina. We're a close bunch. I hope they will be calling you to schedule your network security assessments. And may I offer just one piece of advice concerning your first meeting with a potential client? Try not to set the customer's hair on fire before they get to know you and your stellar abilities. You don't want to alienate these influential individuals before they have learned to trust you, do you?"

Nième, her head now bowed, shook her head slowly back and forth.

"Good. I'm glad you understand. Finally, if you ever need advice or just . . . conversation, please come to me. I wish to be your patron, Adele. I recognize your talent, and I choose this day to invest in you so that you might grow and mature into the brilliant woman whose shape and form I see emerging from deep within you."

Nième couldn't meet Iris's knowing gaze; she was completely undone. Her body trembled, and black mascara and eye liner streaked the wet puddle on the desk between her clenched fists.

Iris leaned across the desk and gave Nième's shoulder a gentle squeeze. "I'll leave you to it now, Adele, but it's going to be all right.

"I'm praying for you."

———◆———

NIÈVE TOOK A city bus to her office the next day. She sat at her desk in a chair she *loved* and checked her phone for new messages. None so far. After an hour, she locked her office door and walked over to Victoria Avenue, then the eight blocks down to Regina City Hall.

After she'd stood in line for twenty minutes, it was her turn to approach the window where business licenses were dispensed.

"I'd like a business license, please."

"Fill out this paperwork and bring it back to me."

Nième smiled inside as she completed the paperwork. *I have an office and an address. Even a phone number. As soon as I have my business license in hand, I'll be able to open a business checking account—and this time I won't need an adult to cosign with me.*

She took the completed forms to the window.

"I'll need your identification now," the clerk said.

Nième handed over Adele Logan's driver's license.

The woman typed away, returned the driver's license, then went to a nearby printer and pulled a sheet of paper from it.

"Here is your temporary business license. It must be prominently displayed where you conduct your business until the permanent license arrives in the mail. You may then tear up the temporary license and replace it with the permanent one. Your fee is $10."

On the way back to her office, Niève made a detour and went into Scotiabank. Half an hour later, she walked out, having opened a checking account for Protect My Network and deposited $200 in cash.

I'll make a modest deposit every week whether I have clients or not, she decided, *so that it looks like my business is growing.*

Back in her office, she again checked for phone messages—none—then used thumb tacks to post her temporary business license on the wall closest to her desk. With nothing better to do, she caught the next bus to the university, and spent the remainder of the day in the computer lab.

First thing after logging on, she checked her symbolics.com email account. So far, no messages had landed in her inbox—and that was fine with her. She'd set up the account strictly as an alert system.

How many banks have Azteca, Syntax, and I hit at this point? A hundred? Eventually, one of the banks will figure out they've been hacked and robbed and report it to the police. Given enough of those reports, the police will hire someone smart enough to go looking for our hack, but dumb enough to trip one of my alarms.

What if they do fall into one of my traps? What then? We left nothing on the banks' networks that ties us to those ops, nothing that could lead the police to us. We'd have to be caught in the act for the police to identify us.

She frowned. Something tingled at the back of her mind, but she couldn't put her finger on it.

Niève spent the rest of her day in the lab on her latest project—research her fledgling business would benefit from. Slowly and systematically, she searched for computer companies that sold computer security code, scribbling what amounted to a hit list.

One by one, I'll hack these companies and their code. I'll study their methodologies, identify and exploit their vulnerabilities, and design a means to defeat every security measure in use, she told herself.

I'll build myself a library of code—programs customized to circumvent every security measure out there. And thanks to the "traps" I leave behind, I'll know if anyone spots my incursion.

She snickered. *A **library** of code? I'm going to need more disks.*

Staring at her screen, she sighed. *This process would go faster on a better machine. Can't believe how great I thought this lab was when I started using it. Azteca's computers have totally spoiled me. What I really need is a machine of my own. In my office.*

When the idea hit, it hit her hard.

Well, duh.

—●—

WEDNESDAY, NIÈVE repeated her previous morning. She took a bus to her office, sat down at her desk, checked for messages—

The light on her phone was blinking.

Heart pounding, Nième retrieved the message and listened.

"Good day. This is Suzanne Parsifal, administrative assistant to Noreen Oliver of Oliver Catering. We are interested in scheduling a—" Nième heard the rustling of paper. "—a network security assessment. Please return my call at your earliest convenience. Thank you."

Nième jotted down the number with trembling fingers. She took a moment to compose herself, then dialed the phone.

"Suzanne Parsifal speaking."

"Good morning. This is Adele Logan of Protect My Network returning your call regarding a network security assessment."

"Ah, yes. Thank you for calling back. Mrs. Oliver would like to schedule the assessment. What would that entail and at what cost?"

Nième described the process and quoted her the fee for the assessment. "This is a special introductory rate, Ms. Parsifal.

"Once the assessment is complete, I will meet with Mrs. Oliver to deliver my findings and recommendations."

"Very good. When can we expect you?"

Nième wanted to tell the woman that she would be conducting the assessment remotely, but before she could open her mouth, Iris's advice popped up.

And may I offer just one piece of advice concerning your first meeting with a potential client? Try not to set the customer's hair on fire before they get to know you and your stellar abilities. You don't want to alienate these influential individuals before they have learned to trust you, do you?

On top of Iris's advice, the memory of waylaying the woman outside her offices followed, as did their initial and contentious conversation.

*So you're a **hacker**.*

The derision dripping from Iris's mouth had been palpable. Even now, Nième shifted with discomfort. Her first meeting with Iris had come within a hairsbreadth of disaster.

You don't want to alienate these influential individuals before they have learned to trust you, do you?

"Proposing a remote assessment might do just that."

From inside her phone Nième heard, "Pardon me?"

"Oh. Sorry; I was interrupted. Would tomorrow morning work for you? The assessment will take two to three hours. During that time, I will need to use one of your company's computers with access to your network."

"We'll set up a computer in an empty office, and I'll make arrangements to get you a login. We don't have IT employees; we use an off-site IT contractor."

Niève had a sudden and prescient vision of Ms. Parsifal telling her IT contractor organization that a *different* contractor would be performing a network security assessment on *their work*. The IT contractor organization would balk and issue a stern caution against the idea simply to protect its turf.

She put all the confidence she possessed into her reply.

"Please don't go to the trouble. I won't require a login to do the assessment."

"You won't?"

"No, ma'am. Any computer connected to your network will suit my needs. I will also require a printer. You may expect me tomorrow at 9:00 a.m."

"Very good. We shall see you then."

———◆———

WITH HER first client appointment looming and Iris's words on *wardrobe* ringing in her ears, Niève had no choice but to "bite the bullet," so to speak. She pulled $300 from her floor safe and caught a bus to Cornwall Centre, Regina's relatively new shopping mall. Niève dreaded the wasted hours ahead but, according to Iris, it had to be done.

As wasted as those hours were, they were also eye-opening.

Niève had never been shopping for new clothes. When the kids in the Northams' house needed something, Maude took them to the Salvation Army's thrift store. So, the selection Niève found within the confines of the mall—the sheer volume, color, textures, and styles on display—left her breathless and jittery.

At the same time, wherever she looked, nothing suited her. She felt like she was browsing in Iris's closet.

I can't wear this stuff, she grumped. *Not my style.*

But wasn't that what Iris had said? *You'll want to upgrade your wardrobe. You don't need to dress like me—I can see that you are developing your own style, a 'look' that works for the type of work you do.*

Niève frowned. "My own style? For the type of work I do?"

Maybe she meant my hair and makeup.

An image of Tozi, elegant and edgy, rose before her—and not just Tozi. Her entire salon. Her employees *and* her customers.

Niève found a pay phone and fed coins into it. Dialed the number of Tozi's salon. "This is, er, Genie. Is Tozi there?"

"No, sorry, Genie. Wednesday is her day off. Perhaps I can help you?"

"I—" Niève felt stymied. Thwarted. Verging on angry. She swore under her breath, repurposing one of Maude's preferred curse words.

"Hello? Genie?"

Through gritted teeth, Nième answered, "Yah. Sorry about that. I was wondering . . . where Tozi shops? For clothes, I mean."

"Oh, sure. I can help with that—but it's more than one place. At least a dozen shops, but I'm familiar with only six or so. Do you have something to write with?"

"Yah." It was easier for Nième to say yes than to say, "No; I'll remember half a dozen places and their addresses without even trying."

Tozi's clerk listed off the shops and their addresses, each one boasting a unique name like *Vintage Exchange, Alice's Secret Closet, Moroccan Mystique,* and *Black Velvet.* The longer Nième's mental list grew, the more intrigued she became.

"That's about it," the girl said. "Can't recall the rest."

Nième almost didn't remember to say thank you before she hung up. She sprinted to the bus stop and studied the route map, finding that the shops seemed to be clustered among the cheap eateries, head shops, and used bookstores around the university—and if Nième knew any part of Regina, it was the university.

It's a good thing I have the rest of the day.

An hour later, Nième was swimming in Regina's counter culture . . . and she couldn't get enough of it. She discovered that the shops she sought were small, hip boutiques owned and operated by women—women who looked Nième up and down, took hold of her, loaded her arms with clothing, and sent her into curtained stalls that barely qualified as changing rooms.

Nième didn't care. *I've found my people,* she realized, trying on pants, skirts, and blousy tops, loving what she saw reflected in old, often cracked mirrors. But before she made any purchase, she ran it through Iris's criteria.

I recommend that, whatever your style, you choose high-quality clothing. Clean lines and in excellent condition. Clothing that reflects the quality of service you intend to deliver. The right wardrobe will instill confidence in your prospective clients.

She piled her selections on chipped and scarred countertops, and the shop owners wagged their heads in approval. "Girl, you have good taste."

When Nième caught her bus home, she wore a sleek new outfit and was loaded with shopping bags. The shop owners' words were ringing a bell in her heart. *Girl, you have good taste.*

"I have good taste?" she whispered, wanting to believe them but not quite getting there.

Two young men farther ahead on the bus turned to ogle her.

Huh, she told herself, *Maybe I do have good taste.*

———•———

OLIVER CATERING'S network assessment was eye-opening and required more time than Nième had anticipated; the debrief afterward took a solid hour. As for the initial client interaction, Nième felt it went about as well as could be expected—all things considered.

Ms. Parsifal escorted Nième into a meeting room where Mrs. Oliver and her junior partner, Joseph Mayfield, waited. The two of them examined Nième in much the same way Iris had at their first encounter. She could almost hear their unspoken misgivings.

How could Iris Dunwoody have recommended this girl? Why, she's barely out of high school . . . and that hair? The overdone eyeliner? That look?

Despite their shocked expressions, Nième knew she cut an impressive figure. She wore a tailored black leather jacket that showed off her tiny waist, and she had loosely twined a silky teal and gray scarf around her neck to provide the perfect pop of color, accentuating the same touch of color in her hair. Black pants and boots completed her chic ensemble.

She also didn't give them an opportunity to express their discomfort.

Don't act like Brie; act like Iris. Iris is just another role, so play it out! Take control of the meeting, and walk them slowly through the assessment, delivering the results one digestible bite at a time—particularly the bad news.

And whatever you do, don't give them time or opportunity to freak out.

"Mrs. Oliver, Mr. Mayfield, good morning. I'm Adele Logan, owner of Protect My Network. Thank you for allowing me to perform a security assessment on Oliver Catering's computer network. As I'm certain you already know, a large part of your business' success depends upon its unique services. That makes the privacy of your network and its information vital to your continued profitability. I'm happy to report that, with one exception, your network is secure."

She hadn't realized how tense Noreen Oliver was until the woman's features began to let down.

"I'm relieved to hear that, Ms. Logan." Then Ms. Oliver's brows twitched. "But did you say, 'with one exception'? What exception might that be?"

Nième didn't realize how tense *she* was, until a globule of sweat ran down her back. "May I preface my answer with a question or two?"

When Mrs. Oliver nodded, Nième sucked in a deep breath. Success hinged on presenting her findings in exactly the right way.

Nième folded her hands on the table, channeling Iris's voice and mannerisms, casting herself in a relaxed, confident manner. "Mrs. Oliver, I imagine that the catering business is competitive. Who might your strongest competitors in Regina be?"

Mayfield laughed uneasily. "I'll field that one, Noreen. Regina Catering is our chief rival. Our only close rival, actually."

"I see. Thank you. Have you also experienced any unexpected trends recently? Trends that have negatively impacted your business?"

The mute exchange between Mayfield and Mrs. Oliver confirmed what Niève already knew. She didn't relish pushing ahead, but she had to.

"Mrs. Oliver, Mr. Mayfield, I've graphed your bookings over the past twelve months." She selected a sheet from the folder in front of her and passed it across the table. "Prior to last quarter, you had been fully booked for the year. However, around three months ago, your reservations began to decline."

Niève saw that the information did not come as a surprise to her clients, so she continued on. "For the past three years, Oliver Catering has been Regina's preferred wedding and event caterer. You were booked every weekend eighteen months ahead of time—again, until three months ago."

Picking up yet another sheet that showed a downward trend in future event reservations, she slid it across the table. "In fact, over the same three-month period, you have experienced an unprecedented number of wedding and event *cancellations*. According to this graph, your bookings going forward eighteen months are down a full twenty percent."

She said nothing more until her clients' attention was fully fixed on her. "Statistically speaking, this is an inexplicable finding, one that requires investigation—because such a downturn must have a cause behind it."

"A cause?"

"Yes, a cause. And I believe that you agree with my statement. I think that over the past three months, you began to suspect that something or someone was behind this decline in your business. You were already wondering if your network had been hacked before you hired me. Those concerns are why you were quick to seize upon Iris Dunwoody's recommendation that I perform a network security assessment."

She paused, then added, "I am glad you did. You see, I, too, found reason to suspect a leak of some kind . . . so I went looking for that leak."

Niève cleared her throat. "Speaking of your competitor, Regina Catering, four months ago they began offering a beef entrée strikingly similar to one of your signature dishes. A month later, they began promoting a new wedding cake. It, too, is nearly identical to *your* special cake recipe, Mrs. Oliver." Niève watched the woman's reaction. "The recipe you inherited from your grandmother, I believe."

She slid a sheet of paper across the table, a printout of a wedding cake recipe.

"This is my cake," Mrs. Oliver whispered, "my grandmother's cake. Where did you get this?"

"I printed it directly from your network where you store it to keep it secure."

She slid a second sheet across the table, alongside the recipe. The second sheet was a copy of an email sent to Regina Catering, containing the same recipe in the same format as the first sheet.

"Do either of you recognize the sender's email address?"

Mayfield flinched. "I do. It belongs to our IT contractor's owner, Bob Billings."

Mrs. Oliver began to tremble. "Miss Logan, are you saying Bob Billings gave my recipe to Regina Catering?"

"Gave it to them? No." Nième passed across yet another sheet. "This is a printout from Regina Catering's accounting program."

"How in the world did you get this?" Mrs. Oliver demanded.

Nième's one-sided smile dripped sardonic humor. "Let's just say I'm demonstrating to you that your competitor needs a network security assessment as much or more than you did."

Mrs. Oliver and her partner gaped at Nième. Respect—and a touch of awe—bloomed over their shocked expressions.

Nième gestured toward the printout. "Note that the highlighted entry shows Billings sold the cake recipe to Regina Catering for $1,000. Of course, that's not all he sold them."

Mrs. Oliver's temper flared. "You don't need to spoon feed me any longer, Miss Logan. Out with it—all of it. Whatever it is? I can handle it."

Nième folded her hands. "I'm glad to hear you say that. The bottom line is that Bob Billings also sold your bookings to your competitor. Regina Catering received your customers' contact information and reservation dates, the detailed event menus they selected, and the price you negotiated with them. Regina Catering then invited *your customers* to visit their showroom and sample the same menu—after which Regina Catering substantially underbid you. Hence your recent cancellations."

She slid her folder across to them, leaving only one sheet of paper on her side of the table. "I have documented their actions, although not all of the documentation was obtained through strictly legal channels. Your attorneys will advise you on how to proceed, what can or cannot be used in court, although I suspect that all of my documentation can be used privately as leverage against Regina Catering.

"As for Bob Billings? We *can* verify that he accessed your recipes and emailed them to an account outside of your company's network—and that, in itself, is theft of intellectual property. But first and foremost? We must secure your network."

"You mean fire Billings and his organization," Mayfield growled.

"I mean *secure* your network. I sat in an office in your building, without a login, and hacked your network myself." Nième chuckled. "And if *I* can hack your network, it is not secure."

She slid the last piece of paper over. "My invoice for today's assessment. If you wish me to strengthen your login processes in a way that will ensure that Bob Billings and his employees cannot breach your network and that will also alert me to attempted intrusions, I have listed that price and the fee for a monthly monitoring subscription that includes security updates as needed."

Mrs. Oliver didn't bother checking the pricing. "We'll take you up on the strengthened login process and monthly monitoring subscription. We'll cut you a check before you leave today."

"Thank you."

Mayfield asked, "Since we're firing Billings' outfit, what do we do about regular IT support? You know, new employee accounts and so on?"

Nième hadn't planned on becoming a company's IT provider, and she wasn't thrilled with the idea. It was dull, unchallenging work. "Protect My Network is a security business only, Mr. Mayfield. That said, I would be happy to, in the coming week or so, recommend someone to you."

Mayfield nodded. "Should we schedule your monthly visits before you leave today?"

"You won't need to do that. I will dial in remotely and send you a report by the tenth of each month."

When Nième stood, Noreen Oliver got up and walked around to her. She held out her hand. "I want to thank you, Miss Logan. I will certainly thank my friend Iris for recommending you. She suggested that if I benefitted from your work, you might appreciate a reference letter? A testimonial?"

"Uh, yah. I mean, yes, please."

"I have your business card and will send the reference letter to your office. Again, thank you. If you don't mind waiting in the lobby a few minutes, Ms. Parsifal will bring your check to you."

Nième left Oliver Catering with a fat check in her pocket. She caught a bus and headed for the university's computer lab. She had email to check and a more secure login process to build for Oliver Catering's network.

Now I just need to locate and recommend a reliable IT contractor for them. Huh. Perhaps this is an opportunity for St. Lawrence Office Supply to branch out. I will mention it to Iris.

CHAPTER 19

FRIDAY EVENING as they prepared to go to work, Azteca made a stunning announcement. "Tonight is our last bank hit."

"You mean our last bank op for now, right?" Syntax asked. "You need time to prep another city?"

"No; I've decided to put the bank ops behind us altogether. I'm cooking up something new that holds the potential for bigger hauls."

Nième sighed with relief. She hoped he had something far safer in mind. The logical side of her brain, however, was not comforted.

We're still way too exposed. As long as I hang around with Azteca and Syntax, I could get swept up with them in a police raid.

I should get out now. Quit Azteca and Syntax altogether.

Instead, she asked, "What are you thinking?"

Azteca shook his head. "I'm not ready to reveal it yet; I have details to hash out. I'll let you in on my idea next Friday. We can brainstorm the fine details at that time."

After they finished the day's op and Azteca handed out their cuts from the previous week's work, she approached him. "Can I talk to you for a sec?" Nième used her chin to gesture toward Syntax. "Alone?"

Azteca glanced to the side. "Hey, Syntax. I need a moment with Jinn. We'll be back in a few."

Nième and Azteca climbed out of the basement and walked outside. Now that it was late November, fall was fully upon them and the air was downright chilly. Nième pulled her sweater tight and wrapped her arms around her middle.

"What's up?" Azteca asked. "Why the secrecy?"

"Not secrecy. Privacy. I prefer to keep my personal business to myself."

"I can understand that, I suppose. What's the deal?"

Niève gathered herself. "I'd like to buy a computer from you."

"That's all? That's what you want to keep private?"

"Yah. I want my own machine, and I like how you build your models." She handed him a slip of paper. "Can you add a couple of specs to a machine you have on hand? I only need the box. I will provide my own monitor, keyboard, and cabling."

Azteca ran his eye down the list. "The hard drive you want is new. Top of the line too. I can get the drive, but I won't lie to you—it will be pricey."

"I figured as much."

He studied her from under his hooded eyelids. "You're moonlighting, aren't you?"

Niève had prepared herself for this question. "If I've found work on the side, that's my affair."

Azteca chuckled. "Right. Gotta say, Jinn, that you're good—very, very good—and you're only getting started. Who am I to hold you back? Sure; I've got everything you asked for except the drive, and I can buy that from a friend. I'll put a machine together for you."

He took a pencil from the workbench and wrote on Niève's list. "This is what it will cost you. My machines don't come cheap."

Niève's mouth curved into a small smile. "You could make a decent living going straight, you know. Build, install, troubleshoot, repair?"

"Nah. Not for me. But I am interested in what you're doing on the side. I doubt you'd be into it if it wasn't paying well."

He waited, giving her opportunity to share, but Niève knew better. She kept her mouth shut even while she answered silently, *Not a chance, Az. Knowing you, you'd sell network security to my clients then turn around and rob them blind.* Not *the way to grow a legal livelihood.*

She said aloud, "When can you have this finished and how would you like to work payment?"

Azteca nodded slowly. "Nice deflection, Jinn. All right; have it your way. Half down before I begin, half on delivery." He laughed. "Guess you'll be returning a chunk of your cut from last week's op, eh? I can deliver the box to your place next week, after we finish brainstorming our new scheme."

Niève pulled out her little cat purse, unsnapped it and removed ten of the one-hundred dollar banknotes Azteca had just paid out to her.

"Here's the half down. I'll pay you the balance next Friday. Oh. And there's no need to deliver the machine to me. I'll take it with me when we've finished our brainstorming session. Would you have it packed up for me?"

Azteca nodded. "Yup. Will do."

190

WEDNESDAY MORNING the next week, a driver from St. Lawrence Office Supply knocked on the jamb of Nième's open doorway. "You Adele Logan?"

"Yah. That's me."

"Got a delivery for you." He grabbed a hand truck loaded with boxes and wheeled it through the doorway. Plopped a smaller box onto her desk. "Your miscellaneous office supplies."

He pointed to the rest of his load. "Where do you want me to put these?"

"Against that wall."

After Nième had signed for the delivery and the man left, she opened the box on her desk. It held pens, pads, more yellow highlighters, hanging file folders and labels, and other desk bric-a-brac. She kept a pen and pad on her desktop, dumped the rest into a drawer, and surveyed her real treasure trove, the boxes stacked against the wall to her right. The boxes contained a computer monitor, keyboard, modem, cutting-edge SCSI document scanner, dot matrix printer, case of continuous feed printer paper, and an erasable wall calendar.

She shivered with excitement. *Two more days. Two days until I have my own computer setup.*

Later that day, a florist knocked on her door jamb. "Adele Logan?"

"Yah."

He set a stunning flowering azalea on the corner of her desk.

Nième swallowed. "Er, wow. That's for me?"

"Uh-yup. And this too." He laid a flat mailer on her desk. "You have a good day."

Nième grinned when she opened the mailer. It contained two items, a beautiful thank you card from Noreen Oliver and a gratifying reference letter from her company. Still smiling, she dropped them both in the file folder she'd labeled Oliver Catering hanging in her bottom desk drawer.

———◆———

NIÈVE WAS surprised when Iris stopped by her office later that day. As she sat in one of Nième's client chairs, a smile tugged at her mouth. "I heard back from Noreen Oliver, and she sang your praises to the heavens. Well done, Adele. Thus far, you are exceeding my expectations, and I'm very pleased."

Nième wasn't comfortable with compliments, admiration, or the emotions they triggered. She had received so little approval in the Northams' home that she wouldn't know how to react if it landed like a twenty-pound weight on her big toe. She fidgeted under Iris's congratulations but knew enough to make an obligatory reply, "Thank you . . . for everything."

Seeing her discomfort, Iris pointed to the azalea. "And is this gorgeous plant from Noreen?"

"Yes, and she sent a thank you card."

"I should think so. She told me what you found. You've probably saved her business, just as you saved mine."

Nième couldn't think of a reply, so she was silent.

"Well, I thought I'd just drop in. See how you're doing." Iris got up to leave. "Oh. And after our last conversation, I recalled another bit of wisdom to share."

"Oh?"

"Intuition. Don't discount your intuition, Adele."

"I'm not sure what you mean."

"Ah. Intuition is that little voice in the back of your head. It may counsel you to take a risk or venture onto a new path. It will even, from time to time, warn you of impending danger. If the same thought comes to you again and again, don't ignore it. Consider it. Perhaps take a step in that direction. See what happens when you do. In my experience, if you learn to listen to your intuition, Adele, it will serve you well."

"Okay."

Half-way out the door, Iris stopped. "One more thing? It's about your, er, habit."

"My habit?"

"That gum you chew."

"Oh?"

"Yes. You may, in future, wish to abstain from chewing it before and during your client meetings. As it turns out, black teeth and tongue are not as universally appealing as is commonly believed."

Iris had delivered the line with perfect aplomb, and Nième snarked under her breath. "Okay. I get it, Iris."

⸺⬦⸺

BY FRIDAY, Nième's phone had rung multiple times. Her newly hung wall calendar had three appointments for network security assessments scrawled on it, and she had a modest deposit to her business account waiting in the floor safe. But this evening?

This evening I get my new computer from Azteca. It was also the Friday Azteca had promised he would reveal his new money-making scheme. Nième wasn't nearly as elated about the new op as she was to take ownership of her computer.

But I am super glad to get out from under the bank ops.

She hadn't told Azteca about the traps embedded in the code she'd used to hack the last several banks—traps, which, if tripped would send an email alert to her symbolics.com account. Azteca was still somewhat miffed over her revisions to his code, and she didn't want to further rock the boat.

He thinks I merely modified his code and wants to share credit for my work. He doesn't want to admit that I rewrote ninety percent of his original code and that what I added to it quadrupled the file size. I think he's worried that my skills have exceeded his . . . and, well, they may have.

At the moment, she was grateful that Azteca was pulling them out of the bank ops.

Surely whatever new plan he's come up with will be miles safer than scamming half the banks in Canada. "Half the banks in Canada" may have been blatant hyperbole, but Nième didn't care. To her way of thinking, the bank ops were synonymous with walls and bars closing in—and she wanted no more of that.

She left her office early enough to meet Syntax at the library and catch a ride with him to Azteca's place. As she walked down to his basement computer setup, she scanned the room for her machine.

That has to be it, she thought when she spied a sealed box on the workbench.

Azteca paid them out for last week's final bank op. Then Syntax and Nième settled into their chairs to listen as Azteca outlined his new plan.

"I want you to know that I have been very selective of our marks. They must be married men, not too prosperous, but each one well able to 'donate' the amount we decide upon. As before, if we don't get greedy, if we keep our demands reasonable, I believe we can keep this op rolling for months, or even longer."

He grinned. "What we have to determine is how much each man will pay to prevent his wife from finding out about his dirty little proclivities."

Nième was surprised. "Dirty little proclivities?"

"Ah, yes! You see, these men like *porn*," Azteca answered, waggling his brows. "I mean, who doesn't? But rather than buy magazines from under the counter, these men like the hard stuff, and they frequent establishments where they can pay to view it. You're thinking, *so what? Right?*"

Nope. That's not what I'm thinking, Nième said to herself.

"Well, here's where we catch them. See, these same guys also get off on discussing what they like. They join exclusive online chat forums to talk about it—and that's their big gaffe.

"I've selected our first marks from two of these forums. They are men who live in or around Regina and who can afford the penalty we will impose upon them."

"What has this to do with computers?" Nième demanded. She was already disgusted with Azteca's idea and particularly unenthused by a plan that wouldn't enhance her skills.

"Wait for it. After we photograph the mark entering and leaving peep shows and brothels and after we print out screen shots of their posts on the forums or chat rooms, we'll mail the photos and printouts to him and include instructions for where, when, and how much to deliver to the place we specify. Our warning, our very real threat, is that we send a duplicate package of photos to his wife at her place of work. Easiest cash we've ever scored!"

Nième hated the entire thing, and Azteca's warped enthusiasm appalled her.

Syntax, though, was focused on the money. "How much will we demand?"

"Like I said, we'll base our monetary demand off the balance in the mark's bank accounts," Azteca replied, "but we'll never pick a mark who can't readily put his hands on $30,000. Split three ways—forty percent for me and thirty percent each for you two—you'll each walk away with no less than $9,000 per op."

Nième was as stunned as Syntax.

Nine thousand dollars per op? Minimum?

Avarice twisted Azteca's grin. "I have already prescreened our first four marks, meaning I've hacked their banks and checked their balances—but that's not all. Are you ready for this? We're going to hit all four of them during the same two-week period."

"At the same time?" Syntax echoed.

"Yes, and get this: Three of the marks are worth more than $30,000. We're going to lift a total of $170,000 from the four of them. That's $51,000 a piece for you two."

Syntax's excitement was palpable, while Nième fought the urge to get up and leave. Simply walk away right then.

I need to hang here until the end of our meeting so I can pay Azteca for my computer and take it with me.

He went on. "Four marks in two weeks. That's the plan. We'll refine our methods throughout the op, then move on to the next set of marks." He nodded to Nième. "That's where you come in, Jinn. Going forward, Syntax and I will haunt the porn boards and provide us with a list of possible marks. You'll be in charge of refining the list by hacking their bank accounts to determine how much ready cash they have."

He waved a hand at them both. "What do you two think?"

"This is a brilliant plan, Az," Syntax enthused. Nième shivered and didn't answer.

"Thanks, dude. Now, four marks in two weeks might seem like a lot to manage, but with three of us keeping an eye on them, we can do it. Keep after them until they pay. What do you say? Are you with me on this?"

Syntax nodded. "Absolutely."

Inside, Nième replied, *Absolutely not.*

A sudden roar of relief rolled across her shoulders loosening a tightness she hadn't appreciated was there. *Wow. Now I know I should have gotten out sooner. Iris is right; I need to listen more closely to my intuition.*

"No," Nième said aloud. "I don't like it."

Azteca frowned. "What's not to like?"

"It's super dangerous for starts, and it's-it's-it's, well, it's *gross*. Sorry, but I'm . . . out."

"What do you mean, *out?*"

"I mean it's been fun and all, but I hate this op. You do know, don't you, that blackmail is a lot more serious than lifting a few thousand dollars from a bank? You get caught at blackmail, you'll do time in prison—or worse. I want no part of that, so I guess I quit."

"You *guess?*" Through clenched teeth, Azteca growled, "I've put a lot of time and effort into this plan. I've invested a lot of time and effort in *you*."

Niève shrugged. "You don't need me for this op, Az. There's no real hacking involved. You and Syntax can handle everything, and your profit will be higher split two ways instead of three."

Syntax nodded thoughtfully. "Yah, you know what? I think she's right, Az. We don't need her for this op. More moolah for us."

Azteca just stared at Niève, his jaw working.

Niève shivered again but for a different reason. "Yes, it means more money for the two of you but listen. *Please* listen. Computer security is evolving. I know because I've been studying all the latest security code. Soon banks will be trickier to hack—even just to check someone's balance—and the police will be catching on too. And like I said? Blackmail is a serious crime. Please watch yourselves. Be careful."

"Don't worry about us," Azteca said, his manner cool, his voice frosty.

"Okay. *Fine*. In any event, I need to get going. No hard feelings?"

"Not from me," Syntax replied. "You, Az?"

"Not a problem. Not at all."

Not entirely convinced, Syntax looked from Niève to Azteca, and back to Niève. "Uh, you said you needed to go, Jinn? Need me to drop you at the university?"

"Thanks, but actually, I have something else I need to do, so I have a cab coming to pick me up. And . . . I need a moment with Azteca."

Syntax stood. "No worries. I gotta jet anyway. Best of luck, Jinn. Been good working with you."

"Yah, you too, Syntax. See you around."

As soon as Syntax left, Azteca said casually, "You know, Jinn, there's no need for you to spring for a cab. I'd be happy to drive you home. Maybe we could catch some dinner? I could help you with your setup?"

They had been alone only once before, just the two of them, when Azteca gave her a private lesson in hacking the banks. She'd gently but firmly let him down then when he'd made a move. Regardless of her rebuff,

Azteca had continued to drop hints over the past months, subtly signaling his interest in her.

And considering how displeased he'd been only minutes ago when she quit his new op, Nième was surprised at this more overt overture, asking herself why he was making nice with her.

Azteca's hiding his anger, but why?

Then it came to her. *He's making nice because he wants to horn in on what he calls my "side gig." Little would he appreciate that I've gone about as straight as I can manage.*

She cleared her throat. "Thanks for the offer, Az, but I've got it handled." She counted out ten hundred-dollar bills. "Payment in full. Thanks—and I'll see you around."

Azteca sneered at her. "Sure thing, Jinn. That's your machine on the bench. Enjoy."

Nième grabbed the box and headed up the stairs, feeling the weight of the box on her arms and the heat of Azteca's molten glare on her back with every step. When the cab arrived, she was relieved to put the box in the cab's trunk and get moving. Twenty minutes later, the cab stopped at Nième's office building.

She spoke to the cabby. "There's an extra ten on top of your fare if you wait for me."

"Sure, but don't be too long," he said. "The meter is still running."

By the time Nième had lugged the box into the elevator and down the hall to her office, she knew full well she needed to turn right around and head for home. The cabby was waiting for her. The Northams expected her for dinner. She could unbox and set up her computer in the morning. She glanced at the phone on her desk.

I don't want to wait.

She ran back to the cab, gave him his fare and the promised ten and sent him on his way, then raced back upstairs. She picked up her phone and called the Northams' number. Albert answered.

"Albert, this is Nième."

"Oh? Where are you calling from, Nième?"

Nième ignored the question. "I'm calling to say I won't be home for dinner."

Silence. Then, "Maude won't like that, Nième. What am I supposed to tell her?"

"Tell her I'm working late."

Albert sucked in a breath. "Guess that'll have to do, but it'll grow dark outside soon. Are you being careful?"

"Of course I am. I'll be home by nine o'clock."

She hung up before he said anything further, and the sight of unopened boxes put Albert and Maude straight out of her mind. Grabbing a pair of scissors, she sliced through the tape keeping each box closed. Soon she was engrossed in the pleasure of configuring her own computer setup.

When she had placed the machine and its peripherals where she wanted them and had made all the connections, she powered them up. After the boot, she ran a diagnostic, then checked to ensure the computer recognized the printer, fax machine, and scanner. The printer's test page printed correctly, but for some reason, her computer didn't "see" the scanner. After fussing with the scanner's SCSI connector for forty minutes, trying repeatedly to establish a connection between the scanner and her computer, she decided that the scanner's SCSI cable was defective.

"Great. Need to return it for a replacement."

Everything else was working, but she hadn't yet connected the modem line to her computer. Niève glanced at the clock.

Already 8:10? Crud! I'll have to grab another cab and will still barely make it home by 9:00.

She wanted in the worst way to jump online, but she knew if she sat down to browse her favorite chat rooms for even a moment, she would be there all night. Besides, her eyes were growing heavy. It had been an eventful week.

"Good thing I called earlier to say I'd be late this evening."

She hadn't considered that, with a single phone call from her office, she had broken one of her own inviolate rules. *Keep the lines between all ops clean and separate.*

———◆———

NIÈVE MOUNTED the Northams' porch steps at five minutes to nine—just under the wire. Maude and Albert were waiting for her in the living room when she closed and latched the front door.

"You get yourself in here right now, missy," Maude hissed.

Niève sighed. She was tired and didn't feel like dealing with the Northams, but she had no choice. She joined them in the living room and sat down across from them.

"Exactly where have you been?" Maude demanded.

"I called. I told Albert I was working late."

She cut her gaze toward Albert, but he wouldn't meet her questioning eyes.

"You, working late? Ha! And where, pray tell, were you 'working'? What kind of place would hire a high school kid and expect her to work after dark? Only one kind I can think of!"

Niève had been interacting peer to peer with adults as of late, and she found herself rebelling against Maude's caustic and heavy-handed remarks. As she weighed her options, she unwrapped a stick of gum and—

Maude stood and slapped the gum from Niève's hand, then slapped her face. "Filthy habit! And your nasty clothes and slutty makeup! The only possible 'work' you might be engaged in is out on the street. Am I right? Have you been selling yourself on the street, Jenny?"

Something inside Niève snapped—the last vestiges of childhood restraint and obedience toward this woman who was supposed to have raised her with a modicum of love and tenderness, yet had not.

Niève rose to her full height and stood toe to toe with Maude.

"You, Maude Northam, are a fat, pompous cow. Don't you ever call me Jenny again. You will call me *Niève*." She leaned into Maude's face. "And if you *dare* lay a hand on me again, I'll personally report you to the police. I'll *make certain* that you lose your foster care license."

Albert appeared at her elbow. "Now, Niève, be reasonable," he interposed. "Maudy didn't mean it. She's just distraught."

Niève studied Albert, seeing him with fresh eyes, how he was aging. She saw kindness lurking under the surface—but it was a kindness as much afraid of Maude's temper as the children in their home were afraid of the back side of her scathing tongue.

"Albert, I'm almost sixteen years old. I'm out of here in a few months. What the two of you need to accept is that I'm already a functioning adult— an adult in every way but the legal age requirement."

She took a deep breath. "I'm willing to stay on here until my birthday so you can keep collecting the monthly stipend CPS pays you for me, but I'll only stay *without restraints*. So unless you want me to leave first thing tomorrow, I will come and go as I please and answer to no one. Do you hear me? *No one*."

She started to leave the living room, but Maude wasn't finished.

"Perhaps it's we who should call CPS in the morning. Report you to them *for dropping out of school*."

Surprised, Niève turned around slowly. Somehow or other, the Northams had figured it out—or was Maude just guessing?

"If you make that call, Maude, I'll simply disappear. No one will ever find me."

"Now, Niève." Albert again tried to get between her and Maude.

Niève waved him away. "How much, Maude? How much do you want now? A hundred a month?"

"Make it three hundred."

Maude was shrewd, and Niève realized she shouldn't have put forward a number. The only way for her to retake and maintain control of the 'negotia- tion' was to refuse Maude's demand outright. Thwart her and keep thwarting her. Never give her the upper hand.

"No. I'll go pack my things."

Maude hesitated. "Two seventy-five."

Niève folded her arms. "No."

"Two fifty."

"Two hundred—take it or leave it."

Maude held out her hand. "I'll take it. Right now."

Never give her the upper hand.

"You'll take it on the first of the month or not at all. And if you try to control me? You'll get nothing."

Maude pressed her lips tight while her eyes raked Nième with undisguised contempt. "Fine."

Nième turned on her heel and climbed the stairs. As she did, she caught the soft patter of bare feet on hardwood as they scampered back to their respective rooms.

The littles had listened in on the confrontation between her and Maude.

Good.

———◆———

NIÈVE LEFT the Northams' early Saturday morning while the rest of the house was still sleeping. She buttoned her jacket against the cold wind blowing through Regina. Winter wasn't that far off.

Before she had gone to bed the night before, she had revisited her confrontation with Maude.

I'm glad things are out in the open now, glad I no longer need to follow Maude's rules.

In her eyes, Maude had broken the rules too and didn't deserve to be obeyed.

She has never liked me, has never cared or been kind. Well, I'm as good as an adult now. Maude just doesn't see it. She doesn't know that I have a business and my own income. Even my own computer. A computer just waiting for me to get to it.

A thrill shot down her back. *My own computer!* Then she remembered the concern that had crept into her head before she drifted off to sleep the night before.

By hook or by crook, by any means necessary, Azteca wants in on my side gig. He built my machine . . . and he thinks he's smarter than me.

"We'll see about that."

Forty minutes later, she let herself in the front door of Iris's office building and entered the code to disable the alarm. All was quiet within. No one else was around this early on the weekend, if at all.

In her office, Nième closed and locked the door behind her, then powered on her computer. While she waited for it to finish its boot, she sorted through her stacks of floppy disks. Found the one she was looking for. Inserted the disk in her computer's disk drive and pulled up its content in a programming window.

Niève smiled to herself. "I admit that you're good, Azteca, but you forgot that I am Jinn, fire and air, a shape-shifting spirit. If you've tampered with my machine, I *will* find you out."

Ten minutes later, she found the code Azteca had planted deep within her boot sector. The moment her computer shook hands with her modem, the code would grab her dial-up info and shoot it off to IncanMan@think.com.

"Why, lookie there, Azteca. You have an email account now too."

But Niève hadn't yet connected the modem to her machine.

For the briefest of moments, as she purged his code from her boot sector, she recalled how close she'd come to plugging in the cable the night before. She wondered at her decision to wait until this morning to plug it in . . . and the serendipitous little suspicion that had crept into her mind before she nodded off to sleep.

He built my machine . . . and he thinks he's smarter than me.

Had it been intuition? That vague thing Iris had told her about?

She spoke aloud as if Azteca were in the room. "You were put out when I wouldn't share my side op with you, right, Az? So you inserted code in my machine that would report my location to you. I'll bet you planned to hack me and hijack my side gig—as if you're clever enough to hack *me*. You still don't know that I hacked you weeks ago to get to Bodie."

Angered, Niève took her hands off her keyboard and gave herself over to thought, to a proper response. She'd been the oldest kid in the Northams' group home for a while, so it had been a few years since she'd felt the need to punish anyone for bullying her. Those feelings had lain dormant during those few years, but today they revived. Oh, yes, they were still *very* much alive.

With a nod of decision, Niève sorted through her disks and pulled out one she'd never used, one she'd labeled Pac-Man.

I had no reason to use you . . . until now.

Niève took her time configuring her "message" to Azteca. When she was ready, she plugged the modem cable into the back of her computer. A minute later, she began her hack into Azteca's machine via his dial-up connection. Eventually, she pulled up the contents of the Pac-Man disk, copied the code it contained, and pasted the code into the boot sector of Azteca's machine, the same place Azteca had secreted his code on her machine. Then she installed a screensaver program of her own design on Azteca's computer, a screensaver that included an *homage* to her hacker handle, Jinn. She launched the program and left it running when she withdrew from Azteca's computer.

Niève unwrapped a stick of gum and sniggered aloud, "Back atcha, bud."

———◆———

AZTECA GENERALLY slept late each day, having spent most of the previous night scouring bulletin boards, haunting his favorite chat rooms, and playing video games. Today, he had slept through the morning, not rising until noon.

No matter. He rubbed his hands in gleeful anticipation of today's results and grabbed his first cup of coffee.

She will have logged on by now. The deed is done; I'll check my email and will soon know where she's hiding and what side gig she's into.

Yes, the deed *was* done—sadly, not the deed he expected.

He'd left his computer on all night, and it had gone into sleep mode. He tapped the space bar to wake it up. The monitor sprang to life . . . as did an unfamiliar screen saver.

The caricature of a scantily clad female genie, sitting cross-legged on a flying carpet, bounced lazily from one corner of the screen to another. Each time the genie floated past the center of the screen, she blew Azteca a kiss.

"What the—"

Azteca tapped his space bar repeatedly. Nothing disrupted the screen saver. He pressed Ctrl Alt Delete multiple times, but his computer would not respond.

Frantic and out of options, Azteca pulled the machine's plug, which forced a hard reboot of the machine.

As his computer booted and sprang back to life, the screen saver was gone. In its place was a programming window. Scrolling within the window was code. Following after the code was a rough imitation of a black-and-white Pac-Man character—a chomping Pac-Man in the process of devouring the contents of Azteca's hard drive.

One line at a time.

All of it.

Azteca screamed and cursed, but nothing he did stopped or slowed the process. He yanked the power cord out of the wall yet again, then rebooted, trying to take control of the system prior to the boot.

It wouldn't let him.

Instead, the Pac-Man character continued eating his files. When his files were gone, the Pac-Man went to work on the computer's operating system. Then the programming window vanished, and his monitor went dark.

Azteca howled in impotent rage.

CHAPTER 20

Vyper

1986

JANUARY GAVE way to February, and March blew in with renewed winter weather. As Nième's client list slowly grew, her astonishment grew along with her income. She solved problems that to her were child's play, and her clients paid her invoices without complaint. And she referred the same clients to St. Lawrence Office Supply's newly launched IT service department, earning herself a nice referral fee. What could be better than that?

Nième's expenses were few, so she banked most of what she earned and watched in awe as her balance doubled, then tripled. The money was great, her sense of independence wonderful, but most important to Nième was the growth of her skills and her confidence in them. Having her own computer meant she worked and learned whenever she had a moment to log on.

This is what I was born to do, what I was born to excel at. Maybe not tomorrow, but someday soon, the hacker community will know of me, and the best of them will see me as their equal. I will, at last, have a place where I belong.

Nième should have been happy and content, yet she wasn't entirely. As positive as her life was shaping up, a prescient *something* gnawed continually at the back of her mind. She wondered, *Is this the intuition Iris spoke of? What should I do about it?*

She often tried to focus on what was niggling around inside her but, like an itch she couldn't reach, it proved elusive. The work she did on her computer temporarily distracted her, kept her from finding "The Itch" and scratching it.

Frustrated that morning, she switched off her monitor and gave her full attention to what concerned her.

What is it? What is bothering me?

She rethought her daily routine. In general, it was so mundane that nothing about it could have sparked anxiety. *Get up and dress. Do my chores. Get the littles out the door to school. Leave for school myself, but really come here. Work all day. Go back home. More chores. Help the littles with their home-work. Make sure they bathe and get to bed. Go to bed myself. Do the same the next day.*

She studied her wall calendar and noted with approval the scattering of assessments coming up. But when she looked more closely at April, she was shocked to realize that her birthday was less than eight weeks away.

I'll be sixteen. I'll be free! I can move out of the Northams' house and . . .

And what? Where would I go? Not away from Regina. Not now that I have this business.

But where? Wait—could I . . . could I rent an apartment? My very own place?

She recalled her bank balance and whispered, "Oh, yes, I could. I've heard that landlords want a damage deposit, but that won't be a problem either, and I have Adele's driver's license, so—"

The Itch in her mind sprang to life spouting her mantra.

Never mix ops. Not ever. Never allow an op to bleed over into my real life. Keep the lines between all ops clean and separate. Start every op fresh.

"Is this business a kind of op even though I'm using a fake ID instead of my real name? Or is it an op *because* I'm using a fake ID?"

She thought a moment. "Wait—should I keep *all* the segments of my life separate? Isolated from the other parts?"

A chill crept up her spine, and she didn't like where her thoughts were taking her. "Except for the cash in my safe and the little bit in my savings account at the Northams' bank, all my money is tied to Adele Logan and her ID. That would only be a problem if her ID were blown—but if it were?"

Niève scrubbed her eyes with her fists. *Could the bank ops I did with Azteca and Syntax ever be traced to me? I mean, to Adele Logan? To this office and the business I'm building?*

"What good would the money in Adele's bank account do me if I lost access to the account? If I had to relocate . . . in a hurry."

She squatted by the credenza, spun the dial on her floor safe, and counted out the cash inside. "Seven hundred dollars. Not enough. Adele Logan is not enough, either. I need a backup ID and . . . and I need a plan to jump ship, to retreat to a different life. Just in case."

Never allow an op to bleed over into my real life. Keep the lines between all ops clean and separate. Start every op fresh.

She sat back on her haunches. "Yah, another clean and separate life in case I need to start fresh. Again."

The sense of urgency within her hummed its soft approval.

Nième sat at her desk and picked up her phone to dial a number from memory—and stopped. Cold sweat beaded on her forehead and upper lip as realization hit her. "Every number I dial from this office is recorded in the phone company's usage logs."

She shuddered. *That's what has been bothering me—I blew it! I called the Northams' house and spoke to Albert the evening I brought my computer here. That means the phone company has the Northams' number in* this *phone's usage logs. I need to—*

She scrambled to find a way into the phone company's network. It took her an hour to hack in, only to discover that usage data was backed up onto tape at the end of each month and sent off site to a storage facility.

It had been months since Nième made the ill-advised call from her office to the Northams'. Months since it was backed up onto tape and removed to their storage facility.

She shook her head in denial. "There's no way I can purge that call. No way. But . . . but I doubt the police would ever look at Adele Logan. Why should they? I think I'm safe here."

The Itch disagreed.

That blackmail plan Azteca hatched is worse than stupid. It's foolish. The police will find them out and arrest them. Then they will raid Azteca's house and find all his computers in the basement . . . and tie them to the bank ops.

And if Azteca or Syntax were to get arrested, would they keep quiet about me? No, if baring all would grant them lighter sentences, they'd give me up in a heartbeat.

She shook her head in denial. *So what if they did? They know me only as Jinn.*

As tenuous a possibility as she believed it to be, The Itch continued to pose the same question to her.

Could my relationship with Azteca and Syntax lead the police to Adele Logan?

I don't think so . . . but should the police somehow *trip to Adele Logan's identity and come here? My office phone logs would lead them to the Northams' house. To me. The* real *me. They would hunt me down and arrest me right along with Azteca and Syntax—all because of that one stupid phone call!*

Nième came to an unhappy conclusion. "Adele Logan is a single point of failure teetering on the brink. My entire life hinges on her identity! I cannot afford to risk everything I have on her."

She still couldn't believe her stupidity, using her office phone to call the Northams' home. Her intuition had been bugging her for weeks, telling her she'd messed up, yet she'd ignored its warnings.

One thing is certain. I do not want to lose my freedom. I never again want to be held prisoner by those who scarcely tolerate me, locked up by the rules of those too stupid to understand me.

Dropping her head into her hands, she groaned aloud, "You *idiot!* You've put the life of independence you've worked so hard to achieve in jeopardy."

I no longer need a backup ID for a "just in case" scenario. I need a fresh ID as preparation against the inevitable.

Nième grabbed her bag. She left the building via the stairs next to her office and an exit door on the ground floor. She caught a bus and rode it to the next stop on the line, then located a pay phone.

"Bodie? Yah, it's me. I need an appointment. Same as before. You can? Good. Tuesday morning, nine o'clock? Same price? Okay. Um, how about Montréal, Quebec? Yah. Thanks."

She hung up the phone and muttered, "While I wait for Bodie to make me another ID, I must take steps to diversify my finances."

That afternoon Nième took a cab to the Northams' bank and withdrew five hundred dollars and change, everything in her savings account except the required minimum balance. She couldn't close the account without Albert's signature, so removing most of the funds was her next best move. She took a second cab to Adele's bank and withdrew $2,000. She zipped $500 into an inner pocket of her bag and put the rest in her floor safe.

"Once I have my backup ID, I'll open yet another bank account and start making regular cash deposits to it. Then I'll rent an apartment using that backup ID and pay for it out of *her* bank account. I want to ensure that I always have an emergency stash in my bag and three pots of funds to fall back on at any given time—two bank accounts under separate IDs and the contents of my safe."

Keep the lines between all ops clean and separate.

"Yah. Clean and separate."

In other words, *safe.*

———————◆———————

BODIE PLACED the ID in her hand for inspection. "Eugenie Danté," Nième read aloud, tasting the name for the first time. According to Eugenie's driver's license, she lived in Montréal, as Nième had requested, but the photo was the same as the one on her Adele Logan license.

The Itch returned with a vengeance and brought his pal Anxiety along for the ride.

"You . . . kept the photos you took for my last ID?"

"I don't keep photos, but I do keep the negatives on file. It's convenient when I get a repeat request, such as yours."

The Itch whispered to her, "Bodie has your photo negatives on file. That's not good."

"I'd like to buy all my negatives from you."

He blinked several times. "Well, sure, I guess. I'll . . . I'll get them."

He went into his office and came back with an envelope. "Here you go."

Niève counted out bills for the new driver's license and placed them on his worktable. "How much for the negatives?"

"Nothing; you can take them."

"This is all of them? You don't have any photos or other negatives of me? You're sure?"

"Yah, *I'm sure*. Like I said before, I don't want any trouble. *Sheesh*."

Niève was beginning to know the power she wielded as a first-class hacker. She was beginning to learn the influence of money too—how it opened doors and shut mouths. How it calmed tempers and soothed perceived slights.

With effort, she was able to moderate her tone. "Thank you for your attention to detail, Bodie. You do great work and, um, I appreciate you." She laid an extra fifty on top of the fee for the license.

He brightened. "Hey, no problem. Thanks for the tip."

Niève left Bodie's house by the back door, already feeling better. Less stressed. Before she returned to her office, though, she headed to the closest RBC branch to open an account for Eugenie Danté.

Two hours later, having opened the account with a sizeable deposit, she sat at her desk, a bowl of curried noodles on the side for lunch and the Furnished Apartments to Let section of the classified ads under her gaze.

That afternoon she viewed three apartments, picked one a few blocks from her office, handed over the damage deposit and first month's rent, then signed the lease as Eugenie Danté.

She couldn't move in right away. She had to wait until her birthday so that the Northams didn't report her missing to the CPS who would, in turn, alert the police. At least the place was as ready for her as she was for it.

Niève had completed the tasks pressing on her with the exception of one detail. *Bodie*. She had to ensure that nothing in Bodie's possession connected to her. For a second time, she hacked into his computer, located the file containing his client list, deleted the names of her two aliases from the file, and resaved the file to his computer. Lastly, she saved a copy of Bodie's client list for herself.

Information is power. And I didn't break my agreement with you, Bodie. I left your records intact. Well, mostly intact.

Before she backed out, Niève scoured Bodie's dial-up history looking for anything else that might be of use to her. Her search was rewarded when she hit upon a chat room not of Bodie and his customers, but of Bodie and three others like him.

They were discussing pending upgrades to passports and driver's licenses and how they could incorporate those changes in the documents they produced.

"Oho, Bodie!" she whispered. "These are your pals, aren't they? Your fellow counterfeiters?" She then hacked each of Bodie's compatriots, collecting them and their information like some people pinned butterflies on felt and displayed them in glass cases.

"I won't use Bodie again," she muttered to her collection of counterfeiters. "Later on, when I need new ID documents, I will employ one of you to provide them."

Niève continued to look and listen within herself, but The Itch was quiet. She believed herself safe.

CHAPTER 21

APRIL 1986

"HAPPY BIRTHDAY, Niève," the Northams, accompanied by the littles' sing-song, called across the breakfast table. Albert handed over her birthday card. All birthdays with the Northams meant a card at breakfast signed by everyone in the house and a cake after dinner—a cake so small it afforded each of them only a single slice.

She should know. This was her eleventh birthday with the Northams. They had all been the same. Today, however, would be her last birthday with them.

This birthday meant the end of mandatory public education. Of greater import, it also meant she was no longer a Permanent Ward of Child Services, Saskatchewan.

Not for the first time or even the hundredth time, she thought, *When I am sixteen, by law no one can force me to go back to school. Even if they were to uncover my hack of the school district and if they found out I'd skipped an entire year of school, when I am sixteen, I will be free.*

Today, she added, *I'm finally sixteen. It's time for me to move on.*

She'd put a lot of thought and planning into this step, and it was time to execute her plan. A clean break came first.

She opened the card. It was the same card she'd received two years ago, but it didn't bother her. She knew the Northams shopped discount stores and bought their cards in bulk.

I guess it's the thought that counts.

"Nice. Thank you, everyone," she replied. "And, uh, just a heads up?"

She waited to say more until she had the Northams' attention. The littles sat quietly, sober and hunched down in their chairs. They already knew what was coming; she had gathered them together last evening at bedtime to tell them.

But first? She'd given each of them a gift, something for them to remember her by. She'd wandered a toy store, lost and bemused by the shelves of toys and games unfamiliar to her. She'd settled on books, two books each, all with interesting tales and lots of pictures. Recalling the present Miss Timmons had given her on her twelfth birthday, Nième had paid the store to gift wrap the books.

"We've never had wrapped presents," the kids had declared with wonder. And once they'd torn open the wrapping paper, they obsessed over the books, passing them around, sharing their joy with each other.

Then Nième had ruined the evening by telling them she was leaving.

"I don't want you to be alarmed at breakfast tomorrow morning when I tell Maude and Albert, okay? And no tears."

That hadn't stopped them in the moment. As her news penetrated and they understood what she meant, Nième was unprepared for the sudden gush of sentiment.

Tears. Disbelief. Wails of protestation.

Nième had gritted her teeth. She hated displays of emotion.

"But we don't want you to go," Donny had whimpered. "You're the only one who can talk back to Maude when Albert isn't around! What will do we do when you're gone and she gets mad at us?" And as a unified, blubbery mess, Kit, Mary, Trey, and Donny had sobbed. "Please don't go!" over and over.

Nième had hardened her heart against their pain. "Everyone grows up and moves away. That's just life. You guys are growing up too. Listen, if the four of you stick together, if you gang up on Maude, you can manage her whenever she throws a fit. And if they bring in a younger kid, you will know how to protect whoever it is. Now, suck it up. It's time for bed."

Nième really disliked having to repeat herself, but this morning she had no choice. She had to break the news to Maude and Albert. She didn't expect them to take it lightly, either.

Maude finished buttering her toast. "Yes, Nième? What is it?"

It came out of her in a rush. "I'm moving out today. Done packing. My things are waiting on the front porch. Cab coming for me at eight o'clock."

There. Done. *Whew*.

Maude's mouth swung open. She and Albert looked like they'd been struck by an asteroid.

Sure, Nième had expected shock from the Northams, but only because it meant the end of Nième's two-hundred-dollar payment the first of each month.

And there it was, the reason Maude would pitch a fit.

"You can't be serious!" Maude protested.

"My cab arrives in ten minutes."

"Albert? Albert!" Maude was winding up. Approaching apoplectic.

Albert wasn't angry, though. All Nième saw was regret . . . and a little sadness? "Where will you go, Nième?"

"I'll stay with friends for a while, and I'll work. Maybe take some classes at the uni."

The lies rolled off her tongue like warm oil.

Maude glared at her husband. "Don't just sit there! Do something!" she hissed.

Albert did. He stood up and walked around the table to Nième. Held out his hand. "Nième, you're a good girl, you are, and I'm gonna miss you. Truly."

Nième stared at his hand. She slowly rose to her feet and overcame enough of her "touch" aversion to let him take her hand. "Thank you, Albert. You . . . you have always been fair . . . and kind."

The cracking, bursting dam around her let go and the kids rushed in. Weeping. Clinging. Pressing against her. Nième withstood it as best she could, meting out a couple of awkward pats on their backs or shoulders.

Albert saw her discomfort and after a minute stepped in. "C'mon, kids. That's enough now. Be brave and say your goodbyes."

"Goodbye, Nième," Mary managed. Trey and Kit followed suit. Donny was last.

"Don't want to say goodbye, Nième," he whispered. "I'm trying hard to grow up, honest I am, but it's really hard. Thank you for everything, for the books and for showing us how to be strong. An' thank you for loving us. You're the only one who does."

He pulled away, leaving Nième thunderstruck and, for the first time in years, uncertain of her path forward.

Thank you for loving us? You're the only one who does?

She was astounded. *Is it true? Am I all they have?*

More astounding, *Do I love these kids?*

She couldn't bear it. Didn't want it.

I don't do goodbyes! I can't . . .

She shunted the unfamiliar and alarming feelings aside. That didn't work, so she shoved them down. *Hard.* Down into her chest, then farther down, into her gut.

She was already standing—halfway to the door, so to speak. She picked up her birthday card from the table. "Thank you again for the card," she mumbled, backing up as she spoke, needing to escape.

Their murmurs came back, a mix of "Goodbye, Nième" and "We love you, Nième."

Unexpectedly, with panic in her voice, Mary piped up, "Wait, Nième! What about your birthday cake? If you aren't here for dinner, you won't get any of it!"

What Nième figured Mary was *really* saying was, "Wait, Nième! If you aren't here for dinner, *we* won't get any of it! Maude will keep the cake all to herself."

Nième crooked a smile at Mary. "We can't let that happen, can we? We should have my birthday cake now—what do you think?"

Maude immediately objected, and Nième ran straight over her.

"Albert? May we have my birthday cake now?"

He slowly grinned. "Yes, I think so. Kids? How's about you fetch that cake and some plates, forks, and napkins for us. Everybody, now. Pitch in, okay?"

As the four kids scampered off to the kitchen, Nième nodded once to Maude and once to Albert. "Thank you, Albert."

Maude sneered.

Albert smiled his sad understanding.

Nième slipped away before the children returned.

⸻⬦⸻

NIÈVE SETTLED into her furnished apartment, rejoicing in the novelty of her independence and wondering over her hard-won solitude—alternately reveling in it and despising it. She missed the littles more than she would admit to her-self, so she buried herself in her work.

Buried herself in making money.

She obsessed over the balances in her two bank accounts and in her safe, not for what she could buy with them, but for what those figures represented: her enduring freedom. She kept to the shadows as much as possible, living frugally and carefully, paying cash for anything personal. Whenever The Itch raised its head, she would deliberate until she came up with new and inventive means to stay ahead of any person or any entity that might try to snatch away her freedom. Nième also recognized that she was more likely to lose access to Adele's account than Eugenie's, so throughout the month, she would withdraw random amounts of cash from Adele's account and deposit it into Eugenie's account, leaving only a sparse working balance in Adele's account.

Her frenetic efforts would calm The Itch temporarily, but days later, it would push its way to the front of her mind, tingling and stinging her into further action, pushing her to find new places to hide, new ways to run should she need them urgently.

Feeling driven to provide herself with escape routes under any set of circumstances, Nième hired two of Bodie's fellow counterfeiters to create new identities for her. Those identities included licenses, passports, and credit cards for five separate women who lived in different cities across Canada.

She joined a gym for the sole purpose of possessing a secure locker and paid a year's membership in advance. She stashed a duffle bag in her locker, a bag containing everything she would need (including four thousand dollars in cash) to flee Regina at a moment's notice. She began carrying a thousand dollars in cash in her handbag at all times and hid another two thousand in a coffee can in her apartment freezer.

And, of course, she checked her symbolics.com email religiously, morning and evening, for if she ever received an alert that one of her traps had been sprung? She would not wait for the police to connect the dots and follow them to her door. She would flee sooner rather than later.

To date, the most audacious of her security efforts had been to rent a second apartment as a last-ditch bolt hole should she need it. She kept nothing of personal value to her in that apartment and furnished it with only the minimum necessary for a short stay, including a month's worth of non-perishable food and a thousand dollars in cash. Even that extreme measure had not relieved her anxieties. Nothing did for long.

Slowly, she began to believe, *I'll never be free from this fear until I leave here, until I hide myself in another city or another country and under so many layers of anonymity that no one alive could untangle them.*

Other than her clients and, occasionally, Iris, Nième spoke to no one. She lived most of her waking hours "online," what the hacker community dubbed being dialed up and active online. In user chat rooms and on various bulletin boards, she "met" and became acquainted with others like herself. She ditched Jinn as her cyber persona (lest Azteca or Syntax spot her online and attempt to hack her location) and rebranded herself as Stiletto, a hacker with a small but growing reputation and following.

She never once suspected that The Itch had tangled her in the potent and merciless cords of paranoia.

CHAPTER 22

Vyper

OCTOBER 1986

NIÈVE CHECKED her email account so habitually that she went through the twice-daily motions as a matter of course, mollified that, to date, no messages had ever arrived in her inbox.

Until one did.

She gaped at the unopened email and its one-word subject line that read "Alert." Hands shaking, she navigated to the message and pressed the Enter key to read it. The body of the message contained the word BREACH followed by the name of the bank and the date and time the trap had been sprung. Yesterday, 7:23 p.m.

Blinking stupidly and shaking with fear, Nième let her eyes roam about the little office she'd come to love, knowing that it and the life she'd worked so hard to build for herself were now lost to her.

I have plans in place. I know what I must do.

All she had to do was choose one of those plans and execute it.

First things first. Warn Azteca and Syntax.

Nième stumbled to her office door; she closed and locked it. She returned to her desk and fired off an email to Azteca. Then she called a cab company. "Can you pick me up in thirty minutes?" She gave the dispatcher the address of the office building.

Next, she turned off her computer, disconnected all the cords attached to the machine, and fetched a flattened shipping box from behind her credenza. She folded the bottom of the box, used strong parcel tape to reinforce it, and set it on the floor. She opened a drawer in the credenza, withdrew the padded packing material she stored there, and added a cushion of padded filler to the box's bottom.

She heavily bound her machine in more padding, taped the padding nice and tight, and place the swaddled computer in the box. She then tossed the computer's power cord in after the machine, added filler until the box was as full and snug as she could make it, and taped the box shut.

With her computer ready for the journey ahead, Nième drew a long, shuddering breath. She placed her handbag on her desk, opened the floor safe within the credenza's cupboard, and withdrew the cash and documents she'd accumulated and stored in the safe. She sorted the money and documents and organized them in her handbag.

Done.

Slinging her handbag crosswise over her body, she picked up the box containing her computer and headed for the elevator. She was in the elevator car, ready to push the ground floor button when her finger seemed to, of its own volition, press the button for the second floor.

Iris's office was on the second floor.

Nième left the elevator and walked slowly to Iris's office. It was still relatively early in the day. Nième didn't know if Iris would be behind her desk or already in meetings. She stood uncertainly in the reception area outside Iris's closed office door. Her secretary glanced up.

"Ah. Miss Logan. Were you hoping to see Ms. Dunwoody?"

"Yes. Please. Only take a minute."

The woman looked her over. "Are you all right, Miss Logan?"

"Of course."

"I'll see if she can accommodate your visit."

A minute later, Nième walked into Iris's office; her assistant closed the door after her. Feeling awkward, Nième set her unwieldy box on the floor.

"You wanted to see me, Adele?" Iris's keen eyesight wasn't on Nième. It was on the box. Then she turned her gaze on Nième. "Are you going somewhere?"

Nième wouldn't meet that gaze. "Yes. I . . ."

She didn't know how to say goodbye or what reasons to give. She shook herself and, after a long pause, muttered, "It's something I did a while ago. Before we met. And for a while after."

Iris was no one's fool. "Something illegal?"

Nième jerked her chin once.

"Are you saying the police are looking for you?"

Nième sighed inwardly. That was the crux of her paranoia, wasn't it? "Not yet. Maybe not for a while." She blew out a breath. "But eventually."

Iris got up and came toward Nième. Stood before her, studying Nième's downcast face. "It isn't something you could, with a good lawyer, overcome? Make a clean breast of things? Pay restitution? Perform community service?"

Nième shook her head. She finally looked up. "Iris . . . we robbed banks."

Iris's lips parted; she stepped back as if struck.

Once she'd uttered those words, Nième couldn't seem to stop talking. "We did it with our computers. Skimmed deposits, then took the money. They are, *the banks are*, just now figuring it out."

"And the 'we'? Your, er, accomplices?"

"They . . . they moved on to worse things. I couldn't do those things, didn't want to, so I got out. Because of my business. Because you helped me."

Iris slowly nodded. "Will the police be able to connect your accomplices to these . . . crimes?"

"I think so."

"Will they be able to connect you also?"

Nième shuddered. "I think the others will tell the police about me, but . . ."

"But?"

"They never knew my name or where I lived. Don't know about my business."

Iris looked hopeful. "So the police won't be able to find you?"

Nième again shook her head. "Oh, Iris. I can't take that chance, can I? I can't wait until they come to take me away. I couldn't live penned up . . . *with other people*." She swallowed. "I need to disappear."

Iris licked her lips. Straightened. "Do you have what you need, Adele? A place to go?"

She nodded.

"Do you need money? I can give you some."

For the first time since she'd opened her email, Nième smiled a little. "I have enough, but thank you. Thank you, Iris, for everything." Her expression again crumpled. "I'm sorry I have to leave everything you've given me. I didn't mean to let you down."

"You did not let me down, Adele. When I was in despair, close to losing everything, I prayed to God for help and he sent *you*. I know you will go on to do good and wonderful things, and that is . . . of great worth to me."

Tears shimmered on Iris's lashes. "My only regret is that I cannot help you make this right, that I will not be able to witness you accomplish those marvelous things."

Already anxious and made jumpy by Iris's unexpected emotions, Nième stuttered, "I-I think my taxi is waiting."

Iris nodded and said nothing further. She lifted her arms as if to put them around Nième, but Nième, already teetering on the edge, instinctively stepped back.

"I'm sorry," Iris whispered. "I won't touch you. I understand. I do."

And perhaps she did; Nième didn't know for sure.

How can she understand what I don't understand myself?

"Thank you for everything, Iris. G-goodbye."

NIÈVE HAD the cab driver take her to within a block of her apartment. "Here is good," she said, pointing to the corner. She paid the accumulated fare, then got out and waved a ten-dollar bill under his nose.

"I'm leaving my box with you, so keep the meter running. This ten is in addition to my fare. Park or circle the block. I'll be back in fifteen minutes."

She ran around the corner and up the stairs to her apartment. Once inside, she pulled out a single rolling suitcase. Into it she folded a quick selection of clothes, toiletries, makeup, and shoes until it was full. She added the cash from the coffee can in the freezer, then locked the suitcase. She was back at the corner in under the fifteen minutes she'd promised the cabby.

"Three more stops," Nième told the driver as she handed him the ten. "Another ten-dollar tip for each stop."

The cabby was enthusiastic. "You got it, lady!"

She directed him to Eugenie's bank. "Back in a flash."

She withdrew all but $100 from the account, slipped the cash envelope into her handbag, returned to the cab, and handed the driver his second tip. Repeated the process at Adele's bank.

"Next to last stop." Nième gave the man the address. While they were on the road, she pulled out a scrap of paper and jotted down a note. When they arrived, she ran up a buckled walkway to a modest house and rang the bell. A moment later the door cracked open.

"Jenny? Is that you?"

"Er, yes."

Miss Timmons didn't know her as Niève, but it didn't matter. Around Miss Timmons, Niève would always be Jenny, an abandoned little girl, a Permanent Ward of Child Services.

"Goodness gracious! Do come in, child. Come in and sit down."

Niève stepped inside and took in her surroundings. The living room was small, its furniture clean but worn to the nub. She hovered near a chair and stayed standing. She was already uncomfortable . . . but she had things to say. If she couldn't get them out, perhaps the note would serve.

When Niève continued to stand, Miss Timmons sank onto the sofa and folded her hands together. "I'm delighted to see you, Jenny. In case you did not know it, I retired in June."

Niève, more anxious than she believed she would be, bobbed her chin.

Miss Timmons tilted her head to one side. "You have certainly changed your look, but I think I like it. And I'll bet you can pass as an older girl now, can't you?"

Niève exhaled. Relaxed a little. Was still too nervous to speak.

"I'm curious. How did you find where I lived, Jenny?"

Niève could easily answer that question. "Phone books. I looked you up. They are on computer disks in the library."

"Are they? My, my. What will they think of next? And is that a taxi out by the curb?"

"Yah."

"I presume you are leaving Regina? Launching out on your own, are you?"

Nième nodded.

"I went by the Northams' on your last birthday. I always remember the date, you know, and I had hoped to take you to lunch and talk to you about your future. But Mr. and Mrs. Northam said you'd already gone and they didn't know where. I was . . . heartbroken to have missed you that day."

Miss Timmons waited.

Nième finally said, "I came to say goodbye, Miss Timmons."

"I-I am glad you did, Jenny."

Nième struggled to frame her thoughts—no, her blasted *feelings*. When she found the words, they poured out in a rush. "You have always been nice to me. I remember . . . I remember when you found me. I was very cold that morning. You sat beside me and listened to me. You *heard* me. You even took me to have pancakes. All I wanted."

Miss Timmons bowed her head. "You were a hungry little girl that day."

"And you . . . watched over me . . . while I was a Ward."

Miss Timmons' eyes grew misty. "More than you know, my dear, more than you know. I would have taken you in myself the morning I found you— how I wanted to!—but how could I? Me, an unmarried woman, already in my fifties, needing to make my own living, barely getting by on the salary I earned? You can see for yourself that I don't have much. And I had no one to watch you while I worked, you know, so they would never have allowed me to adopt you, Jenny . . . but I care about you. I always have. Very much."

The single thing Nième yearned to understand leaped from her lips.

"*Why?*"

"Why? Why do I care about you?"

Nième quivered with emotions that terrified her. "Yah."

Miss Timmons stood. Slowly and carefully, she lifted her hands and placed them on Nième's shoulders. "From the first moment I laid eyes on you, little Jenny, Jesus filled my heart with love for you. He asked me to tell you, to show you, how much *he* loves you too."

"I don't believe in Jesus."

One of Miss Timmons' hands rose to caress Nième's cheek. Her touch sent tingling waves through Nième. Set her to trembling. She was barely able to keep from jerking herself away.

"I know you don't believe, sweet girl. Nonetheless, his love is, right now, flowing through my hands and into you. I am *convinced* that one day, one glorious day, you will meet Jesus face to face, and he will be more wonderful than you ever dreamed of."

Nième spoke through numb, quivering lips. "Even if Jesus were real and I met him, I wouldn't know who he is. I-I don't know what he looks like."

Miss Timmons ever so gently stroked Nième's cheek with her thumb. "Oh, you will know him. You'll recognize him by the same love you feel right now."

Nième had no reply.

"Do you know that I pray for you every morning, Jenny? I pray for the Holy Spirit of God Almighty to fill your heart and mind, and I—"

A puzzled expression flitted over Miss Timmons' face, and she broke off. When she began again, she looked deeply into Nième's eyes. "I realize you don't know much about my Jesus, and yet I feel prompted to tell you something important about him. May I do so, Jenny?"

Nième, trembling and wanting this strange and awful discomfort to end, muttered, "Okay."

"Thank you. What I want to say is this: Almighty God is not the god of confusion. When he sends his Holy Spirit to speak to an individual, he will not speak confusion but clarity. The Holy Spirit will prick your conscience over sin, but it is not his way to confuse or agitate. The devil, on the other hand, loves to create confusion and anxiety. The more he can stir the pot and confound the issues, the more likely it is that he can push or prod a person into making foolish and willful, ill-advised decisions—bad decisions with bad outcomes."

Nième's brow furrowed. "Wait. The devil is real?"

"Very real. He hates Jesus with all his being, and because Jesus loves *us*, the devil hates us too. He will do his absolute worst to keep us far from Jesus."

"Is . . . is the Holy Spirit like intuition?"

"No, not really."

"H-how would I know the difference?"

Miss Timmons thought for a moment. "You can apply the criteria I've just described to determine if any voice speaking to you is the Holy Spirit or if it is something else entirely. The Holy Spirit will lead you into peace, not confusion or anxiety. The devil will most certainly lead you into confusion. The Holy Spirit will tell you if something you plan to do is wrong. He will prick your conscience, while the devil will laugh at and belittle your moral scruples. And the Holy Spirit will lead you toward Jesus while the devil will mock Jesus and prod you into sin—and once he has you there, he will pull you deeper and deeper into a life of guilt, condemnation, and regret."

Nième had been distracted as Miss Timmons compared and contrasted the voice of the Holy Spirit with the voice of the devil—and it had happened so quickly that, before she knew it, Miss Timmons' arms had come around Nième and gently pulled her into a tender embrace.

Nième couldn't return the embrace, though, any more than she could have embraced Iris. She just didn't know *how*. Instead, her arms hung like dead weight from her shoulders. But, for a moment, just a brief moment, Nième rested her head on Miss Timmons' shoulder and felt . . . comforted.

When she could stand the physical contact no longer, she pulled back, and Miss Timmons released her.

Nième let something fall from her hand to the sofa cushions. "Goodbye, Miss Timmons."

"Go with God, little Jenny," Miss Timmons whispered.

———●———

NO SOONER had Nième left the house, than Miss Timmons noticed the object on her sofa and slowly picked it up. A note poked out of the side. She released the snap, unfolded the note, and read,

Miss Timmons,

I have always liked the birthday gift you gave me. No one else ever gave me a present. Please take care of him and remember me.

Jenny

A wad of something else inside made a bulge, but whatever it was, it was too thick for the pocket it was stuffed into. Miss Timmons tugged until the wad gave way.

Ten folded one-hundred-dollar bills sprang apart and fluttered to the floor, startling her . . . but it was the worn yet well-loved cat purse Miss Timmons clasped to her breast and wept over.

———●———

NIÈVE DIDN'T remember leaving the house or getting back in the cab. She came to herself when the cheerful cabbie drawled, "Lady, you gonna tell me where to take you next or do I gotta guess this time?"

"Uh . . . bus station."

He held out his hand. Nième stared at it.

"Oh. Yah."

She laid the promised tip in his hand.

The ride to the bus station, southwest of Regina's downtown, was uneventful. Nième spent the drive staring out the window without seeing. She paid the driver, tipped him again, got out, and fetched a luggage cart, setting both the box and her suitcase on it.

She bought a one-way ticket to Vancouver as Astrid Gettings, but she wouldn't be staying in Vancouver. She would spend a night or two in a Vancouver hotel then board a flight to Taiwan.

A clean break, plus I've always wanted to see parts of the Orient. I'll visit, do the tourist thing, then relocate to Europe, Astrid told herself when they called for passengers to board and she settled into her seat. *New name. New city.*

Never look back.

She'd forwarded the alert email to Azteca's email account, and he would recognize it for what it was, what it forebode. The message she'd included had been short and to the point. It was all the warning Azteca or Syntax needed or deserved.

I'm leaving Regina.
You should too.

The message was signed with the figure of a cross-legged female genie formed using ASCII characters. With that email, Azteca, Syntax, and Jinn were gone for good. She would never again use Jinn as her handle or contact Syntax or Azteca, for that matter.

"A new life," she whispered, "as an adult. No one controlling me."

She would continue to learn, just not in the traditional fashion. Better hackers than her had a lot to teach her, out there in cyberspace, and she was ready to dig in and prove herself.

I don't want to be good or merely great. I want to be much more. My next handle should reflect those aspirations. I want to be the best.

I will *be the best.*

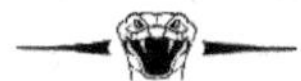

BROADSWORD FINALE

Vyper

CHAPTER 23

SOMETHING WAS up. Something *big*.

Harris returned to Broadsword Monday morning, acting as if nothing were out of the ordinary. But all day long, even while Harris and another Broadsword security guy, Bo, ran her through her PT routine in the gymnasium, the remaining Broadsword employees were hard at work in the yard. Moreover, under Richard and Travis' direction, Broadsword had been a hive of frenetic activity since Sunday afternoon.

The compound rang with shouted orders, the pounding of hammers, and the buzz of electric saws. And whatever they were doing? They were, *literally*, keeping that "whatever" under wraps. Whenever Jaz managed to catch a glimpse outdoors, mounded piles of "stuff" covered by army-green tarps dotted the yard.

"What's going on, Harris?" Jaz demanded.

"Your guess is as good as ours," Harris answered. "Richard sent both of us away Friday afternoon, and we just got back this morning."

"You know as much as we do," Bo added with a shrug.

They sounded truthful, but Jaz wasn't entirely convinced. What she did know was that the activity and noise across Broadsword continued until dusk, which in April is around 7:30 in the evening.

When Harris and Bo weren't pushing Jaz through another round of PT, they pummeled her with endless questions and situations, forcing her to rehearse her cover *ad nauseum*. When they tired of that, they made her practice how she would approach AEA cell members—over and over and over. After that, they ran her through weapons drills.

Jaz was fed up. "If I'm not going to carry a gun during the op, why do I need all this practice?"

"You practice so if you indeed *do* need to use a gun, you won't fumble your response," Bo answered with a cheerful smile.

Jaz wanted to punch him, but she was too tired. "Please. Just let me go upstairs to bed, guys. I'm beat."

"All right, but you'd better take a shower first," Harris observed, leaning in to take a sniff. "You sorta stink—*ow!*"

TUESDAY MORNING while Jaz was eating breakfast, three "security types," two men and a woman she'd never seen at Broadsword, drove up to the lodge and reported to Richard. Since Jaz was sitting at the kitchen breakfast bar, Richard made introductions.

"Miss Walken, meet Devo, Nan, and Bixby. They are contractors well known to us. We bring in trusted operators such as them whenever we have events requiring extra security or when we experience a guard shortage due to vacations, injuries, or extended illness."

Jaz looked them over. "Hey."

They stared back impassively. The three of them offered not a single response.

As if he hadn't noticed the precipitous chill in the air, Richard continued, "Miss Walken, starting today, we'll be engaging you in active training scenarios. These fine people will be assisting in those exercises."

Jaz slowly nodded, her attention on the newcomers. They stared back at her with something like defiance . . . or were they taunting her?

Active training scenarios, Richard? Why am I getting a bad feeling here?

Jaz felt her attitude shifting from polite ambivalence to keen loathing.

Richard, busy with a batch of muffins, gestured the three contractors toward the lodge's rear door in the kitchen. "You know the way to the gymnasium. Travis is awaiting you there and will get you squared away."

The three contractors moved toward the door. Not one of them had spoken a word, but Nan, last to reach the door, turned toward Jaz. She slid something bright blue out of her vest pocket, a color more than a little familiar to Jaz. With her mocking eyes fixed on Jaz, she unwrapped a dark stick of gum and, with agonizing slowness, slid it between her smirking lips. After she had chewed the gum a few seconds, she smiled—and blew a dark-gray bubble.

At the last possible second, her right hand signed a phrase, and Jaz felt her heart jump in her chest.

Best of luck, loser?

Is that supposed to be some kind of warning or a taunt? But how did that tease know that I read American Sign Language or that I like Black Jack?

"What's this all about, Richard?"

"It's about your final spate of training, Miss Walken. Travis and I are teaming you up with Harris and Bo."

"Teaming us up?"

"Perhaps I misspoke. Please consider them your tribe rather than your team."

Jaz guffawed. "My tribe for what, badminton? Tribal croquet, perhaps?"

"More like tribal war games, Miss Walken. Survivor style."

Jaz didn't watch TV, so she didn't snap to the oblique Survivor reference. On the other hand, it did begin to dawn on her that "war games" just *might* require an opposing force—OPFOR, the military called it.

"Wait—what? War games against those contractors? No way! I can't go up against them! That's not fair!"

"Indeed."

"But—"

Harris and Bo surged into the kitchen via the back door. They wore full range gear and yellow bandanas knotted loosely around their necks.

Harris spoke. "You about done lollygagging, Darcy? We've got a long day ahead of us, and our tribe needs to strategize. But first? You need to run up to your room and grab your range gear. Don't bother changing; just grab your stuff and get back here pronto. *Hurry!*"

Jaz stared at the pile of scrambled eggs she'd been forking around on her plate until they were cold and mealy. The eggs, as unappealing as they were, abruptly took on an indispensable quality. *Calories. Protein. Energy.*

"Hold up." She shoveled the eggs into her mouth, swallowing as fast as she could manage without choking.

Her cheeks were bulging with that last bite when Harris and Bo dragged her off her stool and pushed her toward the stairs. She took the stairs two at a time and burst into her room. She yanked her range gear from her dresser and grabbed up her range shoes.

Before she turned to leave, she reached her hand into her purse and snagged something else. It was an act of impulse on her part, but she felt somewhat reassured when she tucked the object between her folded shirt and khakis.

When she hit the ground floor, Harris took her arm and pulled her out the front door. "Let's go!" he shouted, releasing her arm. He and Bo jumped off the porch and jogged diagonally across the yard toward the far left corner of the perimeter where some sort of bright yellow structure stood.

Jaz followed them, clutching her range gear to her chest lest she drop anything. While she ran, she kept looking over her shoulder, terrified that Richard's three "contractors" might appear out of thin air and be closing in on her.

She breathed with relief when she arrived at the yellow building—until she saw the "structure" up close. The thing had no roof, only three sides—a front-facing wall and two side walls that angled outward, away from the front wall. The three walls were about seven feet high.

What in the world? Still, if we're gonna play war games, it's cover, right? Maybe it's protection and we're supposed to shoot from behind it. I suppose that could be fun.

She was even less enthused when she took in what lay behind the yellow wall. A half-dozen piles of "stuff" had been stacked or tossed haphazardly against the perimeter fence. Her eyes inventoried a few canvas tarps, some ropes, a couple of sacks, a heap of blankets, a black kettle, and other junk she didn't recognize—wait! *A kettle?*

Bo handed her a yellow bandana that matched the ones he and Harris wore. "Here's your buff. Change clothes over there. Hustle!"

"Uh, over where?"

He jerked his thumb. "In that corner. We won't look."

"That corner" was between the front wall and one side wall and wasn't even a ninety-degree corner.

"I'm not changing my clothes out here in front of you guys."

Harris rounded on her. "You'd *better*, Darcy. Because we have exactly fourteen minutes left to get organized and appear at the first challenge."

He gestured toward the piles of stuff. "If we're even a second late, we'll lose items from our survival gear. So, unless you prefer sleeping in the rain without cover, *get a move on.* Don't think about us—we'll turn our backs."

Jaz's eyes skittered toward the "survival gear" he'd pointed at. She gulped. "Do you mean we're. . . we're supposed to sleep out here?"

"Sleep, eat, and compete."

"And everything in between," Bo threw over his shoulder. "We even have to turn in the clothes you're presently wearing. If we don't? We lose gear."

"But what—"

"MOVE!" Harris roared.

Jaz fled to the "corner" and hurried to change into her range wear. After she'd pulled on her khakis and long-sleeved shirt, she reached her arm around the side wall and tucked her item of contraband into some tall grass. The last item she donned was the yellow bandana Bo had given her.

"Bandana? This is like hanging a *banana* around my neck," she groused. "And yellow isn't even my color." She tied the bandana as directed anyway. Not only did she not relish being shouted at again, but the idea of sleeping out in the open terrified her.

We're in the mountains here, for heaven's sake! Where bears, cougars, and wolves run around at night killing their food. Are Richard and Travis out of their minds?

"You done yet?" Harris yelled.

"Yah. I mean, yeah, I'm done." Meekly, she handed him the neatly folded pile of clothes she'd changed out of, purple tennis shoes on top.

"Good. Let's go. If we're early, maybe we can scout out the challenge."

Harris began to fast-walk, Bo right behind him. Jaz had to run to catch up. "What challenge?"

"Won't know until we get there," Harris answered. "In case you hadn't noticed, we weren't involved in planning these games. That's why Richard sent us away over the weekend."

Harris led them across the front of the lodge rather than down the side opposite their shelter, and Jaz suddenly saw why. Out of nowhere, an eight-foot wooden wall had appeared. It stretched from the nearer side of the lodge across the yard to the perimeter fence. She'd been in too much of a dither following Harris and Bo from the lodge to the yellow structure to have noticed it.

When the three of them reached the far side of the lodge, Jaz spied a blue structure just like their yellow one in the corner of the yard opposite their shelter. The contractors had just emerged from the structure and were loping through the grass, headed in the same direction as Jaz's tribe.

"Faster!" Harris hissed. The three of them rounded the corner of the lodge only to be confronted by a wooden wall stretching across the yard from the far side of the lodge to the perimeter fence, a wall identical to the one on the lodge's other side. In effect, the two walls had cut Broadsword in half with the gym, stables, and back of the lodge on the rear side, the front of the lodge, the guard shack, and the two tribal structures on the other.

At least this part of the wall has a door in it, Jaz noticed.

The contractors (wearing blue bandanas around their necks) tugged at the door. It wouldn't open, so they pivoted to glare at Yellow Tribe.

"My, isn't this awkward?" Bo said softly.

He and Harris sent Blue Tribe the same withering glowers the Blues were shooting toward Yellow Tribe. Jaz instinctively moved closer to her tribe mates.

Any port in a storm—

"Get your game face on, Walken," Harris growled. "Out here, you're either predator or prey, and Bo and I won't tolerate prey in our tribe. We'll eat you ourselves if you roll over and bare your belly. Now act like the predator you are!"

Predator? Prey? You'll eat me?

Badly intimidated, Jaz attempted to bare her teeth.

Harris sneered in derision. "You call that a game face? Looks more like you're sucking lemons!"

Just then the door in the wall opened and Travis appeared.

"Form up!"

Without hesitation, Blue Tribe melted into a front-facing row.

Harris tossed Jaz's clothing to the ground, then he and Bo each grabbed one of Jaz's arms and yanked her into formation between them like she was the rope in a game of tug o' war.

"Ow!"

"Shut it!" Harris snarled. "And stand up straight!"

Travis appraised the Blues, then turned and examined the Yellows. He nodded. "No points forfeited. Your tribes may go through. You will gather on the patch of grass painted with your tribe's color."

The two tribes filed obediently through the door. They spied the painted squares of grass opposite the gym and assembled on their colored square. Down the yard from the color patches stretched two obstacle courses, not at all unusual in their format, featuring tires, beams, rope swings across a pool of mud, and a single tall wall built from the back of the lodge across to the stables. What lay beyond that wall could not be seen.

Richard stood front and center, waiting quietly for them to settle.

Jaz turned toward Harris and mumbled in panic, "Harris, I can't climb that wall; I'm only five foot two!"

Bo leaned in to listen as Harris asked, "Can you run the tires and the beam and manage the swing?"

"I-I think so. Don't know how fast though."

Bo put his hand on Jaz's shoulder. "Focus on those three obstacles, okay? Don't worry too much about speed; just get through them without falling."

"What about the wall?"

"We'll get you up and over the wall."

"But how?"

"You let us worry about that. Focus on the tires, the beam, and the swing. Harris will go first; watch how he handles each obstacle."

Richard cleared his throat. "Listen carefully. I'm about to issue the rules of engagement for these war games. I will state them once and only once.

"First, any time you hear an air horn sound, it is the call to competition. You will have five minutes to assemble on your tribal color patch. We will then explain the rules of the day's competition before it begins. Competition wins are rewarded with food. Losses result in the removal of some element of the survival gear we've provided in your tribal areas.

"Please do note that stepping off your tribe's color patch except when actively competing, will result in loss of gear."

He glanced with meaning toward Jaz. She looked down, horrified to find her right foot on green grass. Before she could react, Bo jerked her onto the yellow.

"Thanks," she gasped. Anxiety coursed through her blood, making her shudder.

What does Richard mean when he said we'd be rewarded with food? What do we eat if we don't win food?

"Second, except when participating in competition, tribes must remain on the front side of the lodge. You are not permitted to breach the compound's perimeter, access any Broadsword building, cross the wall to this side of the compound, or enter an opposing tribe's camp.

"Get caught breaking any of these rules of engagement, and you will lose gear.

"Third, these games will last three days. Any questions?"

Jaz hand shot up.

"Yes, Miss Walken?"

"What's the point of these games? What's our objective?"

"The objective is to survive."

"But—"

Richard ignored her. "Now for the rules of today's competition. What you see before you is an obstacle course. Each of you will run the first three obstacles alone and in succession. Succeeding tribal members cannot start the course until the previous member touches the wall. Should you fall while attempting and before you complete the first three obstacles, you must return to your tribe's color patch and start over."

The Blues hooted and pointed at Jaz. Bixby yelled, "Count this as a win for the Blues. Little Miss Priss over there probably can't make it to the wall, let alone over it!"

Harris stepped between Jaz and the Blues. "Don't count your chickens before they're hatched, Bixby. Oh, wait—I see you already have chickens. Yeah. Three *very* blue chickens."

"Why you—"

Richard's voice cracked like a whip. "Silence! Listen up, because I will not repeat myself. You may assist each other at the wall and may work together on the final obstacle of the course, an obstacle you cannot see from here. You will receive additional instructions when you complete the final obstacle.

"Any questions? No? Get ready. The competition will begin when the whistle sounds."

Harris crouched and prepared himself to run. So did Devo over on the Blue patch.

"Take your mark!"

Richard blew his whistle, and Harris shot from the yellow patch like an arrow. When he reached the tires, he had to slow down in order to place a foot in each tire without tripping as he ran.

"Did you see that?" Bo asked Jaz.

"See what?"

"How the tires are spaced! Harris had to really shorten his stride. That means the tires are spaced more for your stride than for ours."

"Well, isn't that special."

Harris reached the beam. He raced up a short ramp, sprinted across the beam, then jumped down and ran toward the swing.

"Bo . . . I don't think I can keep my balance on that beam!"

"You can dance, can't you? In fact, we heard you are an accomplished dancer. Light on your feet. Agile. Coordinated."

"You heard what? Who—"

Harris shouted from the rope swing. "Get ready, Darcy!"

He grabbed the rope, swung over the muddy pool, dropped, and landed on his feet. He raced to the wall and touched it.

"Go!" Bo shouted.

Jaz ran toward the tires. When she got closer, she tried to fit her stride to the tires, but failed miserably. With her foot in the first tire, she fell forward.

"Darcy! Get up!" Bo shouted.

She picked herself up, ran back to their color patch, and started again.

"Dance, Darcy, dance!" Bo yelled.

This time she managed—not quickly, but at a respectable pace—to "dance" her way through the eighteen tires. When she cleared them she ran up the ramp to the beam.

And stopped cold.

Harris, from the wall, shouted, "Just point your face toward the end of the beam and run!"

Jaz gulped and did what he said. All except the run part. Slowly, a step at a time, she inched her way across. When she got to the end and jumped off, the Blues were already sitting atop the wall, pointing and mocking her. They were still jeering as they dropped down to the other side.

"Go, Darcy! Don't stop!" Harris yelled.

She ran up another ramp where a rope was looped around a post, waiting for her. She grabbed the rope as far up as she could reach, then ran forward, off the platform. She swung over the muddy pool, looking down instead of what was ahead—until Harris' voice reached her.

"*Jaz!* Let go! Let go! Let go!"

Hey! Did he just call me Jaz? After insisting that I mustn't break character while I'm here?

At the last possible second, she realized what he meant—and why he was stressed to the point of using her real name. She'd reached the arc of her swing and was headed back across the mud!

Her hands let go of the rope like it was a snake. She landed awkwardly, falling on one hip. One foot had missed touching the mud by scant inches, but she was across.

"Come on!" Harris screamed.

Jaz got to her feet and limped to the wall. As soon as she touched it, Bo was away. He flew through the obstacles like he was born to them. When he reached the wall, he and Harris grabbed Jaz by her pant legs and arms and lifted her off her feet. They swung her forward and back multiple times to gain momentum—not unlike two orcs swinging a battering ram at the fortress gates of Helm's Deep.

"Wait! What are you doing?" Jaz screeched.

"Straddle the top when you get there," Bo ordered her.

"What? No, stop! I—"

But she was already flying up, headed for the top of the wall. She scrabbled at the top board and threw a leg over the wall. For a second she nearly went all the way over, and she shuddered when she saw how far she would have fallen.

Harris backed up. "Here I come," he called.

He ran at the wall, used Bo's bent back as a stepping stone, and vaulted to the top of the wall, pulling himself up. He then turned himself around, laid across the top, legs dangling on the far side, his hands reaching out on the other. Bo raced toward the wall, jumped, and caught Harris' hands.

Harris let himself fall toward the grass on the far side, using his own weight to pull Bo up onto the top of the wall, then dropping to the ground. Bo clambered over, hung by his fingers from the top for a second, and also dropped to the ground.

"Hang by your hands, Darcy! We'll catch you!"

But Jaz was looking beyond them to the last obstacle. It began with a steep ramp topped by a wide platform. The Blues were gathered on their side of the platform, but they seemed frozen. They glanced over and saw their opposition gaining on them, but they were . . . stumped?

Jaz knew what desperation looked like—and she was staring right at it.

She laughed aloud. "Stupid jocks!" she chortled with glee.

She laid along the top of the wall on her belly, threw her other leg over the wall, let herself dangle, then dropped.

Harris and Bo caught her and lowered her to the ground.

"Come on," she shouted, limping toward the ramp.

Harris and Bo easily caught up to her. They each grabbed an arm and more or less carried her the rest of the way up the steep ramp. When they crested the platform, they discovered a table, a puzzle frame, and a pile of blocks, all shapes and sizes. The competitors were supposed to arrange the blocks inside the frame so that they all fit together and formed a statement. Jaz immediately began sorting the blocks. On a sign in front of the table were the instructions, but she didn't need them. She'd already read them from the top of the wall.

Solve the puzzle.
When your puzzle is complete,
call for a referee to verify your solution.
Once verified, proceed to your color patch
and run the course a second time.

A Broadsword security guard, serving as referee, stood by, waiting.

"Holy cow," Bo muttered. "I'm not good with puzzles."

"But I am," Jaz exulted. She was making fast work of it, too. Inside of forty seconds Yellow's completed puzzle read, "Beat the Competition, Win Reward."

"Done!" Jaz shouted.

The referee lifted a hand. "Yellow Tribe, go!" He pointed to the side of the course near the lodge. "Return and repeat!"

Harris, Bo, and Jaz scrambled down the ramp and over to the side of the course. Jaz was still limping, so Harris and Bo hoisted her up by her elbows and carried her. Back on their color patch, they lined up again.

Richard blew his whistle. "Go!"

Harris took off, and Bo leaned toward Jaz. "Remember, get into the rhythm of the tires. Don't feel like you need to rush. Because of you at the puzzle table, we have the lead right now. Take enough time so that you don't fall. When you reach the beam, fix your eyes on its end, and dance across. Hit the rope swing, keep your eyes forward, and let go when you're across the mud pool. Got it?"

"Got it."

Harris touched the wall, and Jaz started forward. *Dance, Bo said*, she told herself. *Well, I know how to dance!*

She hummed a tune to herself and danced a perky, lighthearted jig through the tires. Still humming, she focused on the end of the beam and skipped across in confident fashion. At the swing, she kept her eyes on the far edge of the mud. When she released her grip on the rope, she landed on both feet and hobbled to the wall.

Seconds later, Bo joined Harris and Jaz. She was ready this time when she flew to the top of the wall, straddled it, then looked toward the puzzle instructions.

"Huh! Different kind of puzzle."

She glanced behind her, toward the course's start. "What in the world?"

About ten of Richard's men had swarmed the first part of the obstacle course and were tearing it up. They were even running a small 'dozer with a shovel in front.

She didn't have long to study the course alterations, though, before Harris and Bo shouted for her to hang and drop. They caught her, then ran up the ramp, dragging Jaz along with them. At the top the guys stopped and stared.

The instructions had changed. The puzzle had changed. But Jaz already knew.

"Harris! Bo! Get on the other side of the table. We're building a vertical puzzle this time. I need you guys to keep it from falling while I push the pieces into place and balance them."

"Yes, ma'am!" they fired back.

Jaz glanced over her shoulder. The Blues were cresting the ramp. She worked faster. Forty seconds later she shouted, "Done!"

But instead of the referee sending them directly back to the beginning of the course to run it a third time, he sent them to a bench on their side of the course, not far from their completed puzzle.

"You won't lose your lead," the referee assured them. "We have your completion time and will have Blue Tribe's completion time shortly. They will have to wait until the difference between their completion time and your completion time expires before they can continue."

Harris, Bo, and Jaz cooled their heels for nearly an hour. While they waited, they hydrated, rested, and used the facilities. They also avoided looking at the Blues opposite them, because the mood "over there" had shifted.

To say their opponents were *unhappy* would be like saying those who stormed the Bastille were merely *miffed*. No, outraged, bitter, and vindictive were the descriptors that came to Jaz's mind. She was relieved when the referee blew his whistle and sent them back to the course beginning.

Except that the course was substantially different.

Harris nodded. "I've got this. Watch me and do what I do."

The tires that had laid flat on the course now stood on end, buried in sand and clustered tightly together but staggered. It meant that Harris had to get on his belly and crawl through and between all of them. Harris dragged himself through the sand and gravel to navigate the eighteen tires. He got up on the other side, spitting and shedding sand and grit, and ran onward.

The beam was gone.

As Harris crested the ramp, he encountered two ropes—one rope to walk on, the other to hold on to for balance. The rope to walk on was about six feet off the ground; the other rope was six and a half feet above the lower rope.

Harris, at six feet in height, faced forward and held the upper rope with both hands. He stretched his arms wide, one ahead, the other behind, which put his head and body slightly to one side. He began to crab walk across, his feet angled on the lower rope.

"That top rope is too high for me to grab!" Jaz moaned.

Bo shook his head. "Nope, it's not. The fact that it's above your head is actually an advantage. See how Harris' body is turned slightly to the side and how he has to stretch out his arms in both directions to maintain balance? You won't need to stretch out your arms like that. Just face forward, reach up over your head, grab the guide rope with both hands, balance yourself, and walk across. Oh, and scoot across as quick as you can. If your feet are on the rope too long, they will start to hurt."

"Sure, pal," Jaz growled.

Harris reached the muddy pool and found that the rope swing was also missing. It had been replaced by a series of wide posts. The only way across the muddy pool was to jump from post to post. Harris measured the distance with his eye, then hopped to the first post.

Tears appeared unbidden in Jaz's eyes. "Bo, I can't do that! I can't! I'll fall!"

"We heard about you and Brian, you know."

"W-what?"

"The tango you two did at your team's party."

Jaz flushed red and her tears vanished. "Who told you about our party? I'll break their bloody arms!"

"Who told us? Don't you mean who didn't? Harris and I keep in touch with Resolute members, and I received no fewer than three emails describing the highlights of your party—yours and Brian's tango, *in detail*, being the hit of the evening."

He laughed. "I thought Harris was going to punch a wall or something. Talk about green!"

He pointed. "Speaking of Harris, he's almost across the mud."

"What has our party got to do with this-this-this *impossible* course?" Jaz demanded.

"It's not impossible. Everyone in Resolute says you're an awesome dancer —you even proved it to us on your last time through the course."

Harris was across now. He ran forward and slapped the wall with his hand.

Bo nudged her. "Get going, Darcy."

Jaz moaned, "Oh, man!" then raced toward the first obstacle. She hated every second in the sand as she crawled through the first two tires, but she soon realized that she could "monkey walk" from tire to tire, only dropping to her belly to crawl through each tire. She started upping her pace and finished quickly, spitting out sand as she approached the ropes.

It was scary to reach so far over her head for the guide rope, but Bo was right. Once she stepped out, the guide rope gave her enough control to move ahead. She slid her feet along the lower rope at a decent pace, then ran down the ramp.

She crossed the short span of grass and up the third ramp where she came face to face with a series of eight posts, the only way across the muddy pool.

Oh God! If you are listening, please help me!

Jaz couldn't believe she was praying, but she was.

Please?

Harris shouted at her, "Ever play hopscotch? Hop from platform to platform like you would in hopscotch. You can do it!"

And she did—nearly overbalancing on the first platform, but nailing the rest of them. When she ran down the ramp on the other side, she looked back.

I did it.

But you helped me, didn't you?

Thank you. I won't doubt you the next time.

"Move it, woman!" Harris yelled.

With a grin on her face, she skipped up to the wall and slapped it. Moments later, the three of them were over the wall, headed up the ramp. They mounted the puzzle platform and surveyed their last puzzle.

A thick vertical pole stood solid in a tire filled with cement. Sticking out of the side of the pole were ten dowels spaced evenly from the bottom of the pole to its top, not unlike a flag flying from its pole. Each dowel had a number of square blocks skewered on it.

The blocks themselves had letters on all four sides, and the individual blocks could be turned on its dowel to display one of its four letters until the blocks on each dowel formed a single word. The ten words, from top to bottom, were supposed to create a sentence. Unfortunately, the ten blocks in their present state formed ten scrambled words.

Jaz reread the instructions and muttered, "We have to turn all the blocks on each dowel until the blocks form a word."

Harris added, "So, we'll know we have the right words when, from top to bottom, they form a complete sentence?"

"Yeah, a complete sentence."

Bo, agitated, tugged on his hair. "Man, I hate this stuff!"

"Never fear; Darcy is here."

"That's my girl," Harris grinned.

Jaz blushed, but she kept her eyes on the puzzle, starting with the shortest of the words, the ones more likely to be "the" and "and." The third word was definitely "the." The second word had to be "to."

She looked to her left. A wood partition kept the two tribes from seeing the other tribe's puzzle progress, but the teams could see each other as they worked.

Blue team stared at the puzzle, motionless.

You dorks seem poleaxed—and ain't that a shame?

Two minutes later, she yelled, "Done!"

Yellow Tribe's flag puzzle declared,

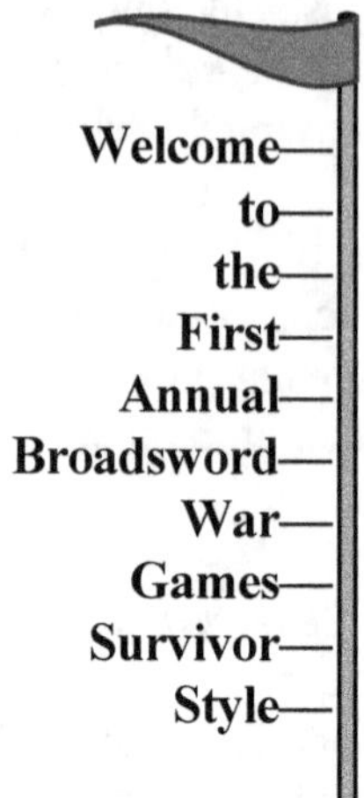

Richard, with a nod from the referee, blew his whistle. "Winner, Yellow Tribe! Both tribes please return to your color patches!"

Jaz glanced back and saw Devo shove the puzzle pole, toppling it to the ground, scattering blocks across the puzzle platform.

Whoops. Guess I caught Devo mid-tantrum!

Harris and Bo didn't notice. Shouting "Ooo-rah! Ooo-rah! Ooo-rah!" the two men lifted Jaz to their shoulders and raced down the incline—nearly dumping her in the process. The Blues, cussing a streak of their own color, followed at a slower pace.

When both tribes stood on their designated square of colored grass, and when Yellow Tribe had stopped gloating, two grinning Broadsword guards entered the course from the kitchen door. They delivered a sizable cloth-covered tray to Richard, who directed them to place it on a stand near him.

"Yellow Tribe wins reward!" he announced, whipping off the cloth. "A complete roasted chicken dinner including mashed potatoes, green beans, apple pie, and as a side benefit, twelve protein bars."

He added with a wry smile, "I recommend that you keep back the protein bars for tomorrow and the third day of competition. You're going to need them."

Jaz's gut lurched, and the low-calorie diet Richard and Harris had put her on went straight out the window. *I don't think I've ever been this hungry in my life.*

"Man, I just caught a whiff of that chicken, and my stomach is singing the national anthem," Bo declared.

"Yeah? Well my stomach is singing Darcy's praises," Harris replied. "We wouldn't have won without her to solve those puzzles."

"Amen to that."

"Listen up, tribes," Richard said quietly. "Whenever you hear an air horn sound, it is the call to competition. You will have five minutes to arrive on your tribal color patch.

"Blue Tribe? Better luck next time, and I will remind you that a loss in competition means a loss of gear. You'll discover that something is missing from your supplies when you return to camp. Yellow Tribe? Come get your reward.

"I remind both tribes that you are restricted to the front side of the lodge until the next competition. You had better not get caught in the other tribe's camp."

Harris and Bo went to get the tray of food. Jaz, however, slid a quick look toward Blue Tribe to gauge their reaction.

The three Blues weren't watching Bo or Harris.

They weren't eying the chicken dinner, either.

Their glaring animus was fixed on Jaz.

Uh-oh. Those guys are seriously ticked off.

At me.

CHAPTER 24

Vyper

JAZ, HARRIS, and Bo returned to their structure and gorged themselves on roasted chicken, mashed potatoes and gravy, green beans almandine, and Dutch apple pie. Not a crumb remained. However, they decided to heed Richard's advice and held back the protein bars for later. They would each eat one bar when the air horn sounded, signaling the start of the next competition.

"We haven't had a chance to inventory our gear and supplies yet," Harris commented with a burp. "Should probably do that next."

"Yeah. We definitely need to get some cover over our sleeping area ASAP," Bo replied. "No telling when it's going to rain, but we generally get a mountain shower here every afternoon in the summer."

Jaz was thinking about something else. "I wonder what gear the Blues lost. And what did Richard mean when he said the losing team wouldn't get food? Did he mean no food at all?"

Harris answered. "I opened the sacks over there and took a look inside before we went to get you. One sack holds a hammer, some nails, a wooden spoon, and other small items. The other sack holds a big plastic bag of uncooked rice. I suppose the rice is what the kettle is for. The bag *might* hold enough rice to get three people through three days, but if so, just barely."

"And it's all carbs besides," Bo said.

"We should probably hide them," Jaz said quietly.

Harris tilted his head toward her. "Hide what?"

"The protein bars. If Blue Tribe doesn't get enough calories and some protein on board, they'll be working from a deficit at the next competition. They won't like that."

"Well, they can't come over here," Bo said, giving his stomach a complacent pat. "Richard said so."

"I think you're wrong."

"Oh? Wrong how?"

"What Richard said before the competition started was, and I quote, 'Except when participating in competition, tribes must remain on the front side of the lodge. You are not permitted to breach the compound's perimeter, access any Broadsword building, cross the wall to this side of the compound, or enter an opposing tribe's camp.

"But then he said, 'Get caught breaking any of these rules of engagement, and you will lose gear.'"

"The Blues wouldn't risk losing more gear."

"You think so? Then why did Richard repeat himself at the end of the competition? It almost sounded to me like he was goading the Blues to take the risk when he said, 'You had better not get caught in the other tribe's camp.' Better not *get caught*. And did you see the looks the Blues were giving us when Richard revealed our reward? Those people hate losing."

Harris, hands on his hips, frowned. "You think they'll come snooping around, like when it's dark?"

"Yeah, I do."

"Then we'd better set a watch before we go to sleep."

"Speaking of sleep," Bo said, looking at the sky, "the sky may be clear at the moment, but the forecast said we'd get a bit of rain later this afternoon. Let's get our shelter up, cuz I don't fancy sleeping with a wet blanket."

"You're talking about Harris, right?" Jaz deadpanned.

"Very funny, *Darcy*," Harris growled.

Jaz grinned and then they all laughed and set about getting their camp organized. They found two tarps, several lengths of rope, three blankets, a few tools and nails, a box of matches, a long wooden spoon, a tin cup, the sack of rice, three gallons of water, and the kettle.

"Not a lot, but I certainly wouldn't like to lose any of this," Bo observed.

"One tarp under us, one overhead?" Harris asked.

"Yeah, but I don't see any firewood, and it gets chilly out here after the sun sets. And we can't cook rice without something to burn."

"You're not wrong." Harris gestured to Jaz. "While we're getting our sleeping area set up, do you feel like rounding up some fuel?"

"Sure, except I haven't ever seen firewood just laying around inside Broadsword's perimeter."

"Then you'd better scout it out quick. I wouldn't put it past the Blues to take whatever is available and leave us shivering when the sun goes down."

Jaz emerged from behind their wall and started off by scanning the yard from left to right. She was heartened to spy two bundles of firewood stacked by the front porch in plain sight. She also spotted Nan running toward the wood.

"Oh, no you don't," Jaz whispered.

She headed toward the wood, then realized she wouldn't reach the bundles before Nan did. She could, on the other hand and if she really hustled, cut Nan off. Pouring on more speed than she'd ever done, Jaz cut across the grass, aiming at a spot out ahead of Nan where Jaz anticipated they would intersect. Nan saw her coming and sped up, but Jaz was too close already.

Jaz hadn't thought yet about what she'd do with Nan once she caught her. *I can't fight her and win, but all I need is a few seconds to grab one of those bundles!*

With that goal in mind, Jaz did the only thing she could think of. She tackled Nan.

As they went down, Jaz rolled away from Nan's thrashing fists, hopped up, ran and grabbed one bundle of wood, then took off, Nan screaming curses at her back.

Harris and Bo, having heard the commotion, were waiting for her outside the structure.

"Way to go, Darcy!" Bo said, slapping her on the back.

"Thanks . . . I think." Jaz's back smarted where he'd delivered his good-natured slap.

———◆———

FOUR EVENTS of note occurred that evening.

First, whatever was happening on the other side of the wall was noisy. Loud in fact. Loud and incessant.

"Gotta be heavy machinery," Bo opined. "Hear the backup alarm?"

"That beeping?" Jaz asked.

"Yeah. That."

"You think they're doing something for the next competition?"

"What else could it be?"

Not long after, the sky over Broadsword filled with dark, water-heavy clouds that rained down on both tribes for around a quarter of an hour. Harris, Bo, and Jaz squatted under their makeshift shelter and stayed reasonably dry.

"At least the noise from the other side stopped while it rained."

"You don't think they'll keep it up all night, do you?"

Third, when the rain let up, Yellow tribe built a fire and cooked up two servings of rice apiece, one for dinner, the other for breakfast.

"Cooked rice heats up fast," Bo said. "By cooking it ahead of time, we won't be waiting all morning for it to cook, maybe getting called to a competition before it's done."

Last, but not least, about two hours after Harris and Bo went to sleep and while Jaz had first watch, Bixby snuck into their camp.

Jaz was ready for him.

She had insisted on taking first watch because she'd convinced herself that either Devo or Bixby, feeling the unaccustomed clawing of hunger pangs in their bellies, would gamble further loss of gear to steal Yellow Tribe's protein bars.

Those people hate losing.

Huddled in her blanket, deep in the shadows with her back against a tree, Jaz waited for one of the Blues to show up. For a while she revisited the competition, shaking her head when she recalled falling on the first tire obstacle, chuckling to herself when she thought how Harris and Bo had tossed her up to grab the top of the wall.

That was almost fun, she admitted to herself.

When she'd exhausted that vein of thought, her mind returned to the long hours she'd spent alone over the weekend . . . hours spent reading the Gospels of Matthew and Mark. She was surprised to find herself wishing she had her Bible with her. She was more surprised to realize she was praying.

Sort of.

Bella said reading the Bible would change me. I guess I'd really like that, Lord. The change part.

Not too far away, she thought she heard a soft *snap*. It was followed by a surreptitious footfall.

Jaz picked up the object resting in her lap, the device she'd hidden in the grass outside their structure earlier. Eyes wide, seeking movement in the dark, Jaz waited. She glanced once at the waterproof sack that had at one time contained their bag of rice. Instead, the sack bulged with small sticks, dead leaves, and a couple of fist-sized rocks.

Besides the kettle, the sack was the only item the tribe had left out in the open, the only dry thing in the Yellow's camp other than their tight sleeping area. Unless the Yellows were snoozing with protein bars as pillows, the coveted food bars had to be stashed in that sack.

Jaz was hidden less than two yards away, a clear route between her and the sack.

As quiet and stealthy as a shadow, a body stood over the sack. Then the dark body bent to grab the sack.

"Psst!"

The form's head jerked up, and Jaz depressed a button, propelling a mist of pepper spray directly into the intruder's eyes. The intruder yowled like a cat whose tail had been run over by a rocking chair.

At his howl of pain, Harris and Bo shot from their blankets.

"What! What is it?"

"It was Bixby," Jaz told them, pointing. "He took off that way."

"Let's get after him!" Bo said.

Jaz answered. "Don't bother. We can point him out to Richard tomorrow."

Harris objected. "That won't be proof, and while we stand here jawing, we're letting him get away!"

Jaz yawned. "Trust me, we'll have proof. Man, I'm really tired. Someone else take watch now."

———•———

ON THE second day of competition, the Yellows wakened to the renewed roar of heavy machinery.

Jaz lifted her head from beneath her blanket. "What *is* that racket?"

Harris yawned and stretched. "Dunno. Still sounds like road machinery."

"Well, make it stop!"

They got up reluctantly and prepared for the next competition, scarfing down the cooked and reheated rice, doling out protein bars, heating extra water to wash with, stretching, trying to limber up after an uncomfortable night. All morning, they waited for the air horn to blow, but the signal for the next competition didn't sound until the sun was straight up.

Harris, Bo, and Jaz burst from their shelter and sprinted through the door in the far segment of wall. They slid onto their color patch just after Blue team reached theirs.

The Yellows observed the Blues with blatant interest, while the Blues steadfastly refused to look in their direction. Instead, they gave their attention to studying the competition setup.

Jaz smothered a chuckle. Even from where she stood, she noticed two things, the first being that all three Blues appeared decidedly . . . rumpled.

"Somebody got rained on last night," Bo snickered. "They're all dried out now, but hooey! Sleeping wet? No fun at all."

"Yeah, they definitely got rained on," Harris added softly. "Check out Nan's hair. She slept on wet hair, and now it's flat on one side. Their tarps must have been missing when they returned to camp yesterday."

The other thing Jaz noticed was that Bixby' eyes were a swollen, mottled red. "Check out Bixby."

Bo leaned toward her and whispered, "So what did you do to him? His face looks sorta off. Puffy and red."

"What did *I* do? Who, little ol' *me?* While I might agree—and only theoretically—that he appears to have taken a blast of pepper spray directly to the eyes, wouldn't possession of pepper spray go against the competition rules?"

Harris gaped, but Bo guffawed and, for a second time, slapped her on the back. "I assume said illegal device got tossed over the perimeter wall?"

Feigning offense, Jaz answered, "Well! I should think so. And by the way? If I need a chiropractic appointment followed by massage after we've finished these war games, I'm sending you the bill."

"What! Why?"

Harris stepped in. "Stop pounding Darcy on the back like she's one of us guys, Bo. Her back isn't made of lead pipe like yours is."

A sheepish Bo muttered, "Sorry, Darcy."

Jaz waved him off. "Forget about it. We need to get our head in the game."

She stared at the new course. Bulldozers had taken a wide swath of grass from the yard, and an oval track, stretching all the way across the yard, had emerged. Jaz's gaze followed the track over small hills and mounds, through puddles and pools, and around some seriously intimidating obstacles.

Wherever the course curved or ran close to the lodge, the perimeter fence, or the stables, the track's outer edge was built up and canted toward its lower inner edge.

They don't want anyone flying off the designated route or crashing into the lodge.

Two dune buggies waited at the starting line.

No wonder they didn't start the competition today until now. Richard's people had to work all yesterday afternoon plus this morning to create this monstrosity.

Just then, Richard blew his whistle, and Jaz checked to make sure both of her feet were firmly on the yellow patch.

"Good day," Richard said. "Welcome to our Day 2 competition." He ran an eye over the two tribes and stopped at Bixby.

"What's the problem with your face, Bixby?"

Harris and Bo snickered through their teeth. Jaz studied her feet and chewed the inside of one cheek. She didn't trust herself not to break into an incriminating chortle.

Bixby answered Richard. "Dunno. Woke up this way. A mild case of contact dermatitis. I'm fine, though. No worries."

"Medic!"

Moments later, a guard with a first aid kit emerged from the gym. The medic studied Bixby's face, but his patient refused to answer questions.

"He won't admit it, but I'd say the guy's been dosed with pepper spray," the medic reported. "He may be hurting, but if he says he's okay to compete, I'll allow it."

"Very good. Thank you." Richard eyeballed both teams. "If I didn't know better, I'd say that some form of *socializing* between tribes occurred during the night. Care to comment?"

"I didn't see a thing," Harris said.

"Me neither," added Bo.

Jaz shrugged noncommittally while the Blues shook their heads in unison.

Richard snorted. "All right. Have it your way. Here are the rules for today's competition. Each tribe will select a single member to drive their tribe's dune buggy around the track ten times, racing against the opposing team's cart. Whichever tribe finishes the ten circuits first, wins reward.

"During the race, the remaining two tribe members are to defend their own tribe's vehicle and driver from attack. But since the best defense is a good offense, designated Defenders may elect to attack the opposing tribe's driver and vehicle, attempting to slow or stop their progress. Alternatively, they may split their members between the two actions.

"Defenders' weapons are the padded pugil sticks you see lying on the grass in front of your color patch. Drivers' weapons are their vehicles. These are the only weapons allowed in the competition.

"Defenders will wear padded head, chest, and groin gear. Drivers will wear crash helmets and chest protection and will use the provided four-point camlock seat belt safety harness.

"Please note that, for the sake of safety, your cart's engine will not start if the safety harness is not correctly engaged. And if, at any time, a driver releases his or her safety harness, the vehicle's engine will automatically shut down."

He paused. "You have ten minutes to select your drivers and gear up. Drivers may not start their vehicles until I blow the whistle."

Jaz cut her eyes toward two dune buggies, one yellow, one blue, waiting at the starting line, facing counter clockwise down the track. The three Yellows walked over to their cart and examined it.

Jaz grimaced. "One of us has to drive that?"

"I vote that you drive," Bo announced, "while Harris and I keep Devo and Bixby off of you."

"No, see, I don't know how to drive—not really."

Bo stared. "What do you mean, *you don't know how to drive?* Were you plucked from a cabbage patch as a kid? Marooned on a desert island until recently? Everybody knows how to drive!"

"Obviously *not* everyone, since *I* don't know how!" Jaz fired back. "I've never owned a car and have only driven a rental a couple of times . . . short distances and not very well. I don't even have a real license."

Bo snorted. "Hope you're a quick study."

Jaz was starting to hyperventilate. "But I've certainly never driven a dune buggy or cart-thingy or whatever you call it!"

"You have to drive, Darcy," Bo insisted. "This isn't gonna work if you don't. Look over there. The Blues have chosen Nan to drive. That means Devo and Bixby will be defending and attacking—and you don't know the first thing about real fighting, nor are you anywhere near a physical match to Devo or Bixby. They would crush you—ergo, you *have* to drive."

"But I-I don't know how!" Jaz was gasping for air.

Harris grabbed Jaz by the shoulders and shook her. "Get a grip, Darcy. Bo's right. You have to drive." He put his finger under her chin. Forced her to look at him as he pointed to their cart's driver's seat. "See? The carts have automatic transmissions. No shifting needed. Just point the vehicle down the track, step on the gas, and go like a bat outa that reeeeally hot place. You can do it."

As though the matter were settled, he turned to Bo. "Instead of playing defense exclusively, what would you think of one on one? You take Devo and I'll take Bixby? Whatever they do, we counter. And if we put them 'out of service' temporarily, we attack Nan."

Bo nodded. "Yeah, that might work best—but it means our success depends upon Darcy making her ten circuits faster than Nan does. It also means she'll be one-on-one against Nan—and that woman doesn't know the meaning of mercy."

Jaz shuddered. "Wh-what do you mean by I'll be one-on-one against Nan?"

Harris took over. "Look, Nan can make only a limited number of moves on you. She will try to climb up your backside, run you off the track, or knock you into obstacles, that sort of thing."

While talking, Harris had wrapped Jaz's chest protection around her and buckled it tight, then placed a helmet on her head, snapped the straps together, and snugged them up.

"Your best option is to get ahead of Nan and *stay* ahead. Whatever you do, don't let her get on your tail where she can ram you. *Stay ahead*—got it?"

"Oh, yeah! I've got it, all right," Jaz mumbled as she turned away. "I'm dead. All that's missing is the cause of death for the certificate—rammed, run over, crushed, or any combination of the above. Throw in heart failure for good measure."

She climbed into the dune buggy's driver's seat, looked about her, and noted the two padded and reinforced roll bars above her head. She scowled. "In case I flip over? Like that's real comforting!"

Harris wasn't done. He pulled two seat belts over her shoulders and fed their hardware into the camlock, then did the same with the two lap belts. He grabbed the ends of the belts and pulled them hard. "You'll be jerked and tossed around a lot, so I'm belting you in good and tight. Remember, punch the gas and keep moving. Get ahead of Nan. Stay ahead of her."

"Yeah, yeah. Get ahead. Stay ahead. Got it."

Richard called out, "Two minutes! Defenders, gear up!"

Harris and Bo hustled over to the yellow color patch; they donned their gear and took up their pugil sticks.

"Tribes ready!"

Jaz stared straight ahead, too fearful to glace in Nan's direction, terrified of what was before her.

Jesus, please help me!

"On your mark!"

Please!

Richard's whistle sounded, shrill and loud.

Jaz cranked on the dune buggy's key, and the engine roared to life. Then she did as Harris had ordered: She punched the gas. Fighting the steering wheel and weaving erratically, she sped down the track, Nan in the Blues' vehicle close on her right.

Halfway down the near straightaway, Jaz encountered her first obstacle, a low hillock. Fearful of going over it full-throttle, she let off the gas. Her buggy slowed abruptly and barely made it over the mound. Nan, on the other hand, raced up the mound, caught some air as she came off the top, and flew many yards down the track before landing with a bounce and hurtling onward.

Jaz *was* a quick learner. *Don't slow down. Got it.*

She drove as fast as she dared over mounds, through muddy puddles, and around the several obstacles dotting the course. She was figuring out how to steer, but she did *not* know how to corner. When she approached the first turn, she started to panic and, knowing it would cost her, she slowed to navigate the upper portion of the oval, speeding up when she hit the far straightaway.

She was appalled to see that Nan had already completed her first circuit.

Must go faster!

Jaz did go faster, and her driving improved marginally as she did, but all in all, it was too little too late. No matter how she pushed herself to get the most out of her cart, Nan remained ahead of her. As Jaz began her eighth circuit, Nan was nipping at her heels, close to lapping her.

I have two laps to go, but she only has one. It's time to pull out all *the* stops.

This time, when Jaz reached the far turn, she yanked the steering wheel to the left without braking or letting up on the gas. To her chagrin, her cart, instead of cornering, flipped and rolled—with her in it.

Behind Jaz in the Blues' vehicle, Nan braked violently to avoid Jaz's roll. She hit the brakes so hard that her engine stalled out.

Far down the course, Harris and Bo saw Jaz flip and roll. Harris broke off his scuffle with Bixby to run to her aid.

Jaz, however, was belted in so snugly, and the vehicle—somewhat miraculously—had landed on its wheels and was pointed in the right direction. Even before her head stopped ringing, she stomped on the gas again and took off, but Nan couldn't get her buggy to restart.

As Jaz raced down the second straightaway, she could hear Nan's faint screeches of frustration.

If I can cross the finish line and get to that first turn before she gets moving again, I might have a chance to beat her!

That's when she saw Bixby running along the course ahead of her, waiting for her to come abreast of him. Jaz yanked her head around, looking for help, but Devo had Bo engaged, and Harris was too far away to defend her!

As Bixby came alongside her buggy, he grabbed one of the roll bars and used it to pull himself into the dune buggy's passenger seat.

He stood on the seat, eyes red and swollen, face glistening with perspiration, and shouted, "Now I'm gonna make you pay for that cheap shot last night!"

He lifted his pugil stick to swing it at Jaz's head. She responded with the only weapon she possessed.

She braked.

Bixby flew over the front of her buggy and cartwheeled down the straightaway, coming to rest face down in the dirt at the turn. Even before he'd rolled to a stop, Jaz had punched the gas and jerked the wheel to go around him.

The finish line was on the other side of the turn, and Nan's stalled buggy was still down the straightaway, near the far turn. Once Jaz reached Nan, they would be tied up, both of them with half a lap remaining. Whoever reached the finish line first would win the contest.

Jaz whizzed by Nan and navigated the far turn with a bit more care. At the same time, Nan's engine roared to life. With a stomp on the accelerator, Jaz headed into the course's second straightaway—but Nan was moving quickly now, making up time.

Jaz didn't realize that Nan was coming up directly behind her until Nan nudged her from behind. Jazz recovered, but that was only Nan's first attempt. With time running out, Nan hit the gas and ran her cart's right front wheel into Jaz's left rear wheel—sending Jaz's cart into a wild spin.

"Oh no! Lord, please help me!" Jaz struggled to bring her cart under control, but when the cart came to a stop, she was off the track, and Nan was closing in on the turn before reaching the finish line.

Unfortunately, although Nan had seen Bixby unceremoniously cartwheel over the front of Jaz' buggy, she hadn't seen where he'd ended up—smack-dab in the middle of the last curve. He had been stunned by the impact and was finally getting to his feet, staggering and shaking his head like the landing had rung his bell, when Nan realized she was on a collision course with him. She yanked the wheel while braking hard, but her efforts were fruitless.

The Blues' cart slid sideways into Bixby, knocking him high into the air. For a second time, he crashed to the ground.

As Jaz wrangled her cart back onto the track, she despaired of catching up with Nan before she crossed the finish line. All she could make out ahead of her was the cloud of dust from Nan's precipitous stop. She also couldn't locate Harris through the dust and flying debris.

She stomped on the gas anyway.

But Harris had witnessed Nan's cart mow Bixby down. When he realized Bixby was out of commission, he took the opportunity to attack Nan's cart. She was coming up to speed again when Harris grabbed a roll bar and swung himself into the back of her cart.

Devo, seeing Harris leap aboard Nan's cart, tried desperately to disengage with Bo and come to Nan's aid, but Bo was having none of that! He countered Devo's moves again and again, stymieing and frustrating his opponent's efforts to break off. Devo had no other option than to leave Nan to Harris' tender mercies.

Harris slid under the roll bars into the passenger seat. Before Nan realized what he was about, he'd reached over and whacked the safety harness' release button on her chest.

The cart's engine stalled out immediately.

But, Harris wasn't done. He put his back against the passenger door and kicked the buggy's driver-side door open. While Nan pounded him with both fists, Harris planted both feet on her thighs and torso and used his legs to shove her right out the door and onto the dirt. He then slid behind the wheel, clicked the safety harness in place, restarted the engine, and whipped the Blues' cart into a U-turn that took it off the track and toward the gymnasium.

While Nan sat in the dirt weeping and Devo and Bixby screamed and cursed, Jaz zoomed her way around the curve and across the finish line. Travis was waiting with the checkered flag in his hand.

"Winner! Yellow Tribe wins!"

Harris and Bo dragged Jaz from the cart and the three of them hugged madly. They joined arms and jumped up and down, shouting their victory.

Jaz couldn't believe they'd won. Then she couldn't believe she was hugging Harris and Bo—*hugging anyone!*—with every bit as much fervor as they were hugging her.

What in the world? I don't do hugging.

Bixby limped off the track, cradling his right arm, scowling and grumbling as he went.

"That's it. I'm packing up. Gonna blow this blasted popsicle stand. You aren't paying us enough for this-this-this—" He embellished his rant with a gush of curses. On his way toward the door in the wall, he shouted, "And I need something to eat!"

Nan and Devo looked at each other. Nan swiped at her drippy nose and nodded, then Devo yelled, "Hey, Bix! Wait up! We're outa here too. Pretty sure these stupid war games are rigged anyhow."

A minute later, only Richard, Travis, and Yellow Tribe, grinning and laughing, remained in the arena.

Richard signaled Travis to come over to him. The two of them put their heads together and engaged in low, animated conversation. When they finished, Richard approached Yellow Tribe.

"Well done, all of you. And Miss Walken? Double accolades. Since your opponents have quit the games ahead of schedule, we consider your training with us complete. We're sending you home tomorrow."

"Way to go, Darcy," Harris said quietly for only Jaz and Bo to hear. "You're the sharpest gal I've ever met, and you're going to do great on your op."

"I agree," Bo said. "You'll do great."

To punctuate his assurance, Bo came *that close* to punching Jaz's upper arm. He caught himself in time, and laid a gentle tap on her arm instead. "See you around, kiddo."

"Thanks for everything, Bo."

"Anytime—and Yellow Tribe rules!"

After Bo walked away, Harris tugged Jaz into one of those awkward side hugs. His arm gripped her shoulders just a little longer than necessary, and he tipped his head over to lightly rest on hers.

Then he whispered, "I'll be praying for you, Jaz."

Jaz's drew a breath of surprise. *You'll be praying for me? What? Are you a Christian too?*

Before she could respond, Harris gave her a last squeeze and strode away.

Jaz sighed.

Gotta say . . . that wasn't awful.

CHAPTER 25

Vyper

WHILE THE sun was still rising the following morning, Travis drove Jaz down the mountain to her Germantown apartment. Bella was sitting in her car in the apartment complex's parking lot, waiting for them. She got out and waved when Travis pulled up.

Bella greeted Jaz with a smile. "Hey, Darcy. I see you survived."

"Hey, Bella. Survived? Is that what they call it?" Jaz grumped. She hurt all over, especially her hips. "Not used to sleeping outside on the ground."

Or running obstacle courses or overturning dune buggies.

"*You* roughing it? Sleeping on the ground? Now that's a sight I'd pay to see."

Jaz only snorted while trying to work out some of the kinks in her back, so Bella turned to greet Travis. "Good to see you, Travis."

"You too, ma'am." He popped the trunk and removed Jaz's bag. "Here you go, Miss Walken. Take care, now."

Jaz nodded. "Thanks, Travis."

Travis drove away, leaving Jaz and Bella on the sidewalk.

"Shall we go on up to your place?" Bella asked. "We need to discuss your next steps."

Jaz grabbed her rolling suitcase and led the way. Once inside her door, Jaz dropped the suitcase. "I need a cup of tea in the worst way. You?"

"Yes, please. And just a reminder, we need you to stay in 'Darcy mode.'"

"Yeah. I get it."

Bella sat at Jaz's little dining table and waited until Jaz joined her with two steaming mugs. Neither of them spoke for several minutes. They shared the companionable quiet until they had both finished their tea.

"Ready?" Bella asked.

"Sure. You said next steps?"

"That's right. We've made a few changes to the op's structure, and I think you'll appreciate them. I convinced Director Wolfe to let Resolute support your mission—with the exception of any armed response, of course. His people will handle that.

"Also, I am now your official handler and will liaison with Wolfe and his tactical team, should we need them. You will take orders from me; however, Rusty is available should you require Resolute's tech support. He will keep me up to date on your needs and bring me in when I'm needed."

Jaz blew out a breath. "I like those changes. I wasn't looking forward to being 'out there,' dependent on Wolfe's other people, people I didn't already know and trust."

"Pretty much what I told Director Wolfe."

"Thanks for that, Bella."

"Of course. Now tell me how you got on with Harris and Bo."

"Royal pain in my backside, both of them," but Jaz smiled as she said it.

"And here I thought that was *your* MO."

"Very funny. At least . . . at least I understood by the end of our war games that those guys had my back."

"Which was the actual point of the war games."

"Was it? Huh. Interesting."

"It's also why they will continue to have your back."

"What do you mean?"

"We will deploy Harris and Bo to Houston ahead of you. They will shadow Wolfe's Houston surveillance team and let the team familiarize them with AEA's cell members and their daily routines, but their primary mission is to support you."

Jaz sat back, relieved. "Best news I've heard today."

"Glad you approve. We also want Harris and Bo as able to recognize our targets in a crowd as you are. We intend for them to "troll" AEA's preferred clubs ahead of you or following behind you, three sets of eyes being better than one. You won't see Harris and Bo until you go out partying, but you'll catch glimpses of them then."

"Out partying because that's where I will first approach the cell members."

"That's it exactly. AEA members tend to socialize together, and Wolfe's surveillance people have nailed down their preferred drink and dance haunts. Back to Harris and Bo. When you notice either of them in a club, do not approach them or give any indication that you know them. Alternatively, don't be surprised if one of them asks you to dance. They may use a dance as opportunity to exchange information; just don't get too friendly with them. Treat them exactly as you would any guy who asks you to dance."

Bella laid a manila mailer on the table and withdrew a stack of full-color photos. She spread them out on the table in three rows. "All of these individuals are suspected Houston AEA terrorists. That said, it may not be an exhaustive display of *all* of our Houston suspects.

"According to our surveillance folks, AEA holds regular weekly meetings. AEA bills their gatherings as public meetings—you know, acting out 'Nothing to see here. We're simple social justice advocates,' and yet newcomers may attend by invitation only.

"What has frustrated Wolfe's four surveillance people is that the meeting locations are not publicized. The surveillance team splits up and follows four of the known cell members, supposedly on their way to cell meetings, yet these members manage to slip our surveillance folks every time. Bottom line? We don't know where AEA meets. We are confident the cell includes these twenty individuals, but additional and heretofore unseen members may very well exist.

"Notice that the surveillance team has numbered these photos one through twenty. The numbering is in order of each member's presumed importance or authority within the cell. We should be careful to remember that the numbering is a 'surmised' ranking, since it is based entirely on the tasks the surveillance team are able to observe.

"For example, whenever the cell meets, surveillance team members frequently spot this man and this woman, numbers nineteen and twenty, purchasing some kind of refreshment, pastries and such, after which the surveillance team invariably loses them. That said, fetching coffee and donuts is a task that puts these two members at the bottom of the hierarchy."

Jaz nodded slowly. "I can get on board with that logic."

"I agree. Now, although Wolfe's surveillance team admits that they may not understand the cell hierarchy perfectly, they *are* fairly certain that the photos numbered one through three, these two men and this woman, are the cell's leaders."

"Confidence level?"

"Ninety percent. If you are able to engage with cell members while out dancing and succeed in receiving an invitation to their weekly meeting, numbers one through three are the individuals who will decide if you are recruitment material or not."

She tapped one photo in particular. "And according to surveillance, photo number one is the 'big dog.' I'm sure Richard and Harris have already drilled you on how to make an effective approach, but I cannot understate this one fact: This op hinges on you engaging successfully. If you blow the approach, that's it. No remedy. No fixing it."

"Wow. The 'big dog' is a woman. That's sort of a surprise—given Chinese culture and all."

"Uh-huh, and following canine pack logic, it behooves you to remember that a new dog hoping to be accepted by the pack must first convey submission to the alpha *by showing her belly*, her vulnerabilities. Along the same line of thought, Darcy Walken, if you disrespect or anger the alpha, you're done."

"No pressure here," Jaz murmured. She scrutinized the woman's photo, committing to memory her dark, monolid eyes, a common genetic effect in Asians created by an epicanthic fold in the inner corners of the eyes. Jaz's eyes, in contrast, had no epicanthic fold, only a noticeable cant that caused her wide-set green eyes to "tilt" upward slightly, from the inside corner of her eye to the outside.

The noticeable genetic contribution of my supposed paternal grandfather, Jaz recalled from her undercover legend.

Bella pushed a sheet of paper toward Jaz. "Memorize this chat room URL and login info. We've placed copies of these target photos on that site. Continue to refer to them until you are certain you can spot these cell members in the flesh. The sole members of the chat room are the five of us: Rusty, Harris, Bo, you, and me. You are to post regular reports in the chat."

"Got it. What else?"

Bella slid an envelope toward her. "Our phone numbers are inside. Memorize them. If you are in trouble and need an *urgent* assist, you can reach Harris and Bo at their numbers. But only call from a pay phone or an otherwise randomly chosen phone.

"You'll also find three emergency meet-up locations detailed inside. Memorize how to get to these three locations and the codewords we've selected for each. If, for some reason, you require an immediate extraction, Harris and Bo will handle it. When you call, say, 'I need an immediate evac.' Whichever of them is on the other end of the call will speak the codeword that identifies one of the three locations and will meet you there. Harris and Bo will also be tied in to Resolute. What they know, we'll know, and vice versa. You'll be continuously supported. Destroy this information after memorizing it.

"We'll be working here, out of your apartment, this afternoon and tomorrow. It's after ten o'clock now. We'll step out for lunch around noon, then you have an appointment with a stylist at 2:15."

Jaz opened her mouth, but Bella held up her hand, forestalling Jaz's protest.

"I'll be blunt. Your current look doesn't mesh closely enough with Miss Walken's cover. Yes, Darcy is supposed to be somewhat avant-garde, but she's neo corporate, not Goth. That means the purple-tipped hair and heavy eyeliner have to go. You'll get a classy, upscale cut and color today, and we'll spend tomorrow buying you appropriate work *and* evening attire. You need to walk, talk, dress, and breathe Darcy Anne Walken—sedate corporate worker by day, party animal by night."

Jaz downed the dregs of her tea. "Okay. I concede. What about my tats? Do I cover up the ink or no?"

Bella's mouth opened. "Goodness. Here I thought I'd have to beat you within an inch of your life to gain your grudging cooperation."

"Sorry, but Richard and Harris 'beat' you to that at Broadsword—pun intended."

"Ha! I must write them a thank you note."

"Don't push it, Bella," but the corner of Jaz's mouth quirked upward.

Bella grinned. "To answer your question, yes, do cover what tats you can, but only at work. We'll make that easy for you when we select your work wardrobe. Outside the office, don't be afraid to let your artwork show.

"The plan is for you to fly to Houston over the weekend. You'll have Darcy's phone and ID on you and will pick up 'her' car in one of the airport's long-term parking lots."

"Great. More driving," Jaz muttered.

"Sorry?"

"Nothing. I'm fine."

I'll muddle through . . . somehow. Hope I don't trash Darcy's pristine driving record.

Bella continued. "Even though you, Darcy, supposedly, started your employment at Parish less than three months ago, you started at the corporate office, not the power plant. Most recently, however, you've been away for several weeks of compassionate leave. Your grandmother, your mother's mother, was killed in a car crash. Your grandfather was driving and remains critically injured."

Jaz nodded. "My *American* grandparents."

"Yes. The basic story is that your mother, widowed several years ago, was so overcome by these events, and being that you're the eldest of your siblings, you were expected to manage things for her and the family—your grandmother's funeral, your grandfather's care, and so on. Your new company was willing to grant you extended leave without pay after you had used up your bereavement leave."

Bella handed over a swipe card. "Your Parish employee badge and entry card."

She slid yet another sheet of paper toward Jaz. "Where to find your car when you deplane, the address of your apartment a few miles from the power station in Thompsons, and the names of the clubs our spotters say the cell members frequent most often. This Club Hyperion seems to be the current rage. Be prepared to dance a lot in order to blend in."

"Club Hyperion? Sounds like techno music. I can get down with that—although I prefer a Latin dance scene when I can find it."

Bella leaned her elbows on the table and cupped her chin in one hand. "You know, before Resolute's celebration party, I wouldn't have believed you. No one on the task force, including me and *especially* Wolfe, ever suspected you could or would dance, had *ever* danced. Well, you demonstrated otherwise, and how! Kind of threw us for a loop there. When and where did you get into the party scene?"

Jaz looked away. "For me, dancing was just another role, a part I played. But I found that I could close myself in and zone out to the music, with or without a dance partner. I could be one with the music, even while surrounded by a crush of strangers."

She cleared her throat and looked away. "If you don't mind, I'd rather not talk about it further."

"Sure. I suppose I just wanted to mention how watching you dance at our celebration party may have solidified the Director's decision to put you in the field—considering that we hope your first contact with AEA members will occur in a dance club."

Jaz said nothing, so Bella placed a final sheet on the table over the first three. A name and photo were printed on it.

"This is your HR contact at Parish. She's one of ours," Bella said.

"I have a contact inside? How did you manage that?"

Bella's mouth tightened. "The answer isn't a good one. Even though Wolfe's intelligence departments, including Resolute, operate with little or no Congressional oversight, the danger posed by AEA was too potent to keep under wraps. Wolfe was obliged to report the threat. When he briefed AEA to the House Intelligence Committee, the news set their hair on fire. And in much the way a forest fire shoots up a dry pine tree—and in the same way forest fires "crown" by jumping from treetop to treetop, we're now detecting serious leaks. It appears that our elected US representatives and their unelected, *politicized* staff members are known for their appalling OPSEC. To put it in real terms, *Congress leaks like a sieve*.

"We've plugged what we believe is the worst leak and put the fear of arrest and prosecution into a bunch of congressional staffers. That said, Congress, in turn, had to brief the President—and we're concerned the info will leak from the White House too. Who knows how much time we have until the media sinks its teeth into this story, spreads it far and wide, and we lose our tactical advantage?"

Jaz frowned. "If media speculation about AEA's plans were to leak to the public at large, AEA might push forward their attack timeline, and we'd lose our window to stop them."

"That about sums it up—which is why, when the intel committee heard that we believe AEA's primary cell and top leadership reside in Houston and that we were attempting to infiltrate that cell, they authorized Wolfe to contact the senior management of Parish's parent company and read them in on the threat and our plan.

"Wolfe swore the company's Chairman, CEO, and CFO to secrecy first and made them sign a stack of NDAs that promised stiff penalties, including jail time, should they disclose their classified knowledge of AEA before we take them down. And when Wolfe briefed those top managers and they understood the threat and how grim an outcome we are looking at? They were, shall we say, exceptionally motivated to help us.

"They arranged for us to insert one of Wolfe's seasoned agents into Parish's HR department. Ostensibly, she's from the parent company's corporate offices—where Darcy Walken recently began her employment—and has been sent to Parish to audit their HR processes. She will meet you inside the front door when you arrive for your first day on the job and will remain available should you need anything."

"Have we learned anything further about AEA's timetable, Bella? Anything at all?"

"Not with much confidence, no. Rusty, during a Resolute brainstorming session, came up with what might be a plausible trigger event, a date the terrorists might choose to launch their attacks. It's based on the national heat index. July is, historically, the hottest month overall in the continental US, making July the month that puts the greatest strain on the nation's power grid—and July 26 is the average hottest day in the nation. We're not saying we *know* July 26 is the date of the planned attack, but we are suggesting it has a certain logic to it."

"Hottest day of summer? Makes sense, but it doesn't leave us much time to figure out and thwart their attack strategy—nor can we rely on a date that indeterminate. Not without confirming evidence."

"You're right, but we have to at least keep it under consideration. We're under tremendous pressure now, and to add to that pressure, Wolfe's spotters have reported an uptick in private meetings across all AEA cells in the US. We need you to gain access to the Houston cell as quickly as can be managed, Darcy. It is your sole priority."

Jaz saw that Bella wouldn't press her further. Instead, Bella gazed deep into Jaz's eyes, conveying the gravity of the situation.

She thinks additional stress might cause me to push harder than what is wise—and she's right. If I blow my first approach to cell group members, a second approach on top of a botched one? It won't likely work . . . but it could get me killed.

Jaz nodded. "I understand." She looked away, breathed deeply, then deliberately changed the subject. "How's everyone back at Resolute?"

"Doing well, but missing you."

Jaz held her empty cup in both hands and stared down into it. "It's weird. I miss them too. A lot more than I thought I would."

"And that's weird?"

"For me it is—or at least the old me."

Bella nodded. "You mean BC?"

"BC? Before Christ? Oh. I get it. Yeah, maybe that's what I mean. Is that weird too?"

"Nope. In fact, I think you'll find that, for the rest of your life, every experience will fall into one of two camps, before you knew Christ and after you began living for him."

"Huh. Well, I have thirty-odd years of BC, Bella, and none of it is pretty. It . . . well, sometimes it haunts me."

Bella studied Jaz's serious expression. "That's not uncommon either, and I, probably more than most, *get you*, Darcy. When I lived in Sweden and Russia, my assignment was to steal emerging Russian tech. My MO was to seduce the men who had it—and I was, I'm sad to say, hugely successful at my job. Now, whenever I read what Paul wrote in 1 Timothy where he says, *Christ Jesus came into the world to save sinners—of whom I am the worst?* Well, memories from *my* past stand up and shout, 'Oh, yeah? Hold my beer.'"

Jaz twined her fingers and lowered her head, then said, "Bella, do you remember when I found photos of you as Linnéa Olander in an online Moscow society newspaper and shared them with Resolute?"

"You mean the day all of you figured out that I'd been Petroff's mistress?"

"Yeah, that day."

"I remember. What about it?"

"I was thinking . . . here's someone I can relate to."

Bella leaned forward. "Oh?"

Jaz ducked her head and continued to stare into her empty cup. "See, for a while I did some similar things. When I found those photos, I thought maybe I'd found someone a lot like me. More recently, I thought you might understand the . . . feelings I'm struggling with as a new Christian."

"Feelings like guilt?"

"Yeah. Do you . . . did you have those feelings?"

"I did, even before I committed my life to Jesus. See, as commonly as sex is used in espionage, I wasn't raised . . . that way. I knew what I was doing was wrong. The guilt I barely kept at bay was crushing."

"How did you get over the guilt and the-the-the shame of it?"

After a quiet moment, Bella asked, "You remember Ruth Graff, don't you?"

Jaz's lip curled. "See, of all the things I don't do? I definitely don't do therapists."

"Join the club. I only agreed to meet with her because the alternative was a life sentence in a maximum security facility somewhere outside the US. I'd been betrayed by my own agency; I was angry and rebellious—and that made me a security threat. Wolfe was that close to chucking me out the door."

Consternation replaced Jaz's disdain. "No way! I didn't . . . I didn't know that part."

"And I'm not saying you need a therapist, but maybe . . . maybe a trusted listener could help?" Bella reached over and put her hand on Jaz's, but only for a moment. "You say you're struggling with shame, Darcy. Well, you're right. I do understand those feelings—and I'm here if you ever want to share them with me."

Jaz said nothing. She fiddled with her empty cup. Stared out the patio doors. Heaved a sigh. "It's just that I . . . I cheated a lot of people out of their money."

"By hacking?"

"Yeah. I started with two hackers several years older than me. They taught me how to skim small amounts from bank deposits, but those small amounts over several thousand deposits really added up. When those guys moved on from simple theft to blackmail, I dropped them like a hot potato. I was terrified of going to prison."

Bella nodded. "You and me both."

"Well, I tried to go straight after that, I really did. But when the banks caught on to what we'd done, I was afraid the police would trace our hacks back to the guys I'd worked with—and I was convinced those guys would rat me out if given the right incentive, so I left town in a hurry."

"You needed money to relocate?"

Jaz shook her head. "Believe it or not? I had squirreled away thousands of dollars and had purchased some clean IDs. I took a bus to Vancouver, BC, under one name, then hopped a flight to Taiwan under another. Lived in Asia a while. Wanted to see Australia, so I spent some time there too. Eventually migrated to London.

"I had provided cybersecurity for a few companies in Canada and had cultivated some good clients before . . . before I had to move. I knew the business, so I started doing the same thing with new clients in Europe, working exclusively remote. But oftentimes I also took advantage of the data I had access to. I built multiple stock portfolios under different aliases using insider tips I gleaned from my clients. Other times, I hacked shady companies and uncovered information that I passed on to people . . . who were in the business of fixing what's broken."

"You mean law enforcement?"

"Some, yeah, but I preferred to feed leads to activists who rescued women and kids. I also traded in information. For profit. I stole or bought personal and financial data belonging to the wealthy or powerful, then I sold it on the black market, employed it for my own purposes, or secreted it away for future leverage. I chose to extort those individuals or organizations I felt deserved it.

"Often, when I found blatant corruption I . . . well, I stole from the corrupt rich, gave away a bunch, and pocketed the rest.

"I made a name for myself and took on a new handle: *Vyper*. As time went on, Vyper developed a fearsome rep, revered by many, dreaded by the rest. Other hackers wanting to make a name for themselves learned the hard way not to cross me. Oh. And I gathered followers . . . like thousands of followers—not that I encouraged that kind of nonsense."

"Ah."

She looked down at her hands. "But when it became known that I could track down just about anyone, I became a contract hunter. I never killed anyone myself, but I'm not stupid. I knew that the contracts I accepted, contracts to locate specific individuals, ended in their deaths."

Jaz took a deep breath. Without actually deciding to, she had begun to unburden herself.

CAMINA

Vyper

CHAPTER 26

Vyper

GULF OF AJACCIO, THE ISLAND OF CORSICA, FRANCE SUMMER 1993

CAMINA JACQUARD stretched in lazy abandon. The fine-grained sand under her towel was nicely warm, the sky dotted with fluffy clouds, the sun a distant, hazy glow through her closed eyes. The skimpy two-piece swimsuit she wore showed off her tan and her shapely figure to their best—particularly her small waist.

She had deliberately set herself apart from others on the beach and had greeted no one. Her objective was to promote the sense that she was alone, should anyone be watching. And she did so hope someone was watching.

The better for you to see me, my dear.

A shadow crept over her face. "*Pardonnez.* Would mademoiselle care for a fresh *apéritif?*"

"*Oui,* mademoiselle would."

"Perhaps another of the mint grapefruit mimosa?"

"Please. And charge it to my account."

He returned quickly with her drink.

As the waiter had noticed that morning, Camina kept a short stack of 20-franc notes under her beach bag. She slowly withdrew a single note and handed it to the young man.

The tip ensured the kind of attention to her needs she relished.

An hour later, when the attentive waiter again appeared with an offer to refresh her drink, she replied, "*Non.* I believe I will go up to my room for a while."

She gathered up her things and strolled along the edge of the water where she would catch the eyes of other sun bathers and individuals farther up the slope within the hotel patio. When she was opposite the patio steps, she turned toward them. She wended her way among those reclining on the sand, rolling her hips in an indolent manner, until she reached the hotel patio.

The patio boasted shaded tables and two lines of chaise lounges, most in use, facing the gentle ocean rollers. Camina wound her way through them, choosing a path that passed by a young man and his father, both of them sunning themselves upon lounge chairs.

Time to dangle the bait, Camina dearest.

The dark-haired and dark-eyed young man, perhaps all of sixteen years old, smiled in frank admiration as she approached. She smiled back and lifted her chin in coquettish fashion. She then dropped the same smile upon the young man's father. He, too, smiled his appreciation. Camina nodded to him before she passed by.

Two hours later, after a light lunch, Camina returned to her place in the sand. She did not have to wait long before the young man and his father approached her.

The boy spoke first. "Good day, mademoiselle."

Camina lowered her sunglasses and raised herself up on her elbows. She looked pleased to see them . . . because she was.

"Hello there."

"It is a lovely day, is it not?" the boy asked.

"I cannot fault any part of it," Camina replied, turning her gaze upon the father before looking back to the boy.

He smiled. "Would you permit me to introduce us? I am Vanya; this is my father, Alexi."

"Hello, Vanya. Hello, Alexi. I am Brigitte." She gestured to her extra towels. "Would you care to sit a moment?"

"Thank you, yes."

The two of them sat cross-legged on the towels. Camina turned on her side and propped her head up on one hand and elbow. The young man and his father ran their eyes from her chin to her toes and back. Both of them seemed to approve of the view.

Vanya asked, "You are American, Mademoiselle Brigitte?"

"I am, though I hardly consider myself one these days. I live in London now. Knightsbridge, to be exact. And you?"

"We have several homes. We spend much of the winter in Switzerland to ski St. Moritz and Zermatt. When we tire of the cold, we go to our Caribbean villa in St. Croix. Later, in the hot weather, we spend time at our dacha or on our yacht on the Caspian. Of course, Switzerland is also pleasant in the heat of summer, as is Corsica."

Must be nice.

Camina smiled again. "Such beautiful places! With a dacha on the Caspian, I must assume you are Russian?"

Vanya's father answered. "We are loyal members of the Communist Party and have many friends in Russia, even though our family's roots are in Ukraine."

It was a carefully worded, politically correct response, but Camina already knew they were Ukrainian and, *of course,* filthy, stinking rich oligarchs. It was, after all, why she had chosen them.

Open the trap now, Camina.

The father nodded for the boy to continue. "We could not help but notice, Mademoiselle Brigitte, that you are alone here while on holiday?"

"Ah, yes, but only because I enjoy my own company. However, as an additional benefit to traveling unaccompanied, the solitude allows me the freedom to make new acquaintances . . . when I am desirous of companionship."

Set the hook, dear girl.

The young man practically vibrated with excitement. "Would you . . . that is, we, my father and I, would like to extend our hospitality to you. Would you care to join us for a late lunch . . . in our suite?"

"Oh, bother," Camina replied with a pretty, annoyed huff. "I have already had my lunch. Also, when I have rested here a bit longer, I have plans to snorkel for a few hours."

She sighed and added, "What a shame."

The boy's hopeful expression fell, but his father stepped in to save the day. "If that is the case, would you care to join us later for dinner, Mademoiselle Brigitte?"

"I . . ." Brigitte hesitated. "I see from your wedding ring that you are married. Will your wife be joining us also?"

Alexi laughed aloud and pointed to the patio. Camina sat up and followed his finger to two stodgy middle-aged women, nodding side by side in sleepy harmony under the same umbrella.

"My wife's sister is traveling with us, you see. As it turns out, they will be taking our motor car to a helicopter awaiting them at the nearby airport. The helicopter will fly them to Lille Rousse on the north side of the island, after which they will take the afternoon ferry to Nice. From there, they will travel to Paris for several days of shopping."

Camina shook her head. "I confess I am somewhat envious of your wife, Alexi. I would enjoy such a trip to Paris!"

"Not as much as I would enjoy taking you there."

Camina laughed and touched his arm. "And you say they are leaving before dinner?"

"The car will depart about two o'clock."

"How . . . convenient," was Camina's breathy reply.

"I can promise that dinner will be everything you could desire," Alexi added. "We travel with my personal chef and a wide selection of wines and champagnes from my own cellar."

Camina grinned. "How delightful! I do so love champagne."

"Then I shall have my chef chill several bottles of my very best," Alexi grinned back. "Shall we say, 6:30?"

"What a treat. I look forward to dinner, but I warn you. After snorkeling all afternoon, I will have a voracious appetite." Camina dimpled as though she spoke of an appetite for something more than food.

Alexi stood. "We will not disappoint you, mademoiselle. Come, Vanya."

------●------

AT 5:10 THAT evening, Camina stopped by the hotel's front desk. The clerk was instantly attentive.

"How may we help you, mademoiselle?"

"Just letting you know that I will be checking out later this evening and would like to settle my bill at this time."

"Of course. One moment, please."

It actually took him several minutes to print up the bill, but when he presented it to her, she opened her purse and paid for it in cash. Camina knew she was not the only guest to pay exclusively in cash. As close as Corsica was to the casinos of Montecarlo and as celebrated as the French Riviera was to the very wealthy—many of whom were also very corrupt—cash was often the preferred tender.

"May we be of service for anything else, mademoiselle?"

Camina slid three 100-franc notes across the counter. "Could I prevail upon you to have my bags brought down and given into the care of the concierge until I call for them later this evening?"

Without looking down, he placed his hand over the bills. "But of course! Think nothing of it." When he withdrew his hand, the bills were gone.

"Thank you."

"*Au revoir*, mademoiselle. Safe travels."

------●------

ALEXI'S SUITE took up half of the top wing of the hotel. Its entry was down a long hallway, far from the distracting noise of the elevator. Two men wearing loosely cut coat jackets to better hide their sidearms stood post outside the entry.

Camina purposely delayed her arrival by ten minutes and took her time walking down that hall. The royal blue gown she wore clung to her hips; it glistened and moved in a hypnotic cadence as she glided toward the guards.

"Good evening, mademoiselle," one of them said.

"Hello. Am I late for dinner?"

"I am certain your hosts will not complain. And I beg your pardon, but we must check your bags before we announce you."

"I understand."

Her handbag was small, an evening purse containing only lipstick, a small perfume atomizer, and a few sundry items. The guard twisted the clasp open, used one finger to move the items to one side, then closed it.

Her other bag, however, was larger, more like a high-dollar beach bag. The bag, like her purse, had a clasp at the top, but it was much heavier, and Camina preferred that the guards not notice its weight.

She smiled. "Because your hands may be a tiny bit rough, perhaps I could remove the contents and show them to you?"

The guard, not following, frowned. Camina giggled. "Please. Allow me." She set the bag on the carpet and unsnapped it. Carefully, she drew out a full-length robe of sheer, gossamer fabric and held it toward the guard. "If you would extend your arm, *s'il vous plait?*"

After she laid the gown across his arm, Camina removed several more delicate items. "Well, there's this, and this, oh! And these."

The other guard, who had said nothing but was looking on, stifled a chuckle. The guard with the gown still hanging from his arm reddened.

"Thank you, mademoiselle. That will be all," he muttered. He jerked his chin to tell the other guard to open the door. "Please enjoy your dinner."

Camina nodded and placed the items back in her bag. Just before she went through the double doors, she purred, "Perhaps it would be best if, after dinner, you did not disturb us for the remainder of the evening?"

The first guard cleared his throat. They both nodded.

———◆———

AS CAMINA entered the suite's salon, her senses were pleasantly assaulted. She noted a small table intimately set for three and, to the side, a chef who was putting the finishing touches on something that tickled Camina's nostrils and caused her to salivate.

Vanya and Alexi rose from a sofa together.

Alexi spoke first. "Ah, Mademoiselle Brigitte! We are so pleased to see you." He leaned in and kissed her on both cheeks.

Vanya echoed his father's sentiments. "Yes, we are delighted you could come." He, too, although a little awkwardly, kissed her on both cheeks.

In return, Camina drew her gloved hand along his cheek and winked.

Moments later, they took their seats at the table. The chef served the food, and Alexi plied Camina with wine and conversation.

Acting out a role she had devised for herself came easily to Camina; what fatigued her and wore her down was carrying on longer conversations, deeper, more intimate exchanges or tête-à-têtes without specific objectives. She had learned how to tolerate the drain of dinner dialogue, however, by perfecting the art of asking personal questions and listening with rapt attention. Men did so enjoy talking about themselves. She also complimented the food and wine and spoke knowledgeably on both scores, which came easily when one had a near-photographic memory.

Finally, the chef and his assistant cleared the dinner things away and placed an ice bucket and two magnums of champagne at Alexi's elbow. Camina's eyes followed them as they departed through the service elevator near the back of the suite.

"Would you care for a glass of champagne now, mademoiselle?" Vanya asked.

"Oh, yes, my dear. Thank you."

Show time, Camina.

"I shall decant it for us," Alexi said.

When he stood and opened the bottle perfectly, Camina clapped her hands.

"Well done, Alexi! Well done."

She lifted her glass for him to fill, as did Vanya. When all three glasses were charged, young Vanya toasted her.

"To the loveliest woman to grace the beaches of Corsica," he said, at first shy, then happy he'd brought it off.

"You are too sweet, Vanya, and I thank you."

He liked her compliment too, she saw.

She downed half her glass, then looked around the suite. "Would you please excuse me and point me to the facilities?"

"But of course."

Camina took her little handbag with her. When she returned from the restroom, she declared, "My, what a lovely dinner—and I salute your choice of champagne, Alexi."

As she walked to his chair and bent as though to kiss him, he looked up expectantly. That was when a light mist dampened his face.

"W-what is that?"

Camina turned away before the young man realized anything was amiss with his father. She leaned into the young man and sprayed her "perfume" in his face also.

Within seconds, both men had slumped over in their chairs, Alexi onto the floor, Vanya onto the table, upsetting his glass of champagne.

The next part was tedious. Camina was strong, but Alexi was heavy, and she needed to drag him into his bedroom.

"Thank goodness I don't need to put you to bed, you oaf," she said aloud.

Soon, with some exertion, she had both men lying on the carpet behind Alexi's bedroom door and had made three lifelike lumps under the covers in his bed. She even shimmied out of her dress and draped it across the end of the mattress to aid in the desired appearance.

For good measure, she returned to the men and sprayed a second dose of "perfume" into their faces.

"That should hold you for a while."

Out in the living room she dumped the contents of her larger bag onto the sofa. The last articles of clothing to fall from the bag were a pair of capris, a button-up sleeveless blouse, and a soft pair of flats. She dressed in them, then removed the fake bottom of the bag and withdrew her laptop computer.

Computers had come a long way since she'd bought her first machine from Azteca. Her skills had grown in the meantime. She built her own computers now—always on the cutting edge of emerging tech.

Connecting her laptop to Alexi's computer and using the laptop to hack his machine was child's play. And once she was in Alexi's computer, she went to work.

An hour later, she had everything she'd come for. She'd bounced eighty percent of the balances in Alexi's three bank accounts around the globe before splitting the money into nine discrete amounts and dropping those amounts into nine separate accounts. She had also located proof positive of Alexi's role in trafficking young boys and girls from poor former Soviet states into Europe and the US. She copied the evidence onto her machine, then shut it down.

Fifteen minutes later, having used the service elevator to leave the suite, she collected her luggage from the concierge and took her waiting taxi to the airport.

She, like Alexi's wife and sister-in-law, also boarded a helicopter to Lille Rousse.

It was, in point of fact, *the same* helicopter. Apparently, the helo's engine had suffered a "malfunction" that had delayed its takeoff for several hours.

As Camina took her seat opposite them, the two stodgy middle-aged women found it hard to contain their excitement.

"Did you get everything you needed?" That question came from Dinara, Alexi's wife.

"Yes, more than enough. I will forward the information to those who can best deal with it."

"Good. I will pray to God that the children are saved and every evil man punished—but especially that brute I am saddled with and who wishes to corrupt my son!"

"And did you steal his money?" asked her sister, Lubov.

"Of course. Your cut has been transferred to your individual accounts in Morocco and Switzerland. What you do with the money is up to you; however, I would advise that you wait at least a year before you touch it."

"Do not worry about us," Lubov said softly. "I have a strong premonition that on Alexi's next birthday, he may suffer a fatal heart attack. Oh, dear! Ah, but then my sister will be free of that monster, you see, and perhaps her son will grow up to be a good man."

Camina's eyes widened in respect. Perhaps even admiration. "Er, wow."

Lubov exhaled. "We may not have the skills or the youth you have, *moya dorogaya* (my dear), but we are not lacking in courage."

"I begin to see that."

No longer holding back her tears, Dinara caught Camina's hand in both of hers. "Thank you, thank you, thank you! God bless you!"

"Uh, it has been my pleasure."

Now that the game was successfully complete and her role had expired, it took all of Camina's self-control not to yank her hand away from the emotional woman opposite her.

Ack! I don't "do" touch!

———◆———

FOR THE next two hours, while Bella listened breathlessly, Jaz related instance after instance in which she'd used her growing computer abilities to enrich herself and increase the height and breadth of her hacker reputation.

"As my status in the global hacker community rose, my skills were lauded, my services sought. I was Vyper, the Venom Queen. To the world, I was cold and deadly, simultaneously worshipped and emulated. In the early days, upon the successful conclusion of a contract, a number of my clients thought themselves wise to get rid of me. Tie up loose ends, so to speak, and claw back the bank transfers by which they'd paid me. They soon learned that their 'wisdom' was misguided. You see, I never took a contract without first gathering a thick layer of protective data and establishing mechanisms to release that information in the manner that would be most damaging to those people should I disappear or die prematurely. I called it *Clause Thirteen*."

She chuckled softly. "As my client list grew and, my processes matured, my SOP was to frankly discuss Clause Thirteen with new clients. After a time, those who sought my services were already familiar with this mechanism. It had become part and parcel with my reputation.

"But eventually? I became bored. The intrigue no longer excited me as it once had. The victories felt hollow and left a bitter taste in my mouth. I acquired properties in the UK, Switzerland, Spain, and Italy. I had plenty of money—and still do—and I bought whatever I wanted, Yet I had never felt poorer.

"Moreover, with every risk that came with a contract, another niggling anxiety took root inside me. On the one hand, I was bored. On the other? Apprehension and a nervous unease became my continual companions."

She turned a lopsided smile on Bella. "You're having trouble believing what you're hearing, aren't you."

Bella shook her head side to side. "I am . . . astounded."

"Yes, well, seeking a quieter, less stressful life, I returned to Canada. Bought a condo and a few investment properties in Ottawa." She laughed a little, but sadly. "Despite the many countries in which I'd lived, the contacts I'd made online, and the individuals I'd helped, and regardless of my lofty reputation across the hacker community, I had to admit how alone I truly was. I had made no real friends. Had not allowed anyone to get close to me.

"Oh, I could enter a club and dance for hours without uttering a word, and I could, over short intervals, act out a role or play a part. Why? Because they weren't real. I considered them mind games or fantasy. But authentic emotions and real relationships? I have always experienced difficulty navigating . . . genuine social settings. It has a name, this . . . malady I have."

Bella touched Jaz's hand again. "I understand. Yours is a little understood condition."

Jaz blew out a resigned breath. "While living in Europe, I read extensively on what is termed the autism spectrum. I found myself identifying with Asperger Syndrome—high functioning, often considered 'brilliant.' Ha! At last I knew what I was and how I differed from neurotypical people. Did that knowledge help me? No. I was empty and lost. And nothing helped or changed me. Until . . ."

Her words trailed off.

"Until the Ukrainian mob in New York put a hit on you for stealing their data? Until you joined the task force? Until Jesus?"

Jaz nodded, a far-away expression in her eyes. "Yes, yes, and yes. From this vantage point in my life, I can look back and see God's hand at work. Moving me and moving others—including you, Bella—like pieces on a chess board, setting in motion the events that would lead to *this* moment. To us sitting here today, having this conversation."

"Will you finish telling me your story, Darcy? You are a great treasure to me. I want to hear how Jesus did it, how he brought you out of your, shall we say, less-than-legal lifestyle?"

Jaz nodded. "Okay, but I left out the linchpin, Bella: *Zakhar*. He was my introduction to *you*, the contract I accepted to hunt you down so that Zakhar might eliminate you. It may not have been God's first move, but for me it was the most vital."

Bella asked, "But what came before that?"

"Ah, yes. God had to set the board first."

She drummed her fingers on the table. Sighed again. "So, there I was, minding my own business . . ."

CHAPTER 27

OTTAWA, ONTARIO
AUGUST 1996

CAMINA JACQUARD lifted the cup of hot tea and held it under her nose, breathing in the sweet spiciness before taking her first sip.

Perfect. Just perfect.

Perfect also described the little sidewalk café where she sat. The dinner rush had ended, the crowds had thinned, and the evening was balmy and peaceful. Camina was enjoying the pleasant albeit somewhat distant view of the Rideau River, its waters moving in a timeless journey northward, pouring itself as a curtain of water into the Ottawa River at Rideau Falls, the Ottawa River later merging with the St. Lawrence, and eventually, the Atlantic.

She had returned to Canada in early March. Since then, she'd located and bought a small condominium from which she'd fashioned yet another temporary residence for herself. She didn't consider it a home, a place where she might put down roots, for she never stayed in any one place longer than a year.

How could she? The Itch no longer tormented her day and night. It did, however, require her to obsessively monitor her back trail and relocate regularly.

Camina also owned a small apartment complex in Ottawa. She had set aside one unit in the complex for her personal use; the remainder of the units were rented out. The rents and maintenance of the complex were handled by a property management company—a company with strict orders to never enter her personal unit.

Camina had made such an intrusion difficult. The only entrance was a steel door set in a steel frame, locked multiple ways with the best locks. And should a determined party succeed at gaining entrance? She would know. Motion-activated cameras would record the intrusion; code she'd written herself would send an alert to her cell phone and several email accounts—although a common thief, looking for cash, jewelry, or items to hock would find the apartment odd. It was, in fact, *empty*, with the exception of an encrypted computer and a sizable server array located in the bedroom.

That Ottawa apartment was where Camina kept her data backup, an expansive library of incriminating or otherwise useful information she'd painstakingly accumulated over the past decade. Camina thought of the data stash as both passive income stream and insurance policy. Present and former clients who paid regularly for Camina to keep her accrued data private also knew she could make it public with a few keystrokes.

She was alone at her table—just as she preferred it—enjoying her tea, overlooking the pleasant tableau and loving both the view and a welcome moment of peace when, with no fanfare, a man holding a cup and saucer stopped beside her.

"Pardon me, Miss Simard."

Jolted from her tranquil reverie, Camina looked up.

<hr>

JAZ'S EYES were fixed on her hands and her empty cup clenched in their death grip. She tore her eyes from them and looked into Bella's face. "You have to understand, Bella. I hadn't used that name—hadn't even heard it spoken—since I was sixteen years old. For this *stranger* to call me by my birth name, rocked me to my core."

Bella blinked. "Your birth name isn't Thérèse Benoit?"

Jaz laughed aloud. "Not even close. So I have a birth name I don't use. You've had so many names that sometimes I get confused."

Then Jaz scowled at her. "You're not the only one on the task force who's lived numerous secret lives under a heap of fake identities, *Linnéa*. Or perhaps I should call you Marta Forestier? How about Elaine Granger?"

Bella chose to overlook Jaz's little fit of temper. "Stop that, you brat, and get on with your story. Who was this man?"

Jaz cooled quickly. "I didn't know; he was completely unknown to me. And I didn't know *what* he was either. Not until he said, 'My name is Bernard Dupont. I work for the Canadian Security Intelligence Service—CSIS. May we talk?'"

Jaz's laugh was filled with irony. "Well, Bella, at that point, you could have knocked me over with a feather."

Bella fell back in her chair. "Wow. I have always wondered how you came to work for Canadian Intelligence."

"It wasn't by choice, let me tell you. But at that moment, I was so tongue-tied, he just set his cup of café au lait on my table and pulled up a chair next to mine, all cozy-like. He didn't even let me recover my wits before he went at me, hammer and tongs."

Jaz screwed up her mouth and affected a prim voice, "'CSIS has been following your exploits for two years now, Miss Simard, and I must tell you how impressed we've been with the creativity and sheer panache of your work, and how often we have applauded your, shall we say, *unique style* of handling certain criminal types. Did I say types? Yes, your exploits do seem to gravitate toward specific types, you know. Traffickers. Abusers of women and children. Senior management of greedy and unethical corporate entities. Corrupt politicians and bureaucrats.

"'We particularly admire your handling of bureaucratic corruption. CSIS and our international counterparts are frequently hamstrung by political corruption, which is a great frustration to those of us who resist bribes and other inducements to *go along to get along*. So, whenever one of our intelligence or law enforcement entities received enough evidence—supplied *anonymously*—to bury a known but heretofore untouchable bureaucratic criminal, well! It was a good day for us, let me tell you.

"'Of course, for a time, we could not discover the identity of our benefactor, since you hid yourself so thoroughly, Miss Simard. Nonetheless, we cheered for you. And when wicked men found themselves in inexplicable financial ruin and we attributed their misfortune to your unseen efforts? Why, whomever you were, we toasted you with drink after hours.'"

Jaz shook her head. "He said they eventually heard rumblings, just rumors at first, about a hacker who was waging war on traffickers and corruption, someone who called himself Vyper." She snickered. "They initially believed Vyper to be a man, because only a guy could be that good, right?"

Bella checked her watch. "Drat! I *have got* to hear more, but perhaps this is a good place to pause our conversation? Either that, or we'll need to reschedule your hair appointment."

Jaz's stomach rumbled. "Hey, you promised me lunch!"

"And yet you talked us straight through lunchtime. Come on; let's get you to your stylist. We can eat afterward. What sounds good? You pick."

"*Everything* sounds good. Those jokers at Broadsword tried to starve me—and now you're dead set on erasing me. New hair style. New wardrobe. *Gah!*"

Bella laughed and picked up her handbag. "Well, actually, I think you look pretty good as you are, *Darcy Walken*. Just a slight makeover and a wardrobe update should complete your prep for this operation."

"*Fine*. Have it your way, but when we're done for the day? I want Chinese, and it had better come in the form of an all-you-can-eat buffet."

———◆———

TWO HOURS later, Jaz gazed into a mirror to evaluate her new look. "I see what you meant about texture, Allison."

Her stylist, standing behind Jaz, ran her fingers through Jaz's freshly colored and styled hair. Multihued layers fell from her fingertips in shimmering waves.

"Oh, yes! By adding fine strands of deep brown and vibrant auburn, we broke up the stark monotony of solid black. Now your hair possesses depth and interest."

"I thought purple-violet was plenty of interest," Jaz grumbled.

"But it was something of a dated interest, Sweetie. You have now a cosmopolitan look about you."

Jaz spied Bella's reflection in the mirror. "Wipe that grin off your face and pay the lady, Bella. I'm starving."

<hr>

JAZ AND Bella found a table in the corner of the Chinese restaurant where they could talk privately. First, though, they ate. Bella picked through the items she'd selected, thoughtfully sampling one dish after another, while Jaz dug into her loaded plate with fervent gusto.

Neither of them talked until Jaz slowed down.

"Whew! I was famished. Not only did Richard and Harris starve me, you wouldn't believe the grueling ordeal Richard and Travis put me through over the past couple of days."

"Oh, I know. I received their after-action report. Well done, Darcy!"

Jaz ducked her head. "Thanks. I . . . well, honestly? I prayed a lot. I had to. In my mind, most of the competition tasks were just this side of death-defying. I think he helped me, though. I mean, somehow I did things I'd never done before, so I'm pretty sure he helped me."

"You think he helped you? He who?"

"You know. *God.* God helped me."

"See? Isn't that better, acknowledging *God* with more than a nonspecific pronoun?"

"Yeah, yeah. I need dessert."

"Or maybe you don't want to regain the weight you lost during your training program? You're looking positively 'cut' at the moment. Instead, I'd love some coffee while you tell me the rest, how Canadian Intelligence recruited you."

With reluctance, Jaz set aside her fork. "Right. I was telling you how I 'met' Bernard Dupont. And I suppose this part in my tawdry tale is the prelude to when I first heard the names Elaine Granger and Linnéa Olander . . . When I began to hunt you for that evil man, Zakhar."

<hr>

THE MAN had the audacity to sit down at her table? Worse yet, to crowd her? Camina tried to freeze him with a look, but, unfazed, he smiled pleasantly instead. He was, she realized with a start, honestly pleased to be horning in on her privacy.

He doesn't see how he's destroying the tenuous peace I've fought so hard to find! Now I have to flee this place. Buy yet another fake identity. Start over.

Dupont used the moment while sipping his café au lait to scan their surroundings. "The three of us at CSIS who have avidly followed your exploits were gratified when our cyber folks, after many months, connected the illustrious Vyper to your Camina Jacquard alias. And so, you cannot imagine how delighted we were when Camina bought a ticket to return to Canada."

His eyes met hers. "Tracing you back to Geneviève Zenibaa Simard, however? That took more time and manpower than you might suppose. Trust me, we were duly impressed. We would probably never have backtracked you had you not made one tiny mistake. You called the house where you grew up—a group home run by Albert and Maude Northam—from an office phone belonging to Protect My Network, a startup business registered to one Adele Logan. From there? We began to, finally, piece things together."

He smiled in what could have passed as genuine appreciation. "Really, the number of aliases and how you employed them at such a young age? Brilliant. Inventive. Tenacious."

Camina bared her teeth and snarled at him. "I have no idea what you're talking about. I've done nothing wrong! I have a peaceful, uncomplicated life. What gives you the right to accost me publicly in this manner?"

His pleasant exterior fell away. "Why don't you ask me why I'm here, Miss Simard."

"I don't care why you're here."

He pretended he hadn't heard her. "Fact is, we'd like to recruit you."

"I don't care and I—what?"

"Recruit you. Right here and right now. We invite you to come work for CSIS. You see, we are in desperate need of your 'hacking' skills. Yours will be a unique position, of course, in line with your own unique and individual personality. We'll place you within another Crown entity, a sister to CSIS. You'll be an invaluable asset with a legitimate job positioned inside an unassailable organization.

"Ostensibly, you'll be a highly paid—emphasis on *highly paid*—cybersecurity specialist, a white hat protecting us from the black-hat world. We don't believe doing so will require all that much of your time, though, nor would any sort of mundane work make the best use of your skill set—and, let me assure you, we do *not* wish you to be bored.

"Accordingly, CSIS will assign you certain tasks, but only the most complex and *interesting* of problems. We will not tell you how to solve those problems. Rather, we'll grant you the liberty to accomplish our tasks with no questions as to how."

The sheer magnitude of Dupont's offer stole her breath away. It took her a moment to gather herself.

"I don't want your job."

"I presumed as much, but my admiration for you being what it is, I wished to invite you first."

"First?"

"Well, yes. A well-mannered, courteous conversation, followed by the extension of our gracious offer."

Suddenly it was Camina who was scanning her surroundings. "And what comes *second* if, say, *first* doesn't work out?"

He spread his hands as if to say, *I apologize; however, I am not in control.*

"Sadly, Miss Simard, my people, who are numerous and nearby, will escort you to a facility where the working conditions are not nearly as amenable to a free spirit such as yourself."

"You can't do that! I have done nothing wrong!"

He nodded. Slowly. "I am sorry to report that Geneviève Zenibaa Simard is wanted by the Saskatchewan RCMP. It appears that she is implicated in a large number of bank thefts from years past, thefts accomplished by hacking the deposits of those banks and altering their records."

Fear flooded Camina, filling her bloodstream with ice, chilling her body. Her cold fingers on the table trembled while The Itch screamed in the back of her head. Bernard Dupont placed a steady, warm hand over hers, while Camina struggled not to throw up.

Well, if I hurl, I'll aim for his suitcoat. It would serve him right!

He went on, as though unaware of her distress. "But why go to disagreeable extremes when what we offer can be entirely pleasing all the way round? Ah! Did I also mention, should you accept our invitation, that you could continue your, how shall I phrase it? your *freelance work* on the side? Make all the money you like after business hours and dole out justice to those to whom the justice system turns a blind eye—*we don't care*—as long as you handle the problems we assign you. So, really, why would you turn down such an agreeable proposal?"

"Why, indeed," Camina ground out between her clenched teeth.

He seemed genuinely delighted. "We have a deal then? Perfect!"

"Oh, yah. Just *super*."

———◆———

OVER THE next two hours and several cups of tea, Jaz regaled Bella with tales from her time as a "white-hat" hacker with Canadian Intelligence—all while, supposedly, she worked as the top cybersecurity specialist for the RCMP in Ottawa.

Bella shook her head in wonder. "But if I understand what you've told me—and please correct me if I'm wrong—you're saying you consulted with the FBI and located a serial rapist and murderer operating in the US Pacific Northwest? Really?"

"CSIS offered the problem to me, hoping I'd succeed and earn CSIS some points with the FBI. It wasn't just me, though. I had the assistance of my many contacts within the hacker community."

"And you helped organize the tens of thousands of women who sued Dow Corning for injuries caused by their breast implants?"

Jaz lifted one shoulder. "All I did was build a website and invite any injured woman to add her testimony to it. As the site began to gain traction and the number of testimonials grew, I gave the lawyers managing the class action suit access to the site. But that job was personal. On the side, not for CSIS."

"What about the human trafficking rings you mentioned?"

"I despise human traffickers."

"As do I, but I'm not the one who infiltrated them."

"I may have hacked a couple trafficking networks. Found out how they 'marketed' their 'products.' Despicable."

"Then sent the FBI the links to those sites?"

"I can neither confirm nor deny."

"Amazing. You also alluded to messing with the bank accounts of several Colombian cartels?"

"Let's just say that Cartel A *happened* to find evidence that Cartel B had stolen a drug shipment from them, and Cartel C was told that Cartel A had muscled in on their territory—and so on and so forth." Jaz laughed with no humor. "*Oy vey*, such a ruckus they raised! All that fussing and infighting, shooting, and killing."

Bella snorted. "You don't say."

Jaz's voice dropped to a whisper. "What I did sent some of those men to their deaths, Bella. How can God forgive me for taking another person's life?"

Bella winced. "Men have died by my hand, Darcy, up close and personal. I know full well the weight you're carrying."

The media coverage of 911 flooded into Jaz's memories, including a hijacking that almost was and that *would* have been, had it not been for the intervention of Quincy Tobin, Sky Marshal, and a mysterious female passenger, a woman whose name the news media declared was one Marta Forestier. A woman who deplaned in Canada and was never seen again.

The same woman sitting across the table from Jaz.

Bella shifted the conversation's trajectory. "And when you went to work for Bernard Dupont, he kept his word to you?"

"Yes. I was given the freedom to solve CSIS problems in my own in-ventive manner, keeping CSIS out of the spotlight. In return, he never interfered with the freelance projects I conducted on the side to pad my bank accounts."

"One of those freelance projects was to hunt me down."

Jaz shook her head. "I'm truly sorry. At first, it was just another job. But then? That weasel Zakhar got on my nerves."

"Yes, he had that effect on me back in Russia."

Jaz snickered. "He irked me so much, that I sent him false sightings of you. Oh, how I led him on a merry chase! But when he deduced that I was deceiving him and hired the Brighton Beach mob's hacker to replace me? Well, I fixed his wagon, didn't I? I fixed all of them. Zakhar. Syla. Even the mob."

"And became the mob's Enemy *Numero Uno*. CSIS had to sneak you out of Canada and hide you in our newborn task force."

Jaz looked down. "I'm grateful to him, *to God*, for orchestrating that situation. It was how he brought me to Resolute and to you. It's the best thing that's ever happened to me. And yet . . ."

"And yet?"

"Nothing good I've done excuses or forgives the thefts I've committed and the many deaths I no doubt contributed to. Because of those things, I still feel a great deal of guilt. Shame."

"I see."

They were both quiet then. Bella used the time to pray.

Lord? How would you have me advise Jaz?

She already knew, though. How could she forget what the Lord had used to demolish the demonic stronghold over her own life?

She finally said, "Darcy, the thing that truly set me free from years of guilt and shame was a time of deep, focused repentance. No rushing, no glossing over. No blanket prayer to cover my many sins. Instead, I asked the Lord to lead me, to bring each sin to mind, one at a time. As he did, I confessed those sins aloud. I named them. I acknowledged them. I brought them to the feet of Jesus. I asked him to forgive me, and I made a sincere vow to turn away, to never return to that lifestyle.

"That day was like a stake in the ground for me, a place I could point to and remind myself, 'This is where I turned away from sin, this is where I turned to Jesus and he forgave me. This is where he set me free.'"

"And after that you were truly free? No more nightmares or fears that your past would catch up to you? No more guilt?"

No more Itch?

"Yes, I was finally free. I don't mean that those accusing voices in my head disappeared right away. I had to remind them, too, of that day, my repentance day, my deliverance day. When I declared to those voices that I had already confessed those sins and that Jesus had paid for them? Well, they shut up. They had to."

"You said, 'accusing voices.'"

"Satan employs many strategies to condemn us. To torment us. Ugly memories and accusations in our heads that try to yank us back into guilt and shame, that try to haunt or drive us."

"Drive us?"

"Yes. Torment does that. It tries to make us disbelieve or distrust the salvation Jesus has given us. Torment urges us to run away from the Lord instead of to him. The Holy Spirit isn't like that. Moreover, he doesn't bring us into confusion, because confusion is not of God."

Instantly, Jaz felt like she'd been walloped over the head. Her senses whirled, and Miss Timmons' admonitions flooded into her mind.

"I feel strangely prompted to tell you something . . . What I want to say is this: Almighty God is not the god of confusion. When he sends his Holy Spirit to speak to an individual, he will not speak confusion but clarity. The Holy Spirit will prick your conscience over sin, but it is not his way to confuse or agitate.

"The devil, on the other hand, loves to create confusion and anxiety. The more he can stir the pot and confound the issues, the more likely it is that he can push or prod a person into making foolish and willful decisions—bad decisions with bad outcomes."

Jaz, with wonder in her voice, said, "Bella, I-I think I've been listening to the wrong voice all along! Since I was a teenager, I believed 'intuition' was keeping me safe, but now I think that what I *thought* was intuition was actually torment, like an itch in the back of my head, an itch I could never scratch or satisfy. Torment drowning me in fear. Torment driving me to run, always run."

Joy broke out in Bella's smile. "Only the Holy Spirit could have revealed that to you. From this point forward, you will know his voice better and better, and you will learn to discern between him and the voice of the accuser."

"I want that, Bella. I want to know God better. And I want to repent like you did. Will you help me do that? Right now?"

"It would be my honor." She glanced around. "But why don't we go back to your apartment where you'll have the privacy you need to 'get it all out on the table' so to speak."

Jaz's eyes swept the restaurant. "Probably a good idea."

They gathered their things and headed for the door.

"Say, Miss *Darcy Walken*, do you have tissues at home or should we stop on the way and buy a box or two?"

"A box *or two?* Are you saying I'm going to need that many?"

"Hmm. Yes. Very likely."

COVERT OPERATIVE

Vyper

CHAPTER 28

MAY 2002

MONDAY MORNING, Darcy made her way through the WA Parish Generating Station's employee entrance and stopped at the security checkpoint. Her eyes sought her inside contact, the woman who was to meet her. *There*. She recognized her from a photo and nodded. The woman nodded back.

"Welcome, Miss Walken. Let's walk to the HR Department and complete your leave paperwork before I show you to your workstation, shall we?" She said it loud enough that anyone nearby would hear it.

The woman led Jaz through several hallways, then closed her office door to give them privacy. She held out her hand. "Beverly Hollis."

"Darcy Walken."

"Nice to meet you. When we're done here, I'll escort you to your workstation in the IT Department. This isn't supposed to be the first time we've met, however, so be sure to act like we've been acquainted for a while. First off . . ." she pulled a sheet of paper from her desk drawer and placed it on her desk, "follow along with me. We're here. Your department is here. Restrooms, cafeteria, first aid, here, here, and here.

"Now, even though you're listed as being a Parish employee of three months, you and your three coworkers here haven't met because we were just bringing you over from our corporate offices when your cover family's accident occurred. In an emergency situation like that, we wait until the employee returns to complete the necessary paperwork."

"Nice touch."

"Yes. Your ostensible three-week hiatus will smooth your entrance here a bit. I'll introduce you around, but your coworkers have already been told why you needed to take the time off. They will be sympathetic and helpful, if you allow them to be. I've been told that you know, in principle, what your position requires. Larry is the IT Department lead and will assign your tasks, but if you need anything outside of your department, I'm here. The sole reason I've been temporarily placed at Parish is to support you."

"Thanks, Beverly. I appreciate that."

"Let's get you settled, then."

After Beverly had walked her to the small IT Department, introduced her to the three men who were her coworkers, and showed her to her cubicle, she again offered her hand.

"Good luck, Miss Walken. We expect good things from you."

Jaz knew Beverly's well wishes applied to more than success at her new job.

WHILE SETTLING into her new role, Jaz was careful not to say or do anything that might bring down suspicion of any kind on herself. For the first three days she watched and paid attention to what went on around her. She was dying for a stick of Black Jack, but she knew better than to give in to the impulse. As a poor substitute, Jaz purchased a pack of spearmint gum and had to content herself with it.

By her fourth day, she had oriented herself to Parish's network, had done whatever Larry asked of her, had taken her coffee and lunch breaks with the IT team, and had worked hard to mask her boredom. She'd even dawdled over the tasks Larry assigned to her lest she have nothing at all to do.

It was while performing those mundane tasks that she loaded and used her own custom-made diagnostic tools to scan for suspicious code across the Parish network. In addition to plant administrative functions, the various network nodes also contained the generating station's operating software, although the plant operators themselves, employees who monitored and controlled the various aspects of power generation and distribution, sat in another building altogether.

From now on, I'll run this scan daily. If a piece of code even breaks to the next line differently than the last scan, I'll know about it.

Her scans turned up nothing out of the ordinary, which was a positive outcome, but she knew she had to remain vigilant. Unfortunately, the price of vigilance was Death by Boredom.

Somebody shoot me, please! I can't access the Internet from this air-gapped network. Can't reach the boards and chat rooms I usually monitor. Certainly can't send email. Not sure how long I can keep this up before I start babbling nonsense and drooling on my keyboard.

At least the weekend was approaching, and with it, her initial foray into Houston's nightlife. Thursday at lunch, she made an overture to her coworkers.

"Hey, guys? Any good dance clubs around? I've been so immersed in my mom's grief and with handling our family's problems that I have *got* to shake it off for a few hours."

"We heard what happened," Mick said in a consoling voice.

"Yeah. We're really sorry for your loss," Larry added. Mick and Stewart nodded in unison.

"Thanks. I appreciate that. I, well, I just need an outlet this weekend, you know? I want to dance until I'm ready to drop."

"Country? Pop? Latin? What's your preference?" Stewart asked.

"I like it all," Jaz prevaricated, since she about gagged over country music, "but I prefer Latin. And for that, I need decent dance partners. Can you point me in the right direction?"

Out of the corner of her eye, she saw the three guys exchange surreptitious glances. Then Larry nodded to Stewart.

"Straight or gay?" Stewart asked evenly.

"I don't swing that way, if that's what you're angling for. I go clubbing to dance, not to hook up."

She took a bite of the salad on her plate. When she'd swallowed it, she asked, "So, who won the pool?"

Her coworkers, in near unison, froze.

"Uh, what do you mean?"

"You guys have a bet going, right? 'Is she straight or gay'? Which one of you dorks won?"

Larry's chuckle was forced and nervous. "Guess I did. You're not going to report us to HR, are you? It was just an innocent bet. The three of us caught glimpses of your ink." He motioned to her neckline and where her sleeves ended. "Great art, by the way, at least from what we can see. Stewart and Mick figured you were gay. I didn't."

"Well, I'm *not*, and I'll tell you what," Jaz said with a smirk, "Cut me in on half of the action, and I'll forget about your boorish behavior . . . this time."

"Done! Pay up, guys," Larry demanded.

Stewart and Mick, red-faced but grinning, each handed over a ten-dollar bill. Larry passed one of them to Jaz.

"Thanks for being a good sport, Darcy."

She grinned back. "No problem, and I'm glad you appreciate good ink when you see it. Now back to Houston's dance scene. What's hot right now?"

Stewart again answered. "Well, you know you have to drive into the metro, right? Takes forty-five minutes to an hour from Thompsons, depending on the time of day. Actual drive time depends on where you live, how far east your club of choice is, and what kind of traffic snarl you run into. I can write down a few names for you. If you have Internet at home, you can look them up."

"Thanks. I really appreciate it. One of my neighbors did mention a place—Club Hyperion, I think it's called?"

"Yeah, I know it," Mick said, reaching for his fries. "Upscale and pricey, but definitely popular. It's a going concern—and they play a lot of Latin music."

"Great. I'll probably try it and a few other places this weekend. I have *got* to kick these doldrums to the curb."

IN ACTUALITY, Wolfe's surveillance team had already identified the four clubs the Houston AEA cell frequented—Club Hyperion being their most visited. Friday afternoon following work, Jaz got on her laptop, navigated to the secure chat room she shared with Resolute, Harris, and Bo, and posted that she planned to hit Hyperion first.

The idea was for Jaz to dress for a night on the town and call a cab to drive her into the city.

No way I'm driving myself into a strange downtown area, particularly at night. I can barely navigate a dune buggy around a dirt course. Wolfe wants me there? He can eat the cost.

Jaz was to enter a club and start letting herself be seen. While she danced, she would keep one eye out for AEA cell members. She was to remain at any given club for ninety minutes before moving on to the next one. In this way, Jaz would become familiar with Houston's nightlife. Conversely, the bouncers, bartenders, and regulars would notice her and begin to accept her as a regular. Harris and Bo were to follow Jaz, but stagger their visits to arrive half an hour later.

If, after ninety minutes, Jaz hadn't IDed any AEA marks, she would move on to the next club. Bo and Harris would remain at the first club a half-hour longer, then follow her to the second club. Leapfrogging from club to club in that manner, Bo and Harris kept tabs on her while adding additional coverage to each club in case any of the cell members showed up after Jaz had left.

Jaz was in her second club, sipping a ginger ale through a straw, when someone behind her spoke.

"Care to dance?"

Jaz almost snorted the drink out her nose. She recovered and turned. "Sure."

The floor was packed, but her partner was good—*very* good, and Jaz let herself go, trusting his lead. He spun her out then back, so that she was snug against his chest.

"They told me you could dance," Harris murmured.

"They didn't tell me *you* could."

A few moves later, he pulled her in tight again.

"Dancing is important to me. It's how I'll win the girl."

"Oh? How many girls might that be?"

"Just the one. I'm a one-girl guy."

The song came to an end. Harris walked her back to the tiny table. He gestured to a waitress, snagged a fresh drink for Jaz, and dropped a five dollar bill on the tray.

"Thanks for the dance."

He melted into the crowd, and Jaz didn't see him the rest of the evening.

Their efforts that night, however, proved fruitless. Jaz arrived home after 2:00 a.m., wiped out and with nothing to report. Not one of the identified cell members had shown up in the chosen clubs while Jaz or Bo and Harris were there.

Hopefully, we'll have better hunting tomorrow night, Jaz told herself.

———●———

JAZ SLEPT in Saturday morning. After she'd had a chance to wake up and eat brunch, she busied herself with ordinary weekend tasks, doing laundry, cleaning the bathroom, vacuuming the apartment's carpet. Late afternoon, she forced herself to take a nap so that she'd be energized that evening to stay out as late as needed.

Near dusk that evening, Jaz showered, washed her hair, and prepared for the night's work. Dressed in a tight sequined dress, Jaz called a cab to take her into downtown Houston.

When she arrived at Club Hyperion, the place was already rocking. She danced with four different partners, thanked them for the dance, then managed to disengage from them. She spied Bo at a table not far from hers. It was all she could do not to start looking for Harris.

Keep your focus, Darcy Walken, she told herself. *No distractions.*

Oh? And is Harris a distraction?

"Shut up," she whispered.

With a fixed and bored expression, she slowly scanned the room. As her eyes passed over Bo, he tipped his head to his left. Just a little.

Jaz picked up her diet Coke and sipped. After a few moments, she let her eyes pass over the crowd in the direction Bo had indicated.

"Do you mind if we share this table? The place is packed."

Three guys hovered around Jaz. The one who'd spoken added, "Be glad to buy you a drink if you let us share with you."

Jaz smiled. "I'm good, thank you, but you can have the table. I just saw a friend of mine."

She saluted with her Coke and began a slow trek around the dance floor. Eventually she arrived at a table shared by three women.

"Hey! Do you mind if I share your table? I'm here by myself and I'm afraid to leave my drink while I'm dancing. Worried some jerk will drop a roofie in my glass while I'm on the floor."

"We don't mind," one of the women replied.

Harris, with perfect timing, appeared at her elbow. "Hey! I remember you from last night. Want to dance again?"

Jaz looked her question at the three women.

"Sure. Go ahead," a second woman said.

Jaz set her Coke on the table and smiled. "Thanks!"

Harris pulled her into the frenzied hedge of gyrating bodies. "Not much room tonight."

"No worries—by the way, your timing was exquisite."

"That's me. Mr. Exquisite."

Jaz laughed, not sure if she was laughing for show or because he was just plain funny.

Doesn't matter, she told herself. *My new girlfriends won't care—and neither will I if they buy my approach.*

The DJ announced a short break. Harris took her back to the table and, still holding her hand, said, "I'm Rick. Thanks for the dance."

"Darcy. See you around, Rick."

As Harris departed, a grinning Jaz turned toward the three girls. "Eeee! He is sooo stinking cute! And he can dance too."

They laughed with her. The blond said, "I'm Stevie. That's Melly—"

"And I'm Hannah." Hannah was a tall African American. "Please ask Rick to bring his friends next time—but only if they can dance like he can."

"Consider it done!" Jaz laughed.

She held up her drink. "Cheers!" and the four of them clinked their glasses. *And just like that, I'm in.*

———●———

JAZ SPENT another hour laughing and chatting with her new friends, before she excused herself. She didn't want to overstay her welcome; rather, she wanted to leave them thinking well of her. As she said good night, she asked if she'd see them again.

"Without a doubt," Hannah replied. "We're not here every night, of course, but we're regulars."

"Super!" Jaz said. "And I know I'll be back for more of *Rick!*" She blew them a kiss, then started through the crowd.

She was exhausted when the cab dropped her home. The crush of bodies had almost been her undoing. *I can only handle so much smiling and pretending that I'm not ready to run, screaming, away from the noise and chaos.*

The phone in her apartment was ringing when she unlocked her door—and it was after midnight.

As she picked up the phone, she thought, *Only my team has this number, and we're not supposed to use this apartment phone to communicate. Whoever's calling? It's not going to be good news.*

It wasn't.

"Any progress to report?"

"Yes; I made a good approach this evening. Very natural and cordial. Three women. One I recognized from the photo spread, a woman named Hannah. She said they were regulars and would see me again."

"That is excellent news, Darcy."

Bella's voice over the phone had been gentle, but her next words hit like a hammer. "Darcy, our attempts to plug the media leaks are failing; in other words, we're out of time. I hate to ask this of you, just as you've made your first successful approach, but Director Wolfe feels that we must order you to push harder. Both of us comprehend the danger and yet, please know that the looming threat to millions of Americans warrants such a risk."

"I-I understand."

"Darcy?" Bella's voice cracked just a very little. "I'm praying for you. Quincy is praying for you. We believe *God* can do the impossible. Please pray with us that the Holy Spirit will lead you, that he will show you how to unlock this organization and get you inside—for where the Holy Spirit leads, he will not let you fail. Please pray with us, Jaz."

The fact that Bella had broken protocol and called her Jaz instead of Darcy drove home the serious state of affairs.

"I will. I'll pray with you and Tobin."

CHAPTER 29

JAZ WAS feeling the pressure to, *somehow*, get an invitation to the next AEA meeting. *Yet I've barely scratched the surface with Hannah, Stevie, and Melly! We haven't spent enough time together for our conversation to progress naturally, let alone for me to wrangle an invite.*

I must see them again this coming weekend. Find a natural opening to tell them what I do for a living and where. Hopefully that will turn the conversation in the desired direction.

But although Jaz, Harris, and Bo spent the following Friday and Saturday evenings trolling the four clubs frequented by AEA cell members, they spotted not one of their targets.

On those nights and just one time at each club they visited, Harris asked her to dance. For Jaz, it was the sole bright spot to an otherwise dismal and unproductive weekend.

Because, she told herself, *Harris is a great dancer—in a sea of mediocrity, that is.*

"Where are they?" Jaz demanded, her mouth close to Harris' neck.

"Blamed if I know," he breathed into her hair.

"Well, it's almost midnight. I doubt they intend to show up an hour or two before closing—and by the way? One Latin song an hour is not nearly enough, and I despise the 'country and restroom' song and dance they use as filler for the remainder of the hour."

"It is Texas, y'know."

"That has not escaped my notice. *Gah!*"

"I don't know. I kinda like the slow songs." He led her gently into a turn, then brought her back to cheek to cheek. He inhaled. "Mmm. Your hair smells good."

Jaz shook her head. "Fate of the civilized world hanging around my neck and you want to stick your nose in my hair?"

"Hey, it can't hurt, can it? Besides—"

"Shut up and dance, you dork."

———————◆———————

FRIDAY, SIX evenings later, Jaz spotted Hannah, Stevie, and Melly at Club Hyperion. She pushed through the crowd and exclaimed, "Oh my goodness! I'm so glad to see you ladies again."

Stevie laughed. "It's Darcy, right? With the guy-ranking line, 'He is sooo stinking cute! And he can dance too'?"

"Yes; that was Rick. I danced with him last weekend, too. Great guy, but I don't like to dance too often with the same partner. Inevitably they get the wrong idea."

"Tell us about it," Hannah answered. "Hey, have a seat, Darcy."

"Yes," Stevie chimed in. "Tell us about yourself."

Melly, on the other hand, didn't seem as enthusiastic about Jaz joining their table.

No worries. I'll win her over.

"About me? Not much to tell, I suppose. I work in IT, and I don't mean the glamorous side of IT, either."

Hannah snarked. "There's a glamorous side to IT?"

"Right? I specialize in cybersecurity—that's my degree emphasis—but I won't be doing that for a while, I'm afraid."

Melly turned cool eyes on her. "Oh? Why's that?"

"It's sort of embarrassing, actually. The company I work for offered me this great student loan repayment hiring bonus. They would make all my loan payments while I worked for them, then pay off the balance if I stayed with them for five years. The catch is—I only realized after I signed on with them—if I leave the company earlier than five years, I have to return the money they've paid on my loans. I know. Stupid. I didn't read the fine print."

Hannah and Stevie made commiserating comments, but Melly asked, "What company is that?"

"It's an energy corporation, the parent company of WA Parish Generating Station. That's where I work—at a stinking, coal-burning, air-killing power plant."

Suddenly Mel was interested.

Oooh, yeah. Come to me, Melly, Jaz crooned inside. *Vyper is waiting for you.*

"Wow. I'm really sorry to hear that. Sounds like you're stuck in a rotten situation."

"Actually, I'm thinking of quitting, because I don't want to be part of destroying the earth. I'd rather repay the loan payments they've made for me so far than continue to accrue more of them. Besides, I cannot imagine staying the entire five years."

They launched into an interesting and varied discussion then, one focused on the environment, saving the earth's natural resources, and governmental abuse of power. Jaz let them lead the conversation. She followed along, agreeing often, and contributing little bits of information.

Melly studied Jaz. "You know, we, the three of us—and others, of course—belong to a great organization. It's called American Equality for All or AEA."

Stevie nodded. "I think you might fit in, Darcy."

"Why not? I don't have any real friends here yet, and I'd like to get to know you ladies better. When and where?"

Hannah smiled. "The meetings aren't on a set schedule, but we do announce them ahead of time. If I may have your number, I'll call you with the info."

Jaz scribbled on a napkin. "I don't have a cell phone, but here are my apartment and work numbers." She passed the napkin to Hannah, who tucked it into her little handbag.

She couldn't be certain, but Jaz thought she saw Mel bend an approving smile on Hannah, and the rest of the evening passed very pleasantly.

❖

AT THE end of another long and tedious work week, Jaz received a call from Hannah.

"Good news, Darcy! We, that is, American Equality for All, would like to invite you to one of our meetings."

Jaz had trouble keeping elation out of her voice. "Really? I'd like that."

"You should understand that your first meeting with us is what we call an interview. We want to hear more about you—your worldview, your take on the current state of the planet and humanity, and what you might have to offer us."

You want me to share my worldview with you? My take on the current state of humanity? No, I'm thinking that if I want to get inside this cell, I should probably keep those opinions to myself and tell you what you want to hear instead.

"Sounds intriguing." 'Intriguing' was the first word Jaz could formulate that wouldn't cause Hannah to reconsider her invitation.

Hannah's voice sparkled with excitement. "Isn't it, though? Meet me tonight at Club Hyperion, ten o'clock. I'll walk you to the meeting from there."

❖

HANNAH AND Jaz left the club arm in arm, like any two girlfriends out for a good time. The chummy, arm-in-arm part made Jaz twitch and squirm inside, but the façade was necessary. She reminded herself that she'd soon be face to face with the leaders of AEA's Houston cell.

This is it, the encounter Richard and Harris drilled and prepared me for. I can't merely pretend to be Darcy Walken; I must put myself in her skin. No blunders.

"In here," Hannah murmured. The "here" was an ordinary dry cleaner's shop with a bell on the door that jingled pleasantly.

Huh. A dry cleaner that stays open half the night? Convenient.

Jaz followed Hannah through the shop, past rows of suits and dresses, and out a back door that led to an alley. Hannah turned left, walked down three doors, then stopped at the fourth door and knocked. The door had a peephole that darkened as a person inside studied Hannah and Jaz.

The door opened. A hand beckoned them inside what appeared to be a stockroom. One dim bulb lit the room. Overburdened shelves lined every wall, leaving little space to move.

"Stand there."

A tall young man of Indo-Asian extraction pointed Jaz to an "X" on the floor. When Jaz obliged, he picked up a wand from one of the shelves and turned it on. He waved it with meticulous detail over her body.

He nodded to Hannah. "She's clean."

Hannah touched Jaz' elbow. "This way, Darcy."

Jaz followed Hannah, single file, through the stockroom to a second door that emitted a loud *scree* when Hannah opened it. The light on the other side was much better, and the door opened to walls painted a pale, calming yellow and a room both spacious and well-appointed. Expensive prints adorned the walls; attractive potted plants brightened the room's corners. A tapestry-upholstered corner sofa sectional and a number of complementary chairs provided comfortable seating.

A large wingback chair of supple, butter-yellow leather snagged her attention. She knew instinctively that the wingback chair was different. Prominent and special. Placed apart from the rest of the furniture. Jaz counted twelve people in the room, excluding herself, but no one sat in the special chair.

Huh. Almost like a throne.

Hannah introduced her. "Everyone? This is Darcy. She will be interviewing this evening."

"Hey, Darcy," "Welcome," and "Hi," and friendly nods greeted her.

Jaz nodded to Stevie and Melly. She recognized the other five from the AEA photo gallery, but none of them fit the profiles of AEA's three presumed leaders.

"Coffee? Tea?" Hannah asked.

"Yes; tea, please. One sugar."

"The restrooms are just down that hall there if you need them." Hannah pointed to a hallway off to the side, then walked to the lovely kitchenette built along the front wall.

Well, isn't this interesting? Jaz asked herself, staring at that front wall. *Except for the door we came in and that hallway over there, this room has no windows or exits. But shouldn't that wall be facing the street? And surely there has to be something on the other side? I mean, aren't we between another shop and the alley? Just how much of this street's property does AEA control? And no wonder Wolfe's surveillance team couldn't suss out this meeting place!*

Jaz joined Hannah at the counter where she was making the tea. She watched Hannah pour bottled water into two beautiful stoneware mugs then put the mugs in a microwave.

Huh. I recognize that brand of bottled water. It's high-dollar stuff. And unless I miss my guess, those mugs are Lenox French Perle White stoneware.

"I'll be right back," Jaz whispered, pointing to the hallway to the restrooms.

"And we'll be right here," Hannah giggled.

Jaz laughed with her, then headed down the hallway.

If the meeting room was "pretty nice," the two separate but identical bathrooms were stunning. Beautiful ceramic tilework in bone, beige, and chocolate with the occasional scarlet accent covered the floors and the walls halfway up to the ceiling. The sinks and toilets matched the bone tiles; all the fittings were an antique-looking bronze. Thick hand towels in striking scarlet hung near the sinks.

But other than the two restroom doors, the hall was a dead end, and the restrooms had no windows. When Jaz returned to the yellow room, a more thorough scan left her perplexed.

Everything in this place is just too high on the hog for an urban social justice front. And good grief! Only one way in or out? I hope they haven't scheduled a fire drill.

But back to this opulent room and the question it begs. Where does AEA get its funding? Sure, the Chinese Communist Party members live well, but this? And smack dab in an older, mid-class business district? The contrast is off-putting.

How shall I write my report? Let me see . . . 'I was invited to attend an AEA public meeting in a swanky fire trap.' Yep. That should do it.

"Here you go, Darcy."

Jaz smiled and took the mug from Hannah. "Thanks. Smells heavenly."

Mmm. Tienchi Flower Tea, unless I miss my guess. Also pricey.

She sipped the sweet, minty tea, smiled in her blandest manner, and studied the room, committing to memory the faces of those around her.

She didn't hear anyone else join them—no footsteps or *scree* of the stockroom door—but when Jaz put her attention back on Hannah, the young woman's expression quite literally *bloomed*. Then she noticed the others perking up. They rose to their feet, smiling in anticipation.

From behind her, a newcomer spoke.

A newcomer? Not to Jaz.

"Well, well. I didn't expect to see *you* here, but I always did hope I'd see you again. What a pleasant surprise . . . *Jinn*."

CHAPTER 30

JAZ TURNED and spread her mouth in an incredulous smile—one that didn't require much effort. "*Azteca?* Wow! Good grief. How long has it been?"

He was bracketed by two men, obviously bodyguards, and a woman who leaned into him, her body language positively shouting "Mine!" As Jaz took inventory of the individuals accompanying Azteca, another shock rippled through her.

Azteca's companions are the three Chinese Americans Wolfe's surveillance people said were the leaders of AEA's Houston cell—and yet all three are clearly subservient to Azteca, even the woman the surveillance folks thought was the 'Big Dog.' As for Azteca? Why have Wolfe's people never IDed him?

Jaz managed to keep her expression relaxed and fixed, but inside she was flailing. She was fighting to keep her body language calm while desperately wrestling to regain her equilibrium.

Azteca put a finger to his chin as though thinking. "How long has it been? Must be sixteen years, by my reckoning."

Jaz shook her head. "Hard to believe."

Sixteen years? Not long enough for me.

She noted that those years had been more than good to him. The charismatic, dark-eyed hacker with hollow cheeks and a black soul patch on his chin was gone. In his place stood a powerful figure, a man in the prime of life, exquisitely dressed and groomed. Whereas Azteca had been charming and at times sweet, this man was over-the-top hypnotic. Mesmerizing. A man whose presence emanated personal power.

He shifted his attention from Jaz to the others. She watched him "work" the room, and witnessed his impact. As he greeted each individual, he would clasp their hands or shoulders or kiss the women's cheeks and murmur something. Each encounter seemed personal. Intimate, even. In response, those he greeted swelled with pleasure.

What in the world? Why, they're fawning over him as if he were a rock star or a demigod.

And why did I not hear four people come through that noisy stockroom door?

Having finished his little meet and greet, Azteca clapped his hands twice. Apparently, the cell members knew what that meant, because they made haste to quiet down and find seats. Everywhere but the throne-like wingback chair. Azteca took it.

Well, of course you did.

The woman with him perched on the arm of the chair, and hung herself around his neck like a winter scarf. Hannah patted the sofa seat next to her, so Jaz sat beside her.

All the meeting attendees looked to Azteca with rapt expectancy. When he turned his attention on Jaz, they did the same.

"I understand you came to interview with us . . . Darcy Walken."

Jaz shrugged. "Yes. I enjoy Hannah's company. I feel—I don't know how to describe it—perhaps a kinship with her? A sense of shared purpose or ideology?"

He wasn't buying it. "You were Canadian when I met you, *Jinn*. Darcy Walken is American."

Jaz couldn't con a con, and because of their shared history, she'd be a fool to even try.

Now what? Obviously, the closer to the truth I play this, the more likely it is that he'll believe me.

Ditching her meticulous drilled cover, Jaz improvised. "Darcy is just one of the many aliases I've worn through the years. Remember the warning I sent you back in Regina? I left town that day, and Canada soon after. I lived in Beijing for a time where I picked up a bit of Mandarin and Chinese culture. After I left China, I toured Australia. Lived all over Europe after that. Always a different ID."

"And yet you seem to have hardly aged, Jinn. How is that?"

A note of skepticism had crept into his voice, and Jaz, suddenly wary, barely managed to grin on the outside. "Well, how old do you think I was when we met?"

"Suppose you tell me."

The grin was a mistake—nor did he appreciate being questioned. The abrupt chill in the room told Jaz the others didn't like her air of familiarity either.

Bella's warning flashed through her mind. *"It behooves you to remember that a new dog hoping to be accepted by the pack must first convey submission to the alpha* by showing her belly, *her vulnerabilities. In the same vein, Darcy Walken, if you disrespect or anger the alpha, you're done.*

Jaz ducked her head, a small submissive move. "What you didn't know was that I was a CPS Permanent Ward, raised in a group home, Azteca. They didn't understand me, didn't see that I had . . . a gift. I was starving for knowledge and anxious to learn when I met you. And I was all of fourteen years old."

Amazement rolled across his face. "You were *fourteen?*"

Azteca's human necktie sneered. "Itztli, why does this stranger persist in calling you *Azteca?*"

"She doesn't know whom I have become, Jing. It is possible that she may learn."

I don't know whom you've "become?" And what did she call you? "Its Lee?" What sort of name is that?

Itztli gestured to the others. "Those of you here with me are among my most precious possessions. We gather here today to interview and evaluate this woman, to determine if she has the skills and the right heart to help us in the sacred tasks before us. I will depend upon you, my treasures, to advise me concerning this woman."

My most precious possessions? Sacred tasks? My treasures? Crud and double crud. I've stumbled into a cult, and Azteca is channeling Jim Jones.

Note to self: 'Pass' on the Kool-Aid!

Jaz tried to emulate the eager expectation on the faces around her but couldn't manage it. Instead, she allowed her features to relax into curiosity.

Itztli again addressed Jaz. "When I last knew you as Jinn, you had grown considerably as a hacker. You even believed your skills to be . . . superior to mine."

He let his last words dangle without resolution.

Jaz didn't have to check Itztli's followers to sense the icy tension in the room growing stronger.

An abrupt and prescient realization struck her. *I'm not long for this world if I'm unable to turn aside the implied insult to their idol. Bella said it herself. "If you disrespect or anger the alpha, you're done."*

You meant "done" as in "stick a fork in me" done, didn't you, Bella? So I guess if the choice is between taking a mammoth risk or being torn limb from limb by these barbarians, I choose to risk it all.

Lord, please help me pull this off.

Jaz shrugged modestly. "Well, sure. I knew my technical skills would grow beyond yours—and no doubt they have—but in the vision and leadership department? I could never hold a candle to you."

Itztli brushed his possessive necktie aside and leaned forward. "You knew your skills would outstrip mine, did you? Within the global hacker community, have you never heard of, never celebrated the exploits and triumphs of *Obsidian Knife?*

Let me hazard a guess. Itztli means obsidian. Am I right?

Now or never, Jaz. Stroke the ego first, then drop the hammer.

"Obsidian Knife? Wow! Why, your handle's fame is revered world-wide . . . as is mine."

He snorted. "No one has ever heard of Jinn."

Jaz, again feigning modesty, spread her hands. "I abandoned Jinn when I left Canada."

"Of course you did," he chuckled.

Itztli's people sneered with him. She heard someone mutter, "*Jinn.* What a dumb handle."

The woman beside Itztli spoke up. "She has challenged your integrity, Itztli. Will you permit such disrespect?"

Jaz allowed herself a heated response. "It's not disrespect *if it's true*, lady."

The room stilled again. Jaz felt the heat of a dozen pairs of hostile eyes on her.

"Name yourself," Itztli said. "I dare you. Your reputation against mine. Who are you?"

Jaz sat back and crossed her legs. With dramatic leisure, she slid the hem of her dress up the side of one thigh and, from the top of her thigh-high stocking withdrew and unwrapped her last hoarded stick of Black Jack, folded it in half, then in quarters, and tucked it between her lips.

Taking her sweet time, staring boldly at Itztli, she began to chew the gum. He seemed transfixed. He would remember her obsession with Black Jack; would he also connect it to her handle?

She smiled. "We've crossed paths many times in cyberspace, Obsidian Knife. In fact, you know me well. And since your people are tech-savvy, I dare say everyone in this room knows me by reputation."

She paused for effect. "I am *Vyper.*"

No one moved, let alone breathed. Itztli's lips parted in wonder. When he finally spoke, some of the hauteur had leaked out of his little act.

"No way. *No way!* Prove it."

"As you like. Do you have a pager or a mobile phone?"

"I have a mobile phone."

Jaz glanced at the female leech stuck to Itztli's side. "And do you have a mobile phone? Let me borrow it."

"Give her your phone, Jing," Itztli ordered.

Jing sauntered across to Jaz. Instead of handing the phone to her, she dropped it on the carpet near Jaz's feet.

"Whoops."

Not exactly living up to your pretty Chinese name, Jing, Jaz thought, ignoring the woman's insult and her hostile glare. Jaz picked up the phone, and found Itztli's number in Jing's contacts. She keyed in a text message and sent it.

Everyone heard Itztli's phone ping. Without taking his eyes off Jaz, he drew the phone from his suitcoat's breast pocket and flipped it open. He pulled the phone back and stared at Vyper's message, her personal signature known throughout the global hacker community: line upon line of ASCII characters forming the image of a fanged asp's head.

Jing leaned over to see the message and gasped. Jaz let a lazy smile turn up one side of her mouth.

When Itztli looked up and into Jaz's eyes, he was more like the man she'd known long before. Curious. Charming. Humble, even. The illusion lasted all of three seconds before Itztli the demigod returned.

He inclined his head in royal manner. "Welcome, *Vyper, Venom Queen*. We receive you as a provisional member of our realm. We are in need of your services—and over the coming weeks we will gratefully employ them. But first we will test your loyalty to our cause. As our confidence in you grows, so will your access to our plans. I can, however, assure you of one thing: You will be handsomely rewarded and honored for your labors on behalf of our sacred duty."

Jaz, playing her role to the hilt, stood and bowed as a subservient Chinese would.

"I am honored to be provisionally received, Itztli. I look forward to demonstrating my loyalty and providing assistance as directed."

Yeah, yeah, sacred duty.

Blah, blah, riches and prestige.

Yada, yada. Whatever.

I've seen it all. Done it all. Had it all.

Man, the ridiculous stuff I have to put up with.

Itztli also stood, signaling the closure of the meeting. He addressed everyone in the room, including Jaz.

"Remember. When we have accomplished our sacred duty, your greatest reward will be to survive the coming apocalypse, not narrowly or marginally, but *richly*, as every king and queen in my kingdom deserves."

Jaz frowned inside. *What the devil . . .*

CHAPTER 31

HANNAH WALKED Jaz back to the club, where they said goodnight. Jaz hailed one of the cabs lined up outside the club waiting to pick up club patrons too inebriated to drive themselves home.

"I'm beat. Are you going back inside?" Jaz asked.

"Yes; I'm meeting someone."

"I'll see you later, then."

Jaz had stuffed her feelings all evening. Finally away from Itztli, his followers, and even Hannah, she acknowledged a growing paranoia—with reason. Itztli's people would be watching their new "provisional" member to prove or disprove her loyalty. *Or*, given Itztli's exalted "kingdom" delusions, he may have already changed his mind and concluded that Vyper was a threat to his demigod status.

The moment the meeting broke up, he could have given his people orders to take her out.

They could be stalking her.

Following her to her home.

Preparing an ambush or already lying in wait for her.

Right this minute.

Jaz's training dictated her movements. She had her cab drop her three blocks from her apartment complex. She walked the wrong way around the corner, ducked into a shadowed doorway, then doubled back to her apartment. Safely locked inside her unit, she sat in the dark with the window blinds narrowly parted.

Watching for a tail.

Tired but afraid to sleep.

Could all that "We welcome you as a provisional member" garbage have been Itztli's way of lulling me into complacency? What if he's decided to end me at his earliest convenience? What if I don't get this information to Harris, Bo, and Resolute before Itztli's goons make an attempt? And what if they've already bugged my apartment phone?

No one will know what I've uncovered. I can't let that happen.

An hour later, wearing black jeans and a black sweatshirt, she crept out her door. She took the long way around the complex, avoiding the parking lot, and went out a gate in the fence that led to a walking trail.

Ten minutes later, she arrived at a minimart. The store's lights were out, the doors locked. A payphone on the wall out front lay in shadow. Jaz picked up the phone, input a string of numbers to activate a long distance calling card, then dialed Bella's home phone.

A groggy voice answered. "H'lo?"

"Sorry to wake you, Bella, but I have vital information that cannot wait until tomorrow. I'm on a pay phone. Please ring me back at this number to conference me in after you get Rusty, Bo, and Harris on the line."

Bella was awake now. "Got it."

Ten minutes later, the five of them were connected. Jaz began with, "Rusty, are you recording this call? Good. Okay, listen. Tonight—well, last night, I suppose—Hannah, one of my initial contacts with AEA, walked me from Club Hyperion to what she called an interview meeting. I'll provide the approximate location of the meeting place at the end of this call, but here are the salient points I learned during the 'interview.'

"First, the leader of AEA's Houston cell is not the Chinese American woman identified by Wolfe's surveillance people. Her name is Jing, by the way, but the cell leader is actually a guy who goes by the name *Itztli*, a Toltec or Mesoamerican indigenous word that I believe means obsidian. His hacker handle is Obsidian Knife. No, I don't think Wolfe's surveillance people have ever seen him—and it's because he has a secret way in and out of the meeting site. In fact, I got the sense that Itztli doesn't *ever* appear in public, which would explain why he's never popped up on the surveillance team's radar.

"Second, I have history with this guy. *He knows me.* Going on seventeen years back, he and I and another guy did a series of bank hacks across western Canada." Jaz paused. "So I hacked some banks back in the day. Bella already knows, so close your mouth, Rusty, before you swallow a fly. Where was I? Oh, yeah. At the time I knew him, Itztli went by the hacker handle Azteca.

"Third, whatever the Chinese Communists are plotting through AEA in order to take down big chunks of the power grid and send regions of the US back to the dark ages? Itztli and his people are definitely in on it, *but*—and this is the crazy part—Itztli is piggybacking his own operation atop AEA's attack.

No, I don't yet know what Itztli has planned, but I'm on it and will report again when I know more.

"Fourth, Itztli's AEA cell is a downright *cult*, and Itztli is the cult leader."

Bella broke in. "What? How does a cult play into this?"

"You should have seen the meeting, Bella. Those people treat Itztli like a god, and let me tell you: This man sits on his 'throne' like he's royalty, calls his people his 'treasure' and 'most precious possessions,' and raves on about completing their 'sacred tasks' and 'sacred duty.' Totally bonkers!"

"This is a lot to process, Darcy, and I'm not nearly awake enough yet to take it all in."

"Well, I guarantee my next bit will keep you up the rest of the night. See, because Itztli and I have history, he saw right through my Darcy Walken cover. At that juncture, I had exactly two seconds to jump trains, or I wasn't going to leave that place alive."

Jaz heard a low growl from Harris' end of the call.

"I'm fine, really, but I had to get creative."

"Creative how?" Bella asked.

"Creative as in I had to ditch my cover, Bella."

Bella was not pleased. "Unbelievable!"

"Look, I had no choice, because Itztli already knew I was Canadian, not American. Furthermore, I could tell from the hostile vibes around me that I wouldn't make it out of that room alive if I didn't come up with a valid reason for my Darcy Walken cover.

"So, I told Itztli and his groupies that I'd lived under a bunch of fake IDs in various places around the world for the past sixteen-odd years and that Darcy Walken was just one more alias. It was an easy sell since it flies so close to the truth. But then I had to provide my hacker bona fides."

"I'm afraid to ask," Bella sighed.

"Right. Had to tell them the truth there too, because anything less than that would not have been glitzy enough to keep me alive and also get me into the group."

"You gave them Vyper?"

"Yeah, I did. What other handle has the *wow* factor Vyper has? And it was the right choice, Bella. When Itztli accepted my hacker identity, he granted me immediate provisional member status. So I'm in, although they expect me to prove my loyalty."

"Rusty, I'm glad you're recording this," Bella said. "Keep going, Darcy."

"Okay. Last item and the last thing Itztli said to me and the others last night was this, and I'm quoting him. 'Remember. When we have accomplished our sacred duty, your greatest reward will be to survive the coming apocalypse, not narrowly or marginally but *richly*, as every king and queen in my kingdom deserves.'"

"Apocalypse. He said apocalypse? You're certain?"

"As certain as I know every verse in the Gospel of Matthew by heart."

Rusty, Harris, and Bo responded as one. "You what?"

"Forget about it, guys. Point is, I have an eidetic memory, and *I know what I heard Itztli say*. I didn't dare wait until tomorrow to get this intel out to you, because if they smelled anything 'off' about me, if they only pretended to accept me and decided to take me out instead, like *right now*—"

Harris cut in. "Bella! Bo and I will deploy to Darcy's apartment ASAP and—"

Jaz interrupted him right back. "And risk blowing my cover after what it's taken to reach this point? Nothing doing, bub. I'm going to infiltrate this Charles Manson wannabe's operation and circumvent their attack before they launch it. Furthermore, now that I'm inside the Houston cell, ostensibly AEA's *command cell*, I intend to locate and breach AEA's communication methodology. Once we have the communications for the entire AEA organization? We will have their plan of attack."

In her thoughts she added, *Come to Vyper, Itztli, you psychopathic megalomaniac, you and your poor, brainwashed little automatons and the wicked plans you have devised.*

You do not see me, but I see you. I am slithering through the grass, silent as the grave, drawing ever closer to you. You do not sense danger approaching, do you? You think yourself safe—but you are not.

Oh, no. You are not.

CHAPTER 32

JAZ WOKE late on Sunday with the phrase "sacred duty" running laps in her head. "Grr! I suppose I need to decipher what Itztli means by his so-called sacred duty, but with time at a premium . . ."

Just before noon, Jaz placed a call to Hannah's home phone.

"Hannah? Hey. It's Darcy. Yeah. Great meeting last night—I'm pretty thrilled, actually."

Jaz made herself sound as self-deprecating and needy as plausible. "Would you like to meet somewhere for dinner tonight? I have so many questions about what I can do to help Azteca—I mean *Itztli*. Good grief! I need help breaking that nasty old habit. So, dinner? Please?"

Hannah laughed. "Sure. We have to eat, right?"

They picked a place and time, and Jaz hung up.

———•———

THEY MET at a small Indian diner not far from Jaz's apartment and ordered chai lattes to go with their food. When their tea arrived, Jaz began to rave about the previous night's meeting.

"Itztli is so different from when I knew him all those years ago. He's grown—or morphed, I don't know which. I mean, his charisma is striking, don't you agree? When I got home, I couldn't stop thinking about him."

She went on for a while, describing Itztli in glowing terms, rehashing various parts of her "interview." She knew from experience not to overplay her act. Yet, with Bella's injunction uppermost in her mind, she chose to push a little harder than was wise.

Hannah, however, smiled and nodded while Jaz chattered, occasionally adding her own comments and experiences to the conversation.

"Goodness, you sound like me. By the third time I'd heard Itztli speak, I knew I loved him."

She shook her head. "He's totally ruined me for other men."

Jaz effected surprise. "You love him? *Love?* Is that what I'm feeling?"

"You and everyone else in his kingdom. We all love him."

"His kingdom! I like that."

Jaz actually wanted to gag. *I guess Jesus knew what he was talking about when he told us, "If anyone says to you, 'Look, here is the Christ!' or 'There!' do not believe it. For false christs and false prophets will rise and show great signs and wonders to deceive, if possible, even the elect. See, I have told you beforehand."*

When their food arrived, Jaz plowed ahead. "The only thing I didn't understand when I came away from the meeting was this 'sacred duty' thing Itztli mentioned. Can you tell me what he meant and how I can help?"

Hannah played with her food a few moments before she murmured, "Darcy, since you're a provisional member, I can't tell you everything. What I can do is remind you of the night we met. We talked about the problems in the world, remember?"

"You mean how the earth's resources are being stripped away? How we're defrauding her? Slowly killing her?"

"Yes. Those problems." Hannah pursed her lips. "Humanity is raping the earth, violating her, and leaving her naked."

Jaz frowned. "How do we reverse course, Hannah? What is the answer?"

"I'll just add one thing, after which we should leave this topic alone until you're fully vested in the kingdom, okay?"

"Sure. I get it."

"All right, so when I said, 'Humanity is raping the earth, violating her, and leaving her naked,' you asked, 'How do we reverse course? What is the answer?' Well, I suggest that you think on this: Humanity *is* the problem, and we have a duty, a *sacred* duty to the earth, to . . . mitigate the problem."

Inside, Jaz stilled. She kept her hands busy cutting a bite of chicken, dragging it through *murgh kari* curry sauce, and bringing it to her mouth, but inside? She slowly processed Hannah's meaning. She forced herself to chew and swallow what now tasted like soapy cardboard.

Finally, she said quietly, "I think I take your point, Hannah."

After that, Jaz spoke of her job and her coworkers. "I'm the only female in my small department, and my coworkers are *such* guys! Ugh! I'm going to need to find some girls to hang with during lunch because I'm absolutely *drowning* in testosterone all day long."

Hannah laughed and they clinked their glass tea mugs together.

"To girlfriends," Hannah said.

"Long live girl power!" Jaz replied.

When they'd finished their meal, they paid the bill and said goodnight.

Jaz drove back to her apartment, allowing her thoughts to fix on what she'd deduced concerning Itztli's "sacred duty."

"Lord, can I be honest with you?"

She shivered. "I'm scared."

HANNAH FLIPPED open her phone while she drove and keyed in a number she'd intentionally left out of her contacts. When the call picked up, she said nothing. She listened to the voice on the other end of the call until an answer was expected.

"I understand she's a famous hacker and all, and I get that she's got the necessary skills to bring off Itztli's plan, which makes her invaluable to him and the cause. But I'll tell you something else, she's too pushy. Oh, she's good all right, but during dinner she was definitely digging. No, I don't trust her. She could ruin everything."

She listened again. "I agree. Take her. *Now*."

BECAUSE IT was evening, all the parking slots close to Jaz's apartment were full, and she had to settle for a spot farther out in the lot than she liked. She hit the button to lock the car behind her as she got out. She had taken only three steps before she knew she was in trouble.

They rushed her from two sides. Someone grabbed her from behind and wrapped a heavy arm around her neck. The arm tightened into a chokehold. She stomped her assailant's foot and kicked his shins with no effect. She tried to slap his ears and gouge his eyes, but she couldn't reach that far back. She couldn't scream, couldn't breathe, and her struggles were fruitless. Seconds later, she lost consciousness.

CHAPTER 33

WHEREVER SHE was, it was dimly lit. She was sitting up, her chin bowed to her chest, her arms behind her. Without lifting her head and letting her captors know she was awake, Jaz cracked one eye. She tried to get a sense of where she was.

I'm tied to a chair. No lights. My head is pounding, my neck aches, my throat is rough and parched. Yeah, so far, so good.

Jesus? Help, please? I'm really in trouble!

Without planning or intending to, she moaned, and the interrogation began.

A grating male voice behind her demanded, "Who are you? What is your interest in the man who calls himself Itztli?"

Jaz moaned again, on purpose, playing for time. "So . . . thirsty."

"Who are you?"

"Water. Please."

"What is your interest in the man who calls himself Itztli?"

A cough from Jaz's dry throat inadvertently sent her into a coughing fit she couldn't control. Her chest spasmed. She retched and dry heaved twice before she was able to catch her breath.

A hand put a bottle to her mouth. Water trickled over her lips and down her chin. She opened her mouth and caught a sip. Swallowed.

"More. Please."

"What is your interest in the man who calls himself Itztli?"

"I go out dancing to have a good time—that's all! I don't know what you—"

"Who are you?"

She coughed and again retched. The disembodied hand delivered another swallow of water.

"Who are you?"

"D-darcy. Darcy Walken."

"Don't lie!" the harsh voice shouted. "Darcy Walken does not exist. Who are you really?"

Jaz's interrogation training kicked in.

"I'm Darcy Walken! It's my name! I don't know what you want from me!"

Strange. They seem more interested in who I am rather than what I know.

Stranger still, a memory flared in her mind. The recollection was vivid. It felt almost real, and yet why recall it here? Why now?

I was Thérèse Benoit back then, the supposedly dutiful employee of the Royal Canadian Mounted Police in Ottawa. It was morning, and I was coming in to work, had reached the foyer when . . .

———◆———

ARMED RCMP security officers swarmed her from every direction, shouting instructions. She dropped her backpack and sank to her knees as ordered. An officer pulled her wrists to her back and cuffed them. Then they got her on her feet and marched her into the commissioner's office.

She hadn't met the commissioner to date, but the woman was waiting for them, her outrage splashed in bright spots upon both cheeks.

"Would it surprise you, Miss Benoit, to know that we received credible intel late last night asserting that you, our very own cybersecurity specialist, were running your own little cyber enterprise from this RCMP facility? And would it surprise you to know that, in fact, we have found evidence to support such an accusation? An accusation of treason?"

"My wallet. Back pocket. There's a phone number."

———◆———

SHE WOULDN'T listen to me. But soon after, Bernard Dupont showed his face anyway.

Jaz frowned. *Jesus? I asked you to help me in* this *situation. Did you bring that memory to my mind for a reason? Is it because Bernard Dupont arrived in time to rescue me?*

Wait. Bernard Dupont, not of the RCMP, but of their sister agency, *Canadian Security Intelligence Service.*

Sister agency?

Jaz chuckled aloud. "Oh, dear! Is that what we're playing at? Dueling sister agencies? The left hand not knowing what the right is doing?"

Dead silence from her interrogator . . . and then, "Care to repeat what you said?"

"Sorry, but who are you guys? FBI or ATF? DOJ or Treasury?"

After a short silence, Jaz heard her captors engage in a whispered conversation on the other side of the room. She raised her scratchy voice to gain their attention. "Hello? I have a phone number. You should call it."

The male voice approached again. "Why would we be interested in a phone number?"

"A woman will answer. Ask her to put you through to Wolfe. Director Wolfe."

A stunned hush followed before, "Director *Jack* Wolfe?"

"Uh-yup. The very one."

The man swore loud and long. Another whispered conversation took place some distance behind Jaz.

A light flared in the dim room, stinging Jaz's eyes. She twisted away from it. Then her wrists and forearms were free, and she pitched forward, nearly falling out of the chair. A hand caught her. Pushed her upright, back into the chair.

"Here. Drink."

A woman's voice.

"*Hannah?*"

"Yeah. Just drink. Then give us that number."

⸺●⸺

JAZ HAD drained the water bottle and half of a second one by the time they finished playing their game of phone tag. Bella had answered her captors' call. She took their phone number and reported it to Wolfe. Wolfe called Jaz's captors back.

He didn't beat about the bush when they picked up.

"Who do you report to? Name and number. Now."

When those had been provided, he added, "Let me talk to my agent."

"Yessir." Hannah's counterpart, the male interrogator, handed Jaz the phone.

"Darcy Walken," she said.

"Bella is rousting Harris and Bo as we speak. They'll be coming to get you."

"Super. I'm beat. Er, but not literally."

"I'm glad you're all right, Darcy."

"Yeah, me too, sir."

"I need to call these agents' supervisor and throw my weight around, so I'll be hanging up now."

"I understand. Thanks again, sir."

Harris and Bo arrived. Harris, his face set in stone, checked Jaz over.

"I'm okay. Headache. And my *neck hurts.*"

Harris turned a killing glare on the male interrogator.

FBI Special Agent Theo Bruckner blushed. "Sorry about the choke hold." Harris didn't dial back his death ray even an iota.

Hannah, actually FBI Special Agent Honor Adisa, asked Jaz and Harris to join her and Bruckner at a table in the next room.

Agent Adisa began. "The FBI has been following this nutcase Itztli for months now. I managed to get inside his little 'kingdom,' as he calls it. Once inside, I discovered that they have some grandiose plot to destroy the evil humans who are raping and pillaging Mother Earth—with the exception of Itztli and his followers, of course. *They* intend to live in the lap of luxury while the rest of humanity fizzles and dies.

"The problem the FBI has is that we can't discern between what's real and what's fantasy in Itztli's mind—in other words, whether Itztli's big scheme to pull the plug on humanity exists in reality or only in his fertile imagination. I mean, the guy talks a good game, but so far I don't see him as an actual threat."

Agent Adisa smiled. "He's sure excited about you though, *Vyper*. He called earlier today to thank me for bringing you on board. Says you're going to help his kingdom army rebuild the Internet after the demise of the rest of humanity."

Jaz was instantly confused. "Hold up a sec. Rebuild the Internet? I figured Itztli wanted me to help him blow up the WA Parish Generating Station."

"Blow up that place where you work?"

"Yeah, coordinated with similar actions across the other cells."

Agent Adisa frowned. "What other cells?"

Jaz stilled. Beside her, Bo did the same, while Harris took a sudden and keen interest in his fingernails.

"Uh, would you excuse me for a moment?" Jaz asked. "And may I borrow your phone? I need to make a call."

⁕

JAZ RETURNED fifteen minutes later. "It seems that our investigation is further along than yours. I've spoken to my handler, and at this time, I've been authorized to provide the following information. One, my agency believes Itztli is building his kingdom atop a wider plot that predates his little post-apocalyptic amusement park. What we *don't* know yet is if he is aware of the bigger plot, if he's a fully integrated part of that plot, or if he and his cult followers are ignorant idiots being used as convenient cover for that plot.

"Two, after Director Wolfe briefs your agency on the wider, preexisting conspiracy, the powers that be will determine how we are to proceed.

"Three, we believe that the slice of the overall plot designed to affect Houston is centered on the WA Parish Generating Station, where I work as an IT employee. I was inserted there several weeks ago. My dual assignment was to infiltrate Itztli's cell in order to discover how they intend to bring down the station and then prevent its destruction from the inside."

Agent Adisa blew out a breath. "That's Itztli's big plan? Bring down the power grid? I mean, how does that 'mitigate the problem' of us wicked humans?"

"Short answer? It won't—but the results would be horrifying, nonetheless. Parish provides about ninety percent of the greater Houston area's electrical service and for other consumers farther down the line. With the station gone, the cascading grid failures would leave in the neighborhood of two million people stranded in the dark. Houstonians would have about a week to walk out of the city and find safe harbor."

"Or what?"

"Or die."

Agent Bruckner frowned. "Walk out inside of a week or die? How do you figure that?"

Jaz listed the appalling facts in detail. "The end result? Inside of seven days, the strong will have taken what the weak possess, leaving the weak to die. What *will* survive is anarchy . . . leaving in charge the very worst humanity has to offer.

Jaz looked at Agent Adisa. "How does Itztli plan to survive when the power goes out?"

"Did you take a good look at the room we met in?"

"The décor was a little over the top for your common protest group."

"Right. And would you believe that room is just for recruitment purposes? Turns out, Itztli has an extensive bunker down below, fitted up with the best of food, drink, and accommodations. He has promised that those on his good side will get to wait out the end of the world there. What has always struck me as odd is how he could afford to build and stock such a place. Do you know?"

Bruckner signaled a time-out. "Can we get back to Houston minus the power grid for a sec? What about help from the state and federal governments? The military, national guard, FEMA, and so on. Surely they would swoop in and establish martial law? Provide assistance to the victims?"

"If all of Texas turned out to help Houston, perhaps a majority of the city's dwellers could be evacuated and saved, but the city itself would die."

Agent Adisa said softly, "Okay, as bad as the scenario you're painting sounds, New Orleans has survived many tropical storms and hurricanes. I know; I lived there. NOLA always comes back from disaster. Houston could rise again too."

Jaz shook her head. "Listen to me! If *all* of Parish's ability to generate power goes down, both the coal-fired plants and the natural gas plants? Rebuilding the station could take years—that's years of Houston without power. Years of vandalism, looting, arson, squatting, and plain old rot. The damage done to the city's infrastructure would be incalculable. And, unfortunately? We're not talking only about Houston. There's a wider plot, remember? Its objective is to kill power to a sizable number of megacities, Houston being but one of many.

"Say, ten such cities lost their power grid on the same day, and that grid could not quickly be restored. Along with looting and vandalism, fires would burn out of control, water mains break, and gas lines explode—because state and federal bureaucracies do not turn on a dime. By the time the feds brought resources to bear, every one of the affected cities would be kicked straight back to the Stone Age. You don't get over that in a month, a year, or even a decade."

"Who?" Bruckner demanded. "Who is doing this to us?"

"You know them as a group that calls itself American Equality for All, or AEA, a cover for Itztli's cult. What you might not know is that we have identified and are surveilling AEA cells in multiple cities, primarily down the East Coast and inland, and right here. We believe every cell represents a city marked for destruction. In addition, at least until now, our surveillance had led us to believe that AEA's Houston cell was calling the shots."

"Seems way out of Itztli's wheelhouse," Adisa muttered.

"You may very well be right. Again, we see three possibilities. Either Itztli is AEA's top dog in this plot and the other cells get their marching orders from him, or he's running a rogue operation overtop AEA's wider plan.

"The third possibility is that he's the megalomaniac we think him to be—albeit a clueless one—and he hasn't the foggiest idea AEA is using him for cover. The third possibility implies that someone else in his 'kingdom' is actually running AEA's Houston cell—with or without Itztli's knowledge—and is sending orders to the various other cells in the US."

Jaz stopped to take a cleansing breath. "So right now? Identifying that 'someone' is my highest priority."

"Okay, you've officially blown my mind," Special Agent Adisa muttered. "I . . . wait. Hold the phone. Let's say that everything you've said is true. You still haven't said who's behind this so-called American Equality for All front. Who's financing Itztli's end-of-the-world bunker and lavish lifestyle? It would have to be a terrorist organization with deep pockets, right? So who is it?"

"Huh. Guess I forgot the punchline," Jaz admitted. "Although I'm certain Itztli has money of his own squirreled away, we believe AEA is funded by the Chinese Communist Party. We also believe AEA's US organization is led almost exclusively by second-generation Chinese-American CCP sleeper agents. Oh, the CCP plays its cards close to the vest and has kept its financial backing well hidden, but China's money is the only explanation that provides for Itztli's extravagant lifestyle, not to mention his *über*-lavish survival bunker."

Special Agent Bruckner lost it right there. He jumped to his feet and shouted, "By saying the CCP is backing AEA, you mean the Chinese *government? Are you out of your mind? Do you know what you're implying?"*

Jaz waited until he'd calmed enough to hear her. "Yes, Special Agent Bruckner, I know exactly what it implies, which is why we must have concrete, indisputable evidence in our possession before the US can accuse China. Even then, when we have such evidence, we'll need to plan and implement a total takedown of AEA's organization in one coordinated action. Anything less may trigger a partial execution of AEA's terror plan, and we cannot afford even that. Too many lives are on the line. Now do you see why we have not, as yet, raided any AEA cells?"

"But how in the world do you plan to get such evidence?"

Jaz lifted one shoulder. "My agency sent me here to infiltrate this cell, thinking my computer skills would enable me to hack them from within. I was just getting cozy with Itztli when Hannah here—pardon me, *Special Agent Adisa*—decided to don her FBI cap and have me kidnapped."

Adisa winced. "Er, sorry?"

"Yeah, yeah. I'll get over it." Then Jaz grinned, and some of the tension in the room bled off. "In any event," she added, "when we do act? We had better hit each and every AEA cell across the US simultaneously and completely lest a lone cell member evade capture—someone capable of delivering a smaller but nonetheless devastating attack."

Jaz smiled sadly. "Of course, should AEA manage to pull off even one of these attacks, we figure the Chinese government will vigorously deny their involvement or culpability, even though we know better."

Special Agent Adisa gnawed her lip. "First strike?"

"Yes. An act of war."

CHAPTER 34

JAZ WAS short on sleep and shorter on patience when she arrived at work a few hours later. Her neck was bruised and sore, and her body and brain were sleep-deprived. She was downright cranky into the bargain. To put it plainly, she was in no fit mood for human interaction.

I'm about fed up with Darcy Walken and this farcical assignment. Don't ask me how disgusted I am that our government intelligence and law enforcement agencies don't share information with each other and haven't a clue when they are blindly mucking about in each other's ops!

"Dumb feds."

Throughout the morning, her coworkers suffered the rough side of her tongue several times and, after asking her (or at least trying to ask) if something was wrong and getting royally chewed out for their concern, they retreated to their cubicles and left her to her own devices. The guys were still shooting disgruntled glares at her when lunch time neared.

But by then, Jaz was wriggling under stiff conviction concerning her bad behavior. She hadn't, until then, experienced a reprimand of this magnitude from the Holy Spirit; however, she was *certain* she didn't care to repeat it. Ever. In fact, she wanted out from under it ASAP.

Knowing she needed to make the situation right, she approached her three coworkers with well-deserved trepidation. "Uh, guys? Just wondering if you're starting to get hungry?"

Three heads swiveled her way. Mick asked, "Dunno. Do you plan to bite our heads off for answering you?"

Jaz sighed. "I owe all of you an apology."

"Apolo*gies*, plural," Stew snorted.

"Yeah, you're right. I'm . . . I'm really sorry. I've been a complete snot all morning."

"Complete *and utter* snot." Larry supplied.

"*Whatever*—wait. No. I mean, *yes.* Complete and utter snot. But can I make it up to you? How about lunch on me at that homecooked burger place in Richmond?"

Larry swiveled his chair in her direction and folded his arms across his chest, his expression unreadable. "You driving?"

"Sure, if you'd like me to."

He snarked. "Heck *no!* We watched you peel out of the parking lot your first week here, and I thought you were gonna plow through the guard shack for sure."

Mick piled on. "Yeah, Darcy. Where'd you learn to drive—downtown New Delhi?"

No, on a race course for dune buggies, you blockheads.

Oops. Sorry, Lord.

Stewart laughed. "Right? I might be brave, but I ain't stupid!"

Still chortling over their witty repartee, the three of them high-fived.

"Fine. I won't drive, but I'll pay for lunch."

"Let's go," Larry said. "The drive into Richmond will cut in on our lunch break."

They locked their terminals and fast-walked to the front entrance, then to Mick's car. Larry and Stewart let Jaz have the front passenger seat, and they left the parking lot, headed down Parish's long drive . . . only to be halted where Parish's drive intersected Smithers Lake Road. A ginormous flatbed truck coming off one of the plant's utility roads was just making the turn, effectively blocking them and a number of cars in both directions. Whatever was on the truck's bed was enormous and weighty.

"Aw, man! Hurry it up," Mick groused, then glanced into the backseat. "Hey, Larry, Mr. IT Department Lead Tech. Listen, dude, we could take an extra 30 minutes for lunch and leave half an hour later this afternoon—if you authorize it. What do you say?"

"Sure. I'll call it a team building activity. Otherwise, at the rate that flatbed's moving, we'll get to Richmond in time to get takeout so we can bring it back and eat it at our desks."

Jaz pointed. "What is that thing on the truck, anyway?"

Stewart answered. "That, Miss Walken, is a beast of a turbine, the last of the old dinosaurs to go."

"Yeah, you missed all the engineers vs. operators drama and accompanying power supply workarounds while they were changing out the old turbines and generators from both plants," Larry said. "You see how huge those turbines are? Took a lot of time and a bunch of contract workers from the turbine and generator manufacturers to swap out the old for the new. And they didn't start hauling the old turbines and generators outa here until the new ones were running and had been tested up one side and down the other. I think all eight of the old generators are gone now and this is the last turbine. Stewy?"

"Second to last," Stewart supplied.

The flatbed finally negotiated the tight turn onto the road and began to pick up speed, but the car Jaz and her coworkers were in was stuck behind the truck until Mick had an opportunity to pass. Jaz gazed at the turbine as they sped by and idly wondered what unconscious concern was trying to make itself known.

"So, guys, can you explain the job turbines have in generating power?"

"Stew, you want to field this one?" Mick asked.

"You want me to 'mansplain' something to Darcy? Do I look like I have a death wish?"

"Just lay it out, Stew," Jaz growled. "I'm no dunce."

"Uh, sure, but maybe I'll keep my explanation surface-level anyway. I mean, it's just about impossible to explain the job of turbines without giving you a high-level overview of the entire process—see?"

Jaz nodded. "Got it."

"Okay, so, first off, WA Parish Generating Station has two four-unit plants, one coal-fired, the other natural gas. We use only the coal-fired plant at this time, but we can switch to the natural gas plant if necessary.

"We're one of the ten largest generating stations in the US. We buy coal by the train load, grind it to powder, and burn the powder in a boiler, sometimes called a furnace. Add water, and the coal fire inside the boiler creates steam. The steam turns our turbines, and—to finally answer your question—the turbines turn the generators. Like I said, we have four of these coal-fired units in operation here at Parish and four natural gas units as backup. Eight turbines, eight generators.

"Since electricity can't be stored effectively, we have to send it 'downstream' as it's generated until it eventually reaches our end-use customers—homes and businesses. I say 'eventually,' because we don't send electricity directly to the consumers from here. We send it first to Parish's hub substation. The substation has a transformer and the transformer's job is to 'step up' the current to a super high voltage."

"Why? Why a super high voltage?"

"High voltage is the best way to send out *a lot* of electricity at one time. Electricity tends to dissipate as it travels. We send it high voltage to limit losses. Otherwise, we wouldn't be able to get enough juice to everyone who needs it, when they need it."

"Ah. Got it."

"So, at the hub substation, the transformer steps up the voltage and sends it in different directions to several intermediate substations. The intermediate substations also have transformers. Each intermediate substation then steps the voltage down and sends it on to regional substations. The transformers in regional substations step the current up or down as needed for where it is going next.

"Let's say the current arrives at your local substation. It is then delivered through the utility company's wires to your house's circuit breaker panel. The panel distributes the appropriate current to your household outlets 24/7. Most ordinary household appliances use 110-volt outlets while a clothes dryer or an electric oven generally uses a 220-volt outlet."

"I think I understand. Thanks for the lesson, Stew."

"My pleasure."

They arrived at the burger restaurant and, because they had an extra thirty minutes, they took their time eating, talking, and telling jokes. Jaz, though, was somewhat distracted.

What is it? What's bothering me?

———————●———————

BACK AT work in the IT Department, Jaz kept chewing on the information Stewart had provided, kept wondering why she couldn't let it go. Finally, she scooted her chair over to Stewart's cubicle.

"Hey, Stew, can you tell me a bit more about the plant's new turbines and why it was a hassle to switch out the old ones?"

"What are you—a glutton for punishment? That explanation dives a lot deeper into the weeds."

"Please?"

He shrugged. "It's your pain."

"I can handle it. First, give me an overview on turbines and how they work."

"Like I said earlier, we burn coal in a boiler and superheat water to convert the coal's chemical energy to steam or thermal energy. The steam's pressure turns a turbine, converting the steam's thermal energy to mechanical energy. The turbine then turns the generator, converting the turbine's mechanical energy to electrical energy—and that is an *extremely* simplified explanation, by the way. Parish operates four similar coal-fired units, meaning four boilers, turbines, generators, backup generators per unit, and all the water necessary for each production process, plus their waste disposal systems."

"Quick question for you. What would happen if a turbine, for some reason, didn't work right?"

"What do you mean, if a turbine didn't work right? They spin really fast. If there's a problem with the generator, the turbines are designed to automatically slow down. That's pretty much what they do—although turbine failures aren't all that uncommon or catastrophic. I'd be more concerned about a generator failing. As unlikely as that scenario is, it's still a possible horror show."

Jaz chewed the inside of her cheek while she thought. "All right then, talk to me about generator failures."

"Well, if a generating station has only one generator and that generator fails, everything downstream from that station experiences a power outage because no electricity is being passed from the generator to the hub substation, its intermediate substations, regional substations, and so on.

"Since Parish has four coal-fired generating units, if one generator had to go offline—like when we were changing the old ones out—excess power from its remaining three generators would be routed to the failed generator's intermediate substations and so on, that is, if the system wasn't already overburdened.

"But if a generating station has only one generator and it fails? The consumers dependent upon that station experience a power outage. The length of the outage depends upon how long the generator is offline. By the way, most generator failures are due to something relatively easy to fix.

"A catastrophic outage, on the other hand, is the stuff of nightmares. Those can lead to cascading systems failures. I used Parish as a multi-generator example. If one generator failed, the other three could share the failed generator's load. But if two failed simultaneously? We'd be in a world of hurt."

"What if all four generators failed in a way that couldn't easily be fixed?"

"I don't want to speculate on something that gruesome and unrealistic."

"Unrealistic?"

"Sure. Every generating station and power plant has safety mechanisms and redundancies built into its equipment and processes. All the active systems are monitored and alarmed, and power plants have backup generators on standby. That's why we employ highly trained operators and engineers. Besides, what could possibly put all four of Parish's generators out of commission at the same time? Other than a direct and sustained hit from a massive hurricane, I can't think of anything."

Jaz, her head bent, went over Stewart's lesson, looking for that niggling concern in her mind.

"Can you think of any situation in which a generator might, say, explode or melt down?"

"Well, sure, but you might as well buy a lottery ticket too."

"Humor me?"

Stewart glanced toward Larry's cubicle. "Sheesh, Darcy, you're starting to worry me."

"Sorry. Just get on with it. Please."

Stewart, obviously worried about Darcy's weird and inexplicable line of questioning said, "The only scenario I can think of that might cause an actual explosion, would be if the generator were to somehow, like *magically*, suffer a prolonged phase fault."

"A phase fault?"

"Yeah. Inside a generator are magnets that turn or spin copper wire coils. This is the actual creation of the electrical current. I'm not able to explain it well, because it's not my strong suit, but electrical current flows in the shape of a wave called a sine wave. That form has to be well controlled. If two sine waves were 180 degrees out of fault and they interacted? *No bueno*. Colossal explosive response called destructive interference.

"But trust me when I say that the interaction between the turbine and the generator is governed so tightly, with so many safeguards and redundancies, that prolonged destructive interference *could not happen*. In my humble opinion and with my limited knowledge, the only way we could experience a failure of that type here at Parish is if someone, *in person*, somehow sabotaged two or more of the four units in the coal-fired plant."

He rubbed his eyes. "See, if Crystal were still here, she'd be able to run you through the details. As it is? You've exhausted my knowledge on the subject."

"Well, thanks. I appreciate what you were able to tell me." Jaz got up to roll her chair back to her terminal. Stopped. Looked at the back of Stewart's head as he rolled his chair into his cubicle.

"Stew, who's Crystal?"

He turned around. "Oh, yeah. Forgot you didn't know her. She's an electrical engineer, part of the contractor group that installed the new turbines and generators. Sharp lady. Easy on the eyes too."

Jaz arched one brow.

"Right. That was sexist. Sorry."

"Thanks. But tell me this, please. If this Crystal person was involved in swapping out the turbines and generators, how did you become acquainted with her here in IT?"

Stew seemed surprised by the question. "Well, because she sat here in our department and oversaw the update to the operations software that controls the turbines and generators. She used your cubicle, in fact, while she worked here. Sorry. Forgot you didn't know. We were glad to have her here since most of the software installation instructions were in Chinese."

Alarm bells ricocheted off the gray matter between Jaz's ears. A chill ran down her back and puddled in her feet. "Stewy . . . are you saying this woman, this *Crystal*, is Chinese?"

"I guess. Definitely Asian American, although that term could refer to a range of ethnicities. Like I said, super sharp lady, but *man!* Cold as ice when things didn't go exactly how she wanted them to go."

"And the update to the operations software? When was that installed?"

"We uploaded it months ago. Haven't had a single problem with it."

A frown puckered his forehead. "That said, the company that installed the new generators told us they found a small glitch in the software update."

Jaz, her body switching from chills to flushing warmth, pressed him. "Told you *how*, Stew? *How did they tell you?*"

"Sheesh, Darcy! They sent a *registered letter* to Larry, okay? The letter contained a patch disk to fix the grid, but we're not supposed to install it until the twenty-fourth of the month."

"This month? July?"

"Duh! Yes, *this month.*"

Clawing its way up and over the clanging alarms in her head, Jaz heard Bella's voice.

"*During a Resolute brainstorming session, Rusty came up with a plausible trigger event, a date the terrorists might choose to launch their attacks. It's based on the heat index across the nation. July is, historically, the hottest month overall in the continental US, making July the month that puts the greatest strain on the nation's power grid—and July 26 is the average hottest day in the nation.*"

She turned to stare at the department's wall calendar. "July 26 is Friday. Today is Monday, July 22?"

"Yeah, it is. We're scheduled to install the patch Wednesday, the twenty-fourth."

"I need to access that patch right away. I need to see it now! Where is it?"

By now, Larry and Mick had turned their chairs around and were listening.

Stewart glanced at Larry before saying, "You can't access it, Darcy. It's locked down in a secure IT node, and your login doesn't have access to that node—only Larry's and my logins do. It's SOP, a station operations security function and a matter of clearance."

Dumbfounded but not yet connecting all the dots scattered through her mind, Jaz stumbled to her cubicle and fell into her chair. She hadn't sat there for even a full minute before she shot to her feet and retraced her steps to Stewart's cubicle.

"Stewart, did Crystal help with the generator installations? I mean, was she physically there?"

When Larry heard Jaz's latest question, he stood up, and shifted nervously from foot to foot.

Stewart slid his troubled gaze to Larry, then back to Jaz. "I don't think I should talk to you about this anymore, Darcy."

"Yeah? And I'm telling you it's really important, Stew, *so answer the question!*"

Stewart turned his head. "Larry?"

"Go ahead, Stewart, but afterward, Darcy? I'm gonna need you to come with me to HR, because I'm not comfortable with where you're going with your questions."

"Yeah, I get you. Stewy? My question?"

"The answer is yes. She interfaced with the installation crew pretty regularly. In fact, I've known her to spin a few wrenches herself. She's extremely knowledgeable about both the equipment and the operating software."

Jaz heart hammered in her chest. She tried to calm herself by breathing in and out slowly, over and over. "Okay. Thanks, Stewart. And Larry? I'll save you that trip to HR. I'm headed there right now myself."

Because I need to brief my agency contact, Beverly, on this intel. Like now.

"Well, since you've freaked me out pretty thoroughly, Darcy, I'm coming with you."

"Fair enough."

"What is this about, anyway? Can you tell us?"

Jaz exhaled. Lined up her thoughts.

"What's it about, Larry? It's about a terrorist whose pretty Chinese name means Crystal—and about my agency planting me here to uncover and prevent an act of sabotage."

CHAPTER 35

JAZ RACED to HR with Larry close behind her. She pounded on Beverly Hollis' door but didn't wait for her to answer before she stepped inside. Beverly was sitting at her desk.

"Darcy?"

"I need to see the badge photo of a recent contractor named Crystal."

"Crystal Sanchez," Larry suppled.

"One moment." Beverly navigated to the HR system and did a search. She turned the monitor toward Jaz and Larry.

"That's her," Larry said, pointing to the photo.

"Thanks for confirming my suspicion, Larry. Turns out, I know her too. Beverly, next we need an immediate conference call with Director Wolfe, Bella Tobin, my task force, Harris and Bo, and FBI Special Agents Adisa and Bruckner."

Beverly didn't hesitate. "This way. We'll use the HR conference room."

Larry, eyeing Jaz with increasing awe, trailed behind the two women.

Long minutes later, using numbers Jaz supplied, Beverly had Harris and Bo, Bella, all of Task Force Resolute, and Special Agents Adisa and Bruckner on the line via the conference room's star-shaped speaker phone. Jaz gnawed her bottom lip as those on the call waited for Wolfe's administrative assistant to pull him from a meeting.

Finally, they heard, "Wolfe here."

"Director, this is Darcy Walken. I have Bella, all of Resolute, Harris and Bo, FBI Special Agents Adisa and Bruckner, Beverly Hollis, and my coworker, Larry, on this call with us."

"I see. Go ahead, Miss Walken."

"Sir, I believe I can now produce credible evidence of an imminent attack on WA Parish Generating Station."

"You *believe* you can produce that evidence?"

"Sir, the Chinese woman we initially identified as the leader of the Houston AEA cell and the coordinator of all the AEA cells? We weren't wrong about her after all. I have met her, sir. Her Chinese name is Jing, meaning Crystal. This same woman, going by the name of Crystal Sanchez, was part of the crew that recently installed new turbines and generators at Parish. And I have reason to believe this woman sabotaged those generators, sir."

Beside her, Larry shuddered.

"Furthermore," Jaz continued, "The Parish IT Department is scheduled to install a patch to the plant's operations software *Wednesday*. I believe that patch contains malicious code designed to immediately activate the sabotage."

"Again, you *believe* it contains this malicious code?"

"Sir, all I need is access to the patch in order to confirm my suspicions and provide you with the evidence you need."

"Who can authorize your access, Miss Walken?"

"Parish's plant manager or someone senior in the parent company."

Larry spoke up. "No. I can give her access. I'm not authorized to do so, but I can do it anyway. If it's a matter of preventing an act of sabotage, I'll take responsibility for giving Darcy access."

"Good man," Wolfe said. "I'll provide top cover for your actions. Miss Walken? How soon can you provide proof that this software contains the code you mentioned?"

"Within the hour, sir."

"Then what, Miss Walken?"

"Then we need to activate a tactical team, sir, and raid the headquarters of Houston's AEA cell. Areas of those headquarters are in an underground bunker, Director. FBI Special Agent Honor Adisa is familiar with the layout and can guide the tactical team."

"Our objectives, Miss Walken?"

"Apprehend the cell leader, Jing, and a man who goes by the name Itztli, and at the same time apprehend all identified AEA Houston cell members."

Bella spoke up. "Darcy, if you haven't yet ascertained AEA's communications methodology and should a Houston AEA cell member escape the raid, how can we be certain that member won't send an alert to other cells, triggering their attacks?"

"Bella, I'm convinced that the only means of communication Jing uses between and among herself and the other cells is a private chat room—the same way I communicate with you, Rusty, Harris, and Bo. To prove my theory and then ID the leaders of other AEA cells, I need to accompany the tactical team on their raid and, following the raid, search Itztli's underground bunker for his and Jing's laptops, then courier them directly to the task force. Once Resolute has their computers and tears into them, we will have control over AEA's communications."

Wolfe answered for Bella. "Granted, Miss Walken. I will coordinate with our FBI partners to raid the AEA Houston headquarters. You, Harris, and Bo, are to accompany them and find those machines."

He addressed Bella next. "And Bella? The moment your team has evidence of that malicious code in your hands, I want it and the President needs it. Based on the intel gleaned from those laptops, we will then simultaneously raid every AEA cell in the US."

He raised his voice. "Special Agents Adisa and Bruckner?"

"We're here, Director Wolfe," Adisa answered.

"Take good care of my people during that raid."

"Absolutely, sir."

"And Miss Walken?"

"Sir?"

"You won't allow that patch to be installed, will you?"

"Not on your life, Director."

"What about the sabotaged generators?"

"We don't know the exact nature of the sabotage except that AEA's goal, in all likelihood, is to shut down Parish Station more or less permanently. To achieve their goal, AEA will need to damage *beyond repair* every generator Parish has—the four within the coal-fired units, four within the idled natural gas units, and any backup generators."

Jaz added, "Someone will need to explain the situation to Parish's senior management, because removing the danger will require the same precise co-opordination and juggling of power distribution that was required to change out the turbines and generators."

"I can brief the chairman and his colleagues, if you wish it, Director," Beverly Hollis offered. "They know me."

Wolfe answered, "Please do. Take one of Darcy's coworkers with you to address the technical aspects."

Larry dropped his head, and a great sigh of relief whooshed from his lungs.

———————◆———————

WHILE BEVERLY called ahead to alert the chairman of Parish's parent company that she and Larry needed an urgent appointment, Jaz and Larry raced to the IT department to find the malicious code in the operations patch.

Larry, Stewart, and Mick scooted their chairs over to Jaz's cubicle and crowded around her—entirely too close for her comfort. However, it wasn't every day in the lives of these IT geeks that they got to uncover harmful system code, prevent a devastating act of terrorism, and thus save a big chunk of their state from disaster, was it?

Despite her itchy, claustrophobic anxiety, Jaz chose to cut them a little slack. She loaded a floppy disk onto her computer, trying not to squirm as the guys leaned in even closer.

"What's on the disk?" The question came out in near unison.

"Tools. I've designed software tools for specialized tasks. Like seeking out malware."

She navigated to the isolated IT node where the patch waited for installation.

"You couldn't even see that node before I gave you access," Larry muttered. "I'm . . . I'm really sorry."

"It's okay, Larry; you were doing your job as ordered. I'm in the node now, and I'll find that code."

Stewart pointed to a folder. "The patch is in that folder."

"Thanks, Stew."

He cleared his throat. "So . . . *Darcy*. Is that even your real name?" His voice dropped to a whisper. "Like, you're what—a secret agent?"

Jaz started to laugh and nearly choked on her gum. She recovered and said quietly, "Stewy, Stewy, Stewy. If I tell you . . ."

"Then she'll have to kill you," Larry and Mick intoned.

"Not funny, guys. Not funny!"

It may have been a silly, trite exchange, but the four of them laughed anyway.

Jaz opened the patch's code in a text file and scrolled through it. When she reached the end of the code, she muttered, mainly to herself, "I don't see anything obvious, but I expected nothing less."

"I didn't see anything out of the ordinary either," Larry said.

"Same," Mick added.

"Right; the malicious code is disguised or hidden somehow, but no worries. They don't call me Venom Queen for nothing. Watch my tools tear this code apart!"

She navigated to her floppy disk, opened a folder, and clicked on an executable file. As the program on the disk launched, it began searching through the patch's code, copying bits of the code and pasting those bits into a new window.

The guys were breathing down Jaz's neck now, driven by their need to understand what her program was doing.

"Found it!" Jaz chortled. "Look here. Whoever wrote this patch broke the code into small elements then separately nested those individual elements within multiple lines of code.

"This innocuous command pulls the separate elements from their nested locations and reassembles them into a single line here. Doing so embeds a *new* executable command within the patch and initiates a twenty-four-hour countdown timer. Then this line dictates what event will take place when the timer reaches zero. And do you see this?"

Her finger rested on her screen. "This is a detonation trigger."

"Detonation trigger for what?" Larry demanded.

"I suppose I'd put my money on a malleable plastic explosive material such as C4 or Semtex. It wouldn't take much of either to do the job," Jaz said quietly. "The bomb maker would probably pack the material inside a hardened, insulated shell, both to protect the explosive material from premature detonation and to focus the explosion in his preferred direction. I don't know generators, but I assume that the bomb maker would attach the packed explosive to an inside wall of a generator's housing, then wire the detonator to a small electrical source."

She grimaced. "Hey, guys? I count twelve separate detonation triggers in this code, indicating twelve explosive packs, one for every generator on site, active or inactive, primary or backup. Someone wanted to ensure the *total* annihilation of this station's ability to generate and distribute power. Whoever it was also wanted to prevent a switch from the coal-fired units to the natural gas ones, or the ability to quickly replace wrecked generators with viable backups."

She sat back. "Know what else? Crystal couldn't have done the sabotage work on her own. She had to have help building and installing the explosives . . . and she needed a hacker to write this elegant but deadly code."

Jaz peered at her screen for a long minute, searching. "Ah. There you are. Just couldn't help yourself, could you," she muttered. "Had to show off."

"What are you talking about?" Mick asked.

"Those seven lines of code, right there. Take a gander."

The three guys again leaned in. They spotted an icon formed by ASCII characters, the figure of a horizontal knife.

Larry responded. "Did I hear you tell your director during the conference call that Itztli guy's hacker handle is Obsidian Knife? You're saying this is his signature? I guess that answers the question as to the extent of his involvement—nutcase or not."

"Yup, and he's no slouch when it comes to programming." Jaz removed her tools disk from her computer and inserted a fresh disk. Saved both the original patch code and the assembled detonation code to the disk and ejected it.

"This is the evidence my director needs to act. And Larry?"

"Yeah?"

"We may, at this moment, have kept the patch from being loaded into the system, but those *very real* explosives are still sitting inside the generator housings, waiting to be detonated. If I were you? I'd delete that patch code from the network, defrag the drive, and burn any backup tapes—but that's just me."

Muttering dark expletives, Larry sprinted for his desk.

Jaz noticed that Stewart was sweating. "Stew? You okay?"

He shook his head. "Okay? Nope. Not even a little. Like you said, we have explosives sitting inside four coal-fired generators currently in use. Explosions inside those generators *while they are running?* We're talking massive phase failure and destructive interference.

"And if the frictional heat from the alternator rotors grinding to a halt sparks the coal dust the plants burn as fuel? It would cause a secondary explosion. The entire coal-fired power plant would be gone. Not just the generators themselves, but everything around them for quite some distance. Pretty much melted to slag—not to mention, how many people would die."

Jaz nodded. "Beverly has probably already arranged a meeting to convey these findings to Parish's parent company. I think you're the right guy to go with her, don't you? You can explain the details and why this generating station won't be safe until bomb techs locate and remove each and every one of those explosive devices."

CHAPTER 36

BY NINE o'clock that evening, the FBI's tactical team had scoped out Itztli's bunker, verified the location of every known Houston cell member, and planned their assault down to the last detail. The only part of the plan the team and its commander did not like was bringing Jaz, Harris, and Bo along for the assault. Sadly for them? They had their orders.

At the commander's signal, four squads would simultaneously hit four targets. One squad would hit the dry cleaners' shop; two squads would enter the shops between the dry cleaner and the yellow room, front and back; and the primary squad would enter the stock room from its alley door and gain entrance to the yellow room.

Once the primary squad was inside the yellow room, they would breach the concealed door at the end of the hallway, as revealed by Special Agent Adisa, and descend the stairs behind that door leading down to the bunker. The above-ground squads were to ensure that no one in the bunker escaped by way of an unknown route leading up to the shops surrounding the bunker.

Jaz, Harris, and Bo were ordered to wait down the alley during the assault, far from the action. The three of them were "accompanied" by a young FBI agent whose sole job was to ensure that Jaz, Harris, and Bo neither participated in nor interfered with the assault. Nevertheless, Harris and Bo carried their sidearms, and Harris had demanded that Jaz also be armed.

In an aside to her, he told her, "This FBI team may be in charge of the takedown, but make no mistake, this is *your* op, Darcy Walken. Not one of us would be here if it weren't for you. Since you're most proficient with the Mossberg, take it and five shells, and carry that gun like the boss you are. Remember your training, and don't forget our maxim: It's better to have a gun and not need it than to need a gun and not have it."

Jaz didn't mind carrying the shotgun. In fact, its weight was rather comforting . . . as opposed to the wary, distrustful scrutiny of their FBI watchdog.

She glared at him. "Whadda you looking at? We're the good guys. The terrorists are in *that* direction."

Stung, the young man swiveled and faced outward.

Harris shot her a big grin. "Like a *boss!*"

Harris' accolades and confidence in her warmed Jaz inside. She ducked her head, pleased but at the same time *just a hair* concerned.

Huh. When did I start caring what he thinks of me?

Just then, the strike commander issued final instructions to his four squads—and to the agents spread across Houston charged with scooping up every cell member not apprehended in the bunker. "I've been told that if we blow this takedown in any way, that if even one target slips our net, the consequences could be dire. So listen up. The count is *twenty-nine*. Twenty-nine terrorists, from their leaders down to the grunts. Your job is to make certain we hit our numbers."

Now, prior to the start of the assault, the tactical team listened to the commander's voice over their in-ears comms. "Tac teams, get ready!"

Four squads, as silent as death, waited for the go signal. Two of those squads, stacked and prepared to roll, were positioned down the alley from Jaz, Harris, Bo, and their guard.

"Go! Go! Go!"

The four squads hit their assigned entry points at the same time. From Jaz's perspective, for several minutes, nothing seemed to happen. Then bursts of semiauto gunfire reached her ears. Harris and Bo had heard the popping sounds as well. They and their FBI minder, weapons at the ready, inched forward, while Jaz stood perfectly still. Listening.

She'd heard something behind her, a few yards farther down the alley. She focused on the soft sounds. At first she thought the whiffling noise had to be sewer rats.

Yeah, but rats don't whisper.

The soft grate of metal on metal removed all doubt. She crept toward the sound and caught the glint of a hatch rising up from the alley. Lifting the Mossberg, she palmed a shell from her pocket. She slid it into the firing chamber, and automatically pushed the forend away from her.

That nice solid sound she liked so well told her she had one round at the ready. Unfortunately, that sound conveyed the same message to whomever had hoped to come through that hatch. The hatch slammed shut abruptly.

"Harris!"

He came running.

"What?"

She pointed with the Mossberg. "That's an escape hatch. Someone just tried to come through it. Guess I changed their mind."

Harris grabbed the edges of the hatch and pulled. The hatch opened and revealed a dark gaping hole and a ladder.

"Keep your gun on this hatch," Harris told Jaz. "Nobody gets out, got it?"

"Got it."

He jogged back to their FBI babysitter. "Hey, you! Tell the assault commander, that we've plugged an escape route over here."

The man thumbed his mic and repeated the information and location to the commander, while Harris returned to the open hatch. Moments later, Jaz and Harris heard shouted commands echo up from the tunnel beneath the hatch.

Finally, about ten more nail-biting minutes later, the primary squad emerged from the stock room door, herding seven prisoners including Itztli, Jing, and Itztli's two Chinese-American bodyguards. The remaining FBI squads were given the all-clear and began to reassemble in the alley.

The commander walked up to Jaz. "Can you identify these individuals?"

She nodded. "That guy is our messiah complex, Itztli. The woman there is either first or second in command of this cell. The two musclebound goons are also cell leaders. The last three are rabid cult members I met at a recent AEA meeting."

Two agents prodded Itztli and Jing past Jaz. Their hands were secured behind their backs in flex cuffs, but the two prisoners were far from cowed or docile.

Jing laughed when she saw Jaz. "If it isn't the vaunted Vyper! Well, guess what, thou mighty Venom Queen? You haven't a clue what's coming, let alone how to stop it."

"Are you referring to AEA's plans to sabotage the US power grid?" Jaz asked with a smile.

The laughter fell from Jing's mouth like she'd been slapped, but Itztli sneered at Jaz.

"From the first day I met you, you acted like you were so much better than Syntax, better than me."

Jaz shrugged. "I was just a lonely, eager kid . . . who knew she *would be* better than you. You knew it too, Azteca. You as much as told me the day I saved you from hacking that bank protected by Sawtooth's security program."

Itztli scowled. "You quit on us and skipped town. You left us to take the rap for those bank hacks! I spent two years in lockup because of you!"

"*Not* because of me," Jaz answered. "I sent you fair warning—and I cautioned you about that harebrained extortion scheme of yours, too. If, in either case, you chose to ignore me? That's on you."

"Whatever, *Jinn*. We'll see how high and mighty you act . . . after."

"By 'after,' do you mean after Parish IT installs the patch for Parish's operations software?"

Itztli's features froze.

"That's right, Az—or should I refer to you as *Obsidian Knife?* I found your code in the software patch. Very nice. Elegant, even—especially the signature part. By the way? I sent a copy of your code to my boss, who sent a copy to the FBI. Basically, your code—signature included—is all the evidence we need to hit every AEA cell in the US."

While Itztli struggled to regain his composure, a look of desperation crossed his partner's face.

"Are you surprised that Parish won't go *boom*, Jing? Disappointed? Please don't fret. ATF explosives experts are on the way as we speak. They will remove the explosives you helped install in the vain hope of blowing Parish to kingdom come."

Itztli and Jing's captors nudged them to get moving, but Jing resisted. She turned back to Jaz. "Wait. You need to help us! If our missions fail, they won't just abandon us—we'll be dead before you can even question us!"

Jaz held up her hand to the agents and stood face to face with the woman. "Are you saying the Chinese government will kill you if we don't protect you?"

"That's precisely what I'm saying. I'll tell you everything I know, but only if you swear to protect me. Please don't leave me alone with them," she motioned to the two bodyguards, "they *will* kill me! But don't bother with him," she jerked her chin at Itztli. "He doesn't know the half of what I know."

Itztli struggled with the agent's hold on him, and his face twisted between anguish and disbelief. "Don't 'bother' with me, Jing? What are you saying? I thought you loved me! You and I, we were going to survive the cleansing of the earth and live a life of luxury in the aftermath!"

She made a crude, dismissive sound in the back of her throat. "I'm sick to death of your kingdom slash messiah song and dance and the fatuous name you picked. Itztli? Don't get me started. You were a nice distraction and a convenient cover—*that's all.*

She sneered at him. "I used you and your coding skills, but now I'm done with you—besides which? There wasn't going to be any 'life of luxury in the aftermath,' you brainless maggot. The Red Army was supposed to invade and occupy Houston, take control of the shipping and the oil refineries!"

Itztli lunged at her; the agents pulled him off of her and dragged them both away, Itztli screaming and cursing, Jing telling him to shut up.

Jaz shivered. "Wow. That was kinda harsh."

Harris nodded. "You're not wrong about that."

Jaz cleared the Mossberg's receiver and pocketed the unused shell, then moved toward the stock room door.

"I've got laptops to find and crack. Bet you a dollar, it takes me less than five minutes to locate the chat room AEA uses to communicate with their cells—just like we communicate with Resolute. I'll send the chat room URL to Rusty, then courier the laptops to Resolute. The task force will ID every AEA cell in the US, possibly including a few cells Wolfe's surveillance folk have missed."

Harris followed her. "Hey, want to grab some pizza after?"

"Do I ever!"

"Hey, guys! Don't forget me," Bo protested, running along behind them.

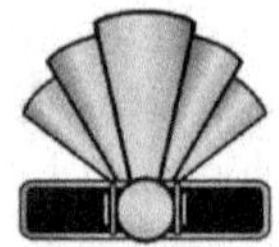

CHAPTER 37

TWO HOURS later, with the laptops safely on their way to Resolute via an FBI agent aboard an FBI plane, Jaz and Harris were ensconced in a cozy booth at a late-night pizza parlor. Bo, shaking his head, had elected to grab burgers with Special Agents Adisa and Bruckner rather than pizza with Jaz and Harris.

"I'm starving," Jaz proclaimed as their large pizza arrived. She picked off a slice of pepperoni and sucked it down.

"Want to say a blessing over the food first, Jaz? Is it okay that I call you Jaz now?"

"What? Oh, okay. Sure. And yes to the blessing. Sheesh, this Christian thing is a lot harder than it looks."

"It's an adjustment for sure, but well worth it."

"So, you're a Christian now? I mean, you've dropped some hints lately."

"I surrendered my life to Jesus about nine months ago. Wasn't confident enough to tell anyone at first, but that's changing."

"I still can't believe it. Why didn't you tell me while you were training me?"

"Uh, if you're mystified about me getting saved, I'm pretty flummoxed about *you*. Why didn't *you* tell *me*?"

They laughed, prayed over the pizza, then dug in. The quiet was comfortable —even cozy—while they ate. Afterward, awkwardness set in. They split the bill, paid it, then left, walking along, looking for a cab as they did.

Harris finally broke the ice. "So what's next for Agent Vyper?"

"Agent Vyper? Has a nice ring to it, doesn't it? *Not*. This was a one-off assignment. No more field work for me. I'm going home to Resolute."

"Dunno, Jaz. You did great, and Wolfe will know that. I wouldn't count on spending the rest of your career in Resolute's bullpen."

"Nope. I turned him down the first time. I can do it again."

"Because turning him down the first time stuck, right?"

Jaz blushed. "He's persuasive."

"Naw, that wasn't it, was it? I heard that *you* initiated a second meeting with him, that *you* had the insight to perceive AEA was after the power grid."

Her eyes narrowed. "You sure hear a lot."

"When Wolfe set up your training at Broadsword, he spoke of you. Highly, I might add, *Agent* Vyper."

Jaz stuck out her jaw. "I won't be using Vyper as my hacker handle in the future. I've decided that I need a new name, one Jesus chooses for me—like when he changed Simon's name to Peter and Levi's name to Matthew. I want my handle to proclaim the work he's done in my heart. 'Course, it's not a complete work, not by a long shot. But I hope to begin talking about him online, telling my cyber cronies about Jesus' grace and mercy over my old, miserable life."

Harris grinned. "That's my girl."

Jaz blinked and slowly reddened. "W-what did you say?"

"I said, 'That's my girl.' I'd really like you to be my girl, Jaz. Will you?"

Right there on the sidewalk, he carefully stretched both arms around her, gently tugged her to his chest, and with his eyes wide open staring into Jaz's startled orbs, laid a single kiss smack-dab on her lips.

From Jaz's shocked perspective, the kiss wasn't rough or demanding. It was just . . . nice. Still, she had no intention of letting Harris get away with it or anything else—whatever *it* was or whatever *anything else* meant.

"What do you say, Jaz? Shall we pray on it?"

She pulled away. "What do I *say?* Honestly? Look here, you dope! I don't do—"

"Yeah, yeah, yeah. You don't 'do' kisses. Is that it? Well, good! Because if you were going around kissing just anybody? See, that would upset me. I mean, if you and I are going to ask the Lord what *he* says about us—if we're going to ask him if there even *is* an 'us'—I would expect any and all kisses to be mutually exclusive. Oh. And chaste."

Jaz folded her arms and screwed up her mouth. "You are *way* too far out over your skis, buster. In fact, I predict you're about to snowball straight down that hill. What I was saying was that I don't do kisses, *period.*"

Harris just looked at her, all bland and unconcerned, his jaws moving slowly while he watched and waited.

For what? What's he waiting for? Gah! Men! I don't get them. Not even.

Unexpectedly, her nose twitched. *Hang on. What's that smell? Is that—*

"Harris, are you chewing gum? *My gum?* The gum you *stole* from me?"

He shrugged. "Maybe. I thought I should probably get used to it. You know, if we were gonna kiss and all."

Jaz felt her head was about to explode. "Do you have a hearing problem? I said I DON'T DO KISSES!"

"Yeah. Okay. Got it. Probably best anyway until we get engaged." He just stood there, unconcerned, chewing *her* gum . . . but not walking away either.

And neither was she for some stupid reason.

Jaz tried to stretch her neck, which seemed unaccountably taut. "Well then, that's that."

Wait—did he say engaged? *Engaged?*

Harris inched toward her. Lowered his voice. "Are you sure?"

"Am I sure what?"

He edged in a bit closer, and Jaz couldn't help but notice the pretty gold flecks in his brown eyes as he stared back.

"Are you *sure* that you don't do kisses? Not ever?"

Jaz was shocked at how deeply his gaze was searching her, as though he was seeking an echoing response to his heart or hoping to find . . .

What I'm unable to give.

Unable to give.

Jaz felt the sting of tears. "Harris . . ."

"What is it, sweet Jaz?"

"Don't call me that. I can't . . . I mean, it's really hard for me to-to-to—"

"To let me get close to you? To let anyone touch you?"

Jaz felt herself grow hot. Then she shivered as if a cold wind had gusted over her. She puffed out a breath and fought to find some piece or place of equilibrium.

"Yeah, I'm not . . . Harris, I'm not like other people. I-I . . ."

"I know, Jaz. I know that some parts of life are difficult for you to navigate, and it's okay. It's an ongoing struggle. I get it. I understand. More than that? Jesus understands."

Jaz's *present* struggle was to just stay afloat. "You do? He does?"

"Yep. I also know that whatever you ask Jesus to help you overcome? He will do it, one step at a time. So, please. Will you tell me what is in your heart? Is there room in there for me?"

You understand?

Jesus understands?

Jaz stared down the block and closed herself off. Closed herself off so she could ask the question she had assiduously avoided all her life.

Jesus, do you know what is wrong with me?

There it was.

She knew something was wrong with her. Knew she was different, had always been different. Radically so.

Jesus, do you understand me like Harris says you do? I'm asking because I sort of like this man—okay, I do like him!

But I don't know how to show him. Don't know how to let him in.

She blinked and "returned" to find that she was again standing inside the loose circle of Harris' arms, his hand gently stroking her back.

And she wasn't freaking out?

"Is this okay, Jaz?"

"I-I think so."

He pressed a soft kiss on her forehead. "How about that?"

"Um . . . okay. Sure."

"Could you try resting your head on my chest?"

Jaz considered said chest. It was all puffed out, like, with *muscle*.

"Rest my head on your chest?"

"Yup. Right here. Think of it like a pillow."

Hesitant but intrigued, Jaz placed her cheek on his t-shirt and let it rest there a moment. With a sigh, she leaned into him.

"How's that, sweet Jaz?"

"You don't know me very well if you keep insisting on calling me 'sweet Jaz.'"

Harris' laughter rumbled in her ear. She felt it rumble through her too, and it made her snicker.

"So, are you sure you don't do kisses, Jaz? Or could we try one more time? Just to be sure?"

She lifted her head . . . and he closed the gap.

A few moments later, they came up for air.

"So, what do you think, sweet Jaz?"

"Uh, *wow*. I mean, whew!"

"Not too bad?"

Jaz stole another look at those gold flecks in his eyes.

"Well, I suppose I could be wrong . . . about the kissing thing."

CHAPTER 38

THE FLIGHT carrying Jaz, Harris, and Bo landed at Reagan National in DC. Travis, driving a Broadsword vehicle, picked them up at the arrivals gate.

"Where to?"

Jaz answered. "Even though it's Saturday, we have a debrief at Griffin Industries. It may take a few hours. Want to grab some lunch while we're doing that? We'll call when we're done."

"Sure thing."

Jaz, still traveling as Darcy Walken, didn't have her Griffin Industries badge with her, but the guards at the gate had permission to let the car through. Travis dropped them in the parking garage, turned around, and drove off. The elevator opened, sent from above, and Jaz, Harris, and Bo got in.

Harris kept trying to hold Jaz's hand.

She finally had to smack his fingers. "Not at work, *dork*."

"Yeah, *please*," Bo begged. "Bad enough flying with you lovesick pups."

"Shut it," Jaz growled.

The elevator opened, and all of Resolute met them, applauding, cheering, and whistling. Bella stepped forward, smiling. "Not bad for a first op, Jaz. Not bad at all. We owe the three of you a great debt of thanks."

She motioned them forward. "Come on in. We've read your reports, but perhaps we can tie up the loose threads on this end."

They did, but in fits and starts, plus a few chaotic leaps. Even though Bella began in an orderly manner, Jaz's teammates were anxious to provide details and, as usual, talked over each other. A lot.

"As you know," Bella said, "two days ago, the FBI and Wolfe's tactical team executed simultaneous warrants on fifteen AEA cells in fifteen cities, including Houston. They acted on intel provided by Wolfe's surveillance teams, the chat room URL you sent, and both Jing and Itztli's laptops. Thanks for getting those laptops to us via courier, by the way.

"Resolute worked through yet another night this week to tear those laptops apart. Itztli was definitely AEA's coder—more on that in a moment—but Jing's laptop held the information we needed most, including the details of each cell's target, their method of attack, and the AEA members responsible for carrying out the attacks. That information enabled our tactical teams and the FBI to hit every cell and round up AEA members before they could act. In every instance but one, they arrested all suspected terrorists.

Bella glanced up. "Jaz, your thoughts were right on the money concerning this plot. Because many power companies are, to some degree, managed by subcontractors, AEA managed to insert their tech people inside every major target they planned to take out. Those individuals provided logistical intelligence to AEA. They identified the most desirable targets, ascertained those targets' vulnerabilities, and passed that info to their cell's leadership.

"But that's not all those technically competent AEA members did. From inside, they planted Itzli's code in key grid operating systems, code that would lock out operators and administrators, suspending control over power-switching systems so that once the attacks began, *no one* would be able to shift load from one segment of the grid to another to meet sudden heavy demands. Then these same individuals left on vacation in order to exit their city before catastrophe hit.

"When Resolute found the code on Itztli's laptop to lock out the operators, we passed it to the FBI. Their tech monkeys were able to scrub the infected systems and eliminate that threat."

Jaz nodded. "Sounds about right. With the operations controls disabled, intentional generating failures could crash the grid, whereas at Parish, the AEA insider threat coordinated the insertion of shaped charges to physically blow up the generators. What were some of the plans to cause failures elsewhere?"

"Good question—"

Brian jumped in. "What were some of the plans to cause failures elsewhere? Holy Spumoni, Batman! Eight, count 'em, *eight* Chinese HJ-9 antitank missiles! That's how they were gonna blow the Narrows Generating Station and Gowanus Station in Brooklyn, the Astoria Generating Stations in Queens, and the daddy of them all, Ravenswood, also in Queens."

Rusty chided him. "Brian, you interrupted Bella."

"Right." Brian sat down. "Sorry, Rusty. Sorry, Bella."

But Rusty didn't return the conversation to Bella as expected. "Now that we've muzzled Brain Fog, *I* get to tell Jaz about the *suicide bombers*. Yup, real ones, two pilots, each flying a Cessna loaded with C4. One was supposed to crash into Plant Scherer about seventy-five miles south of Atlanta, and the second into Plant Bowen, roughly fifty miles north of Atlanta.

Resolute erupted in boos and catcalls that didn't diminish Rusty's enthusiasm a wit. He actually took a bow.

"And I thought I left an adult in charge," Jaz sighed.

Gwyneth saw her opportunity and grabbed it. "AEA targeted the DC and Chicago power grids too—"

Soraya cut in, "Yeah, AEA members had two up-armored dump trucks filled with ANFO. They were ready to drive them, one to a DC generating station, the other to a Chicago station, crash their way through barriers, and detonate them when they reached their targets."

"ANFO is what the Oklahoma City bomber used," Jubaila provided, "ammonium nitrate fertilizer mixed with fuel oil."

Without missing a beat, Gwyneth picked back up. "*And*, as a total outlier because it wouldn't have devastated a large urban environment like the rest of their plans would, a third suicide bomber was told to fly a plane loaded with explosives into the power switch yard just outside of Grand Coulee Dam in Washington State. That switch yard, as substantial as it is, might not have been as difficult to rebuild as a generating station would have been, but its temporary loss would certainly have put a tremendous strain on the grid that supplies the Pacific Northwest. A tactical team arrested that pilot just as he drove up to the hangar where he kept his plane."

Bella lifted a closed fist. Resolute members quieted, but they chuckled under their breath and grinned at Jaz. Jaz grinned back, feeling a little like a proud mama hen.

In an attempt to restore order, Bella asked, "Jaz, Harris, and Bo? Are the three of you interested in hearing the end result of the FBI's operation to round up all the AEA members?"

"Most definitely," Bo replied.

Bella's fist shot up again—preempting another Resolute free-for-all.

She rolled her eyes, then said, "I had no idea what you go through on a daily basis, Jaz. It's like herding cats."

Jaz winked. "Tell me about it. Glad you survived."

Bella laughed under her breath. "Right. Now for the end results. So far, we know of only three AEA cell members who avoided capture, all three from AEA's New Jersey cell. Yesterday, July 26, was the date set to execute concurrent attacks across all the cells—large attacks on generating stations or major power plants. But as we discovered from what happened, they had a backup plan, vulnerable substations that were targeted as Plan B if Plan A failed.

"The three at-large cell members, females armed with high-powered automatic weapons, shot up a sizeable substation outside Newark, then moved on to a second substation about two miles away. As they headed toward their third objective, five miles west of the second, police air support spotted them.

"The police were able to set a roadblock and prevent them from reaching their target. In the confrontation that followed, the three women did not surrender and were, unfortunately, killed. Yes, putting those substations out of commission was a big blow to Newark, but they will recover quickly. We're grateful because we know how much worse it could have been."

"And the attack on the US financial markets?" Jaz asked.

"Ah! Great question. After the director of the FBI alerted the SEC that a concerted market 'short' was in the works—a short being when someone sells a security with the intention of repurchasing it later at a lower price—the SEC commissioners brought in some very savvy market people. They dug around and identified several suspicious movements. More important, they identified the entities behind the suspicious movements.

"Once we had supplied SEC with the date AEA planned to hit its targets, the SEC allowed the suspect entities to sell their securities. But, minutes after they issued their sell orders, the SEC hit them with criminal sanctions.

"When the attack failed? The SEC did not permit them to buy back into the market. Not only will China's penalties be severe and costly, the SEC also suspended them from trading in the US pending a full investigation. In other words, China and its surrogates took a huge financial gamble and lost millions."

"So, what gives with the Chinese government?" Jaz demanded. "They were behind everything! What happens to them?"

Bella grew a small, satisfied smile. "This will be news to all of you. Early this morning, the President summoned the Chinese ambassador to the White House. I understand it wasn't a pleasantly worded summons, either. The ambassador's meeting with the President lasted exactly seven minutes—seven minutes in which the ambassador listened while the President spoke and tolerated *no* interruptions. When the ambassador departed, it was to return to his embassy and pack. He was given twenty-four hours to leave US soil."

Brian expressed incredulity. "Are you saying the President kicked the Chinese ambassador to the curb?"

"That he did. He also gave the ambassador a strongly worded message to take home. Let's hope the message is received as the unequivocal warning it was intended as."

With that, Bella nodded to Vincent, her administrative assistant.

He jumped to his feet and announced, "A caterer is setting up a special lunch in the lobby." He nodded to Jaz and grinned. "It's to welcome you home, Jaz. We've missed you something fierce."

THE LUNCH was pleasant, but after an hour of excessive talking, hugging, and *more* hugging, Jaz was worn to the bone. She went to the bullpen to catch a moment alone. There, she discovered an entire, unopened *box* of Black Jack—twenty packs!—sitting on her desk. A single blue bow adorned the box.

She tore off the wrapper, sliced through the tape, and ripped out a pack. She withdrew a single stick of gum, kissed the blue wrapper, and inhaled the familiar scent. Unwrapped and stuffed the stick into her mouth.

Oh, how I've missed you!

Less anxious, she returned to the party. Harris and Bo were saying their goodbyes.

Harris sidled up to Jaz and said (at normal volume), "So, next Friday. Dinner followed by a movie? How about I pick you up at six o'clock? Chinese okay?"

"Yum! Chinese is always okay in my book—Chinese food that is, as opposed to, say, CCP terrorists."

Harris belted out a guffaw. "Good one!"

Conversations ceased. Eyeballs rotated in their direction and got stuck on the two of them.

Harris pointed to the pack of gum in Jaz's hand. "I see you found my gift on your desk. Mind if I have a piece? I'm starting to appreciate the appeal."

Jaz smiled. "And a very thoughtful gift it was, Harris. Better than flowers any day."

He grinned. "You're welcome. Only the best for *my* girl."

Jaz giggled, pulled a stick of gum from the pack, and offered it to him.

"Thanks, chickie. Can't wait till the weekend." He leaned in and brushed her cheek with a kiss. "See you then."

Jaz pinked up. Her smile widened.

When Harris turned around, he added for the pairs of straining ears, "Yup. Jaz and I? We're an item. Probably should get used to it."

Vincent, Rusty, and Brian, standing together, quietly voiced their reactions.

"Huh. I did *not* see that coming."

Rusty folded his arms. "You ain't wrong, Vinnie. And hear that raucous commotion? That's the sound of my last pipe dream crashing to the ground. Bursting into flames. Not that *I* ever had a shot."

Brian sighed. "At least I'll always have our dance together—I mean, who knew Jaz could tango like that? *Va-va-voom!*"

Rusty slapped Brian on the back and grinned. "Right? That scene was epic, dude. The stuff of legends."

Vincent nodded. "It certainly was." He glanced over his shoulder. "Too bad no one filmed it. We could have taunted Harris forever."

Brian's woebegone expression brightened. "Right? I'd have paid money to see Harris's face when Jaz and I performed the move, '*tango enganche*'! Wowza!"

The three of them cackled long and loud.

"All right, you scurvy crew! Inspection!"

Resolute scrambled to form a ragged line; they puffed out their chests and focused steely eyes straight ahead. With one voice they shouted, "Aye aye, Captain Black Jack!"

Jaz stifled a snort. Then she eyeballed them up and down. "Well. Hmm. Very good. Yes. Er, *well done*."

Turning on her heel she commanded, "Resolute, up anchor! Hoist the main sail and prepare to come about!"

"Aye, Captain!"

The task force disappeared into the bullpen, and Jaz slowly followed. She plopped down at her workstation, exhaled, looked around, and took in the purposeful air of her dorky but precious crew. She laid one hand on her keyboard.

"*Home*. Thank you, Lord."

POSTSCRIPT

◄ *Vyper* ►

SEPTEMBER 2002

AS JAZ'S plane prepared to land, she studied Regina's landscape. The city's boundaries had spread out since she was here last, and she spied tall buildings that hadn't been there sixteen years ago.

I might recognize this town, but things change. People change. She smiled a little. *I've changed too, haven't I?*

The wheels touched down on the runway with a thud, and her heart thudded along with the wheels.

An hour later, Niève Simard checked into her hotel room.

Jaz's ID, using her actual name, was a compromise hammered out between Director Wolfe and Bernard Dupont, with Jaz and Bella sitting in.

"If I understand correctly, the Ukrainians no longer pose a danger to you, Miss Simard," Dupont said over the conference call. "In that case, we'd very much like you to come back home. CSIS has a place for you and important work for you to do."

Wolfe and Bella had avoided Jaz's eyes, probably to sidestep accusations of influencing Jaz's decision. Jaz, though, didn't need to be influenced.

"Thank you, Mr. Dupont. I appreciate the offer, but I'm happy in my present situation."

To herself she admitted more. *I could no more leave Resolute, or Harris for that matter, than I could leave the faith I've found in Jesus. But I do have unfinished business in Canada.*

It was nearing dinnertime, time for her to get going, yet she was undeniably nervous. She sat on the edge of her hotel bed and prayed.

I don't know what will happen while I'm here, but I know you will be with me through it all. I choose to trust you.

With the Saskatchewan driver's license in her purse, courtesy of Bernard Dupont, she pointed her rental car toward the restaurant she'd selected. Toward the individuals she'd invited to meet her for dinner.

Donny would be 24 years old now, and Trey 25. Kit and Mary would both be 26. How would they respond to seeing her after all this time?

Still a bit anxious, Jaz entered the Chinese restaurant and approached the hostess.

"My name is Niève Simard. I reserved a private room for dinner this evening."

"Ah, yes! Your guests have already arrived. This way, please."

Jaz walked into the small room, not knowing what to expect.

Four strangers stood and stared at her. Came toward her.

"Niève?" one of the men asked.

Not a stranger.

It was Donny, all grown up. Smiling. Strong and happy—as were Trey, Kit, and Mary. They gathered around her, remembering her quirks and careful not to crowd her, but wanting to touch, to reconnect. Jaz faced them one at a time and leaned in for a quick half-hug. They received what she offered with joy.

Then they were sitting, laughing, talking, ordering more food than they could possibly eat in one sitting, each of them sharing their lives, their families, and the work they did.

"What about you, Niève?" Trey asked. "Tell us what you do."

Jaz had hammered this out with Bella and Director Wolfe. A pat answer to satisfy the questions—and no more.

"I live in the States now where I'm an intelligence analyst." Jaz made air quotes with her fingers around intelligence analyst and shrugged. "Really, it's pretty dull stuff."

But Donny just smiled. "You can't talk about it, can you."

Not a question.

Jaz smiled back. "No, I can't."

"I have always believed you were special," he said, "more than merely special *to us*. Whatever it is you're doing? It has to be important."

He ducked his head. "The main reason I came today was to thank you— thank you for being my big sister and my knight in shining armor all rolled into one."

"*Our* knight in shining armor, you mean," Kit threw in. "When you slew Maude the Dragon for us, you showed us how to be brave."

Trey laughed. "And here I've always thought of you as our anime heroine!"

"Good one," Mary agreed.

"You do have a bit of an Oriental slant to your eyes, Nivève, and it really popped out that day you dyed your hair pure black. Oh, my goodness, that day! I thought certain Maude was going to—"

"Explode? Implode?" Donny asked. "Maybe launch herself into orbit?"

They laughed as one, nodding at the memory.

Donny put his hand into a bag and brought something out. Two books. Two very loved, well-used books.

"My wife and I are expecting our first in December, a boy, and I will read these books to him."

"I still have mine," Kit murmured. Trey and Mary smiled and nodded.

"Do you know about Albert and Maude?" Donny asked.

"Yah. I read their obituaries online," Jaz said. "I was sorry . . . sorry that I didn't have a chance to tell them what's happened to me. In me."

"Tell us," Trey asked, suddenly serious. "Tell us everything."

Jaz licked her lips. She was about to go off-script—not to reveal anything classified—but in order for Donny, Kit, Trey, and Mary to understand the depth of what Jesus had done in her, they first needed to know what he'd saved her from.

"By the time I was fourteen, I was hacking banks with two older guys. We were stealing thousands of dollars a month from the banks."

Donny gaped. "Hacking? At fourteen? But . . . that's when you were still with us and the Northams!"

"If I'm special in any way, Donny, it's with computers. Long story short? A couple of years ago, I was one of the most feared hackers in the global hacker community."

She took a deep breath. "But then, Jesus . . ."

———◆———

THE FOLLOWING morning, Jaz took her time getting ready to leave the hotel. She dreaded her first visit of the day, and paused several times to pray before she got in her rental car and drove to the address she had.

The building was nice enough, its exterior and grounds impressive, the interior's décor tasteful. But all the expense in the world could not hide the facility's pervasive antiseptic odor. She'd forced herself to push through the heavy, ornate doors.

Lord, please help me!

She spotted the reception desk and walked toward it as another woman was signing herself out. When the woman turned, she and Jaz recognized each other.

"Miss Logan?"

Jaz cleared her throat. "Mrs. Oliver. How . . . how are you?"

"I'm glad to see you, that's how I am! I'd like to give you a big hug, but Iris told me years ago that touching isn't your thing. Speaking of Iris, I assume you've come to see her?"

"Yes. How . . . how is Iris doing?"

Mrs. Oliver's eyes glistened. "Awake and lucid, but in tremendous pain. The cancer is quite advanced now. Would you like me to take you to her?"

Jaz swallowed. "Yes, please."

"Sign in here with the receptionist. Iris is in Room 167."

They walked down a long hallway together, saying nothing. Mrs. Oliver knocked on a partially open door, then stuck her head inside.

"Iris? You have another visitor."

She turned and smiled at Jaz. "I'll leave you now, but I am truly delighted to see you. And I want to thank you again for saving my business all those years ago. My daughter runs it these days, and we are in good shape."

Jaz nodded. When Mrs. Oliver left, Jaz paused at the door to muster her courage. Then she pushed the door open and stepped into the room.

Iris lay in a hospital bed. The bed's head was partway up, but her form scarcely made a bump under the covers. Her head turned toward Jaz, and she squinted.

"Who's there, please?"

"It's me, Iris. . . . Adele."

"Adele? Adele! Is it you? Please! Please come closer."

Iris lifted thin fingers to beckon her.

Jaz drew near the bed. She gritted her teeth and picked up Iris's emaciated hand. Leaned toward her. Met her slowly blinking gaze.

"I'm here, Iris."

Iris studied her. "My goodness! It is you, and you've grown up."

"I suppose I have."

"Please tell me about your life, Adele, will you?"

With Iris's hand nestled between both of hers, Jaz began to talk. "For a number of years I roamed the world. I lived in many places and saw wonderful things . . . but I continued to make money in less than legal ways.

"One day, a man from the Canadian Security Intelligence Service offered me a job as a white hat hacker. Actually, he coerced me, threatened to have me arrested if I didn't come to work for CSIS. At the time, I despised him and his agency. Looking back, I can see . . . how God had his hand on me. How he was orchestrating my circumstances . . . to bring me out of darkness."

Jaz teared up. "I didn't deserve the wonderful things you did for me, Iris. I wanted to see you today because I'm very sorry I left in such a hurry. I must have seemed terribly ungrateful."

Iris's hand in Jaz's squeezed with the little strength she had.

"I do not regret a whit of it. You learned while I had you with me, and I knew you would take those lessons with you. I hoped and prayed that you would grow and achieve mastery of your talent—which is what any patron desires. And have you, Adele? Have you mastered the gift God gave you? Are you using it for good, for him?"

"To the best of my ability, I am," Jaz whispered. "I'm a Christian now, Iris. I've given the remainder of my life to Jesus."

She swallowed. "I cannot share every detail with you, but I can say that eventually I moved to the US and became an intelligence analyst. Where I work, we track down terrorists."

"Oh, my!"

"Yes, it's important work. We save lives."

Iris closed her eyes. "I knew it. I knew you'd do great things! Oh, Adele! I never had a daughter. But if I had? I would want her to be you."

Not 'I would want her to be *like* you,' but 'I would want her to *be* you.'

She felt Iris shifting in the bed, struggling to turn on her side toward Jaz. A moment later, Jaz felt Iris's hand come to rest on her head. With the little strength she had, Iris stroked Jaz's hair.

"Thank you for coming to say goodbye, dear Adele. Your visit means the world to me."

Jaz couldn't keep her tears from dripping onto their joined hands.

◆

HOURS LATER and emotionally exhausted, Jaz parked alongside the curb and stared up the walkway, still old and buckled. She got out and trod up the walk on shaky legs.

She pressed the doorbell's button and heard it ring inside. Eventually, a cracked voice answered, "Coming!" Minutes elapsed before Jaz heard a shuffle on the other side of the door and caught movement through the peephole.

"Yes? Who is it?"

"It's me, Miss Timmons. Er, Jenny."

"Jenny? *Jenny!* Oh, merciful heavens! Is that really you?"

"Yes, Miss Timmons. It's me."

Miss Timmons wrenched open the door. "Oh, Jenny!" the old woman sobbed. "Jenny, my dearest girl! Come in, come in!"

Jaz stepped into the house and closed the door behind her. Miss Timmons, bent and gray-headed, tears in her eyes and leaning heavily on a cane, stared at her. Slowly, she lifted one hand to Jaz's face and caressed her cheek.

"How I've longed to see you again! How I've prayed for this day!"

Suddenly, Jaz reached for Miss Timmons and pulled her close, stretched her arms around the older woman and held her.

Jaz felt the choking discomfort of touching others rising within her, but she chose, in this moment, to endure the discomfort. She was, in fact, slowly learning to give to others what *they* needed from her, even when it was hard for her.

Isn't that what laying down our lives for others means, Lord?

"Oh, Jenny!" Miss Timmons sniffled, resting her cheek on Jaz's shoulder. "I am so very happy!"

Jaz whispered in the woman's ear, "I am happy, too. I came to tell you, Miss Timmons, that just as you prayed for me the last time I saw you, I *did* meet Jesus face to face."

Jaz swallowed down the lump in her throat. "I came back to thank you and because I wanted you to know that Jesus? He is every bit as wonderful as you said he would be."

THE END

MY DEAR Readers,

Thank you for reading *Vyper*. I so appreciate each one of you! I pray that while reading this book you have been built up and strengthened in your faith. I also pray that you take away from this book some bit of God's word that will increase your courage for him.

About this story: While I don't profess to be an engineer or an authority on power generation, I hope I provided enough detail to underscore the essential nature and vulnerable state of our nation's power grid. In addition, for the story's sake, if I used artistic license on that topic or on the evolution of computer technology while Vyper was young, I beg your indulgence.

Two interesting side notes: During 2021's winter storm *Uri*, the state of Texas suffered a major power crisis that included 1,796 energy storage outages or derates, resulting in a series of rolling blackouts. WA Parish Generating Station itself experienced a 664MW loss in generating capacity. Then, on May 8, 2022, one of Parish's coal burning units caught fire, heavily damaging one of its turbines, which took that unit offline for several months.

Finally, what's next? I hope to soon (and at long last) begin a new series, *The Tahoe Mysteries*, based around Lake Tahoe. What can you expect? Danger, suspense, thrills, a little humor, all of it (of course!) bathed in *faith*. By the way? I think you're going to absolutely love this series' protagonist, Miss Finch.

Blessings on you and yours!
Vikki

ABOUT THE AUTHOR

VIKKI KESTELL'S passion for people and their stories is evident in her readers' affection for her characters and unusual plotlines. Two often-repeated sentiments are, "I feel like I know these people," and, "I'm right there, in the book, experiencing what the characters experience."

Vikki holds a PhD in organizational learning and instructional technologies. She left a career of twenty-plus years in government, academia, and corporate life to pursue writing full time. "Writing is the best job ever," she admits, "and the most demanding."

Vikki and her husband, Conrad Smith, make their home in Albuquerque, New Mexico.

To keep abreast of new book releases, sign up for Vikki's newsletter on her website, **http://www.vikkikestell.com**, find her on Facebook at **http://www.facebook.com/Vikki.Kestell**, or follow her on BookBub, **https://www.bookbub.com/authors/vikki-kestell**.